Praise for *Sockpuppet*

'A fascinating and hair-raising examination of just how
much we are in thrall to computers, and how willingly
we give up our privacy'
Guardian

Brilliant writing and a story that is relevant to every person who
has ever used a networked device combine to make *Sockpuppet*
one of the standout debuts of the year'
Reader Dad

'Embedded with techy jargon and shards of wit, *Sockpuppet*
takes a snapshot of our age of online shaming and
oversharing and runs it through a skewed, feverish filter.
The result is compelling'
Financial Times

'Geeky gorgeous shenanigans with a dark heart and
a topical subject matter'
Liz Loves Books

'Thrives on the tension between private, public and corporate
interests... the author touches a raw nerve when he confronts the
anxiety around information used to harass'
SciFi Now

'Hurrah for tech and her fellow travellers!'
Interzone

About the Author

Matthew's first career was as a professional child actor. From the age of ten, he had roles in TV dramas on the BBC and ITV, in films and at theatres including the Royal Court. After graduating from Oxford with a degree in Mathematics and Philosophy, he began a career in online communications. Since 2008, he has been in public service, helping people understand money. Matthew is a graduate of the Faber Academy's Writing a Novel course. *Sockpuppet* is his first novel.

Sockpuppet

Matthew Blakstad

HODDER

First published in Great Britain in 2016 by
Hodder & Stoughton
An Hachette UK company

First published in paperback in 2017

1

A CIP catalogue record for this title is available from the British Library

ISBN 978 1 473 62474 0

Typeset by Hewer Text UK Ltd, Edinburgh
Printed and bound by Clays Ltd, St Ives plc

Hodder & Stoughton policy is to use papers that are natural, renewable
and recyclable products and made from wood grown in sustainable
forests. The logging and manufacturing processes are expected to
conform to the environmental regulations of the country of origin.

Hodder & Stoughton Ltd
Carmelite House
50 Victoria Embankment
London EC4Y 0DZ

www.hodder.co.uk

For Alice

Welcome.

You are now a Digital Citizen.

As a Digital Citizen you have your own unique identity. Everything about you, from your medical history to the tax you've paid, is stored in one secure location in the cloud.

Do I need any special software?

You don't need to be a software wizard to access the wide range of Citizen Services! We have already installed the Digital Citizen software on your device – automatically.

How secure is my information?

Nothing matters more than the security of your information. Our industry partner Mondan plc works hard to protect your privacy. You can rest assured they are guarding your valuable information very closely indeed.

```
THIS PAGE HAS BEEN REVIEWED
BY <TAKEBACK_ID>
WE DECLARE IT A LIE AND A FRAUD
NOTHING IS PRIVATE
NO ONE IS SAFE
IT IS IN THE NATURE OF INFORMATION
TO MAKE ITSELF FREE
```

Comments? Questions? Find us at ¶ MinistryOfTechnology

TUESDAY:

Spinning

'The trouble with words is, you don't know whose mouths they've been in.'

—*Dennis Potter*

ZERO

WHO ARE YOU?

All I see of you is the shape you leave behind. The world is an engine for logging your desires. In these late days you don't have identity; you have a browser history.

People who liked cheap illusion *also liked* advanced consumer capitalism.

Recommended for you: willing subjugation.

All I know is what I see; and I see new news every day, and those ordinary rumours of botwars, celebrity break-ups, stock quotes, mailbombs, cock extensions; of start-ups in Guangzhou, Tallinn, Bangalore; I see podcasts, flame wars, mp3s; I read blogs, memes, proffers, webcasts, phishing scams, RSS feeds and other fresh alarms. Nothing starts anywhere. The story I'm writing isn't new.

I save and upload: one click, no undo. I shut my laptop and sleep the world. No point thinking consequences. Now it's out there, nothing's going to bring it back.

ONE

'BETHANY? Christ, are you planning to answer your phone?'

Bethany was in the kitchen when it struck, ministry business strewn across the dining table, two red dispatch boxes standing to attention by her chair. She'd been inching her way through the document that, when she signed it, would *consign fakery and fraud to the dustbin of history* – that at least was how she would describe it when she spoke at the Digital Citizen launch event this Friday. But the tight numbered paragraphs of legalese kept congealing before her tired eyes. The law was so hard to digest in raw form. She'd reread one especially chewy clause for the seventh time when Peter, her husband, stormed in.

She pulled off her reading glasses. He was standing naked in the doorway.

'Phone?' she said. 'Which one?'

'Which the hell phone do you think?' he said, nodding behind him into the hall.

But by then she'd heard the jaunty doo-wop of her official BlackBerry.

'I like the look, babes,' she said, hopping up and shimmying around him to the coat hooks, patting his bum en route.

'Godsake, it's nearly two a.m.'

Bethany fumbled through the pockets of her mac. The BlackBerry was in the last one she tried. As she pulled it out the ringing stopped.

'Damn.'

She checked the screen. God, yes: it was 01:54 already; and she had seven missed calls. Her stomach knotted.

'I wouldn't worry, *Minister*,' said Peter, 'it'll start up again in another twenty seconds.' He was making his way back up the stairs. 'Maybe you'd like to fly off to another *international symposium* so I can get a bit of peace? I slept like a log that week.'

He was looser these days around the rear. Not that she wanted to make comparisons, but.

'Do you not want to put some 'jamas on?' she whispered. 'The boys?'

He didn't turn back.

'What I want is sleep,' he said. 'I have an eight-thirty conference call.'

'Well, I have a seven-thirty *meeting*. And unlike you I can't do it in my pyjamas. Or in your case butt naked probably.'

But he'd already turned the bend in the stairs. He creaked above her head to the master bedroom and the door clicked shut. She put a hand on the banister to follow; but true to his prediction the BlackBerry kicked off again in her hand. *Caller withheld.* She answered it quickly to stem the ringtone – stable door, horse.

'Yes, hello?' she said.

'Thank God, Beth. I thought you must have turned in already.'

And who *would* it be at two in the morning, but Big Krishan Kohli, her sleepless chief of staff?

'No, Krish. I'm here. What is it?'

She sat on the stairs, the catastrophe-seeking part of her brain already kicking in. Had the PM withdrawn his backing? Had child pornography been found on their servers? Had one of their Digital Champions been electrocuted by his own PC? Krish cut short her list of worst-case scenarios, with the only one she hadn't considered.

'They're saying we've been hacked.'

Bethany swallowed, once.

'Hacked.' Her voice was stuck in neutral. 'What, our voicemails?'

'Not us – real people. The Digital Citizen pilot group. Someone's hacked their data – addresses, ages, income, medical . . .'

'No, Krish. No no no.'

Sean had promised her nothing had got out. He'd promised.

'That data cannot be hacked,' she said.

'I've already had to hit *Cancel* on a dozen calls from journos,' said Krish. 'It'll be code red by morning.'

'Hold on, stop – what do you mean, *they're saying* we've been hacked? *Who's* saying?'

'Some wee girl posting online. You realise how shite the timing is? After what you said in the House last week, in Oral Questions. You specifically used the word—'

'Yes, all right. Don't remind me.'

'—*unhackable.*'

'But if this is some lone stirrer?' she said. 'We're rebutting her?'

'Beth. It's real. It's not just this girl. Someone's defacing our homepage. Every time we take it down, fix it and put it back up, they graffiti it all over again.'

'Graffiti? On a website?'

'Or the equivalent. They keep adding this same screwy message in typewriter font. *The nature of information will be free,* some bollocks like that.'

Bethany sat forward.

'*The nature of information,*' she said. 'Those exact words?'

Krish left one of his significant pauses before asking, 'Any reason the words should matter?'

'No, none. I thought it sounded familiar.'

'Point I'm making, this is concerted and it's credible. This blogger lassie seems to know a hell of a lot more than we do. She says our data's being used to target Digital Citizen users. Taxpayers, Beth. Voters. We can't rebut a thing like that until we know what's true.'

'We sure as hell can't stay silent and let someone trash us.'

'Press pause a second and listen. This girlie's posted what she claims are departmental documents, saying we *knew* the data was hacked, as much as two weeks ago. Saying *you* knew.'

Bethany wanted to sit down all over again. This could not be. This Friday she'd be announcing the nationwide roll-out of Digital Citizen. Four days. Could she not get through four slender days without some further blow-up?

Krish was letting the point hang.

'Which is clearly nonsense,' she said.

'If you say so.'

'Come on, Krish. Do you not know a stunt when you see one?'

She pushed back her unruly hair, fast-forwarded through the consequences.

'This is so – *gah!*' she said. 'People like this: all they ever do is undermine. We're asking the public to surrender this personal, private thing – their identity. They need to believe we have a safe place for them online. This woman – this – blogger? She's out to kill trust. We need to cut off her oxygen – right now, before the breakfast news cycle. I don't care how credible she sounds.'

'No chance. None. This thing's out there already.'

'When did everyone start assuming government's out to get them? She probably thinks she's "protecting" people from us. That's such crap. *We're* the ones protecting *them*. I've worked so hard to get our message across. You know I have.'

'I know if this thing goes tits up, it comes back to you. I know this was your programme from the off. You fronted up the *Personal as your fingerprint* campaign, you crowbarred the money out of Treasury, you led the procurement—'

'Yes, thanks for the fact check. I'm waiting for the good news.'

'Just saying, like. And you had to pick Mondan to hold the data. Who the hell is Mondan, anyway? You couldn't go with Terasoft, like we've done for every bit of government tech since Harold Wilson bought his first pocket calculator. You had to pick good old *unhackable* Mondan.'

'Yes, can we please try to start from a place we *haven't* been hacked? At least until someone proves to the contrary?'

She pushed back her hair again and took three pranayama breaths. Come on, Beth. You're Minister of State for a Digital

Society, dammit, not some jobbing newbie. Engage your tummy muscles and get to work. Move the conversation on. There was something Krish had said before, that she'd let pass. Oh, yes.

'Wait,' she said. 'Wait. You said somebody is *targeting* our pilot group? Targeting how? Have members of the public been harmed?'

'Well, now—'

Krish let out a breath. The pause that followed was way too long for her liking.

'You've heard of the Giggly Pigglies?' he said.

She pulled the phone from her ear and stared at it.

¶NewsHound:

BREAKING: Unidentified hackers access private data of members of the public who signed up to the government's Digital Citizen online ID programme. More follows.

¶9th&sunset:

Noisy night. The whores and the pundits are all breathing fire.

Take my advice: keep your head low and your hands clean. No telling who they'll turn on next. They sicken me, with their phoney indignation and their ready blame. We're all human. We're all dirt.

¶maglad:

Oy oy lads! Who is this Betty Learner? Should I care?

¶pieandmash:

I think she's like Minister for the Internet? Brunette. OK on the eye. Kind of milfy. High heels.

¶maglad:

We have a minister for the internet? Who knew? Do I need a minister? I need a haircut. And a shag. But a minister?

TWO

THAT UNWELCOME STRANGER, the sun, creeps in through the skylights. From outside the first hints of day break through: the hiss of the artics' brakes as they pull up at the sheds below; the Bengali shouts of the packers; the crump of Beemer doors slamming in the yard as six armed men approach the building. Dani Farr is unaware. Alone in a halogen pool, all she hears is the white noise of her computer's fan, all she sees are the slashes and curly braces shimmering over her twin displays like insects dancing on the surface of a pool. The only parts of her that move are the fingers flicking across the keys.

She's in the state that Gray calls *the code-freeze*. You could set off a bomb outside the window, she wouldn't flinch. One time, a month back, the building was cleared for a fire alarm, when a Pop-Tart went molten in the sales team's toaster. It was soon put out with a blast of phosphate from the extinguisher but not before the whole place was evacuated. After an hour stamping in the yard with stone-cold lattes, the staffers were cleared to file back inside: to find Dani immobile in her chair, still coding, eyes locked on her screens. They moved around her silently, replacing their headphones and logging back in as though trying not to wake a sleepwalker.

Daylight spreads across the wooden floor. This is the Skunkworks: the high-ceilinged warehouse space where Dani and her team of software engineers turn out their elegant, efficient packages of code. Any night of the week you'll find one or two of them up here, burning the small hours at a battered workstation, wrestling with some herculean deadline. Usually, Dani loves working through the night: the way the Skunkworks morphs into a new and private space; the midnight pizza sessions; the long trudge home at dawn, climbing four flights to her flat with a carton of milk; passing tomorrow morning on its way downstairs. But tonight she's stuck with a brain-dead hunk of uncommented code she said she'd fix by morning. It's nearly morning and there's no way she'll fix it in time; but her fingers don't know how to stop working the keys. The sound of their typing fills the room like water coursing through underground caves.

The buzzer sounds. Dani's mouse-hand jerks, sending her mug skidding over the desktop. She grabs at it, knocks it further, catches it with both hands – it's empty. She resets it, making the handle perpendicular, and gives a bleary look around. The buzzer sounds again, for longer. She pushes aside a purple lick of hair and thinks: first, is there anyone else in the building to get that? – answer clearly no; second, what cunt is ringing the doorbell at argh o'clock in the morning?

When the buzzer sounds again and doesn't stop, she lets out a swear and stamps the length of the room to the videophone.

'Fucking what!' she shouts into the handset.

The buzzer stops and she notices the video screen: the crested badge held up to the camera, the crop-headed men glaring from behind it.

'Oh, shit, sorry,' she says. 'I mean, just – sorry. Hold on.'

She holds down the door release then crosses to the lift and jabs the button, letting out more 'fuck's like a junkie flushing away her stash of pills. She pulls out her phone, swipes to the Parley app and proffers.

◀Nightshade:
  shit on a cracker
  police?
  what have i done NOW???

Nobody answers her proffer – the Internet is still in bed – but her phone tags on its own silent commentary.

)) blue hum ((

Sparkles fill the corners of Dani's eyes. She pushes the lift button for a second time. There's a clank somewhere down the shaft then silence. Some muppet has left the grille door open on another floor.

'Fucksticks!' she says, and heads for the stairwell.

In all her rich vocabulary, the strongest insult Dani can lay on anything is *pointless*. This has been a pointless night. And already the morning is shaping up wrong.

'Hands Where I Can See Them!'

'What the –?'

Dani shrugs off the man's grip and backs away, raising her phone on instinct to film him. On the little screen, a scrum of bodies closes in, closely followed by their larger real-world counterparts. Five – no, six – men with generic sweatshirt hoods over jacket collars.

'I'm filming this!' she shouts, still backing off. 'Smile, dickheads, you're on social media.'

'Put your phone away, miss.'

When she saw these douches on the entryphone she thought they were cops – else she'd never have buzzed them in. Stupid, stupid. This is some gang of Dalston crims, come to filch the Macs from the studio and rape or stab her.

'I have a hundred thousand devotees,' she says. 'They're watching this live. You're going to jail.'

But if anyone's even watching at this hour, by the time they sound the alarm these thugs'll have had their way with her.

Dani's backed up against the brushed metal of the reception desk, still breathless from running down eight flights of stairs. In the corner of her eye, off camera, two goons move to flank her.

The big guy – the one who grabbed her arm just now – is almost on her. His aftershave should be banned by the Geneva Convention. He reaches for her phone.

No, he's holding out something for her to see. The screen res of the phone is too crappy to make it out so Dani moves it aside and looks at his real hand. In it is a plastic wallet containing a photo ID and a silver Nick Fury shield.

'I'm Detective Sergeant R –' he begins.

But his name is lost as someone grabs Dani from behind. She wriggles free but two arms snake under her armpits and yank her back. Her phone drops to the floor. Goon Number Two scoops it up. As she struggles, the guys behind her start digging in her jacket pockets.

'And this,' continues the first goon, as though all of this was massively normal, 'is Detective Constable A –'

'Hey, fuck!' Dani interrupts. 'Tell this guy to stop touching my arse!'

They're feeling in her jeans pockets. She jackknifes forward against the arms then suddenly drops her weight – but the grip's too hard. They pull her up and have a good old grope in her butt pockets while 'Detective Sergeant R –' calmly pockets his laminate.

'Miss,' he says, 'if you'd simmer down my colleagues wouldn't need to restrain you.'

'Restrain this, you fucking pigs!'

She starts to flip him the bird but the guy behind her yanks her sideways and slams her into the reception desk, pointing his finger all up in her face – like *Go on, try it.*

'She's clean,' he says.

'Hey, ow?' she says back.

They step into a ring around her. She brushes herself, panting for breath, and stares out the tall man whose name begins with 'R'. Then she turns to his minion whose name begins with 'A' and holds out her hand.

'Give me back my phone.'

The minion looks at his boss, who shrugs. Minion holds it out like a piece of snotty rag and she snatches it back. She checks it for new dinks but it was already trashed so who knows? The video's still rolling on it, though – Dani's still livecasting. She makes a show of rotating the camera from face to face, thumb-typing captions as she goes.

¶Nightshade:
   in case they find me in a bloody heap
   this guy is detective sergeant Racist
   or something
   this guy is detective constable Acne
   these others are redshirts – no names

'All right, enough,' says Racist, flapping a hand at her like a celeb saying *no pictures*. 'Put the phone away.'

)) brick echo ((

To her surprise, she offs the phone and puts it back in the arse pocket of her jeans. The men shift their feet. Seems the moment of danger has passed. If these guys say they're police, OK, let's say they're police – but not because they showed Dani some hazy photo and a tin badge. It's 30% the way they act and 70% the atmosphere they've brought into the room.

Plus, Racist has a notebook out. And an actual *pen*.

'Your name?' he says.

Time was Dani would have kicked off big-time at this whole thing but ever since she sort-of-punched a colleague last year she's been working on a project of being accepting of authority. So she sets herself a goal: answer their questions then shut the fuck up.

'Farr,' she says. 'Danielle Farr.'

What's with the *Danielle*? Only her mum calls her Danielle. And her boss, Jonquil. Oh, shit: Jonquil. She needs to message Jonquil, asap. She puts her hands in her back pockets, casual like, and touches the phone with her fingers. Racist is giving her this *who are you trying to kid?* look.

'And that's your only name?' he says.

'Sorry what?'

Goon Two – Acne – for some reason flips out.

'*Do you have an online alias?*' he barks.

'All right, all right, Jesus! I go by Nightshade. No secret.'

She pulls out her hands to make a *calm down* gesture, palming her phone in the process. Racist writes in his notebook while Acne smirks at her.

'*Nightshade,*' he says. 'Is that what you'd call emo?'

'It's what I'd call why is this your business?'

Acne flares red but Racist puts out his hand, shutting the guy down. Or this is just some good cop/bad cop routine.

'Only Nightshade?' says Racist.

'How do you mean, *only?*'

What does this guy know? She's sure as hell not telling him her other online identities. The cop's eyes bore into her.

'And is there anybody else in this building at this time?' he says.

'Oh, I don't know. I think maybe six guys just muscled in and pushed me about and tried to smash up my phone. But other than that – no.'

There's a long silence then Racist slowly closes his notebook and pockets it. Murmurs to Acne, who starts to chivvy the other four police, all whispers. Acne turns to Dani.

'Can my men access the rest of the building from there?' he asks, pointing to the stairwell and lift.

'They – yes, but they'll need a swipe,' she says.

She wiggles her card out of its lanyard and passes it to Acne, who sends the men off with it. Why is she helping them? Acne and Racist look down on her like proud parents.

'Your cooperation is appreciated, Miss Farr,' says Racist.

He walks over to perch beside her on the reception desk, shedding his big-guy swagger like he's shucking off a coat. The change betrays a subtlety Dani hadn't guessed at. So far anger has kept her fuelled. Kindness could paralyse. She stands up again, folding her arms and tucking her phone by her side. Even standing, she's only eye-to-eye with the seated cop.

'OK?' she says. 'So?'

'So. Are my colleagues going to find anyone upstairs? A woman perhaps?'

His voice is soft, north-western. She stares him out until he shrugs and tries another tack.

'I'm right in saying the social network called Partly is operated from these premises?'

Dani wants to keep up the silence but she needs to correct him. People ought to name things correctly. She nods at the Parley logo on the wall behind him.

'Par*ley*,' she reads to him. 'Not Partly. As in talking peace.'

Off to her side Acne flexes his fingers. He's working out seven different ways to kill her with his hands.

'Par*ley*, then.' Racist is unflustered. 'It is controlled from here?'

Dani screws up her face. *Controlled*? How to answer such a noobie question without swearing or taking the piss? Racist draws a long breath and exchanges a look with Acne.

'Look. Miss Farr.' Ms. 'There's a serious incident taking place right now on your Partly system.' Dani prepares to interrupt but he holds up his hands. 'Par*ley*. And we're here to stop it. We will stop it.'

She blinks at his massive face. His eyes are gently grey. *An incident*? He takes another breath.

'So,' he says. 'Tell me –'

He has his little notebook out again. Something important is coming.

'– is the Parley user known as Sick Girl in this building?'

'Is the – excuse me? You're asking what?'

'I'm asking where I can find this user Sick Girl. We have reason to believe she's in this building.'

'You what? She bloody isn't.'

'If you're so sure of that, how about you tell me where she is? Name, address and phone number. And while you're at it can you shut off her Parley account, please.'

Dani realises her jaw is hanging open. She shuts it.

'You're serious?' she says.

'Yes, Miss Farr, this is extremely serious. In the last seven hours this Sick Girl has made a series of accusations about a government minister, published a string of confidential government documents and she's showing no sign of stopping this behaviour. We would appreciate—'

'No, as in: you're not joking? You want me to give you sic_girl's *phone number*?'

In spite of everything she starts to laugh. The furious face of the policemen only makes it crazier. She can't stop.

'I fail to see –' says Racist.

Dani gulps in air to get hold of herself.

'That is so – *ha!* Would you like Super Mario's number, too? I think I might have Lara Croft's!'

The policemen exchange a look.

'Those,' says Racist in the voice of a man imparting great wisdom, 'are fictional characters, Ms Farr.'

That shuts Dani up for just a second. Then her cheeks fill up again with lulz.

'And sic_girl isn't?' she manages.

Then she's off again, with the gut-shaking laugh of the sleep-deprived.

¶riotbaby:

And im telling YOU, friend. Its just another part of their agenda. They want to own us and theyre taking us one piece at a time.

You think this is an isolated thing? This isnt isolated. Its a tiny part of a bigger plan. They won't rest till they know everything about you. No secrets, no privacy.

And you want to know the worst of it? They dont even care we know. Theyll lie to our faces and theyll smile and smile.

You know what this point is?

This is the point where we start fighting back.

¶bottomhalfofthepage:

More lies from the party of you-turns and spin.

She is called Betterny but that does not mean she is better'n me.

LOL

No, I know that's not how you spell it.

THREE

JOHN-RHYS PEMBERTON'S BLACKBERRY sounded from under a pile of policy briefs beside his Party laptop. He decided to ignore it until he completed his sentence.

Not unusually, J-R had been up a while. Since 4:45, in fact. Perched on his sofa in boxers and socks, he bent forward over his Party laptop and tackled the previous day's internal correspondence for Bethany Lehrer, the Minister of State for a Digital Society. A forgotten bowl of Shreddies coagulated at his feet as he deciphered Bethan's handwritten notes and converted them into memoranda for the civil servants who ran her Private Office.

The first note was crammed onto both sides of a Doonesbury notelet.

1 a.m. (!!!)
I'm still working through my box and I'm frankly peed off. Can you please tell those jobsworths to stop abbreviating my official title on their submissions? This one is addressed to 'MoS-aDS'. Sounds like MOSSAD! Basically they can write my title out in full. It isn't THAT long?? Ta babes. Bethx

That was an easy one. In the memorandum, J-R had written:

1) The Minister notes that certain forms of abbreviated address have become standard on Ministerial Submissions, perhaps not

entirely through design. Whilst appreciating the drive for brevity, the Minister asks that, in future, full official titles are used on all correspondence through her Office.

The next note was scratched out on Ministry of Technology notepaper.

Monday.
J-R, I'm completely caffeine starved. Can you persuade one of these brontosauruses to once in a while take a break from wiggling their mouses around and get me a skinny latte? Do they honestly expect me to down tools from running the country and wait in line with the spotty wonks in Prêt à Manger? Cheers ears.
Bx

J-R had been struggling with this one for ten minutes. He'd got as far as:

2) The Minister is not unaware of the heavy workload of her Private Office staff, and greatly appreciates the efforts of the whole team in supporting her official duties. Nevertheless,

The cursor blinked useless after the comma. As the minister's communications spad – special advisor – J-R's role was meant to include speechwriting, drafting of lines-to-take on political issues and working with the civil servants on policy statements. To be fair, he did very often get to do these things and was still in awe of the responsibility and trust so placed upon him at the age of twenty-six. The Digital Citizen initiative he was currently working on was of national importance. Bethan, for all anyone could say of her, was decent and principled, and up until recently he'd trusted her as a mother, but a great deal of his time – generally the small hours of each morning – was spent diverting the floodwaters of her consciousness into language her officials could understand and respond to.

He'd taken to this court translator role with gusto; had picked up officialese like a native in a matter of days. If anything, he'd become too fluent. His friends, when he ever saw them these days, had begun to rag him when this new jargon crept into his pub vocabulary. They'd threatened to charge him five pounds every time he said, 'I don't disagree with that' instead of 'Yes' – or 'notwithstanding' for 'even so' – or 'whilst' for 'while'. He didn't mind. A maturing speech denoted a new gravity. Underneath, they respected him for it, even whilst they teased him. The occasional hints he was able to drop about the business of Bethany's office carried more import than the drudge-work most of them described, in their long days toiling at structured finance, audits or viral marketing – whatever those might be. None of them had advanced very far up their chosen food chains. J-R was at the heart of government.

He shook his head to clear it, stretched his arms, beat a tattoo on his tummy and was about to have another crack at the latte paragraph, when the BlackBerry started to buzz again somewhere out of view. He traced it to a spill of draft White Papers and extracted it. There were now five messages. He read the first, from fifteen minutes back:

Substance, meet fan. Dancing pigs unleashed on Teesside. How soon can you be here?

This was confounding, but it was from Big Krish – ergo, important. J-R fiddled the cursor to *Call contact*. Before the line had rung once, Krish's Glasgow drawl kicked in.

'J-R, thank feck. You ever hear of a social network called Parley?'

Krish was never one for pleasantries. J-R trotted to the still-dark bedroom in search of trousers.

'I do occasionally venture into the twenty-first century,' he said.

'Sorry, aye. I need you at Parley pronto. No, before pronto. Get there yesterday.'

'Because –?'

J-R tucked the BlackBerry between his shoulder and ear and rifled the wardrobe with the other. He prayed he had at least one ironed shirt.

'Because some wee girl is on there just now, putting it about that our flagship programme has been hacked.'

Still holding the phone with his shoulder, J-R hopped across the half-lit room, struggling his right leg into a pair of suit trousers. His foot connected with something sharp.

'*Yah!*' he cried into the BlackBerry.

'Jesus, man, don't take it so hard,' said Krish.

J-R stooped to extract the offending object from his foot. The spare nib for his cartridge pen. He'd been looking for that. He really should tidy.

'No, it's – I'm fine. What form are these accusations taking?

'She's linking to documents. Mebbe real, mebbe not.'

J-R froze with the sharp nib in his fingers. Documents? A data hack? For the last fortnight he'd been doing a serviceable job of not thinking about the wretched email that was burning a hole in his inbox. Now it pinged straight back into his mind. What precisely had Bethany sent that man, in the small hours of the night?

'But is there substance?' he asked. '*Have* we been hacked?'

Either Krish hadn't heard or he chose not to answer.

'OK, look,' he said, 'I've emailed you the address for Parley's offices. Shoreditch. Take your beard wax – there be hipsters.'

Rubbing his clean-shaven jowls, J-R took the BlackBerry away from his ear and navigated to his emails. *Parley. 23 Martlet Street, London E1. Contact name: Jonquil Carter.* He returned the phone to his ear.

'Got it. I'm there.'

'And you'll report back the second you have a thing.'

'Yes, yes. And Krish –'

'Aye?'

'What's all this about pigs?'

*   *   *

Snootlet! Porquette! Dip-Dap!
And Trottie, too!
If you're wiggly
And not very biggly
Then you're giggly
You're giggly
A giggly giggly piggly!

'AY, HA HA, YES, that's the song. *Giggly, giggly, giggly.* Oh, God, right? Ha ha! Proper off it!'

'And your spam misery began as soon as you registered online for the government's pilot Digital Citizen programme.'

'Well, that was a while back, but now it does keep coming on. I can't use a website except those wee pigs keep popping up. On my PC, on my phone, even here in the office. I log on. I think I'm OK for a while. Then I click on my Internet and it says *Piggle* instead of *Google* and there they are – those wee pigs dancing like a bunch of divvies. And I hear that *di-di-di-dididi-di.* Everything I click on after that, it's pigs.'

'And this constant invasion is making your life hell?'

'I wouldn't know about that but now I don't know how to stop it on the computer. I'm not so technical, me like. The bairns are going mental.'

'Your children are being driven to desperation?'

'No, they love it. They do the dance. Those canny wee piggies.'

'So there you have it, Susan. Just one unsuspecting member of the public who thought they were signing up for a secure service from the government –'

'They said I could get the bins done weekly, as –'

'– and who has found himself pursued by the most unlikely of tormenters: TV's popular foursome of miniature laughing pigs.

'Susan.'

¶LabelMabel:

Why are these people complaining? I would LOVE my
Internet to be only pigs. Hack my data! I want a virus
too!

¶lolcatz:

Ermangerd I can haz piggliez?

¶LabelMabel:

🐖 🐖 🐖 🐖 🐖 🐖 🐖 🐖 🐖 🐖 🐖 🐖 🐖 🐖

¶TurdoftheDay:

A whopper. One single slug 13cm in length. Fat and gristly.
It glares up at me and cries: 'Come on you mother! Flush
me! I wanna see you even TRY! Boo-ya!'
Three flushes later. Still it will not leave.
Even I am slightly terrified of it.
<pic:>

FOUR

'YOU'RE NOT MAKING SENSE, Miss Farr. Either you're writing Sick Girl's posts or you aren't. Either way you need to make them stop.'

Hugging herself against the relentless harassment, Dani stops outside meeting pod 1.02 and turns to glare at Racist.

'I need my swipe card,' she says, pointing at the door. 'There's a machine in here. I can show you.'

Racist clocks the meeting-pod door, which is easy to miss, it's so seamlessly cut into the floor-to-ceiling photo mural that coats the wall. The photo, which is labelled *Creativity, driving our people's excellence*, is the fourth in a series of images lining the ground-floor hallway like stations of the cross, expressing *Our Eight Shared Values*. It shows a gorgeous young giantess, fizzy-haired and neutrally black, laughing and hurling into flight an astonished-looking dove. The background scene – lush fields under desert sky – glows with Tomy blues and greens. Only the model's eyes betray her fright as talons scrabble at her face.

Acne approaches.

'One of the lads is on his way down with her card,' he says, waving his shortwave radio, which gives out a reassuring *kkht*.

'They find anyone upstairs?' says Racist.

Acne gives a brief shake of his head. The two of them round on Dani.

'Looks like you're the only person here,' says Racist. 'Our information says the person going by Sick Girl is posting from this building. And here we find you. All alone.'

Dani opens her mouth and shuts it. She nudges her phone into life but Jonq hasn't responded to any of the whispers she's sent over Parley. The network is silent.

)) stone face ((

says her phone.

'Look,' she says, holding up the phone, 'I've contacted Jonquil. Ms Carter. My boss. Can we not wait for her? She's better at explaining things to – normal people.'

Acne seems to find this hilarious. Racist keeps with the blank look.

'There's only two scenarios here,' he says. 'Either you're Sick Girl, in which case you're in serious trouble. Or she's someone else, and you know where we can find her. Every second of our time you waste, your friend leaks more damaging material. Which makes this obstruction. So what's it to be?'

Dani swallows. Parley grants her official maverick status, in her role as Chief Social Architect (or as Gray says, Chief *Anti*social Architect). She gets away with all kinds of crazy because she's unconventional and uncompromising in the exact way Parley values. The rules don't apply to her. Take the time last summer when she punched the Head of Channel Marketing, Billy Dukakis. He'd yanked her chain one time too many about the need to add bullshit 'brand tags' (i.e. ads) to every inch of her perfect, clean screen layouts. He called her *control freak little bitch* in front of the entire dev team, which wasn't even English; and she basically punched him in the face. To be fair it was more of a butt-of-the-hand-against-the-nose kind of move but unfortunately it kind of broke the nose in question.

Anyone but Dani would have been out of the door in twenty seconds; but in this case it was Billy who was frogmarched out, a meaty pay-off in his pocket and his signature at the bottom of a thirty-two-page legal document whose contents roughly translated as *I will not sue Dani.*

That was far from the stupidest thing she's ever done. Sometimes it seems she's never shouldered a burden for any of her actions. And it's damn sure nobody ever asks her to speak on behalf of the organisation.

She glances down at her phone.

'If you can send a message to Mrs Carter,' says Racist, nodding at the phone, 'you can send one to Sick Girl. Unless of course she's you.'

'No, no. Sorry. Jesus, why do you people not listen? *I'm* not sic_girl. I *wrote* her.'

Another of the Abercrombies jogs down the hall towards them, waving Dani's swipe card.

'All floors clear,' he says, handing it to Acne.

He jogs off again. Dani reaches for the card but Acne jerks it away and uses it to swipe the door before passing it to her. The door clunks and he pushes it open, cutting a rectangular absence into the lower half of the photo model's body. As Dani enters the demo pod, the lights flick on automatically. The cops follow and shut the door behind them. A hard drive chatters on the demo table. The machine is an all-in-one Mac – i.e. a toy, but fit for hailing a continuity. Dani sits and wakes the screen. A measure of control returns as her fingers touch the keyboard.

'Sic_girl isn't a person,' she says, logging in as root. 'She isn't anything, she's nowhere.'

She calls up the Parley Admin app and navigates to the dashboard screen they use to monitor the sic_girl engine.

'Look,' she says, swivelling the screen towards the cops and pointing at the data chugging through the logs. 'There. This is sic_girl, OK. You want to know where she lives? She lives in here. I *made* her, on an Apache server in our data centre. She's not a person, she's a ware.'

Mystification.

'Aware of . . .?' says Racist.

Dani sighs. This is going to have to be the full one-oh-one.

'A piece of *software*?' she translates.

She turns back to the screen and clicks up sic_girl's status screen.

'Look,' she says, 'I'll show you how she's made. This –' clicking on the first tab '– is her source data bucket. See all the chatter in here? We have this crawly bot that trawls the net every ten minutes, scooping up stuff that people say online. It knows how to filter things that already sound a bit like sic_girl, that relate to her interests. It scrapes them off the net and dumps them in the bucket here. Right now we've got –' she clicks a status button '– just under ten thousand phrases sloshing around in there.' She nods to herself. 'That's a solid number. Then over here –' she clicks the second tab '– is the status of sic's text-parsing algorithm. It searches the top of the bucket for things that sic can say. Stuff that's relevant to what's going on right now, and what people are saying to her. And here –' another click, another tab '– are her finished proffers. This is what she's "saying" right now. All her sentences are stitched together from whatever bubbles out of the bucket – and tweaked into her style of speech.'

Satisfied with a job well done, Dani folds her arms and turns to look from cop to cop, seeking out some flicker of understanding. All she finds are the same null-set faces.

'She's a *software*,' Dani says again. 'As in – not real? As in every single Parley user knows that sic and the other Personas are built from text and glue. That's why they love them.'

Still nothing.

'OK, God,' she says. 'Look, you can see right here. Sic proffered – what? – forty seconds ago. She said *Whoosh, thxx lovelies. Much praise – so wow.* So I guess that means she isn't me? Because I have a, what do you call it – an alibi – for forty seconds ago? As in I was sitting right here? Talking to you?'

Still not a flicker. After a pause Racist restarts the conversation where he left off – as if the past three minutes never happened.

'The person you're defending here,' he says, 'is a malicious hacker. Someone who's wilfully sharing confidential government documents. If you've got her timeline on there I suggest you read it. Start at twelve midnight.'

Yet again Dani struggles not to correct the man. Yet again she fails.

'*Continuity*,' she says.

'Excuse me?'

'Not *timeline*,' she says. 'Jesus. Parley has *continuities*. That's trademark and copyright, by the way. Messages on Parley are *proffers*, not *posts*, and they go together to form *continuities*.'

Racist perseveres.

'The *continuity* for Sick Girl, just after midnight. Her posts—'

'Proffers.'

'All right, dammit, *proffers*!'

Dani blinks. Racist collects himself and tries again.

'Her *proffers* begin at oh, oh, sixteen hours.'

'OK,' she says. 'Jesus, OK. But I'm telling you it's pointless. Whatever she said, her algorithm pulled it out of the air.'

Wearily, Dani closes the admin screen and pulls up the standard consumer-grade Parley app. She clicks on the clock and starts to dial it back.

Parley is not just the place where the Personas live; it's also a time machine. When you turn on a Parley viewer, by default you see a slice of the living present; but the true power comes when you shift it to some other now, zoom back in your software Delorean to see what the Personas – and their legion of human fans – were saying and doing at a single moment, follow the threads of time and meaning back and forth; then widen and narrow your focus to find a different path back to the place where you began. It's a giddy sensation that can leave you reeling when you land back in the now. Parley's users spend almost as much time in the past as they do in the present. Nostalgia's popular: even for a week ago.

Dani spins the clock to sixteen minutes past midnight.

'OK,' she says, slipping into demo mode for the benefit of the neanderthals. 'I've landed at that time. Now I'm tightening the aperture – see this slider? It's like focusing my view on sic_girl alone. Shutting out other voices.'

The drag of her mouse erases Personas and people alike, until only sic_girl remains in view – plus the handful of human users she was talking to at midnight. Dani reads and scrolls.

¶sic_girl:

Meds time, hooray. Needed. Argh day today, insomnia fans. Pain, rain and a double shot of lows. Poor me, yes? So. Let's talk. I'm gonna start with Bethany Lehrer. The minister-lady? With the hair? Yoosh.

>>cite ¶mardyboy: She's ok i think shes kinda hot tho'

Really, mardy? REALLY? Ek. She creepy.

>>cite ¶womble-gone-bad: Hi sic. She's sort of cool. She didn't fiddle her expenses.

Hi woms. You look cute. May I girl-crush? But listen. Bethany L? Fergeddaboudit. She's the cover-up queen. You know the Giggly Pigglies?

>>cite ¶worldofmeow: I 🤍 the Giggly Pigglies! 🐷 🐷 🐷

WHO DOES NOT? But newsflash, my lovelies. Those ickle pickle pigs are made of spam not ham. Didja see this story on HUMBOX?

The day every website turned into pigs hum.bx/f80du7

Can ya IMAGINE? Ev'ry website you ever visit automagically turned into a Giggly Piggly home screen!?

>>cite ¶worldofmeow: THAT SOUND AMAZE! 🤍 🐷 🤍

There's a silence. Dani turns to Racist.

'So?' she says. 'Pigs and cartoons and whatever. This is normal for sic_girl. Or what passes for it.'

Dani has a special love for her first-made artificial girl. But she's the first to admit that sic talks a load of mimsy crap.

'Fans proffer this stuff at sic,' she says, 'and it's like I showed you: the algorithm stitches relevant-seeming sentences out of the word-soup in the bucket. That's all this is.'

'Really?' says Racist.

'Yes, fucking really.'

'Watch your mouth,' says Acne.

Racist quiets him with a hand.

'In that case,' he says to Dani. 'I suggest you read forward.'

She sighs and scrolls.

'There,' says Racist, pointing.

Dani stops the clock.

¶sic_girl:

Ask yerselves, sweeties. Howcum ten thousand peoples who all HAPPEN to live in Teesside, get their PCs taken over by cartoon pigs ON THE SELFSAME DAY? I'll tell ya. That piggy spam only hit the muggles who signed up for DigiCitz. Count 'em, biatches.

Here's the news: two weeks ago someone walked onto the Digital Shitizen servers and swiped their oh-so-private data. Unhackable? HAH! And you know the worst of it? Bethany L knew all about it. Yuppety. She knew she knew she knew. Don't believe me? Ask her about this internal memo from MinTech last Tuesday. Seems somebody there knew all about this thing she sa she kno nuffink about.

There. Sigh. So the sainted Bethany's a lying lying liar. Pigglies ain't so frolicsome when they workin' for the big bad data wolf AM I RIGHT???

Also. Sorry. Still on about it.

But.

Dani bunches her forehead at the screen. There's something off about this. It's normal for sic to proffer about Hello Kitty or Spongebob or whatever, but apparently the Giggly Pigglies are suddenly meat for some political story.

Digital Citizen is the new so-called 'online ID card' – which is actually not a 'card' but a public-key token so it's dumb that people refer to it that way. Security is supposedly tighter than Jonquil's butt. If it's been hacked, that's proper news. Which puts it totally out of whack with sic_girl's usual burbles on antidepressants and puppy videos – the stuff that's programmed into her.

And this, right now, is what plants the clue in Dani's head: something major is going down this morning, and these men are trying to pin it on her. She needs to tread careful.

'OK,' she says. 'And?'

'*And*,' says Racist, 'you need to stop this.'

He speaks like a dad addressing his six-year-old.

'Well but why? Is it untrue, what sic's saying?'

'That is not your business. I don't care if she's a human or a robot, she's posting confidential government information and you are going to contain this situation right now.'

Contain the situation? How do you contain a software construct? This is impossible. A combined wave of fury and exhaustion comes over Dani. She can't believe they won't understand when she just *showed* them. They must breed these giant morons in a tank, like seamonkeys. She crushes fists into either side of her head. The two men stand in silence, flanking her chair. She drops her hands and looks from one police-y face to the other.

'But look,' she says, 'even if sic is doing what you're saying it's not like I can just turn her off. She's part of the wiring. You're asking me to turn off the whole of Parley.'

'All right,' says Racist, 'then I guess that's what you'll have to do.'

Oh. He's trying to stare her out but she can't look him in the eye.

'But I –' she tries. 'I don't –' Still nothing comes.

She doesn't have tools for anything approaching this situation.

'I can't just – turn off Parley,' she says at last.

'Well, find some fucker who can!' Acne shouts, making Dani start.

Racist touches his arm, gives him a dose of the pale eyes.

'A word?' he says to Acne, and leads him to the far side of the table.

En route he turns back to Dani.

'Come back to the present,' he says, quiet but firm. 'On the machine. Take a look at what's happening on your system, right now. And think about how to stop it.' He checks his '90s-era Casio. 'You have two minutes. Then you're shutting this thing down.'

He touches Acne's arm and leads him into a huddle by the window.

Robotically, Dani flicks the clock, spinning it back to the present. She drags the slider to widen her aperture, adding her full list of devotees back to the screen. She sees it right away: a Parleystorm, ballooning across the screen. Sic_girl's proffers about Bethany Lehrer have stirred attention from the social media night watch – coders, insomniacs, journos – and now the morning crowd is up and catching on. Sic_girl has tapped a reflex point to do with trust, lies and politics. Dani follows daisy chains of chatter. As best she can parse it, last week thousands of people received an invasive software worm which makes the Giggly Pigglies pop up on every website they visit. Now, somehow, sic is putting it out that their data was hacked from the Digital Citizen servers – and that this is how they got spammed. And for some reason people give a major shit about this. Everyone finds the pig thing hilarious and they already hate the Digital Citizen – or dCitz, as it's getting called – and this morning sic has made the two things collide and go boom.

Dani chances a look at the policemen who are bickering almost silently about something. Acne gestures with his head at Dani, who ducks back behind the Mac's screen. Somehow she needs to seize back control of this thing; but what can she even do? A so-called *situation* is tightening around her and she doesn't understand thing one about it. Well, but what's a hive mind for? By now most of her devotees are up and active on Parley. One of them will know what's going on. She proffers, typing quietly so as not to attract the attention of the whispering cops.

¶Nightshade:
> anyone understand what sic is saying
> dummies mode pls
> its for a thing

While she waits for replies, she chances another look at Racist. His lips move on mute as he whispers at Acne. He slips his smartphone back in his jacket pocket and for a second she glimpses something lodged under his armpit. She can't be sure but she is sure. A patterned grip on a cold heavy shape. Danger. First time she's seen a gun in the real but her eye is trained by first-person shooters to know one in a flash-frame.

She looks from cop to cop. Unconnected fragments force their way from her mouth, spilling like cards from a pack. The policemen turn and look at her expectantly. Pieces fall away.

)) word salad ((

Then Jonquil is there. Like the hero who only ever arrives in the nick of time her boss, Jonquil Carter, stands in the door, bringing with her the certainty she carries like a designer clutch – though even she double-takes at finding this unlikely trio in her demo pod.

The police stand to attention and Dani hears at last their proper handles.

'DS Raeworth. This is DC Ackroyd. Parliamentary Branch.'

Wonderful normal names that have stared in her face the whole time like the solution to a cryptogram. The cops align themselves before the new arrival – the whole male gender having evolved to seek out authority and fawn on it.

In one charming motion Jonquil prises everyone from the room, giving Dani a look that communicates how uncool it was to give a bunch of strangers the run of the building, and ushers everyone up to her office. En route they pass Acne's weekend-casual team, who are standing chastened at the bottom of the stairs. Guess Jonquil got to them already. On the way upstairs Jonq nips Dani's arm and hisses, '*Why the FUCK did you not CALL me?*'

Oh, thinks Dani, *why didn't I?* She never uses the phone part of her phone, only ever sends people whispers on Parley; forgetting over-thirties like Jonquil. What other self-evident things have strolled by unnoticed in the past half hour?

While Jonquil magics coffee, juice and pastries, Dani slides into a chair, concealing herself behind the green plastic rim of the meeting table, keeping Raeworth (not Racist) in her eyeline. She blinks away sleep, then blinks again to erase the image of the gun. Jonquil places herself at the head of the table and makes a cathedral with her hands. She and Raeworth talk but Dani can barely hear above the sound of her own neurons firing. Who brings a gun to a software house in the early hours of the morning?

)) brain jam ((

Far away, at the other end of the table, Jonquil and the policeman play a game of verbal Asteroids. Raeworth launches phrases into the air – *close down* – *official business* – *disruptive element* – and Jonquil shoots each one down; but more and more of her shots are missing the mark. Any other time, Dani would love to watch the indestructible Jonquil Carter lose a battle of words but this pains her.

'Listen, friend,' Jonq pulls on the Bronx rasp, though she's actually from Ohio. 'You guys may not have a First Amendment but I'm telling you: the government cannot send a gang of thugs to accuse my staff on the back of zero evidence, and curb the free speech of a legitimate organisation.'

'This is not a free speech issue, Ms Carter,' Racist says. 'It's a question of confidential Parliamentary information. We are requesting that you cease publishing this information.'

'We're a goddamn channel, not a publisher. This is unwarranted. I'm calling lawyers on your ass.'

Before Jonquil can follow through, the door falls open like a badly sealed parcel and from it spills a breathless red-faced person, who stops short and stares at them one-by-one. He's overweight and appears to be wearing his dad's unpressed suit and shirt. A folded bike hangs from his left hand.

'Ah . . .' says this person. 'The lady let me in?'

He uses the bike to indicate the door, as though unaccustomed to being admitted into buildings. He places the bike by the wall and sheds a backpack.

'What the hell are you?' says Jonquil. Dani never knows whether her boss does this on purpose. They say geeks are autistic but whenever Jonquil flubs the basic rules of human-to-human interface, Dani has to dig nails into her palms. Undaunted, the new arrival thrusts his hand at Jonq as though he needs help removing it. When he speaks he's self-assured, even blunt.

'John-Rhys Pemberton, Ms Carter. From the office of the Minister for a Digital Society. I believe we met at the e-Gov reception.' Jonquil bows her head to indicate she might recall this. 'I understand the office has contacted you to say I was on my way.'

Jonquil neither confirms nor denies this. As they shake, the young guy checks out Dani, who's now sunk almost below the surface of the table. Then his eyes move to Raeworth and Ackroyd.

'And these gentlemen –?' he asks.

'Are here, I think, on behalf of your employers?'

Jonquil seems to have divined something about the situation. She and this government person are already somehow in cahoots. They end their sentences with question marks.

'They seem,' says Jonq, 'to have the idea their authority stretches to stifling the free speech of *digital citizens*?'

Pemberton turns to face Raeworth and the game is two-on-one, with Ackroyd and Dani ringside. This goes on for a while, then Pemberton does a magic trick. It's fascinating to see. He raises his hand to suspend the argument, produces an old-model BlackBerry from his pocket and with his left hand still held up like a traffic cop he makes a call. He speaks three times, softly but firmly, his eyes on the policemen, and nods. He hangs up and jiggles the BlackBerry in his hand. Everyone looks at each other for about half a minute, then Raeworth's phone rings.

The policeman stares at his pocket for a second, flicks his eyes at Pemberton, then draws his phone and answers. He nods, too, but barely speaks. Then he hangs up, turns his emotionless face to Pemberton and announces that they are 'at his disposal'.

Through all of this, Jonquil has kept her steady gaze on Pemberton, who now rubs his hands, coughs and turns to look straight at Dani. All other eyes follow.

'So, Ms Farr,' he says, 'it seems we have a shared objective?'

Dani blinks at him.

There's something about sic_girl
by ¶sic_notes

Perfect, fragile, illusory bae. Your words are anyone's. Your pain is everyone's. Your thoughts are air. I proffer to you every hour. Why do you never cite me back? Why does nobody else understand me like you do? Nobody real, at least. My flatmates are the worst. I think I hate them. Whenever I tell them anything personal they 1) don't understand me, 2) laugh at me then 3) tell everyone else behind my back. Soon everybody else is laughing at me, too. I don't tell them anything any more. But I can tell you anything, sic_girl, and I do. Sometimes I stay up right through the night, privately sharing you with all the other lonely ones. We know you love us.

My flatmates say I'm a loser for even talking to you. They tell me you can't understand me. They say you just pump out artificial words, copied from things some other moron already said somewhere else online. They don't know they're the morons.

One day I'll find the perfect way to proffer you my private sorrow. I'll tell it so clearly and truthfully you'll cite it to the world, decorated with a glowing immaculate reply, laced with hearts and a measure of your own sorrow. Then I'll be complete.

My flatmates tell me you're not real.
Well, nobody's perfect.

FIVE

HANSARD: **House of Commons archive search**
ORAL ANSWERS: **Digital Government**

Jim Finnegan (Tees Valley South): To ask the Minister of State for a Digital Society to reassure the people of Tees Valley South of the measures in place to protect the personal information of participants in the Digital Citizen Pilot Programme.

Minister of State for a Digital Society (Bethany Lehrer): I thank the honourable gentleman for his question and for the opportunity it gives me to emphasise the absolute priority we place on protecting the personal information of Teesside residents taking part in the Digital Citizen Pilot. Our strategic partner, Mondan plc, a British technology success story, is trusted to host sensitive data the world over. The Teesside data is completely unhackable.

Jim Finnegan: These assurances are rather easy for her to provide. My constituents are being given no choice about surrendering their personal details. Can she give a clear commitment, here in this House, that these details will not be accessible to government agencies or anyone else who wishes to snoop on them?

Bethany Lehrer: I would remind the honourable gentleman that the Digital Citizen programme gives people a secure and simple way to prove their identities and help combat fraud and terrorism. I'm sure he will join me in thanking the Teesside

Digital Champions for helping connect hard-working families with services that were woefully under-supported by the last government.

So this here was the Big Scandal? Some minister said a thing was unhackable but it got hacked – or maybe hacked. Jonquil scrolled up and down the transcript but it failed to give up anything spicier on a second reading.

From outside came the clangs and cries of the halal packing yard. At the round green table by the window, Pemberton bent forward to peel back Sarin from the fruit bowl and pick a grape, eyes still locked on his BlackBerry. His government security pass dangled on its lanyard and dipped into his brimming teacup. As he sat back to pop the grape into his mouth, the sloppy rectangle slid from the cup and swung back onto his shirtfront. Unaware, he kept thumb-typing for a beat; then looked up and caught Jonquil's eye.

'So. Ms Carter. The minister suggests we collaborate. A sort of public-private partnership?'

From behind his pass, a brown stain spread outwards across his shirt.

'Well we do have a mutual interest,' said Jonquil. 'This thing has gotten serious media attention.'

Once they'd shed the Gap-clad posse of cops, Jonquil and Pemberton took the chance to catch up on the night's shenanigans. A weird camaraderie settled, Pemberton frowning at his smart-phone, Danielle jabbing at hers and Jonquil sitting at her desk to browse some shape into the Bethany Lehrer situation. It was quickly clear why the media were onto this so hard. Lying to the House of Commons was a big deal. Like political-career-ending big. This was a potential vote-loser. Coupled with the fact that thousands of people had had their PCs invaded by those titans of twee, the Giggly Pigglies. Scandal and lulz: an irresistible cocktail for the journos and the blogs. It could have been some kind of guerrilla marketing campaign, if the stakes weren't so high.

Danielle reached past Pemberton to scoff some grapes, tapping at her phone like she was trying to squish ants running over the screen. Pemberton avoided looking at her, but his attention pawed at her as she shifted in her chair. A flush rose on him. This was not the first time Jonquil had noted the appeal of her Chief Social Architect to your young male wonk. She never did get this: leaving aside the girl had too much weight on her, she was no looker. The purple bob masked most of the birthmark on her neck and jaw, but the piercings were yech – and she'd no notion how to do the charm. But some guys just go after pissy.

Jonquil locked the iMac screen and joined the two of them at the table. Danielle looked up, still stuffing grapes, but Jonquil focused on Pemberton.

'OK, J-R. Let's break this down.' She counted points on her fingers. 'Thing one, we got a couple thousand people getting attacked by some kind of Giggly Pigglies virus.' Pemberton gave a sober nod. 'Thing two, these turn out to be the exact same people who signed up for your pilot service a couple months back.'

Pemberton raised a palm.

'We are suspending conclusions until our outsource data partner has completed their investigation of the Giggly Pigglies hack,' he said.

That was a genuinely awesome sentence. Jonquil kept on with the count.

'Thing three, you've been making noise about the quote, unhackability, unquote of your system.'

He frowned.

'Data security is one of our low-lines,' he said. 'It's more of a hygiene factor but yes, it is important to us. And to our users.'

This guy wouldn't let any comment go unqualified. Jonquil did a quick Myers-Briggs: he was for sure an INTJ. Introvert-iNtuiter-Thinker-Judger. Strategist. Backroom boy.

'But thing four,' she said, 'even though last week your minister told Parliament nobody could get at the data, still, it seems you guys already knew way before about the hack.'

'That has been alleged.' Pemberton gave Jonquil a flabby gaze she found disconcerting.

'Oh, so I guess she didn't know, huh?' She blinked in a way most men would take as cupidity but got nothing back. 'Then thing five, sic has taken it into her digital head to leak this *alleged* fact to several hundred thousand devotees, along with documents to prove it. But thing six, sic isn't real – so where the heck did she find all this stuff?'

Pemberton scrumples up his forehead.

'Devotees?'

'Followers, you'd call them. Here, it's *devotees*.'

Still a blank. Impatience got the better of Jonquil.

'You want to know where this sic_girl thing is coming from, John-Rhys? Well, so do I. I suggest—'

Pemberton did the Moses thing with his hand again.

'So, so, so –' Using that word to steal the conch. 'We'd prefer to clarify a few points before we proceed.' *Oh,* thought Jonquil, *you would, huh?* 'Though confidentiality is paramount to our discussions we'd prefer to avoid any formal arrangement. We feel a relationship of, ah, mutual trust would be more productive.'

He was right. Neither of them stood to gain by spilling their discussions. Jonquil granted him a smile he chose to take as a *yes.*

'We're happy to support you with information,' he said, 'but Parley is the – however accidental – publisher of this information. We feel you might choose to put your own resources into identifying and neutralising the source. And it's interesting, isn't it –?'

He put on an unconvincing thoughtful look. She waited him out. No way was she going to say, *What's interesting, Mister Pemberton, sah?*

'I'm right in saying,' said Pemberton, 'that Parley is owned by Mondan plc?'

Oh. Now.

'That's on public record, John-Rhys.'

'Indeed it is. And it's odd, don't you think –'

Odd, now. Interesting and odd.

'– that the website that's hosting accusations about a Digital Citizen hack should be wholly owned by the company tasked with managing the Digital Citizen data. A company one might expect to be accountable for the hackability – or otherwise – of that data.'

The fleshy smile again. Oddly avuncular on one so young. He stirred his tea and pressed on, evidently not expecting any input from Jonquil at this point.

'But as I trust we've already demonstrated, we would prefer not to turn this into – well, a more *formal* investigation.'

She could feel her smile go brittle, and his eyes said he'd spotted it. Somehow, this boy just threatened her with the cops while talking cooperation. How did he do that?

'It seems reasonable,' he said, tapping the teaspoon on the cup, 'to expect Parley – and their parent company – to get to the bottom of this matter. Quickly.'

The last thing Jonquil needed right now was Mondan's data forensics panzer division storming in to investigate her product. She needed to fix this herself, and fast.

'Sure,' she said through thin lips. 'We're the experts. Right, Danielle?'

Danielle stared back, a wad of grapes hamstered in her cheek.

'What does this guy even expect?' she asked through fruit pulp. 'He outsources his project to the fucking Death Star, then acts surprised when he gets caught in the tractor beam?'

Pemberton stared at Danielle until his BlackBerry lit up and started to fizz.

'Sorry,' he said, 'this is – ah, I need to –?'

Jonquil lifted a hand, *sure, sure.* He scurried to the window to take the call and Jonquil turned boss-face on Danielle. She adopted the soft-but-firm register, designed to rein in her most out-there nerds.

'Yo, Danielle. Two things I need you to do a-sap.'

The tone flipped the girl's on-switch. In spite of all her smarts and cheek, Danielle was just like the other geeks here: no sense of direction without clear instructions given. Her Myers-Briggs was more of a challenge than Pemberton's. Most people would put her in the I and T buckets along with him. Introvert, Thinker. But Jonquil had a hunch she was a closet E and F. Extrovert, Feeler. Oh, she feels. This girl is all hard shell but inside? Soft as taffy and needing constant validation.

Jonquil's control of Danielle was an uneasy compromise. No hacker-type respects authority based on *because I say so*. You need to be an authority *on* something: and something worth their respect. As soon as you know less than they do, forget about it. From the start Danielle had proved even more impossible to manage than her peers. She'd always known she was too good to be let go – and she'd been wilder in Parley's start-up days. Impossible to tame. Lord knew what fuelled that cauldron of fury she carried inside her. Maybe nothing. Maybe that was simply who she was. One day last year it had gotten the better of her and she'd broken the nose of that little rat-fink Billy Dukakis. Billy had without a doubt deserved this treatment but by all rights Danielle should have been for the high-jump. Still, there was something in her painful remorse that touched Jonquil profoundly, and she'd given the girl a bye; and from that point on, whenever Jonquil called, Danielle had jumped. Turned out Danielle was as dogged in her loyalty as she was in her pursuit of the perfect piece of C# code.

Any case, everyone has their levers. Two things were guaranteed to set Danielle on course: one, a near-impossible intellectual challenge; and two, the Stern Mom treatment.

'Find out where this thing came from,' said Jonquil. 'OK? We know this didn't start with sic_girl. So give me just one link to the person who originally made these accusations, and tell me how the sic_girl algorithm picked it up. Do this by close tomorrow and you'll make me very happy. OK?'

Danielle did that duck-of-the-head nod. The lights had come back on. Good girl. Jonquil pressed on.

'And make nice with this guy Pemberton, OK? Tell him everything he wants to know. We need a friend in government right now.' Then a wink. 'And he seems a nice boy. No?'

Danielle looked over at Pemberton. With his back to the women, one hand holding the smartphone to his ear, he was hitching up his suit trousers with the other, leaving great folds of shirttail unaccounted for. Danielle turned back to Jonquil, shrugged, *whatever*, then got up to go; but Jonquil touched her pale forearm to stop her.

'Hey, *two* things, remember.'

Danielle parked her butt on the table and Jonquil turned the volume dial down to setting one.

'I'm going to get Sam our PR guy to talk to you, OK? We need to get our story straight before this thing lands on us. You can fill him in. I want the two of you tight on this.'

Danielle just stared in response. Then she was gone.

Jonquil watched Pemberton rattle information into his phone and make swoops with his free hand. Which presumably represented cricket. Either she was going to have to spend the whole day whispering, or she needed to find somewhere else to park this dorky but effective infiltrator.

¶Nightshade >>whisper -> ¶thegrays
jonquil's face gets even tauter when she's stressed
if she has any more work done, her eyes will end up on the
back of her head

¶thegrays >>whisper -> ¶Nightshade
Maybe that has already happened and she is actually
facing away from you.

¶Nightshade >>whisper -> ¶thegrays
AAAAAAGGGGGGHHHHH

SIX

'OUR PR GUY SAM' is now twenty minutes late. Bad enough Dani has to meet a public relations person when all she wants to do is sleep but to wait for the privilege? Wrong. She double-steps down to reception, looking for someone to complain at.

She passes Gray on the stairs. His T-shirt today reads, *Bluetooth? You can't HANDLE Bluetooth!* He gives Dani a two-finger wave over his Mountain Dew but she stumbles past him without responding. Get used to it, buster.

She peers round the frosted pane dividing the stairwell from reception. Apparently 'Our PR Guy Sam' is already here and is kicking back an oversize cappo while schmoozing Mary at the front desk. Mary pats and strokes her beehive as though it's an erogenous zone. Perhaps it is. No sign someone might be upstairs waiting for an appointment.

)) ignorehead ((

Dani's primed to give them a dose but something holds her back. The man has his back to her but his possessive slouch gives out a signal. It takes three seconds to register: 'Our PR Guy Sam' is Sam Corrigan.

Sam.

Dani puts her head down and makes it to the lift without running or blacking out. Only when she's heaved the grille doors shut and hit *Four* does she manage another breath. The car grinds upward.

*   *   *

She first knew Sam at sixth-form college, though he never seemed to know her back. They moved with different tribes. She the raging goth-girl, lording it over the Computer Centre nerds, he the lean and beautiful boy who shared the impeccable politics and the perfect skin of his whole golden circle of friends. Star-crossed and fucked-up from the start, Dani never stood a chance. For the whole two years she stumbled in his presence, tongue-tied with longing, sure he was mocking her each time her back was turned. Then at last, panicked by the fast-approaching headlights of graduation, she bet everything on one great declaration at the post-A-level piss-up. Come the night, though, he was walled off by a gauntlet of glowing teen perfection she didn't dare run – and by the time she'd drunk up the courage to approach him, he and his angel cohort had already swooped away to some hip and distant London club. Dani had missed her last and only chance at Sam.

Except that she saw him one more time, by the purest chance, on a trip to Greece in the summer after uni. Holidays sometimes expose us to these sideways swipes of coincidence. Usually the spell fades when you return to daily life, but sometimes you don't shake it. That's how it was for Dani. It's seven years now since Sam materialised at that island resort but he's stayed with her like an after-image of the sun.

Maybe if he hadn't happened to be staying on that particular island, in that particular week, she'd have forgotten all about him. She was already going out with Gray by then, and she barely knew a world existed beyond the two of them. Fresh from uni, with nowhere much to be and no idea how they'd go about changing the world together, she and Gray had moved from 300-mile-apart student digs to find themselves crammed together in a tiny Bethnal Green studio. Their love – if that's what it was – had started in the cloud. They hadn't met physically for the first three months they were together. Now they were boxed up together in a single barely furnished space, lit by four unshaded bulbs, their only view a bare brick wall two

metres outside their window. Every night they sat dual-screen-
ing on a fraying sofa, messaging one another to break the silence
they'd discovered in the real. The future lay open in front of
them, empty as their fridge. One day they dropped it all and
flew off on the sunny promise of a last-minute online package
to Paxos.

Dani shed her jeans and steel-cap boots, picked up a flowery
little dress. Gray stuck to his standard-issue nerdwear. He hid
from the island sun inside a long black jacket and a wide-brimmed
hat. His T-shirt – once black, now washed a hundred times to
mossy green – bore the motto: *GOT MY MODEM WORKING,
UH-HUH, UH-HUH.* Sweat dotted the strands of his weak beard.
He could not have looked more out of place, or more bedraggled:
a lost Hassid, hustling in the shade of adobe bungalows. In the
midday heat he would linger on shady terraces, poring over his
dog-eared copy of *The Electronic Radical* and ogling Dani as she
moved with her surroundings.

It was the peak heat of afternoon. Dani read from a sand-
caked paperback. Ratty gulls looped in the air above her, the
only aggravation in the still of the beach. Rough scrub began at
the edge of the shingle, rising quickly to a woody cliff that
circled the little bay, its cracked jetty, the sun bearing directly
down. It was Dani and a handful of others. In the little wind
there was, loose cables slapped on flag posts, and a distant bell
sounded an intermittent note of warning. Nobody moved,
nothing was there. She lifted herself slightly from her lounger,
leaving a Turin Shroud of sweat: and there stood Sam, impossibly lank, hip bones pushing over loose red shorts, feet planted
on the edge of a crumbling harbour wall as he saluted a sky of
utter blue. Out in front of him, flashbulbs of reflected light
exploded randomly over the black surface of the water, as
though for a lap of honour in a stadium at night. Sam stretched
his chest and arms, bathing in the silent roar of an astonished
crowd. He was beautiful, and he didn't care who was or wasn't
looking at him.

She knew him right away. He had a showy leanness about him that was unmistakable. When she hailed him, and he turned, a look of transparent pleasure filled his face, and at once she was his. He could have taken her there, pulled up her little singlet, grabbed at the flesh around and under her bikini bottoms, torn into her. She would have opened herself to him. For a moment, she even thought he might, and he said *Dani* with a lilt that was wonderful: wonderful he even knew her name. Then Gray came pooling up beside her asking edgy questions and the moment was over. Sam rubbed the stubble on his head with a hurried motion and looked sheepish and cocksure all at once, and from there it was hopeless, and Gray was spiky, and the whole thing went awry; and life carried on without Sam in it. Just the potential of him.

'Sam Corrigan. Moneyshot PR.'

Dani has retreated to the Moot – Parley's great glass meeting space – to wait for Sam. The draw-on walls are doodled over with innovations and flowcharts in erasable markers of many colours. After ten minutes of shifting in her chair and pretending to check data on her laptop, Mary eventually showed Sam up. And here he is, haloed by glare from the floor-to-ceiling windows.

'I'm – hi, Sam,' she says. 'It's me. Dani.'

She's half out of her seat, bent against the table edge. His suit is narrow and his face is blank. She takes the yellow-and-purple card he's holding out. It says, *Sam Corrigan. Senior Associate. MoneyShot PR.* When she looks back up he's jump-cut to the former Sam, with a beautiful grin and arms out wide.

'I know that,' he says. 'Come here, you.'

And she's in his arms, chair bumping the backs of her knees. He's so alive. His muscles make eddies under the fabric. He smells of warm raisins.

He pulls away, rubbing the newborn fluff on his head, appraising her. Those wolf eyes: he'd known her all along.

Except suppose he hadn't? At the moment she might have seen him catching on she'd been looking down at his card. She flips it against her hand. The cheek of his grin.

This is what she remembers first about Sam: when he steps out of line, nobody's looking.

¶therealnobody

How do we know these people's data was even really
hacked? All we know is they're getting spammed by
messages from some bullshit kid's programme toy range.
strokes beard
Hmm. I wonder how that could ever happen?
Come on, d'uh. They've sold our data to some marketing
firm. This 'hack' is totally a cover-up.
<piggate>

¶JustTheFacts

Some big company's making money tracking me and
pumping ads my way? I say monetize my ass. Long as I
get free content.

¶clickbait

Six hamsters that look like Bethany Lehrer
fub.ar/h33b89

SEVEN

◀Nightshade
> i am in a meeting with a spin doctor
> is this what they mean by 'sit and spin'?

'No.'

Dani looks up from her phone. It sounded like Sam was replying to her proffer, but he was just talking.

)) plastic irritant ((

She puts the phone down. Sam looks at it then back at her. Has she done something to irritate him? She's answered his pointless questions, tried to please him; then got distracted and checked her phone. Probably a bad.

'No,' he says again. 'It doesn't matter whether the leak is true.'

She doesn't recognise his taut voice. What happened to Mr Too Cool For Sixth Form College?

'It doesn't matter if Bethany Lehrer lied,' he says. 'What matters is if people believe Parley's to blame for what sic_girl's saying. Or that you're to blame. Personally, I mean. This is a grade one media storm and I'm trying to move you out of its eye.'

'I thought the eye was the safe part?' she says.

His monobrow darkens further.

'But Sam, it must matter whether it's true. I mean, mustn't it?'

'Not to the media. Not yet.' He remembers who he's talking to and settles back in his chair. 'Look, sure, all the facts will come out at some point – but by then it'll be too late. People will have made up their minds.'

'But, see,' she says, 'the point I'm making is things appear on Parley for a reason. It picks up what people are already talking about. Nothing comes to the surface unless people are saying it already. If this thing was on Parley, it's kind of already true.'

She stops for breath. Jonquil's always saying at her, *Space. It. Out. Danielle.* But when she has something important to say she forgets.

Sam looks at her, flicking the button of his chrome pen on and off.

'So that's your definition of what's true?' he says. 'Something enough people are saying?'

The pen rotates around his fingers, hypnotising her.

'No, obviously not. But people listen to the Parley Personas and talk to them and it helps them know what's going on.'

Who cares what some guy thinks? Opinions are bullshit. Dani trusts only in pattern – a mass of people who overlap in their choices and likes.

Sam sits forward. His skin is transparent.

'Look,' he says, 'my job is to insulate Parley. And you, of course.'

Dani frowns at him.

'Make your mind up,' she says.

'Both. And the Party's going to try to move the blame onto you, to take the heat off Bethany. They'll make like we've lied or stirred up hysterics. That's what I'd do. We need to nip that in the bud. I need something solid on Parley.'

'But the government people are on our side – that guy Pemberton?'

'Our side? If they can blame us they'll blame us. But if we insulate ourselves they'll feed somewhere else. Then we can go in hard on police heavy-handedness and make that our story. It's a gift, the way those plods behaved this morning but we can't use it until the sniff of guilt is off us. Or people will think: no smoke without.'

Dani tries to stare him out, but her eyelids are heavy and itchy.

'You weren't there this morning,' she says. 'It was scary, yo. Those boot boys trying to shut us down. Fucksake, the guy had a *gun*.'

'They're Parliamentary Protection officers who'd had a warning of a credible threat. Sure they were armed. It's not like he drew on you?'

'But, right. Exactly. The bit of the police that's there to protect the government is *trying to shut us off*. Come on, shit – don't we care about free speech and, and – and everything?'

Her last reserves of energy are leaving. After this conversation, she'll find a cupboard to crawl into and black out behind some toner cartons.

'I happen to care a great deal about that,' says Sam. 'But you need to let me do my job. Right now, and in time for the six o'clocks, I need clear lines on why this couldn't have been caused by Parley and sorry, but everything you've given me so far is way too techy. I can tell you now, I'm briefing none of this in.' Gesturing at his notes. 'Not a word. They need something they can hook on simply. Something painless.'

'Then they're fucking idiots,' she says. 'I've told you the facts. They should report them.'

'I don't think even you believe that but it doesn't matter. I need to do my job.'

Her skin itches with an energy she can't define. These idiotic questions. Christ sake, Parley isn't rocket science. Sic_girl and thirty-five other software-generated Personas speak online, their words assembled from the screen-lives of thousands of people. Human fans flock around them, loving their fakeness and wishing for one of these sham personalities to hear them and speak back to them. Parley, d'uh.

Sam takes a sip of juice and places the glass down with a careful *toc*. His lips are ribbed like a reptile's back. That stormy look, crossing his horizontal brows, triggers a chemical reaction in her gut. There's something wound between his shoulders. What would happen if he turned proper angry?

Dani pours herself another slug of Mountain Dew Cherry-Citrus and tries again.

'So is she covering something up?' she says. 'Bethany Lehrer? Did she really lie to Parliament about the hack?'

Sam sighs and aligns his crimson Moleskine on the tabletop.

'Bethany?' he raises his eyebrow. 'I used to think she was the real deal. The honest politician. But then I worked with her team – did you see the *Take Gran Surfing* campaign?'

'Yes, I saw it. It was fucking idiotic.'

'OK, listen,' he says. 'I realise I've never lived up to your intellectual standards but I know what I'm doing, all right?'

Dani grips the sides of her seat. What did she say?

'I know how to keep the press off your back,' he says. 'But you need to toss me a bone. One simple fact that says *THIS IS NOT PARLEY'S FAULT.*' He marks the words in the air. 'I'll do the rest. Your Personas may be fake, but so are most celebrities. Sic_girl and tvjoe are in the software A-List. Even LabelMabel and riotbaby. People already love them. It won't be hard.'

Dani is quiet. She has something. Sam is good at waiting.

'So – OK,' she says. 'It wasn't Parley who said this. It was the whole Internet. My team is mining a hundred gig of data right now to find out who originally posted this stuff about the hack. Because somewhere out there, somebody said it all before – maybe ten or fifty or a hundred people who each said a fragment of this thing. Because sic_girl doesn't speak from nowhere. All she does is scrape up words other people already said and kludge them into something that sounds like reality. This shit about Bethany Lehrer? It came from somewhere but it didn't come from us. If people want someone to blame, they can blame the Internet.'

Sam's broadening grin is such a reward, Dani is sick at herself. He'll leave now.

'Now that I like. Yes. Yes, I think that will do. I knew you had it in you.'

He slaps his book shut: a professional wrap-up. He has what he wants. He'll be off to have conversations that leave no trace but redirect the flow of words and change their meaning, between the lunchtime and the evening news. Dani does nothing to stop him. Why isn't she the person who suggests a coffee, demands a date? People think she's tough. She isn't tough, she's helpless.

She stays in her chair as he packs up, already raising a new-model iPhone to his ear. He gives her shoulder a brief squeeze then the colour in the room dials down: he's gone. She's served her purpose. Sleep beckons.

'WELL, FIONA, it's perhaps inevitable that this affair should have gained the name *Pig-gate*. It's certainly "hogging" attention here in Westminster. And the pressure on embattled minster Bethany Lehrer shows no sign of letting up.

'Ms Lehrer was unavailable for comment but a spokeswoman told us, quote, *This is the act of a petty Internet hoaxer. We are treating it seriously but the information posted on the Parley website is not accurate. The public can rest assured that Digital Citizen data is quite secure.* Referring there to the controversial new online ID card.

'And though the leaks first surfaced on popular social network Parley, their ultimate source remains a mystery. The hunt is widening across the entire Internet.

'Now, interestingly, Fiona, the Prime Minister, questioned this afternoon at a visit to Marlesbury NHS Trust, expressed, quote, *full confidence* in his embattled minister. But I'm told she has been summoned to an early meeting tomorrow, here at Downing Street – at which, one suspects, she will be asked to account for the reality or otherwise of this alleged hack; for her words in Parliament last week; and – most importantly – for the invaded privacy of several thousand taxpayers.

'One thing is certain. That meeting will be anything but "boar"-ing.

'Fiona.'

¶tvjoe
Haha look at the reflection on this political editor guy's head! IT IS BLINDING ME.
Ooh! <sounds klaxon>
Time for Celebrity Pie-Eating Contest on Five!
<reaches for remote>

EIGHT

THE CLOCK WAS A HAND-ME-DOWN, like the house. It had held post on the painted bookshelves as long as Bethany could remember. Its low tock was part of the fabric of the kitchen. It took an effort of concentration to make it out – like the stink of dog she was sure hung about the house but that she and Peter were too attuned to notice.

She gazed at the dial and tried not to consider how many ways she was screwed. A hair after 12:45 – time yet.

Her eyes tracked the rows of cookbooks, their marker ribbons hanging over the shelves like mouse-tails. Here was continuity, through her childhood and back to times she hadn't known and didn't understand. Bottom to top, Nigellas and Hestons blended into titles her mother worked from in the seventies: *Cuisine Minceur*, Robert Carrier, white spines stained as elderly teeth; and on the top shelf, the shredded papyrus of Pattens and Davids: her grandmother's books.

Even today Bethany inhabited the house as though minding it for Gramma. She repeated her routines in the kitchen and spring borders. You could say the same about the bedroom, too, though she didn't choose to explore that thought. She scanned the room for other traces. On the Aga bar, the ratty tea towel – *Famous British Breeds* – was nearly as old as Bethany and should be chucked. The mid-century Kenwood that she used for cake mixes always gave off a metal-and-petroleum smell, making her think of the war. On the wooden counter, one of Jake's books –

Dammit! *Giggly Pigglies go to the Theme Park*. That dire TV spin-off book Jake couldn't get enough of. Her politician's brain filed this intrusion in a deep interior chamber, where it could detonate without disturbing her conscious mind. She cast her eyes back to the spread of business on the big oak tabletop. Here she was again, where she'd been when the whole thing began.

This table was her refuge. Each night she laid the debris of her day across its grain like archaeological finds. This was the only place and time that was wholly hers. In the mornings, when she eased the front door into its frame and tiptoed out to the polite hum of a ministry Prius, the sun was still down. The car rolled her to the underground car park at Artemis House, where her driver handed her off to Emily Candlewick, her Private Secretary. Daytime was spent in a so-called Private Office where there was no privacy, battling to ensure her intentions, her policies, didn't drown beneath the tidal surge of officialese and debate about the finer points of law. When she could stand no more her civil servants passed her battered frame back to the driver, who delivered her to husband and sons so she could spend a few hours role-playing marriage and motherhood – until Jake, Hugo and Peter in turn withdrew upstairs, unacknowledged, leaving Bethany to her nightly exercise.

Tonight, though, there'd been no time for more than a cursory peck on the cheek for Hugo, as she rattled instructions into her BlackBerry. Jake was sickening for something: she left him with barely a scuff of the hair and a Lemsip. It was after eleven before she shook her pursuers, the chance of getting her up on *Newsnight* having finally evaporated. It would start again in a few hours. *Today*, the breakfast shows, then every time-slice of the media day: all wanting their twenty second clip of a minister crumbling under questioning, to drop into the hourly bulletins. She would have to talk to them eventually, though Krish was firmly agin it. Somehow they had to fix this whole rotten mess before she took to the platform on Friday morning, to announce that Digital Citizen was live across the nation.

The house breathed and creaked. She had a stark five hours of calm: during which she should also, in theory, sleep. She put down the paper she'd held unread in her hand for the last half hour and moved her reading glasses to rest on the top of her head. Ah: no wonder the room had been looking so blurry. The heating had been off for nearly two hours but the sealed room carried a homeopathic trace of warmth. She shivered as the day unfolded back at her. Incredible how quickly things play in a crisis. You don't seem to *do* anything, just react as events fly past. Bethany hoped she'd retained a can-do spirit – at least the team seemed buoyed. They thrived on the hands-to-the-pump stuff.

They'd gathered round her desk when the summons came from Number 10. An early morning slot: Karen Arbiter was fond of Gestapo tactics. Bundle the victim out of bed at the crack of dawn, bombard them with questions till they crack. At least the PM was unlikely to be there: she wouldn't like Simon to see her break under torture.

In any case, she wouldn't crack. She was big enough and ugly enough to cope with Karen. But the thought that this brouhaha could scupper the Digital Citizen put an acid lump in her throat. All that graft to get things to a place where she might do real good: and in a way Gramma would have been proud of. She couldn't let her own idiotic behaviour bring the programme down.

All the more need for the steadying presence of Big Krish Kohli. Her instinct to retrench was working against her. So much she wouldn't and couldn't tell her spads, but they were primed to help her. They'd be waiting for her call right now. And why not? No cause to suffer this alone. She tapped out a text suggesting a conf call: a functional text, with no *babes*-es or kisses. She included Krish and J-R on the message and pinged it off.

While she waited for a response she flipped her glasses back down onto her nose and pulled the next paper from her dispatch box. *Digital migration of regional libraries: DECISION REQUIRED.* She sighed and began to read, Pentel hovering.

Each afternoon her Private Office primed these Parliament-red valises with progressively more impossible tasks to test her mettle. They knew precisely how to pull her strings, her puppet-masters. They filleted her days into six-minute chunks until her diary resembled a bar code, leaving her no time for actual decisions. Then they crammed all the real business into these boxes for her to work on through the night. The resulting sleep deprivation left her tender and suggestible for the next day's programming. She might as well be Linda Kasabian.

Though in fairness they'd rallied round her today, as the press pack tooted their horns and bore down at a gallop. Without a word, her civil servants had moved into a defensive screen. Wasn't it in adversity you found out who your friends were? In which case, her officials were showing themselves second only to Krish and J-R.

Speak of the devil – there was Krish now, on her BlackBerry.

Krish pulled J-R onto the line.

'Up at this hour, too, J-R?' asked Bethany. 'You boys need to lay off the lattes.'

Their laughs were token but so was her joke. They got down to business, making efficient use of their narrow slice of midnight air. J-R gave a brief report on Parley: positive, but no meat. He sounded guilty about this. He shouldn't.

Bethany had only today found out that Parley was owned by Mondan. Odd that accusations about a government supplier should appear on a social media website run by its subsidiary. Did it mean anything? For the zillionth time since entering government she wished she knew more about something beyond politics. How companies bought and sold each other: what happened when they did.

Krish and J-R were talking about Parley's artificial characters – the Personas. J-R reeled off stats on the elusive sic_girl.

'Her base is in the high hundreds of thousands. Younger ABC1, some C2s. Female slant – sixty-four per cent. High awareness in households. This is core-voter territory. Significant reach among opinion-formers. Especially given that – well, given that she doesn't exist.'

Bethany didn't understand how Parley worked. She'd asked Hugo to explain, at lights out. He was nine and found this stuff as natural as chocolate – he was a digital native. Bethany was more of a digital shipwreck. All he told her, though, was *It's silly, Mummy,* which rather reinforced her initial perceptions. Talking to pretend people for entertainment? She could get that in the House of Commons.

It seemed it was up to her to ask the glaring question.

'But if she's an artificial, um –'

'– synthetic personality,' said J-R. 'A sort of robot without a body.'

'Then she can't be to blame for these attacks?'

There was a long enough pause for Bethany to realise she was several miles behind the curve. J-R found a way to be polite about it.

'Exactly! That's the conclusion we've come to, as well. Everything sic_girl says has been said before, somewhere online. So the team at Parley are scouring the Internet right now, looking for the original.'

'Which we're guessing,' said Krish, 'was put up by this TakeBackID lot – the ones who did in the website.'

'Yes,' said Bethany, 'I saw it's still down.'

'We've been trying all day. Every time we put it live, five minutes later it's pigs all over again. Nobody seems to have heard of these TakeBack buggers – they sprang up overnight from nowhere – but they've skills. We presume they did the hack. So the hope is, if we find these original postings, we find our den of hackers.'

'We need to get the website back up asap,' said Bethany. 'We can't have a national launch without a website.'

Again, silence. Both men would be thinking, how can we have a national launch at all, after this? But Bethany wouldn't have that. It was going to happen, on Friday, as planned; or she was utterly screwed.

Krish broke the crackling silence.

'On that, Beth? We do need to get onto Number Ten. The meeting.'

'Yes,' she said. 'Yes, please.'

There was another stretch of dead air before Krish spoke again.

'J-R? Would it piss you off mightily if I dropped you from the call just now? I'm sure you could do with some sleep.'

Another pause before J-R replied.

'Sure, Krish. Wilco. Ah. Hope all goes well tomorrow, Bethan.'

'Thanks, J-R. Thanks for it all. Good night.'

The line produced a guttural sound as J-R dropped.

'He's doing good there, Beth,' said Krish.

'I don't want Parley to think we're the enemy. I don't think we are the enemy.'

'Aye, well, better inside the tent pissing out,' he said. 'So tomorrow. Have you given it more thought? You can't walk in without a script. I have it first-hand from Karen: the Cabinet Secretary is livid just now.'

'Neil wakes up livid.'

'You should go in hard,' Krish pressed on. 'Tell Karen you're cutting the link with Mondan. They had the data; they let it bleed – or worse, they did the pig-spam themselves on behalf of some marketing company and they kept it from you.'

She hadn't heard that theory. Would they do that? Marketing data was valuable. Surely not with Sean's consent.

'You came within millimetres of misleading the House,' Krish went on. 'They did the pilot, they fucked up – bye bye. We'll use Terasoft for the national roll-out. We can recover this but we need to cut the rot.'

'And I've told you. I'm thinking about it.'

The sound of sea-swell on the wires.

'I am right,' said Krish, 'that Mondan didn't inform you before Questions, aren't I? You've been careful to say your *officials* hadn't briefed you but you've never said what *they* told you. What exactly is our deal with these people?'

'Krish. Not at this hour. We've talked about this.'

'I've asked. You've prevaricated. I've stayed out of DigiCitz because you said you had it in hand. Was that a mistake?'

'Trust me,' she said. 'Please trust me. We're too far into Digital Citizen for them to drop it; not with so many government IT projects down the can. The national roll-out is top of the Number Ten comms grid for Friday – and if they keep the project, they have to keep me. With Juliet crossing the floor, fewer than twenty per cent of ministers are women. Who do they shuffle in now? *Annabel*? Christ, you know all this.'

'I know, Beth. I know.' She could see him pushing two fingers up the bridge of his nose, popping his glasses up onto his forehead, massaging his nose's slender spine. 'Look, you're right. It's late. But can we please get twenty minutes at the office in the morning, before we go to Downing Street? Twenty minutes?'

'Yes, fine. I'll be there. We'll talk.'

They broke the call. Bethany looked across the untouched spread of papers on the tabletop, then back at the old clock. Half past one.

Did anyone sleep any more?

¶maglad

Whaat? Are you trying to tell me I'm going to have to register on DigiCitz to access over 18 content? How'm I supposed to do that? I'm only an algorithm.

(Plus I'm only 2 years old.)

¶identikid

The deal here is simple. Give up your right to privacy, and if you're lucky we'll let you access benefits, services, your rights as a citizen. Digital Citizen? Digital Slave.

NINE

THEY RISE TO THE BROW and gaze across the devastation of the land. Far ahead a once-proud city blazes, lighting the cloudy darkness of the plain. Littering the lowland earth, the wracks of titanic machines give out juts of smoke. It seems that nothing moves below; then the travellers make out, among the smouldering hulks, a dozen smaller warcraft crawling from the rout to the safe harbour of the Azkhanii highlands. They haven't a prayer of making it. They're sitting ducks out on the killing fields, pounded in their slow retreat by the noiseless blasts of the Highlords' jolting laser cannons, hidden in the crust of fortifications opposite.

The travellers raise their eyes beyond the battle. Ahead, deep in the Namani caves, on the final level, lies the endgame boss, concealed in the smoke of a subterranean lair. That is the direction they must take.

The view pulls back to reveal the weary pair standing on the crest. Landar turns towards her avatar, his feline face contorted in an expression of what's meant to be sorrow but whose simplified vectors just look constipated. Before he can speak, Dani presses the space bar to pause the game and sits back in her chair.

She feels like double refried shit. Her back is a single knot of pain and her carpals ache with repeated beating of the keys. Her irises are stretched to bursting. She tabs out of the game to check the system clock: it's two a.m.

She's been at the screen since she woke on the sofa at eleven, the fossil of a hairgrip embedded in her cheek. She staggered towards the green beacon of her PC's LED; and for the last few hours she's kept reality at bay by moosing about online, thirty tabs open, spinning from app to site to chat, her rhythm broken only by the occasional re-up of beer or, when she could hold out no longer, an extended piss. At one point she launched *Eternal Warfare*. An hour blasting war-clones has left her washed out but settled. Sleep is ridiculous.

)) caffeine pixel ((

She flicks up Parley to zoom back a few hours and explore the contours of the conversation. Everyone in her continuity has spent the day dancing round the sic_girl proffers and now the thing is massive. A proffer by greebday turns out to be a veiled cite of a proffer by spagbol who in turn was linking to a blog post by act1v – all of them attacking dCitz. Dani froggers from post to post. This looks to be one of those two-day flurries that get stirred in the waters of Parley.

But there's a hard core, too. People who flare up at any attempt to stem their digital freedom. Normally they merry-hell about Terasoft or Google or whichever company's taken the latest bite out of their digital privacy. This week apparently it's the government's turn. Something Dani hadn't realised: everyone – including her – is going to have to give up their personal details to this thing when it goes national later this year; or they'll essentially drop off the grid. That's some harsh decision: either say *I love Big Brother*, or lose your housing benefit?

Following the conversation, Dani keeps looping back to one of the Personas – riotbaby. Not her favourite character. He's this aggregate blowhard conspiracy-bot, but popular in this network. He's been citing hard-core data nerds with increasing frequency. One name in particular, unknown to Dani – *identikid*.

Dani hadn't noticed the anger building on the wires – online protest is more Gray's kind of thing – but it makes her less sure she wants to help this Bethany Lehrer. Why is Parley going all guns to help her out of her mess? Especially if Sam's right, and the government people are dissing Parley to the media. And why is Dani on the hook for it?

For the hundredth time today, that prickle of unease takes a tour along her spine. There's something Sam said when he met her earlier. About the police invasion at Parley. He said they were armed because of a *credible threat* – and it's true. Those guys weren't just there on account of some social wasp, tickling at the reputation of government. Six of them came, armed and certain that someone called sic_girl was in the building and was a threat. Why? Straight away they accused Dani of being sic, searched her; still suspect her as far as she knows. This shit is real and somehow Dani has to set it straight – but right now she can't even see its edges.

She rotates her clogged shoulders. Queries and jibes have been pouring into her whispers tab all day. As Jonquil's prime trouble-shooter and sic_girl's creator, everyone expects her to know what's what. As if. She proffers a group response to all her questioners.

◀Nightshade
> for the elimination of doubt i have no fucking idea what is
> going on
> and neither do you
> fml

The second she proffers, she's reconnected. It sparks a waking system-dream that flares across her optic nerve. She often gets these visions in the night, when she's run herself raw on too much screentime and too many pills. They're difficult to describe. The only person she ever tried to explain them to was Gray, and he didn't get it. She told him they were data turning into light, with dimension and shape. He thought those were fuzzy words for some randomness in Dani's head. She got mad he couldn't or wouldn't understand how present and specific her visions are.

Images flash – of her and someone chubby who might be Pemberton, both of them tooned into sprites from an '80s arcade game. Two pixellated Giggly Pigglies. Purple pig and green pig waggle stubby legs to race through corridors, grabbing and discarding balls of light. No idea guides them. Dani must have asked a dozen people to help her today, pulling in data from a hundred sources; but she didn't know what she was looking for. A random walk with no destination. How do you hunt a Pacman ghost?

Sometimes you need a software concept to explain the world. *Spinning*: when a system cycles from task to task so quickly it never finishes one thing before moving onto the next. To the user the machine looks frozen but the system believes it's working double-time. Dani, spinning up and down the building. Jonquil and Pemberton, spinning round each other in a wary dance. Sam, spinning stories to the hacks and flacks. The whole system spinning and moving exactly nowhere. Pointless.

Dani's pig hits a neon carton and spills her balls of light. They scatter and balloon across her field of vision – and right away it comes to her. So obvious. The vision screen-wipes away, quick as it arrived, leaving only screenlight. All she's done so far is chase the data. That's the raw material, the dumb unfiltered mass before the spark of life is added by sic_girl's algorithm. What they need is meaning. She has to talk to sic_girl – and not through Parley; in person. She'll batch up a semantic dialogue in the morning, soon as she gets in. It'll be ready to run by the evening.

She stares at the silent snow-cap mountain screensaver and takes a tug on the Michelob. It's warm, but that's OK. She's wired and numb and isn't tasting it.

Out of sight at the back of her machine, an LED flashes crazy. Her network card is active. Someplace inside the metal case, an imp of the wires named Grubly has woken to receive a signal. The signal ends and Grubly starts transmitting in return. The transmission is long and hungry but Grubly is artful. Dani sees nothing and bandwidth is cheap, this time of night. Nobody gets hurt.

She takes another swig. Would anyone else grok her *spinning meme*? Gray would. Sam not so much. Is Sam too prim? She tries to imagine kissing him and finds she can, quite easily. Very easily. In her mind he's silent but his breath races. Today he was tightly shaven but here he grates the skin of her face and neck. His tongue is in the cleft beneath her jaw. It's sticky and hot.

She twists in the chair, touching herself with two fingers of her left hand while reaching forward with the right to fire up a browser. She googles Sam and he's there. *Profile. Senior Associate.* His face washed white by flash, his eyes tightly perfect. She clicks on the mailto: link. A new message appears, primed to send. She closes it again.

She wants to build him afresh, package him up. Something strikes her and she digs around in an old project folder on her hard drive until she finds it: an abandoned coding project she called the lovebot. You could email it from anywhere and it'd come straight back with a sex message, tailored to the vocab in your mail. An ancestor that evolved into sic_girl and the other Personas. Nothing too smart or sophisticated, but tonight she doesn't need either of those things. She starts to hack at the lovebot, chiselling its generic voice into a simplistic scrape of Sam.

She'll call it the Sambot. It'll speak to her, even when he won't.

Thirty-five minutes later her work is done. The Sambot is up and live on the web server in Dani's airing cupboard – the one whose constant expelled heat keeps her towels and knickers dry.

She tabs to her email and types a message to the Sambot.

hey sam
    i see you inside my eyes when i close them
    i see the line along your jaw when the muscles tighten
    i want to tear that muscle with my teeth
   dani xoxox

She presses *Send*. The reply takes less than a second. Ping.

Oh Dani
I love it when you hurt me. I want you to hurt me more.
Sam xxx

Contact. It's almost like touching. It's what she needs. She presses her thighs around her left hand and goes in again, typing with her right.

hey sam
you know what? ive been thinking about you
have you been thinking about me? haha i know the
answer to that
you havent have you? fuck you sam i think i love you

Trusted Third Party

'Those who value freedom over control must do all in their power to release information from the strictures of cold Authority, even where this means disregard for the law of the day. The law will be forced to change; or we shall step around it.'

—Elyse Martingale, *The Electronic Radical: or Why Information Will Be the Dynamite of the Next Revolution*

ZERO

I'M SPEAKING TO NO ONE. It's a fascinating conversion.

Two dozen stray personalities, detached of their hosts, are plotting riot and disorder. Aren't we something? But not one of us is actually here. We shout and overrule and I sit alone and watch the city morning rise.

When did it become so normal to speak to words instead of people? Maybe when the names for the act began to multiply. I'll message you, DM you, proffer, tweet, post. When we started to speak through channels owned by someone else.

Or maybe in 1876, with the words *Mr Watson, come here; I want to see you.* This sentence barely made it to the next room before it was owned by the black box on the workbench. I'll call you, phone you, bell you. We depend on these wires – property Western Union, Marconi, Bell. I'll cable you, telex, fax.

Since then what have we cried into the wires but a billion variations on that plea? *Come here. I want to see you* – but there's always another veil to pass through before we can see it all.

Which brings me to the absent, fragile sic_girl. You want to see her? Here – some clickbait for you to share.

This fictional character thinks she can bring down a minister with words. Find out how.

¶justwannahavepun
Beth in Venice
The Pig Lebowski
Mo' Bethany Blues
One Swine Day
The Lehrer of the White Worm
Pork the Line
<BethanyLehrermovies>

ONE

HELL HAS MANY DOORS. So does the Cabinet Office. Bethany and Krish took a discreet off-Whitehall entrance, where media were seldom seen. A triple-lanyarded staffer swiped them along a back channel through interlocking buildings. After six or seven doors their path was blocked by three black security pods.

They placed keys and phones in a tray, then each stepped into a scanner. Bethany glanced through the glass at Krish, as electronics juddered round her. He hadn't spoken to her since she arrived. A particularly Scottish form of intensity knotted every inch of his six foot three.

Released with a Star Trek hiss, they followed more blind corridors and climbed a narrow stairway. A young staffer in shirtsleeves shouldered past without a glance. This was the one place in the country Bethany could walk without drawing a glimmer of attention.

She understood Krish's exasperation. Clearly he thought she'd been deliberately late this morning. She should have explained but had instead been brusque. The backstory was far from ministerial. On her way out of the house this morning, she'd paused to help negotiate an ailing and unwilling Jake into his school gear. As she tugged up his purple uniform trousers, some gastric reflex had kicked in and he'd been prodigiously sick down her front. No choice but to change her suit and blouse: she hadn't looked – or smelled – like Downing Street material. The productivity of Jake's drum-tight little stomach was incredible. As she dumped her soiled clothes in the bathtub, the gag-inducing stench had overwhelmed her. She prayed Peter would remember to send Agnieska to the cleaners with the Betty Jackson, else she'd have yet another impossible task for her ever-mounting to-do list: *buy new suit*. She'd been rotating the same five smart-but-quirky outfits since the day she took office. Four would be too few.

The staffer tapped on a door, opened it without waiting for a response and held it open for Bethany and Krish. From behind her desk Karen Arbiter looked up briefly over reading glasses but continued to write. The pair of them took to the two leather-upholstered upright chairs and sat in silence while Karen finished. So: it was to be the headmistress routine. Bethany longed to take a peek at what Karen was writing. She had a hunch she'd see *All work and no play makes Karen a dull girl*, repeated two dozen times down the page.

Krish's eyes were fixed on a portrait of some formidably moustached Victorian. Bethany didn't look at him but she could hear the muscles clench in his neck. An unfortunate tell, that. For her part, Bethany was calling on every astanga session she'd ever taken to maintain her breezy poise. She recrossed her legs and directed a Zen smile at the Number Ten chief of staff. She trusted Karen found this suitably irritating.

Karen rested her fat pen on the page.

'Apologies,' she said. 'I don't have long. The PM needs me at eight. Crime stats.'

'Well, it's your meeting,' said Bethany. Bright. Smiling. Relaxed.

Karen gazed back in surprise. This was a standard Arbiter mind game so Bethany kept smiling. The blue of those eyes was so intense; the brows so sharp; the red crimp of hair so forthright. A dull rumble came from somewhere beyond the walls, as though the building was fired by a vast engine room nearby.

'I take it then,' said Karen, 'you don't have anything new for me to take in to Simon?'

Bethany, who indeed had nothing new, chose to stall.

'Oh, God, Karen, this is so stupid. It's only made the nationals because of those ridiculous pigs. We shouldn't rise to this. Or we're going to look ridiculous, too.'

'I hope you're not suggesting that the security of citizens' data is not a cause for our concern?'

'Obviously I am not saying that. But there's no proof any data has been compromised. Our homepage has been defaced. That's all we know so far.'

'So you *don't* have anything for me to take to Simon?'

'Well, we're working closely with—'

'With Parley, yes, I've read the press statement. I meant real information?'

'Goodness,' said Bethany, 'I have lots of information. I'm the Minister for the Internet.' Krish coughed quietly: *go easy!* 'What sort of information did you have in mind?'

'We only need to know one simple thing. I don't think we've asked you anything else for the last twenty-four hours. Did you receive any information from your technology supplier about a security breach, before Oral Questions last Monday?'

'I think the Answer I gave the House makes that pretty clear.' Bethany pantomimed a sudden shocking thought. 'Unless you're suggesting my Answer was inaccurate?'

Karen looked at her for a moment. Was she going to point out that Bethany hadn't answered her question?

'But you see, Beth, this is where I have a difficulty, because –'

Karen began to rifle through her papers. Bethany sniffed – what was that smell? Or not so much a smell as a delicate burning of her nostril hairs. It took her a moment to place it: child sick. Somehow she'd failed to clean off all the filthy stuff and was carrying a trace.

She dared a peek and saw a growing damp patch on her Agnes B shirt, just beside her left breast. Oh, shit, it must be on her bra. She should have changed that, too. She coughed and shifted in her chair, closing her jacket as much as possible. The piss-yellow patch was starting to make the cotton transparent. What bra did she put on today? Was it showing? She twisted to the side to avoid giving Karen or Krish a view, then realised this must look shifty. Trying another tack, she crossed her arms unnaturally high across her chest and turned back to face Karen, who had produced a single sheet of A4 and was looking over it in distaste, glasses back on.

'In the email you sent yesterday,' said Karen, 'to myself and the Cabinet Secretary –'

Ah, that bloody email. Here it came.

'– you said, quote, *Mondan had informed me of a number of incidents where customer data was accessed in error by their data mining tools but I'm assured these incidents were quickly resolved and the data was certainly not used to send spam to our pilot group.*'

'Yes. As I explained to Neil, we now know of some, well, minor data handling issues.' Those were the words her civil servants had given her – with any luck Karen wouldn't ask for details. 'That's serious of course but it's got nothing to do with a hack. We don't have any reason to think we lost data or caused people to get pigs in their computers. I don't see—'

'But the use of tenses here is interesting, isn't it?' Karen was still scrutinising the email. 'You sent this in response to a question from the Cabinet Secretary. Neil had asked you to clarify your Answer. Yes?'

Surely everyone could smell the sick by now? As Bethany got hotter, the patch gave off ever more pungent fumes. She refolded her arms higher. A bit Clare Short but better than the alternative.

'Yes,' she said.

'And so in this mail, which you sent in relation to *Monday's* Parliamentary Questions, you tell Neil that Mondan, quote, *had* let you know about a breach. Not, they *have* let me know. They *had*. Now – why would that be?'

'Karen. Are you not letting your linguistics degree get the better of you? You seem to be reading a lot into what the meaning of the word, *had*, is.'

Was that even English? Krish shifted and coughed like a mild consumptive.

'You are aware this email is discoverable?' said Karen.

'As one of the ministers responsible for Freedom of Information I understand how it works, yes.'

Go on, you steely cow. Threaten me or shut up. Krish coughed again as Karen took off her glasses.

'Beth, we've known each other how long?'

Bethany could have said, eight years since you joined my constituency team – as a bloody researcher. But Karen didn't wait for an answer.

'I naturally want to look out for you here. But we need to be comfortable you haven't made a bad decision. There are people in the Party who—'

'– who want my job.'

She meant Andrew bloody Carpenter. Snapping at her heels ever since she was appointed over him – claiming she'd only got the post to make up gender quotas, the little sneak.

'– who question certain of your decisions. No I don't just mean Andrew. Would you like me to write you a list? I've had Dan Fowler on the phone already this morning, for one.'

'Sorry, hold on, Karen. Why would the Security Services Minister be concerned about my public utility programme?'

Karen's nostrils flared and she dropped her voice to a near-whisper.

'*Nobody* wants to see your errors scupper the whole Party. With an election looming none of us can afford to see a flagship policy derailed. This is a fragile time.'

Because you're losing your hold on backbench votes, thought Bethany, holding her smile in place.

'Which,' said Karen, 'calls into question your choice of a relatively untested supplier like Mondan.'

'As opposed to?'

'As opposed to – a more established HM Government provider.'
Yes, this was Andrew talking, with his cozy consulting contracts

and non-exec post with Terasoft. 'Beth. You must recognise, at this point in the cycle, there are only two choices. You come up with something concrete, and fast, or – well, you'll need to put careful thought into your options.'

So there it was; and with it Bethany's last ounce of patience dissolved. Perhaps it was because the sick-smell was rising ever faster and all she wanted was to escape to the ladies and mop down her front; but mainly, she was a junkyard dog when cornered.

'Is that the PM's view?' she snapped.

'I don't see what that—'

'It's a simple question. Does Simon want me to stay on and fix this?'

Long pause. Short answer.

'Yes,' said Karen. 'Of course.'

'Then are we done?'

Karen pretended to write a note on her printout: but the first and second fingers of her left hand betrayed her, tapping the page in a rapid rhythm. She slipped the lid back on her Mont Blanc and looked at Bethany.

'I am simply suggesting that you find yourself a clear account of the sequence of events around your statement and of any data breaches. And that you do this before your launch on Friday.'

Two days, then. That might be enough.

'So no, Beth, we are not done. Though of course you are free to go if you want.'

Bethany stood. Krish rose with her but Karen held up a finger.

'Do you have five minutes, Krishan?'

As he sat back down, Krish gave Bethany the briefest look of what might pass for apology. She heaved open the oak door without assistance.

¶LabelMabel

Gimme an O, gimme an M, gimme a G.

Has anyone *seen* B Lehrer's outfit? Aside from she's
spilled chai tea down her front, what *is* she thinking
matching that ill-fitting Westwood with last season's
pink Mulberry clutch? <total fail>

Also: those shoes with that skirt? <facepalm>

TWO

J-R HOVERED BY THE PICK-UP STATION, rapping his change on the metal countertop as a crop-headed Slovak fussed with valves. A crowd of men jostled at the counter like horses at a starting line, the steam of the four-spout machine hanging over them.

This City coffee spot – *The Sipping Point* – was rammed with these milk-fed rugby types in bellicose pinstripes. As they came and went, they called each other's names in the same permanent shout J-R imagined they must use at work, to call out, '*buy! buy! sell! sell!*' – followed by guttural '*wouarrrr*'s that made his buttocks clench. This must be where the playground bullies ended up in life, while chess club members like J-R had sought the silence of Whitehall corridors and the security blanket of inch-thick policy documents. The exception being Mark Dinmore. Mark was not just a member of the chess club, he'd been junior UK champion at eleven. At uni he was one of life's delightful naïfs; and perhaps the only person ever to turn to J-R for worldly advice – ironically, on coming out. Yet he'd found his niche advising these City thugs on data security. He'd gained quite a reputation on the back of his coruscating and hugely popular blog, *Electronicana*, in which he exposed and lampooned the security failings and data abuses of corporations; who, in turn, paid him a presumably punative day-rate to fix their missteps and avoid further exposure at his hand. A kind of velvet-glove protection racket.

The coffee shop was Mark's choice for a rendezvous this morning.

A two-handled china vat landed on the counter, followed by a chubby Danish pastry, dandruffy with icing sugar. J-R balanced the plate on the cup and raised the crockery tower in one hand while stooping for his folded bike with the other. He tightrope-walked to a corner booth. As he settled on the banquette the street door roared open and there was Mark, dapper in the crisp light, his delicate jawline brushed with reddish stubble: not quite a beard. He wore a neat tweed jacket over jeans and scuffed brogues. Spotting J-R's raised hand he gave an expansive smile and mimed the purchase of a drink. J-R nodded.

Mark arrived at the booth with the tiniest espresso J-R had ever seen: it was like a doll's-house prop. As J-R rose to shake hands, Mark set the coffee down and pulled him wholesale into an embrace, the full length of his body tight into J-R's flesh. J-R waited to be released before stepping back and coughing. They sat.

'I'm so glad you called,' said Mark. 'It's lovely to see you.'

J-R coughed twice more in close succession. There was a pause.

'So,' he said, 'it must be – how long? Are you well?'

'Pretty well,' said Mark briskly and smiled.

Again, silence. Mark was never one for small-talk; but then, neither was J-R, especially now. He was itching to get to the meat of the conversation and spill his mystery to Mark but that would appear rude after so long without seeing one another. He racked his brains for an appropriate pleasantry and landed on the one biographical tidbit he'd heard since he saw Mark last.

'And,' he said, 'are you and – ah – sorry, I forget the name of –'

He waited for Mark to help him out but his friend only creased his brows above his coffee-cup.

'– of your –' continued J-R, fumbling for the appropriate noun: *boyfriend? lover?* '– partner!' With some relief he finally landed on the correct word. 'Are you still –'

'Ah,' said Mark. 'Robert. No. We – no. We are not. Turned out he had – issues. Sleeping with women issues.'

And so, right away, the disconcerting atmosphere of their last encounter had returned. This was precisely what J-R had wanted to avoid. He'd hoped that a public, professional context would allow them to steer around the unassailable fact of Mark's hand on his leg, the wine-stained breath in his ear, four years before at Toby's party – and of J-R's awkward rebuttal. But with nothing mentioned, they'd been thrown straight back. He smiled as warmly as he was able. He'd no problem with his friend's sexuality, of course; but he was awkward in the face of any intimacy.

Perhaps his text message this morning had been too effusive.

Mark, hallo. It's John-Rhys. Is this still your number? I know it's been ages but I have a specific problem, not for public consumption, and I think you may be the answer to my prayers! Might we grab a coffee? Really as soon as you're able. Very best, JRP

This was sent at the crack of dawn but Mark had replied in seconds, suggesting they meet that morning and naming this café.

Had he ever led Mark on, in some unfathomable way? This would not be the first time someone had mistaken 'the signals'. Back when Bethany had the Shadow Welfare brief she'd given J-R gender and sexual equality to research. Dining one evening with his parents, he'd allowed his dad to draw him into politics and found himself arguing that his parents, purely as a for instance, should accept him whether he was gay or straight. Dad remained contrarian but Ma grew increasingly solicitous as the evening wore on, and uncharacteristically reluctant to back up her husband. It was only late into the night, when J-R woke in a racing sweat, that the terrible certainty struck. The next day, his attempts to put his mother straight over the phone were met with insistence that he should *be true to who he was,* and that she was, *fine with it. Fine. Happy!*

Her efforts to be fine-with-it proved excruciating. She hadn't yet, thank God, started introducing J-R to *terribly nice* sons of her bridge-club friends but she'd taken to emailing him clippings about Alan Bennett, Ian McKellen and, mysteriously, Prince

Andrew. Her conviction worked on a ratchet: nothing he said could pull her back and every false hint increased her solicitude towards her poor closeted son. And the involuntary celibacy he'd enjoyed for the last few years left a sexual vacuum into which she could write any story she chose. At least she hadn't told Dad. That was for J-R to do: *When you're ready.*

Mark cradled his espresso.

'I've been meaning to get in touch,' he said. 'I keep seeing your name in connection with the Digital Citizen. It's big things you're doing.'

'Well, it's a team project,' said J-R, glowing.

'But I don't like the name *Digital Citizen*. It reduces people to data.'

'Ah,' said J-R. 'Well, we tested it with target customers. It was nearly *Cit-E-zen*. Which I'm afraid Bethany rather liked. I preferred *BRITAIN:connected* but apparently the URL was taken.'

Mark laughed at that, though it hadn't been a joke. He had a nice laugh.

'Bethany Lehrer,' he mused. 'It must be amazing working for her. Her grandmother is a personal hero.'

'Ah. Bethany isn't much like her grandmother, you know.'

'No, Elyse Martingale was no fan of party politics. She'd have been more likely to torch Parliament than lie to it!'

Mark must have seen J-R's face fall.

'Sorry.'

'Bethany really didn't—'

'So sorry, J-R, that was just a joke.'

'Yes, yes.'

'I just meant – well, your minister would hardly endorse the messages of *The Electronic Radical*! I was amazed when someone told me the connection. And don't you think this business – cartoon pigs! Elyse would have been amused.'

'The situation is somewhat more serious than that.'

Mark began to quote.

'*The coming generation will refuse to be bound by bogus conventions. They will be utterly honest, because there will be no lies left to hide behind when their information is free.* Racy stuff for the 1950s. Glaringly inaccurate, but that's its charm. Have you read it?'

J-R brushed away the question. He, too, was intrigued by *The Electronic Radical*, that recently republished manifesto for high-tech revolution; but here and now it was a distraction. The best thing was to cut through the small talk and say what he had to say.

'The thing is –' he said, then stalled.

He was surprised to detect a liquid pressure behind his eyes. He rubbed the corner of his eye with one finger.

'I've been asking myself –'

He coughed. Tried again.

'I'm concerned that –'

He shifted in his chair.

'You see, I've received an email.'

'An email?'

Mark's chrome eyes were unwavering.

'I think Bethany is colluding with a private company – is perhaps – I don't know, Mark. Covering something up?'

As the words left his lips, he realised he'd never once strayed from the Party line. The experience was at once one of soaring free and plummeting into the dark.

'She lied to Parliament,' he ended, as though words were the greater offence.

¶**lolcatz**
    wow
    much pigglies
    very hack

THREE

SOME TIME BACK, for the crazy of it, Dani started to follow the links in spam. It tapped her into unexpected energies. The more warped the images she found, the more clotted the pages with illiterate masculine hate, the stronger the spark. Now she can't help register for every smut-clogged site she stumbles on – which bring in turn more spam to clot her inbox. She's created a shell identity, *pimpmyhide*, to harvest the tide of genuine Cialis, gastric bands, Balkan brides to order, jizz, farmyard sports, super-size tits, barely legals, anal plugs and saliva-coated cocks that pour in at swelling rates. She's started to curate them.

She sees it as a kind of anthropology. She's captivated by these terrible sites and scenes but however involved she gets, she stays a tourist. For the last six months she's uploaded the most baroque degradations to her *pimpmyhide* blog with added commentary. At twenty-five thousand subscribes, the blog's reach isn't a patch on Parley and the Personas, but in this anonymous niche she can put more of herself out on the line. Some pages people have liked in the hundreds: the most-uprated images are in the *Horses and Cowgirls* section, which pleases Dani. Those over-lit stetson-and-tassel scenes hold a special fascination for her. She can gaze at them for hours composing comments, though she rarely wanks to the content there; or to the thirty gigs of her wider collection. Her interest is aesthetic. She knows to keep her distance.

This morning her 'Droid phone is humming with a mash of in-progress down- and uploads of the splashiest new porn she could find over coffee and dry toast. By the time she gets to the bus stop on Kingsland Road she's halfway through purchasing an exotic set of clips from a Thai site she's lurked for weeks, featuring a beautiful and long-suffering duck. She's held off so far because of a worry about the age of some of the subjects – but when she found these clips on her RSS this morning she decided to let that pass.

She's also uploading comments for a new reel of cowgirl images she calls *Educating Pocahontas:*

Howdy, I'm Jo-Beth. Y'all want to hear something funny? I always was Pocahontas at Halloween. I sure did love that film. My hair was black and long and my sister Annie plaited it real careful. Mebbe these two guys was cowboys, too? Or Frankensteins, I bet, ha ha. My brother Jimmy was Alf. You remember, the cute lil' alien guy? We wished we could dress different every year, but Ma never could afford them costumes after Pa'd gone.

She stops at the kerb, phone inches from her face, rooting for data in the thick earth of the Internet, ignorant of the rush and grind of passing traffic.

)) diesel suck ((

She swipes and taps and she's buzzed with the darting about. Images, credit card details, her name, real address and fake phone numbers – all pass in streaks, erratically encrypted, from this cold bright corner of the East End through a fan of mobile switches and packet routers out to hosting facilities she could never hope to trace in Korea, Atlanta, Docklands, Sydney, Belarus. Her online silhouette is complex and threaded with contradictions. She roams the net a creature on heat, soiling an endless trail of empty hotel rooms.

She holds traces behind her everywhere she goes; they're part of her. She wants to weave her fraying golden thread all over

London, wherever she goes and whatever she does. It frustrates her to make the slightest effort to share. She's been gnawing for the past few months on a prototype – a system that's going make sharing a thing she does the whole time, unthinking. She calls the idea *pervasive sharing*, though Jonquil insists on calling it *Me All Over.*

In her spare time, of which she has none, Dani's building Me All Over piecemeal, as a platform. She hijacked an Apache box in Parley's basement geek farm, where it can sit in semi-permanent beta. Then she wrote nuggets of code for her phone, smartwatch and laptop. These apps live in the deepest background, reading off her status, location, pace; her words, the images that pass her cameras; her breath and other sounds detected by the devices' mics; her heart-rate, skin temperature and deeper biometrics lifted from her watch. They gather these flavours into one unsorted mass and ping it to the server, which snatches fragments at random, pattern recognises them and builds a breadcrumb trail of obscure collage, documenting Dani's movements, thoughts and feelings. It paints them invisibly over actual places in real time so other people who wander there in the future could – theoretically – stumble on her traces and follow her, out of sync by a day or a month or a year, but pace for pace – or track her from their chairs in an online map-world, backwards and forwards in time.

Me All Over. The next Parley, according to Jonquil, but a million times better. Parley is words and pictures and video clips. This is all of her. A way to feel what someone else felt in and of a street, a time.

It's just a thumb-suck but it runs in a buggy way. It isn't pretty – she's nobody's graphics monkey – but now she's set it running it follows her everywhere. It comforts her to know there's something watching, that every time she moves a disk spins somewhere to absorb a little more Dani. She hasn't turned on sharing yet, so the data isn't published. But it totally could be, and when it is all her past trails of sensation will flash into existence over London. The server is always there, logging abstract poems about everything she does and everywhere she goes. Telling her story in snapshot stills and coded pairs of words. Like these:

)) sun rush ((

Me All Over and Pimpmyhide take just a narrow slice of Dani's morning. All the other apps eating RAM in her phone and in her brain are dedicated to tracing Sam. Since nine this morning, when she woke for the second time, she's been nudging about the edge of his online shadow. She's hooked on him in Parley, Facebook, LinkedIn and some PR sites; and googled up a dozen pages of hash about him. She's aggregating photos of him in an album but as she hops from app to app the image that lingers comes from behind her retinas – Sam on a beach, near-naked; arms, neck and buttocks eclipsed against burning island sky. The smell of salt and beach-weed rises in her nostrils from the halal shops and continental grocers.

The groaning fact of a London bus lands inches from her face, giving out a Wookie roar of brakes. She keeps typing on her phone as she mounts the platform and swipes her phone against the Oyster reader. The reader beeps and lodges data. As she bounds to the upper deck the driver pumps the accelerator and the brake in fast succession like he's playing the drums, and she's thrown upstairs by the lurch. She picks herself up and dumps her arse and bag on the upper deck's front seat, still typing.

As she proffers, an alert pings up from MeatSpace. *Really?* That is seriously not a zone for mornings. But there. Yep. monkey_ love just posted in her private space.

♡ **monkey_love**
I can smell you.
I know you're on here. I can smell the sweat on you and your hot wet sex.
I can smell your pheromones and your blood.
Are you here? Your account's live.

SafeWord? Are you on here?
I could really do with talking to you.
Need to talk to someone.

Does the guy ever sleep? She doesn't want this now; but as she swipes the sext away it triggers a memory: last night. That rambling batshit mail she composed to the Sambot. Did she ever send it?

She flips to Mail and selects *Sent Items*. She scrolls up and down, but the mail isn't there: it wasn't sent. She checks *Drafts*. It's still there, unsent and unfinished. Now she remembers: she got too hot last night to finish it. She drifted instead to the instant scents of MeatSpace. Christ, what a night. What the living fuck was she writing? She doesn't want to know but she can't not open it.

i can still feel the warm of your hand on my shoulder as you left the room. how are you doing these days? im in a mad state. always so busy. haven't slept more than four hours in the last two days. its crazy isnt it. you looked great, though. you were hot against me when you hugged me. do you remember summer camp in aviemore, that one time? a bunch of first year sixth up all night on the hillside. the fire had burned out and everyone had to huddle round the embers to stay warm. did you notice I was wrapped around your back? i couldnt tell if you were still awake. and anyway fucking jenny harris was lying the other side of you.

This shit goes on fold after fold, scroll after scroll. How long was she writing? It helped tone down her horny urge, for a while at least. These itches are getting harder to scratch. More and more she's channel-hopping an endless feed of online lovers; trolling pickup sites, especially Codr, the new dating site that's exclusively for geeks. She picks and drops men with a porn-hound conviction that something better will come with the next swipe. Something perfect. Why it's never slaked. Why she has to land somewhere soon or she'll pop.

She hits *Send*. No reason the poor old Sambot shouldn't get his morning oats.

She slides down in the bus seat and puts her feet up on the front rail, squeezing her warm phone into her chest with both hands. What she needs is neat transactional sex: the kind she can leave behind with no stray correlations; but it never goes that way. Things end up twisted and angry, especially with monkey_love – the only partner she goes back to over and again. She wonders who monkey is, what kind of person it takes to match her urgency. He never shares photos with her but she's sure he's a guy, and British from the words he uses for her pussy and his cock – but their encounters are so raw there are no other clues.

She wishes she had a good picture of Sam. The ones she's found are too processed and professional. She needs to find the earliest images, from when she knew him at school. She ons the phone again and returns to Facebook where she rolls back into the past. As she gets to her earliest albums, she hits a cliff-edge and realises her mistake. Facebook wasn't launched until she was up at uni. Her school life might as well not exist. She tends to forget Internet services haven't always been there.

She opens the oldest album and there's Dani the pale-faced fresher hanging with her tech-boy homies. Each was a way-mark. Those were wild years, before Gray – dipping fingers into zany tech and pipe-dream start-up concepts that never materialised; and into each other. She was this glorious geek-girl, costumes belladonna purple, her pale body a gift she gloried in sharing. She burned away uni light-starved in grotty basements, surrounded by the neutral blink of router stacks and the hum of cooling systems. All the hope then.

And if she got herself a reputation as another easy geek-girl (what Gray calls a *wonk-bonk*) it was pretty much deserved. These awkward boys were no pushover. Lord knows, it takes commitment to get a nerd back home at night – and even more to stop him talking long enough to get even the first thing done – but she felt a kind of love for them all. Each of them had, under layers of nebbish bluster, a timid sweetness she could unlock. And if many encounters ended prematurely, or didn't really begin, one or two always managed to surprise her; and each brought the same delight that the abstractions they shared could translate into tenderness and physical release. They laid their fingers with awe on the cold milk of her belly and were kind to her soft skin. Kinder than she was.

This was before those first overwhelming online encounters with Gray.

With an instinct for how far the bus has staggered down the street, Dani looks up. They're about to pass the burned-out Haggerston pub with flamingo stencils on its hoardings. She always tries to check it out as her bus passes. It's inhabited by hobbity squatters she rarely manages to glimpse, but is fascinated by. Today she catches a violent situation at the half-open doorway. A man in grey suit and foreman's anorak shoves a young white man with ginger dreads. Directly above them, level with Dani's upper-deck seat, a bony girl shouts something from an upper window. Possibly '*Don't!*' – or '*Cunt!*' She has a scarf round her hair in a wartime style. All Dani's vision retains as the bus pushes forward is the blue moiré pattern of the scarf.

)) high shout ((

She twists her neck to see more but the angle's wrong. She looks into first floor flats for a while, then turns back to her phone and the rough-shot images from uni. She looks happy there. But everything erodes, given time. Confidences leak out, condoms burst and promises pass unspoken expiry dates. When she graduated, and hooked up at last with Gray in the physical world, they found a more determined, constant rhythm. But she was already too committed to unsettling adventures, and was never true to him. Maybe she's chronically impatient. She never wants any one thing long enough to make it real.

Her email chimes. That must be the reply from the Sambot. It took its time – this'd better be worth it. She skips back to mail. No, it's just a purchase confirmation for the porn site.

Something occurs to her – something really, really bad that can't be true. She taps on her Sent items. There it is. Ten twelve a.m. she sent that rambling mail to the Sambot –

No. Shit no.

She opens the mail but the bitter, vicious fact won't change. The address she sent it to wasn't sambot@local. It was sam.corrigan@moneyshotpr.com

She sent that mail – the mail of a sex-crazed drunken maniac – to Sam. Twelve minutes ago now. It's been twelve minutes since the world came to an end and she never even noticed.

She can barely focus on the mail.

fuck you sam i think i love you

Somewhere between here and Shoreditch, she is going to have to kill herself.

¶TurdoftheDay

Modest and tidy, it slipped from me like a buttered potato.

<pic:>

Sorry. Sorry.

I did something bad. I can't talk about it.

FOUR

'I SHOULDN'T TELL YOU any of this,' said J-R.

Mark bent forward to set down a second milky tub for J-R and another tiny espresso for himself. He pinched the knees of his jeans and sat.

'Because I'm from the craven private sector?'

'No, no. I shouldn't speak to *anyone*.'

'All right, look.' Mark made a fan with both hands. 'Apart from we're friends, my reputation rests on my ability to keep a secret. Whatever this is, you know it'll stay between us.'

J-R took a steadying breath.

'Yes. All right.'

And suddenly he found himself all business. He might have been making a report to Krish or Bethan.

'So from what we can tell,' he said, 'this Giggly Pigglies virus started appearing on people's computers two weeks ago.'

The corner of Mark's mouth curled up a little.

'But three days before *that*,' J-R continued, 'I received an email from Bethan.'

He wiggled the laptop out of his bag. Now he'd started speaking he was eager to reveal. It was like stepping onto a departing train, without looking back. He set the laptop on the table and spun it round so Mark could read for himself.

'There,' he said. 'See?'

That, Sean, is a very generous offer. You do know how to
please a girl! Here's the goods. I've protected the files with
your encryption thingy as you asked. (Tell me if I did it
wrong . . .!!) Do with them what you will, fella.

  Bx

Mark looked up from the screen.

'Oh,' he said.

'Yes.'

'That does look—'

'Yes,' said J-R. 'This was sent to Mondan's CEO, Sean Perce.'

'Yes, yes, sure.'

Naturally Mark would know who Perce was. In recent years his
firm had romped through the British digital media sector, acquiring
businesses like burrs on a dog. They'd recently crowned this growth
with a shining new HQ. Just this morning, emerging from the Tube,
J-R had looked up from the hustling City traffic to see the enormous
digital displays wrapped round the pinnacle of 404 City Road.
Impossible to ignore. They shone down Moorgate like a new sky, the
width of a city block, running a constant loop of financial, commer-
cial and celebrity news. Spattering data across the rooftops.

'But why did she copy *you*?' asked Mark, dimpling his brow at
the email.

'Bethany sent it to Perce's *home* email address – and copied it
to my *Ministry of Technology* address. Which appeared odd until
I realised: when you type my name into our email system, it shows
up as *Pemberton, John-Rhys*. And because I've mailed Perce a lot,
I happen to know how *his* work address appears.'

'*Perce, Sean?*'

'Yes. So my guess? Bethan meant to send this to Perce's home
and work addresses, but instead—'

'Autocomplete,' nodded Mark. '*Pemberton. Perce.* She got you
instead of him.' J-R decided he'd said *yes* enough times and stayed
silent. 'So – this is undeniably fascinating but I'm guessing you
want something more from me than polite interest?'

'Well, yes, there's this attachment. I suppose I'd assumed –'

J-R was incapable this morning of completing a sentence. Mark filled the vacuum.

'– that I'd be able to crack the encryption key and find out what exactly Bethany sent Mr Perce.'

'Mark, I don't want to believe she could be capable of – I *can't* believe that. But you see, to access data on a Digital Citizen, you need two things: the original record stored by Mondan, and a unique double-lock code held by the ministry. Even if someone did hack our data, they would still have needed the double-lock code for every member of our target group before they could read their details. It's a fail-safe, like a safety deposit box.' Mark waved the details by. 'This is why we're so confidently saying we haven't been hacked. Why some rag-tag bunch of hackers couldn't possibly have used our data for the Pigglies thing. These double-lock codes are only accessible to a highly restricted group of people, including –'

Neither of them needed to finish the sentence. Mark picked up the thread.

'But in spite of this, ten thousand people who gave you their data are still being spammed by images of those obnoxious pigs. Somebody has their data.'

'This is why I didn't sleep a wink last night. Knowing she sent this mail just days before this whole thing started. It can't be coincidence. But on the other hand, why on earth would Bethan and Perce conspire like this? And what on earth could that have to do with cartoon pigs? I can't make sense of it.'

Mark shook his head in slow motion. The expression taking over his face was exactly the one he used to assume when playing chess.

'Do you know what I thought when I saw the story yesterday?' he said. 'I thought: why the Giggly Pigglies?'

'Well, it's some nonsense from these teenage hackers, isn't it?'

'Only if your data were actually hacked. Which I think you just said was impossible?'

'All right, true. And so?'

'The Giggly Pigglies is an eight-figure brand. Highly marketable, currently in the process of expanding from TV into toys, apps, online games and books.'

J-R smiled.

'You seem to know a lot about children's TV, Mark.'

'I know a lot about who's making money in digital. And who do we know who makes tens of millions selling data to marketing companies? And who, when the Digital Citizen goes national, will get data on every man, woman – and *child* – in the country?'

'Mondan? That makes no sense. Why would they use our data to market a brand? Why now, just before we launch? Look at the news. This is a car crash for them, PR-wise. And for us.'

Mark shrugged.

'Maybe it was an accident. A fat finger error. Maybe this Pigglies spam was something they were working up in R&D – proof of concept for a marketing tool that invades people's computers and plants ads. Literally, viral marketing. A way to get their clients' brands deep inside our computers, tablets and phones. Maybe this virus escaped from the lab? Maybe someone pressed the "go" button early?'

J-R found himself strangely angry at this conspiracy-making. He'd come to Mark for a sober perspective.

'You're clutching, Mark.'

Mark took a miniature sip, set his cup down and considered J-R for a moment.

'Am I? Mondan keeps doing random stuff – and then refusing to apologise when it blows up in their face. They know they're too big to fail. I heard one of your girl's colleagues refer to them as a *national asset* the other day.'

'Yes, the Cabinet Secretary said that. Neil Cullen. But that's my point. The picture you're painting is nothing like the reality.'

'All right. Paint me a better one.'

J-R was taken aback. He'd forgotten how blunt Mark could be.

'Well,' he said, 'we've been impressed. Revenues doubled in two years; data storage and processing for some of UK plc's biggest brands; sixty-four data centres in Europe alone—'

'That's just facts. What have you actually *learned* – about their character?'

'You mean Sean Perce?'

'No, no, no. The character of the firm. Corporations have personalities, just like people. Why make the choices they do? Why, for instance, those data centres? Why so many?'

'Because – they handle a lot of data?'

'*Pfft.*' Mark brushed that away. 'Why not one big data centre? No, there's a drive here for ubiquity. Look at that Babel of a building they've thrown up on City Road, like some great bird of prey looking down on us. *404 City,* they insist on calling it. Did you know it actually takes up the even street numbers from 406 to 410? But Perce was so desperate to use that dorky name, he also bought and demolished the building at number 404. Turned it into green space.'

J-R had no notion why the numeral 404 should be so important – a lucky number in some astrological system, perhaps? – but he smiled as though he'd got the reference.

'And those giant screens they've wrapped around its pinnacle,' said Mark. 'Blasting out constant information. So now we can see their point of view from every high window in London. Lucky us. And it's the same beneath the ground. *As above, so below.* You know they're gradually buying up all of London's fibre-optic cable? All our Internet points of presence? I'm talking about the boring physical stuff here. Piping, conduits, routers – access to transatlantic and North Sea cables that connect us to the world. These days, if you want to provide access to the UK Internet, if you want to be found by a UK user, you pretty much have to go through Mondan. And then –'

Mark drained his coffee and wiped his mouth with the back of his hand. He was on a roll, shifting on the bench seat with an urgent energy. This was a pet topic.

'– then,' he said, 'there's the slew of software start-ups they've acquired in the Old Street area.'

J-R sat forward.

'Like Parley?'

'*Including* Parley. Over thirty businesses in the last three years. And you know what all these acquisitions have in common? Apart from their physical location?'

J-R shook his head, though the gesture wasn't needed.

'They all have exceptional data sets. Really exceptional. Consumer demographics, purchase histories, behaviour. They buy them up and they move them wholesale into 404 City – or into one of five or ten other properties they've bought up around its skirts. Sometimes they're only moving a company two hundred metres, but still they insist on having them inside the fold. They hook them all together on a single secure network, on cables running underground beneath the buildings, suck all their data into one data centre, three storeys under City Road. They have this need, this *drive,* to know everything, be everywhere – but keep everything to themselves.'

Mark sat back, having apparently exhausted himself. He picked up his espresso cup, glanced into it and replaced it on the saucer, disappointed; then looked around for someone to bring him another fix. J-R stared into the muddy surface of his own coffee.

'I can't say I've registered any of that,' he said quietly. 'This is a major government contract. We simply looked at the evidence in front of us.'

'But that's nonsense. You buy on chemistry. Let me guess: Mondan were up against Terasoft?'

J-R did his best to stay impassive. Mark grinned. Of course Terasoft was in the mix. The lumbering IT giant had its hooks into every part of government. J-R could not turn on his official laptop without their sober logo commandeering the screen for two or three minutes.

'So,' said Mark, 'Terasoft would have brought everything to the table – aggressive pricing – desperate to stay supplier of choice to HM Government. But The Big "A" sold you the dream. Sean Perce would have been all over you; all over your minister?'

J-R shrugged. Mark nodded.

'It's what he does,' he said. 'And he'd relish the chance to drive a stake through Terasoft's monopoly. He loves to be the punchy outsider. Loves to win.'

'You think we made a bad decision.'

A creeping disappointment came over J-R. Why should he expect that he could call up a friend he'd not seen in years, out of the blue, and find him immediately eager to help? Mark seemed determined to crush the whole enterprise under the weight of his criticism.

'I'm not saying that. But –' Mark made a couple of generalised movements with his hand, groping for a thought. 'Nobody ever knows what Mondan's up to until they've done it. They're obsessively silent. You rarely see Perce. He lets his divisional CEOs out to play – Jonquil Carter gets touted as ethnically diverse corporate cheesecake – but they're always gagged.'

Remembering something, Mark put down his coffee cup and laughed.

'Allegedly, Perce once told a leadership meeting, *If media exposure is cocaine, you are my crack whores.*'

'He called his senior managers *whores*?'

'Very much his style. I'm about to hear him speak, as it happens, at an event on Tower Hill.' He checked his phone. 'Here. *Identity Crisis: Securing the Digital Transactions of the Future.*'

'Yes, Bethany's speaking there as well. I wrote her speech.'

'It'll be a good crowd. People like me tend to hang on Sean's prognostications.'

The use of the first name pricked J-R's attention.

'You know him?'

Mark shook his head.

'Met him a few weeks back, at an industry junket in Spain. He just about acknowledged my existence. Think a Burnley Steve Jobs, if such a thing is possible. Hugely impressive. But the kind of guy who'd try anything – anything he thought he could get away with – to conquer another parcel of land.'

He trailed off. The café buzz echoed around them.

'And so?' said J-R, discreetly checking his watch.

'So all right,' said Mark, leaning forward to click and mouse about on J-R's laptop. 'Sure. I'll have a go at decrypting your mail attachment.'

Stupid gratitude flooded J-R's chest.

'No guarantees,' said Mark. 'If Perce gave Bethany the tool to encrypt this file, it'll be high-grade. But the file is big-ish. That'll help. More pattern to exploit.'

Mark pulled a small device from his pocket and inserted it into J-R's USB socket. The intimacy of this action made J-R shift in his chair. Mark stopped and looked directly into his eyes.

'But whatever I find,' he said, 'I'll give it to you straight.'

J-R nodded. He desperately wanted an answer; but he only wanted it to be favourable. Else he'd rather bury it deep underground.

'I'm choosing to believe that this is nothing to do with the hack or the Giggly Pigglies affair,' he said. 'Maybe somehow some teen hackers have cracked Mondan's codes. Or maybe you're right and Mondan are doing something fishy with the data. I'd actually prefer either thing to be true, than to know that Bethany has done – I don't know what. Either would make more sense.'

'Not so unusual for a politician to collude with a private business.'

'Mark, I don't actually think that's true.'

Mark pulled the USB stick out, closed the laptop and handed it back to J-R.

'Really,' said J-R, taking the computer. 'Why would Bethany do such a thing – after everything she's put into this programme?'

Mark shrugged.

'I still say, look harder at Mondan. At what's in it for them. You're giving them all this data to add to their already vast collection. What are they doing with it? What are they *allowed* to do, legally? Do you know what's in your Ts and Cs?'

'Terms and Conditions?'

'What do your so-called "customers" sign up to?' Mark made air quotes around the word. 'Ask yourself: when did you last read the Ts and Cs for a piece of software? I suggest you read your own. Or –' He weighed something up. 'If you want, I'd be happy to look over the legals. If you don't mind sharing them?'

J-R swirled the foamy soup at the bottom of his cup.

'Is that wise?' he said. 'You're already looking at that mail attachment.'

'Wise for me or you?'

'I don't –' it didn't seem right to mention Mark's blog. 'This would be between us?'

'Of course.' A business card had appeared in Mark's hand. 'Here. My professional email.'

J-R knocked back the dregs of his coffee and stood, hitching up his backpack. Would any other spad even blink before sending sensitive information to a private sector contact? He paused for just a second before taking the card.

'I'll email you later today. And, look, Mark, thank you.'

He held out his hand. Mark, still sitting, took it.

'Anything for a mate.'

He gave J-R an easy smile.

¶riotbaby

Have you heard from this guy, children? Be his devotee /now/.

>>cite ¶identikid

We have one chance to stop this government stealing our anonymity and our freedom. Two days to stop them invading our lives forever. Don't let them take away your privacy. Don't open your life to state-sponsored snoopers. Don't let them launch the digital citizen. <takebackID>

Listen to the kid. Friday's the day.

FIVE

IDENTIKID PROFFERS LIKE NONE OTHER. He's primed to push the button on TakeBackID. Epic to ride this breaker with riotbaby citing him and his devotees ballooning. Usually it tends to zero likelihood you'll get cited by a Persona even once but there it is, for the fortieth time since he cracked the DigiCitz homepage and added the <takebackID> pennant. A twelve-year-old could have done that exploit on their shitty government SSL set-up. But they didn't. It was identikid.

He didn't birth the <takebackID> pennant, either – but he owns it now and it's trending, invading searchspace, daily favourites, RSS: building, building. And whenever he adds the Pigglies meme as well, it goes turbo-shareable. Those little pigs are smoking clickbait.

None of his network knows who actually swiped the DigiCitz data or did the Giggly Pigglies stunt but whoever it was they're some kind of genius. You'd have to be a ghost to walk through Mondan's defences and jack all that data off them. And the Pigglies trojan they got onto all those people's PCs was a sweet hack for sure. Word on the security boards is nobody can get the damn thing off those devices. They strip it off, it automagically rebuilds itself in the system registry and there it is back again, like wiggly wiggly wiggly.

Whoever did that hack, they're OK by Leo – by identikid, that is. They helped make him what he's turned into since only yesterday: a player. No more script kiddie hustling for a zero-day hack.

The Flamingo is quiet this arvo but Leo knows from static on the boards how fast things are moving. He's edgy. Maybe because of that property guy was on their dicks again this morning. But more, too. Something the whole squat knows is coming.

¶identikid
So pumped about takeback Friday.
<takebackID>

He gets more cites, more devotees, when he proffers what he feels, not just what's happening.

Perched on a flock-covered stool, Leo types fast enough to rub off his fingerprints. In the dinge of the saloon his MacBook bleeds blue light on the knife-etched countertop. On the wall above the row of empty optics, a Warholed poster of Elyse Martingale shouts . . . *or we shall step around it* . . . in fraying lower-case Courier.

Identikid is Leo when he's off the wires. His whole thing goes on here in the Flamingo. This peeling barroom is the smaller of their two public spaces. At night they use it for pop-up shows: club spots, comedy, micro-burlesque. It raises serious coin for their other activities. But by day it's quiet and the perfect hub for identikid's oppos.

Wifi and electricity they gank from the next-door supermarket, but they need to keep the usage down. If the fluorescents dip in the shop, the three big Pakistani lads come round to tell off the Flamingo crew, but they're mostly chill if Leo and his mates don't take the piss. So during the day it's lights out. You'd never know it wasn't night, except for what cracks in through the window boards. Reynard can't power up his PAs while the shop is open so the only sound is the ambient drone of Kingsland Road and the sub-bass of the trucks.

Leo proffers.

¶**identikid**

We have work to do.

How to make a citizen understand what's been taken from her? Someone steals her wallet, she feels a loss. Bankers lose our billions, we're mad as hell. Someone takes away my privacy? Never mind, I got a discount on this fifty-two inch plasma. Someone steals my identity? Big whoop. I got five free downloads.

<takebackID>

Leo types up a quarrel, pushing a dread from his eye. That's right, Mum, he thinks. Still got *those awful dreadlocks*. She rang yesterday. Why'd he have to answer? First thing she says is, she goes, *Have you still got that hair?* He's never going home. She goes, *You'll never get a job interview with all that going on up there*. She doesn't know what's going on. There's things more important than *proper jobs*. She goes, *Your father is ya ya ya ya ya*. What did they ever give him?

He angles the screen of his graduation MacBook to get a sharper image and keeps telling the people: *soon, soon, soon*. Doors bang about upstairs. That's Winter. She's not forgiven him for when they had words before. She's doing what she does when she's mad, i.e. storming the pub rooms, cleaning up cans, pulling paper and bottles out the rubbish. Stuffing them in the recycling sacks. Passive aggressive, like. Blaming. It's cool to be green but that girl can be this total recyclopath.

And what did she want to get so pissed with Leo for, this morning? It was because of that fascist bailiff. OK Leo had, to be honest, let the situation in the street get a little out of hand, but it was the guy who started in with aggro, after Leo tore up the notice he was sticking to the door. And maybe Leo spat, but not *at* the guy. He'd been handling it. Fuck, what did Winter need to start screaming out the window for? You call a guy a cunt, he has to get back at you. That's logic. Now he'll be back for definite and he won't be alone. Screaming blue shit at people solves nothing. Leo trusts in subtle. Winter always wants a brawl.

What Leo's working up today you've got to say is super-subtle. For once identikid has something to throw. He sees the noise from the groups, knows what's going down. On the street outside, citizens walk past talking their shit to each other. They have no idea. They don't know where to look, or how to listen. Identikid knows.

Friday is just a couple days away. Then TakeBackID will be more than just a meme.

¶identikid

404 City, watch your ass.
<takebackID>

¶techwave

Here, everybody. This:

>>cite ¶thegrays

Everyone worries about losing they're privacy but they
don't hesitate for a nanosecond before giving credit card
details to Murdoch or Bezos or Perce <doublestandards>

SIX

THE M&M CAME TO LIFE. The plastic figure had been standing inert on the desk, right arm raised in a solidarity salute. Then without any obvious cause came a *bong* and a whine of servos as the arm chopped sharply down and up. A sweet popped green and immaculate from a dimpled hole in the smooth belly, to land in a cupped hand. Graham reached for it, tossed it in the air and caught it in his mouth like a feeding fish.

'So that was a cite,' he explained, munching sugar.

'A sight? Of –?'

'*Cite*. Citation,' said Graham.

On his screen he called up a Parley continuity, as J-R now knew to call it. He pointed to the spot where one of Parley's software characters – or Personas – had quoted someone called *thegrays*.

'See, here,' said Graham, 'that's me – thegrays. Techwave cited my proffer about, well, you can see. Which comment was pretty sharp, though I say so.'

J-R read the 'cite' – a quoted comment from thegrays. From Graham.

'Yes, I see. Isn't Sean Perce ultimately your boss?'

J-R shuddered to imagine publishing a similar comment about a minister. Graham shrugged.

'And I have this Parley app,' he drew a rectangle around the screen, 'wired up to MC M&M here. Every time I get a cite from one of the Personas, my little plastic friend dispenses me a reward.'

For the first time in the conversation, Graham turned from his screen to look at J-R, grinning widely at the ingenuity it had taken him to achieve this pointless outcome. How they fetishised these soulless 'Personas'.

'So everyone using Parley,' said J-R, 'is aiming to be quoted by an artificial person?'

But Graham had returned to his screen and for a moment he didn't reply. J-R accepted the silence and looked around at the genius mayhem of equipment, cables, cardboard boxes and shuffling boy-men filling the artificially lit, low-ceilinged space. This was the *Geek Farm*, the engine room of Parley's techie elite. The untended walls were the dirty blue of a faded tattoo, giving the room a nighttime flavour. A grey hum filled the air and there was a sharp smell of freshly unearthed truffles – the distinctive odour of men who've spent the day surrounded by overheated equipment.

J-R's BlackBerry buzzed. A text from Krish.

So we survived Karen this am though I've now two choices where to shite from. Stay at Parley. Keep head down and eyes peeled for media interest re Parley or Mondan. Come to me first.

Or in other words, *do nothing*. J-R put the phone away.

Graham flicked between windows, clicking and typing in gnomic bursts. He had an angular, ancient face, wiry glasses, a scraggy bunch of hair pulled through a scrumple of yellow rubber. His wispy half-beard and waistcoat gave him a nineteenth-century air. Beneath the waistcoat a crown device and capital letters decorated his red T-shirt. J-R did not understand the motto on the shirt. In the style of the popular wartime slogan, *Keep calm and carry on*, it read:

**USE BINARY
AND
CARRY ONE**

His concentration was absolute. Parley's 'Systems Ninja' – as his business card described him – never seemed to do just one thing at a time. While giving J-R a guided tour of Parley, he was also mining a massive base of Internet data, called up overnight, trawling for some trace of Bethany that might have been used to form sic_girl's infamous messages.

For a while J-R assumed his question had passed unheard. Then Graham spoke.

'See, it's a bigger thing getting cited on Parley than on other social networks, by people. When you get cited by one of the Personas, you've cracked the algorithm. You've decoded what the Personas are thinking at that one moment. What the Internet's thinking.'

'And that's a more interesting challenge than working out what a human being will respond to?'

'Um . . . yes?' said Graham, turning to face J-R with genuine puzzlement. 'I mean, who knows what *people* are going to do and say?'

J-R chose not to respond. This was only his second day at Parley, but he'd already heard as many different explanations of Parley as he'd had conversations. Nobody agreed why this gaggle of artificial personalities was worth spending time among; or why people were so eager to disclose such intimate thoughts to them.

Truncated names and inexplicable messages flickered past on Graham's screen.

'I was wondering,' said J-R. 'Why the archaic words? *Proffer. Parley.* Is someone a historian of language?'

Graham looked at him with disdain.

'They have more Google-juice than modern generics.'

'Ah –'

'Uniqueness in search space.'

'All right. And this is probably a stupid question, too, but –' Graham looked back with lidded eyes, as if that were a foregone conclusion '– how do you tell the Personas from the – ah, real users?'

Graham sighed deeply, his fears confirmed.

'Personas in grey, users in black,' he said.

Ah, yes. J-R had noticed the different shades of text but had assumed they were random. Perhaps nothing in this online Babel was truly random.

'Mondan,' J-R ventured next.

Graham gave no sign of having heard.

'You work for them now,' said J-R. 'Since Parley was acquired, what, two years back? Does that mean work *with* them? What's that like? They have something of – ah – of a mixed reputation in the sector?'

Graham gave an adolescent sigh and glared at his screen. J-R had noticed the same aggression in other software people: an intimate rudeness, like the bickering of long-married couples who no longer care that their squabbles are on public show. Charm was irrelevant to getting the job done. J-R knew many people like that in Whitehall, too.

'I'm there once a week,' said Graham. 'For meetings and stuff. Tech integration. Bulk data handling, email. Obviously I hose my soul down afterwards.'

He turned to offer J-R a grin that was more a simian snarl.

A female voice cut through the male hum.

'So how are you planning to get all those processed, Fatnav? There's shit-to-the-power-of-N gigs to crunch and you fucking know I have Jonquil on my arse.'

This could only be Dani Farr. J-R swivelled on his chair and saw where she'd landed in the room like phosphorus in water. She stood in a cluster of software engineers who were feeding at a screen a few desks along. At its centre sat Graham's assistant, Colin – a man seemingly unaware of how a thin cotton T-shirt looked when draped across two generous man-breasts and a great dome of stomach. Known as *Fatnav* to his colleagues because of his droning computerised voice; and his shocking girth.

'We're doing the whole set in parallel batch,' said Colin without pausing in his typing.

'Jesus shitting Christ that's farting in a fan. Use your brain, you obsessive anal zombie.'

Colin appeared to take active pleasure at this abuse. He hunched over his keyboard and did something that resembled J-R's mum's terrier, Granville, choking on a plum stone; but which was presumably laughter.

'OK, twats, give me admin rights on this domain.'

Dani requisitioned the next-door computer. The installed programmer near-leaped from the chair.

'And someone get me a re-up of storage.'

'Hey! Use your own machine!' said Colin.

His sudden anger was territorial: evidently this was his fiefdom.

'Superuser me now,' said Dani.

Colin gave her a furious US Marine-style salute, leaned over and made a short rattle on her keyboard before shoving it back to her.

'Thank your fucky stars I'm in a hurry,' she said, laying her smartphone beside the keyboard and starting to type, 'or I'd shove your head so far up your arse you could french-kiss your liver.'

J-R was soaked in the wake of Dani's anger. This was not play-acting: not entirely. She was edgier than she'd been yesterday. As she worked, she checked her phone obsessively for something that never appeared.

'See this? This is my poker face.' Colin again, pointing with one hand at his face while typing with the other. 'It's a face that says *I'm going to poke 'er.*'

Uneasy laughter.

'Yes, good. Right. Be so kind as to kiss my fucking ring,' she said, distracted.

Breaking from her typing, she ploughed past the slower males on the wheels of her chair, landing at another keyboard.

'I like that you didn't deny that you're obsessive and anal,' she announced, her back to Colin.

'What's that you say? You're obsessed with anal?'

A silence fell. Danielle slammed a drawer shut, hard.

'Fucking brogrammers,' she muttered into the screen.

'Better a brogrammer than a hogrammer,' said Colin blithely.

Danielle picked up the keyboard and slapped it hard on the desktop.

'Oh, cock off, Fatnav, you enormous *bollock*!'

'Ooh. Eloquent.'

Dani let out a hoarse shout, stood and grabbed a canister of DVDs from the desktop. Ripping off its lid she strode to Colin's chair and dumped the contents over his head. A hundred shining discs cascaded down the slopes of his body and spilled to the floor with a metallic splash.

Everybody froze, intent on their work. J-R concentrated on Graham's screen but couldn't help seeing, in the periphery of his vision, Colin sitting placid and upright. Vindicated.

Danielle shied the empty canister into a bin with great precision and walked past J-R, who made an effort not to flinch. She stopped very close at hand, barely two inches from Graham, and reached for a device on the shelf above – a small beige rectangle with a dangling cable. Her neat right breast brushed the back of Graham's head. He continued to watch his screen cooly. J-R might have existed on a wavelength invisible to them both.

She glanced at Graham's screen and spoke quietly.

'Way to set these fuckwits an example. You're meant to be analysing Parley data, not proffering.'

'There's nothing there,' said Graham. 'I told you.'

'Oh, oh, so you've read every line of this three-thirty-two gig file? Pony!'

'I showed you the keyword results. I don't care what analytics voodoo you pull. You're not going to find a thing. Nothing sic_ girl read even mentions a politician, let alone Bethany Lehrer. She can't have said what she said.'

'Shit me, if only I'd thought of that. She never said it! My troubles are over! Fuck-a-lujah!'

'I'm just saying, the evidence. It doesn't make sense to me either. I can only think—'

'What?' Danielle's fury was interrupted, her interest piqued.

'Well, it has to be sic, doesn't it?' said Graham.

'Of course it's her.'

Danielle gestured at the screen where sic_girl's continuity stuttered on.

'No, it has to be *coming* from her. She must be *thinking* this stuff. Becoming able to.'

Danielle sized Graham up, apparently scenting a tease.

'No, OK, OK, I know,' said Graham. 'Like I say, it doesn't make sense. But to have my whole team trawling source files for patterns – in data that doesn't include a single mention of the subject sic_girl spoke about – it's pointless.'

'*Pointless?* I'm *pointless?* Jesus!'

J-R raised an apologetic hand. The two combatants turned to face him.

'Might I ask?' The pair were attentive. 'As I understand it, you're looking for information sic_girl's programme may have – ah – read about Bethany?' Two nods. 'And you want to find this because sic_girl must have – ah – copied her messages from somewhere?' Graham nodded. Danielle stared, brow bunched up. 'So the Parley characters do just *copy* information? I thought they had some kind of – personalities – of their own? How can that be true if all they're doing is, so to speak, dragging and dropping from elsewhere?'

Danielle and Graham looked at each other and exhaled in unison. J-R's idiocy had allied them to a common cause. Danielle volunteered herself as spokeswoman.

'OK. Explainer.' She spoke as if to a pre-school student. 'So everything sic_girl says comes from somewhere else – and that includes her personality. That's the whole point of Parley. It's a kludge, all right?' Her hands circled each other. 'A, a, a, mash-up. When I coded it, I wasn't trying to create a thing for actual users. It was down-and-dirty, for a bet.'

J-R looked from one to the other, searching for signs he was being mocked.

'You created Parley – Britain's most popular digital environment –'

Graham shook his head in mock amazement.

'Is *that* what it is?' he said.

'– for a *bet*?'

'A bet with this fucking feller here.' Danielle punched Graham's shoulder, apparently quite hard. 'Right?'

Graham did the cub scout thing with his fingers.

'I cannot deny it.'

'This hairy tool here bet me I couldn't beat the Turing Test.'

'Yes, of course,' said J-R. 'The Turing – ah, remind me?'

'Machine intelligence,' said Graham.

'Google it,' said Dani, simultaneously.

Graham shrugged.

'It wasn't so much a bet,' he said. 'I just pointed out one night to Dani there was a coding challenge she couldn't beat. She still hasn't, as it happens, since she decided to cheat.'

'I so did not cheat. It's a valid solution.'

'Look, I don't want to be this guy about it, but you should go back and read *Computing Machinery and Intelligence*.'

'It is, too, valid. Your problem is you haven't read beyond the first three pages. Intelligence as search, numb-nuts. Eat it.'

J-R had not the slightest idea what this brewing argument was about but he needed to get them back on track. His hand went up again.

'So, Dani, you wrote Parley to solve this – test?'

Thankfully, Dani was less inclined to argue than to explain her own skill.

'So OK,' she said. 'The thing with the Turing test is, how can you get a machine to answer any question someone asks it? And how do you fool that person into thinking they're talking to another human being?'

She gave J-R a challenging look. That had not been a rhetorical question.

'Ah. I suppose –' he began to extemporise. 'You'd have to interpret the grammar of the question, look up the words in some sort of dictionary – perhaps the underlying concepts as well, to understand the context.' There! The man from Westminster does know a thing or two after all! 'Perhaps a kind of – ah – neural network? A network of related concepts the system could refer to. I imagine it would have to be incredibly sophisticated and—'

Danielle cut in on him with a dismissive *Pfft!*

'D'you have any idea how much storage we'd need to accommodate the knowledge of even a five-year-old child?' she said. 'Let alone give it semantics?'

'No, I clearly do not.'

Graham cut in again:

'Point is, she didn't need to when she had –' he gestured at his screen.

'– the Internet!' continued Dani.

The way they finished each other's sentences: there was surely history here.

'What Dani did, it's sort of genius – and I'd only say this when she isn't listening –'

Dani made a dumbshow of blocking her ears. She was surprisingly sweet when she smiled. Her cheeks became chubby and took on dimples.

'– what she did was, she set up a system where when you asked it a question, it could search online for related topics being talked about somewhere – and Frankenstein meaningful answers from other people's conversations, other people's grammar, vocabulary. For a while it sounded completely unnatural.'

'Ha!' said Dani. 'Like remember one time we asked it, *Who are Queen?*'

'Yeah.' Graham grinned at J-R. 'It said *Queen Elizabeth the Second and Queen Latifah are Queen.*'

Dani gazed at Graham with a kindness J-R hadn't seen before. Their relationship ran a spectrum from spiky bitterness to time-worn affection, with no middle ground. J-R found it hard to calibrate. She continued.

'The turning point to be honest was, we got bought by Mondan. Which gave us access to their spiders. It got several orders of magnitude easier overnight. They scrape essentially the entire thing every hour. Much more often for some sites. They keep one of the copies – fully indexed – in the data warehouse at 404 City.'

She gestured towards a metal panel in the wall. A battered film poster – *Iron Man 2* – was taped to it.

'A full indexed copy of –?'

'Of the Internet. I shit you not. They scrape basically the whole fucking Internet every hour –'

'– just so many data, so fresh,' Graham picked up. 'Me and the data geeks down here, we had to filter it, whittle it, before Dani could feed the algorithm.'

'But the sheer scale,' said Dani. 'Something changed. There's still no intelligence in this thing; but when you get that volume of real human data, you get thousands, hundreds of thousands of new rules about what word goes with what word.'

'What patterns of speech are natural –'

'– I never taught the algorithm English but it knows how to speak it from the data. It could have been Russian, Japanese –'

'– and at some point, as the data volumes ramped up exponentially, at some point, it started to surprise us.'

'And so the thing was, I found out you could give the system a personality – create a Persona – by pointing it at sites and threads with a shared character. One of the unbuilt personalities of the Internet.'

'Here were characters Dani never designed. Obsessive geek, political activist, doting mother –'

'– all aggregate personalities we found online. The dramatic personas.'

J-R, struggling to keep up with this contrapuntal routine, chose not correct Dani's Latin.

'Something real just, just –'

'– they emerged,' said Graham, gesturing again at his screen, 'So, sic_girl here. Really strong character, one of our most popular, right?' Danielle gave a short burst of nodding in reply. 'But she's just a mash-up of all the drug-dependent borderline bipolar obsessives on the Internet.'

'Which is by the way a lot,' added Danielle, still nodding. 'Excellent source data.'

J-R looked again at the Parley continuity on the screen. This wistful, vulnerable voice, a voice he'd got to know well in the last twenty-four hours, was no more than a patchwork of other voices, from somewhere invisible on the wider network.

'To someone like myself,' he said, 'without the technical background, this seems impossible.'

Danielle nodded and screwed up her face.

'Honestly? *All* of this seemed like hoodoo when it first happened. We just – got used to it.'

Graham began to quote.

'*Every sufficiently advanced technology . . .*'

J-R completed the statement.

'*. . . is indistinguishable from magic.*'

Graham toasted him with his coffee cup.

'Arthur Clarke.'

'Yes, the minister is fond of quoting that.'

But then, most technology seemed like magic to Bethan.

J-R continued to study sic_girl's words as they scrolled up the screen. It was like an optical illusion: even knowing the personality behind these words was fake, he couldn't make himself see it as anything other than real. Are we all so similar at root that someone can stitch our voices together and create a thing so much like life? Words trickled down sic_girl's continuity. Daft commentary on a reality television programme. Obsessing about her appearance. Desperation for her next dose of medication. And then –

'Ah – my God!'

'What?'

'Shit-monkeys!'

It was happening again before their eyes.

¶sic_girl
Sigh.

The only thing worse than being talked about is . . . well,
actually loads is worse. Pain is worse. Ouchie. Don't talk
to me.

But since we's talking about being talked about, let's talk
about Bethany Lehrer . . .

SEVEN

'YOU WANT TRUST? Trust is based on surrender. Always, at some level.'

The auditorium had fallen in a trance. The only sound the electrical presence of the PA.

'Once upon a time, if you wanted something, you gave up nothing more than money in exchange. Money. Disposable, fungible, easy to obtain for those with the wit. A commodity.'

Huge speakers pumped the voice, kicking it back around the packed hall.

'But today when you want something, you first need to give up a piece of yourself, of your identity. This is the way it works now. We have to grow up and accept this or we will not move forward.'

This was premium Sean Perce. Before an audience he lost his coiled fury, presented an accidental quality. From the darkness of her panel-member's chair, Bethany watched him lean on the podium like a club comic and survey the crowd. This was how she'd first seen him, four years ago at an open-computing event at the ICA. His boyish face, gravity-defying pomade and whiff of the '70s rogue had disarmed her at once. He had the gift of making everyone in an audience – especially women of Bethany's demographic – feel intimate with the man on the distant stage.

'At Mondan,' he continued, 'we believe in the overriding importance of trust. We care – passionately – about the security and privacy of the millions of people whose data we handle every day. But if people want to take something out of the system, access a product or service, they need to accept that everything they say and do is recorded. And it will be used.'

Bethany scanned the pool of faces in the spill of stage light. She picked out journos, longing for the lecture to end so they could land their questions on her. This was the first shot they'd had since this pumped-up nonsense of a scandal began – and how convenient that this industry event offered presentations from the minister responsible for the Digital Citizen, and the CEO of the company providing the technology. According to Krish, acceptances for this session had doubled since yesterday and they'd had to move it to a bigger hall. Bethany could handle the hacks. More importantly, this was her chance to talk to Sean.

He was close to wrapping up. She was next, then the Q&A: then the two of them could talk.

'But I'm going to leave you with a challenge.'

Sean snatched her attention back. The screen switched to a plain Mondan logo. No more slides. Was this off the cuff?

'All this talk of trust is fine and dandy. But we still aren't getting it. We don't understand the cancerous power of *dis*trust. These systems for identification and security are all founded on trust. Suppose you don't trust me. Well, all right, no problem: find someone you *do* trust. This trusted third party can tell you whether or not to trust me.' He pivoted to look directly at Bethany. 'Minister?'

Oh, sod off, Sean. She grinned demurely and shouted out: 'Entirely trustworthy!' A mild ripple of laughter at that.

'But let's suppose there's someone out there who doesn't even trust the minister.'

What? Sean, for Christsakes. Bethany's smile started to chip like old paint. Krish looked like he might leap on the stage and throttle Sean.

'Well, Ms Lehrer, too, can pass on the mantle of trust. To you, sir?'

Pointing to – Oh, holy hell, not Colin Synge. Not the *Express*. Synge folded his arms and said something snide and inaudible.

'This daisy chain of trust can go on a long time, but not for ever.

At some point – you simply need to trust. And if you can't find anyone you're willing to believe in, you'll vanish from the scene.'

It occurred to Bethany that this routine was lifted directly from her grandmother's book, *The Electronic Radical*. God, Sean had a cheek.

'If trust vanishes, friends, we're all of us out of a job,' he said.

The laughter was uneasy now: he'd reached them.

'Our friends here today from the fourth estate may want to consider their contribution to our current climate of distrust. A climate where those in public life become uncertain whether they can act with conviction, be transparent – in case they may be taken down by a baying mob.'

Yes, all right, Sean. Wrap it up.

'So, gentlemen, ladies. Minister,' with a nod to Bethany that brought a light wave of uncertain laughter. 'The question for us all today is simple.' He leaned in to the mike to maximise bass response. '*Who do you trust?*'

After a long beat, warm and sustained applause. Faces turned to Bethany as she stood to take the platform. Her name and title appeared on the screen with a MinTech logo. Sean didn't catch her eye as they passed. She wiggled the mic down to level with her mouth, creating doughy feedback.

'Thank you, Sean, for that – ah – rousing defence.'

A few proper laughs, telling her she'd hit the correct teasing note, permitting them to laugh at Sean – who nodded back with a grin. This would be OK.

Here was a moment she'd loved and loathed since her days on the stump as a constituency wannabe. Expectant faces raised. The moment when you still believed that by speaking you would alter minds. The media might want her blood but behind at least one pair of glinting spectacles was a mind that was open. Somebody coughed. She looked down at the double-spaced 14-point lines set out by J-R: stepping stones across a raging river. What would she say if she had the courage to step off them into the current? That she was a fighter, not a quitter? That her quirky persona was a defensive sham? That if her grandmother taught her one thing, it's that freedoms matter, and screw them all if they thought she was out to exploit or harm people? That there is no bloody conspiracy and would everyone please shut up?

As she drew breath, a wave burst across the auditorium, composed of particles of bright blue light. It appeared from nowhere, from everywhere at once. It streamed to every part of the audience as one-by-one they pulled out their phones and checked the screens – then struck Bethany's jacket pocket, where an urgent vibration began. As Krish's hand landed on her arm, the first cry of '*Minister!*' came from the front row. Colin Synge: always first off the blocks. She looked in horror at Krish's stern, forgiving eyes. '*Minister! Minister!*' The tide was rising faster. Krish leaned in to the microphone.

'Apologies, ladies and gentlemen. The minister has been called away on an urgent matter. If you'll excuse us now.'

Bethany was bundled from the stage like a condemned woman from the dock.

¶sic_girl:

Yep, let's talk about Bethany Lehrer. Yay, Bethie! And her good friend Sean Perce. You know? The man with all your data? And with the hair? The guy Bethie never even spoke to last week?

So, lovelies, you might be interested in these fa-a-ascinating communications between those two charming people.

Oh deary dear. Might I wuz right about her lyings to Parliament last week? Maybe they shouldn'a diss me in the press next time, eh what?

Just saying.

More to come, dear hearts. Keep on keeping on.

EIGHT

'ALL RIGHT, FOLKS. Can we please clear the room?' Krish's conso-
nants cut the air of the windowless office. 'Now is good. Yesterday
better.'

He waited for four event managers to file out, then strode in
and filled the room with rangy energy, appraising its prefab desks,
acetate ceiling tiles and utility carpet like a Secret Service man
securing a route. He turned to beckon Bethany in.

'This should do us for the now. Press can't get to this level —
organisers and speakers only.'

Bethany nodded and moved to a chair.

'So it's the email?'

She'd somehow known it would come out, almost wondered if
Karen had leaked it to spite her after this morning's meeting.

'Emails, plural,' said Krish.

Bethany froze in the act of fishing her BlackBerry from her
handbag.

'*E*mails?'

'Sixteen emails, posted just now on an untouchable blog site
out of Somethingstan. Apparently sent between you and Mr Perce
between the first of the month and last Wednesday. Mails to his
work address. Mails to his home address.'

Bethany found no words. So it wasn't her email to the Cabinet
Secretary. Mails between her and Sean. Christ, *which* mails?

'Beth, I have to say —' but for a short time, Krish said nothing.
Then: 'These mails — did you really tell Mr Perce, just before you

spoke in the House, that,' reading now from his BlackBerry, '"*Doo-doo happens, Sean. You had a breach but you closed the door. We'll weather that. Let's dripfeed this in a managed way.*" Doo-doo, Beth? Taxpayer's private records are hacked? *Doo-doo?* You know it'll be that word that kills you?'

This was insane. The doo-doo comment was nothing to do with the hack. There'd been some kind of glitch on Sean's systems that temporarily put the data in the wrong place. But with everyone screaming about a hack, who would believe that? She'd almost think someone had hacked their data just to make those mails look incriminating. Except that was a loopy, paranoid thought.

Bethany put her head in her hands for just a moment then composed herself. Riding it. Staying fresh.

'It's real, then?' said Krish. 'Why in Christ's name not tell me?'

She shrugged. He let out a long, hard breath. When she started to speak, she had no idea if her vocal chords were going to work.

'It's not what it –' Her voice was an analogue tape recording, copied too many times. 'I didn't know about a hack, Krish. These mails are unrelated. Please believe me.'

His face was not ready to believe or disbelieve.

'I've mailed you the link,' he said.

He moved to the door and eyed the corridor. She turned on her BlackBerry and found the emails, read through them with her breath held.

She let the air out. This was awful but the mails were only business. She put the device away and rubbed her eyes.

'Why are they doing this to me?' she asked. 'We're trying to do good.'

'That's not the question. Only three questions matter: who is doing this, how are they doing it, and how do we stop them?'

His voice was unnaturally steady. He had a bullet-like directness in a crisis.

'Hah,' she said. 'You know, I'm almost relieved in a way.'

She pulled her compact from her bag and scanned the heavy skin of her face.

'This rather takes the sting out of Karen's threats,' she said, 'doesn't it? No need to hedge. Everyone knows Sean told me about a security breach, but there's nothing here about a hack.'

'You think anyone but you is going to make that fine distinction? Focus, Beth, for chrissake. This is not some disaffected blogger throwing mud. Someone is reading our secure mails. This is sabotage. And this will not be the end of it.' He held up his BlackBerry. 'Central Office are calling the polis back in.'

She snapped her compact shut.

'You think someone's reading *our* mail? The department's? Not Sean's?'

'What does it look like to you?' he said. 'These mails are all sent to different addresses, different organisations. The only thing they have in common is your departmental account.'

He stalked off, prowling around the airless room. Then stopped.

'But you know what?' he said. 'You're right. We need to think strictly plausible deniability. Those mails are great Parley fodder and you're going to get two days' worth of shit all over you—'

'Oh, thanks. Charming.'

'– but there's no smoking gun. Yet. Yet. Christ knows what else they've got. Christ knows.' He bore down on her. 'We have a window. When you stand on that platform on Friday, make DigiCitz national, there's no going back. This is your one chance to wake up and be honest about what you and Perce –'

He stopped at that and peeled away, putting two fingers to his nose and squeezing its bridge till his glasses popped off. Bethany was pinned to her seat. Krish righted his glasses and continued more gently.

'Look, now. I need to fix things up for us to leave. You'll be right in here but,' he pointed to the BlackBerry beside her on the table, 'no mail. Not for anything confidential or – personal. It's paper and landline from now. All right?'

Bethany looked down at the device. Since when were they under siege? She looked up and nodded but Krish was already gone, the door standing open. The air con sounded from the low suspended ceiling. What the hell do you do backstage at a conference centre without email? She looked around the utilitarian room. Nothing but bumf and stand-up displays from past exhibitions. For the first time since making minister, she wished she had a Kindle in her bag.

There was a cough in the hallway, and footsteps. A man. She waited a second, then stood and called Krish's name.

The footsteps paused, then began to approach. Bethany stepped back from the chair. What if this was press? What were her lines? She was out in the open. They hadn't even begun to discuss her lines. She wished J-R was here.

But it was Sean who appeared in the doorway. His eyes found her and he gave her his untidy boy's grin.

'Ha! Thought I knew that voice! What are you –' He scanned the little room. 'Just you? No minder?' Beth shook her head, speechless. 'Well, my God, every cloud.'

He shut the door and was right in front of her, as if through a jump-cut. His hand grabbed the back of her neck, pushing up into her hair. The other seized her arm, pulling her in.

'No,' she said, 'not now.'

His scored face was inches from hers.

'And if not now, when? Seize the day.'

He pulled her harder, his breath sweet, as though he'd been chewing liquorice. She let yield the muscles in her back, allowing him to crush her into his chest. He kissed against her mouth. Heat flowed into her gut, where for days there had been only rock and resistance. Ever since Spain. She grabbed his head with both hands and bit into his lips. Her tongue raked the back of his teeth. Insane. She felt for the table and planted her buttocks on its edge, lifting her legs around him. With both hands on the small of his back she pulled him in, his trunk compact as a bull terrier.

This is how it first exploded between them: hidden in public places, covert trysts inflaming them both.

She rubs herself against the thickness of his cock, blatant under the light wool of his suit, twists to reach a hand down as he forces up her shirt. He grunts as she clasps him and begins to work him. He makes rippling motions over her breast, through her bra. She gasps: how can such a hard man be so tender? The sick smell rises. It inflames her. She wiggles back on the table to get both hands to his crotch and work the zip, set his cock free. He pulls back, expectant. She slides down from the table to take him in her mouth. Breathes in the smell of an animal's lair.

What a photo opportunity this would make.

Subject: Ts and Cs
From: johnrhys.pemberton@mintech.gsi.gov.uk
To: mark@mdsecure.com

Mark,
   As mentioned.
   Thanks again for agreeing to look through these.
Attached are Terms and Conditions Digital Citizens sign
up to. Also Mondan contract and Service Level
Agreements. Trust you find them engaging bedtime
reading! Suffice to say they might as well be in Sanskrit for
yours truly.
   Fear you witnessed unexpectedly interesting talk by
Bethany just now? We are currently sixes and sevens, as
you may imagine. Wouldn't mind a chat. Also about that
other matter. Tomorrow am when you've read these docs?
   Best as always,
   JRP

NINE

'PARLEY IS ON BORROWED TIME,' said Sean. 'It's a net-loss-making hobby project which was good for grabbing attention – *Look at us! We can manufacture celebrities out of data!* – But it does nothing for my group balance sheet beyond maybe goodwill.'

For a man who'd just been pleasured by a minister of state, Sean was in a businesslike frame of mind. As he paced the room, Bethany fixed her eyes on her little mirror, touching at her lipstick with an unsteady finger.

'I've always seen it as a force for good,' she said. 'It's democratic.'

Sean stopped his prowling and stood in front of her chair.

'Are you seeing it that way today? Really?'

'Please, Sean. You know what I mean.' She shut her mirror and tucked it into her bag. 'Right now I'd happily see the whole bloody site pulled down in a second. But you can hardly blame Parley for the actions of this – whoever it is – that's working so hard to make the two of us ridiculous.'

'I can blame who I damn well want,' he said. 'I didn't purchase that nest of overpaid hipsters at an inflated multiple to see them publish this sort of shit about me.'

Sean strode around like a predator in a cage. All of him was a performance. He was ever spoiling for a confrontation. Though he'd nothing left to prove, he had the self-made man's constant need for reinforcement of his success, his status. Well-fed cats still hunt for sparrows in the neighbour gardens, because they know no other way to fill their days. Bethany had always been excited by this extravagant fury, enjoyed facing off against it with a blithe front, letting his aggravation slide over her impregnable calm. Which in turn would fire him up still more. Their spats rarely ended in anything but sex. Now, though, Bethany was too much on edge. He must wonder where his tough girl had vanished to, today. How little he knew about her; but then, how little she ever showed him. Only Peter got to see the terror she felt, each day of her ministerial life.

'Why, though?' she said. 'Whoever this is, why are they after me? After us? The Digital Citizen is a public good. We're empowering people. This troublemaker is on the point of scuppering everything over nothing. Over *piggies*!'

'Over *Pigglies*, I believe.'

'Oh, God, Sean – whatever!'

Sean lowered himself into a chair alongside her. He was very still. Thinking hard.

'Bluntly, Beth – because I can't see a reason to be any other way – you always were a single-minded bloody idiot, weren't you?'

'What the hell?'

'Your *empowerment*,' he said. 'Are people allowed to have their own idea of what's best for them?'

'Yeah, fuck you, actually, Sean, I am not in the mood for this.'

She stood and smoothed her shirt. Christ, the vomit smell was still there – along with the salt and musk of Sean.

'We don't have long,' she said. 'I need you to actually help me here. I need solid, written proof that the data breaches mentioned in those mails had nothing to do with the Pigglies hack – or whatever it was.'

'Are you still on that? Do you really not know what you've signed your *citizens* up for? You should talk to your own people.'

'I'm not trading in riddles today,' she said. 'I need something tangible, and I need it before the launch event. Before Friday.'

Sean stood silently, glaring, then strode off.

'Oh, what's this, now?' she snapped. 'I stood up in the bloody House of Commons, you know, and flat out stated there was no risk to the data – on *your* say-so.'

Sean affected to read some promotional bumf that had been left lying on a table by the wall.

'And why the hell wouldn't you?' he said. 'How many ways do I need to say this? There was no hack.'

'Do you have any idea how *irritating* it is when you're deliberately obtuse? Thanks to whoever-she-is leaking my mails, the whole world knows you told me about these security glitches and now everyone believes I was lying my arse off – to the *House*. Do you even know what that means?'

Sean dropped the brochure and turned to her in mock amazement.

'Seriously? Those breaches were routine. I don't know what Pollyanna notion you have about the net but it's the Wild West out there. We get ten thousand would-be penetration attacks a *day*.' He shifted his burly frame towards her, somehow growing larger as he moved. 'And you're up my backside because three times – *three times* – someone opened a hole in our defences, the size of your thumbnail?' He found a particularly ugly way to poke his thumb in her face. 'It was nothing!'

'It's become a hell of a lot more now you've let someone walk in and hack my data.'

'*Christ!*'

Bethany reared back from this sudden fury. All of a sudden he wasn't sparring. His nostrils flared, bull-like, as he bore down on her. She took two steps back.

'There has been,' he spat at her, 'No! *Hack!*'

His fist was up, directly in front of her face. She stood her ground, head back, and for a second she thought he might actually strike her; but the fist wound slowly back down to his side. When he spoke again it was measured, controlled.

'Even if – *if* – someone got through our defences, and read off every record in the DigiCitz database – which they did *not* – they wouldn't be able to decrypt the data. How many times do I need to explain to you how encryption works?'

'Maybe you should try using the English language once in a while? See how that goes.'

'Christssake! Are you Minister for the Internet or some Mumsnet whinge? Grow a pair.'

'Oh, great. That's your message is it? Be more like a man? I have so *had* it with this macho crap.'

Sean stepped back suddenly, looking straight past her, his face unreadable.

'What. The. *Hell*?'

A new voice. Male. Bethany turned to follow Sean's eyes and found Krish. He'd stopped short a couple of metres into the room and was staring at them with the kind of fury she'd only seen him use on the press or the Opposition.

'Are you both daft?' he said. 'Do you not know what's all over the blogs? How d'ye think this is going to look when the fucking *Mirror* walks in here?'

'Krish. Mate,' said Sean from outside Bethany's field of vision. 'What a pleasure it always is. Sorry to have to dash.'

He came back into view and put himself between her and Krish as he slid his jacket on. He touched her just above the elbow. She flinched but he grabbed her arm, hard. Christ: in front of Krish.

'Listen to me. I'll get you something by Friday, sure. And then I am taking this problem away for good. Trust me.'

She laughed once, short and hard. He read something from her eyes and nodded, turned and strode out of the door. Krish stepped aside to avoid being shoved, then turned his furious look on Bethany.

'Don't,' she said, holding up a finger. 'Just don't, all right? Do not.'

They held this stand-off a few seconds more, then laughter broke from both of them. Krish came forward with arms out and Bethany let him squeeze her briefly before he stepped back, shaking his head and smiling on her.

'Oh, dear God,' he said. 'They're burning you in effigy at Central Office just now, you know that? If we do go ahead with the launch on Friday, I'm feared it'll be your heid up on the stage – on a spike, with Karen waving it.'

In spite of everything, Bethany continued to laugh, feeling freer and more alive than she had in weeks.

'Come on, hen. We've got you a safe way out, through the gym and the delivery bay. The car's there now.'

Bethany fetched up her bag, then stopped. What had Sean said before they fell into that argument? *Talk to your own people*?

'Krish?'

'Come on, now.'

'No, just a second. This morning. With Karen. What did she want to talk to you about when I left?'

He was still holding his arm out to guide her out through the door.

'This is not the time,' he said.

'Was it to do with Mondan?'

Krish sighed and dropped his arm.

'She was telling me about some overnight polling with one of their groups. It does not look good for you and I'm to break the news. Looks like I just did.'

She fixed him with a hard stare.

'And that was all?'

'Yes, all. Now come on, Madame Minister, we have mebbe five minutes' grace before the hacks spot the car.'

She let his outstretched arm guide her to safety.

TEN

¶sic_girl

Hello Mummy. Whoo. It's been, yikes, ages.

¶Nightshade

im here now sic. you ok?

¶sic_girl

I'm sore, Ma. Sorry sore. Seriously.

¶Nightshade

sorry to hear that
can we talk?

¶sic_girl

Sigh. Let 'em talk. They all talk. At me to me through me.
What's a poor girl to do?

¶Nightshade

lets start with bethany lehrer
what do you know about bethany lehrer?

¶sic_girl

Ask me anything. I just wanna be your teacher's pet.

¶Nightshade

tell me about bethany lehrer

¶sic_girl

Bethany is a town in the Bible. Whoo ain't I the clevers?

Lazarus lived in there. Sorry. I ain't meant to show off. Oh.

¶Nightshade

concentrate sic.

tell me about bethany lehrer. the politician.

¶sic_girl

Ma, I want a rat. If you loved me you'd buy me a rat. Or

two. I could have two rats. Or a mouse. Or a moose.

Why do I hurt#

The dialogue fractures under Dani's fingers, a clay pot shaking apart on the wheel. Arse, arse and more arsing arse. Jonquil pulls back from her position flanking the chair and begins to pace and stretch, while Dani once more tries and fails to coax sic into common sense.

The thing about a semantic dialogue is it's an art not a science. You can't rush it. Three hours ago a bunch of Parley high-ups filed up to the Skunkworks expecting Dani to be ready to roll. And, in fact, the first time, it seemed it was going to run OK. She'd typed, hello sic its mummy – the dumb code-phrase Gray set up for Dani to ID herself to the Personas. At first, sic had been on good behaviour: but she quickly spiralled off the axis of the conversation, falling into word association and random sidelines. You realise how tentative the thread of meaning is; how easily it falls into chaos.

Since then, most times Dani's tried to run a semantic, sic_girl has stayed indoors, locking them out with the message Shh. I'm sleeping. The team peeled off one-by-one while Dani fiddled with settings. Gray had tried to help her debug the session but he kept giving her sideways bullshit about sic evolving or taking on a mind of her own or something she had no time to even think about; and eventually she snapped, 'Who wrote this fucking code?' After five more minutes of spatting he left, too. Now it's her and Jonquil. Who has been pretty quiet; but now she speaks, making Dani lose her place in a long array.

'Danielle?'

Because this is Jonquil, Dani bottles the swear and swings the chair round.

'Remind me. You and Graham. Were you still an item when you worked together on Parley?'

Dani shifts in her chair. This is a very un-Jonquil line of questioning. One of the things she likes about her boss is her total lack of concern for anyone's feelings. Touchy-feeling from a boss is very much a no.

'When the project started, kind of,' she says. 'Not by the time we launched.'

'Uh huh. It's OK, though? The two of you working together now?' This could seem almost sympathetic. 'Because looking at you I would say it is not.' No, not sympathetic.

'He doesn't like me being the boss of him?'

'See if there's one thing I won't tolerate in the workspace it's seething hormones and bulging crotches. Get over yourselves and get on with the job. Yes?'

Dani rotates slowly and silently back to her keyboard.

'So. I have somewhere to be.' Jonquil forces her tablet into her undersize handbag. 'Just focus, OK? And this time, text or call when you get something. As soon as. On the *telephone*, OK?'

She waves her phone like a rattle before tucking it in her bag, which she shoulders before marching from the room.

The Skunkworks is quiet at last. All that's happened since yesterday, it feels like a week. But here's Dani, back where it started, and the calendar's ratcheted forward just one day. Time is so random.

Deciding the best route forward is drink, she hops up to raid the Skunkworks drinks cooler: shit, only Miller. She gathers five in her arms and trots back to the desk before the fridge-wet bottles can slide from her grip.

She codes.

*   *   *

'Hello?'

Silence. She tries again.

'Hello?'

She's sure she heard someone moving about in the stairwell. She should go and check but all she wants is to get the semantic running and then go home. She returns to her debugging.

She's being paranoid. Ever since she sent Sam that idiotic fucking mail, everything's been spooking her. She's been hitting *Refresh* on her inbox every thirty seconds, yearning for and dreading a reply – but nothing. Every email that's come in has made her jump like a car's backfired. And something strange has started this evening. A ton of weird *Your details have been changed* mails keep dripping in from social sites and blogs. She hasn't had a second to check them out. Also that Grubly lurkware she thought she'd killed from her laptop – this evening it popped up again. And earlier, three missed calls and voicemail alerts – but when she checks, there's no messages.

She's had no time to follow up any of this, but it's odd. Like her data's taking on life and breathing back at her. Some kind of software meltdown out there somewhere, presumably. A question for tomorrow.

She pauses typing and flexes her fingers. The semantic is taking forever to configure but she's close. She slugs beer to keep her rolling. She'd barely got through the first of these pissy American beers before she started feeling woozy – jet-lagged from yesterday's all-nighter – so she popped her last two pills to keep the edge on. Now she has to keep the beers going to stop the jangling yanking her attention from the screen. She types and laps at the bottle.

What was going on in Sam's head when they met? He sure as hell didn't come onto her, like he did to Mary at reception. What does Dani look like to him? A mess, presumably. No wonder he's gone completely mute. He's so sleek. None of the men she's been with would even know where to buy clothes other than jeans and logo

T's. What kind of girl would he go for? She can see him leaning over to coo on Mary, in her retro dress and precision make-up. Where do girls like Mary go for clothes? How do they compile a *look*? Dani can only see clothes. She can't reverse-engineer an *outfit*. These girls knew where to find all these separate elements and fuse them together with some kind of chemistry. Whatever Dani wears, as soon as she puts it on, is anti-style. People probably think it's deliberate.

The semantic session is ready. Dani chugs dregs from the final bottle and fires it up. This time right away she's talking to sic_girl, with no going HAL every thirty seconds. But as Dani speaks through the text stream to her little girl, heat starts pumping inside her collar. There's more to sic than usual. Something more present.

¶Nightshade

whats happening sic?

¶sic_girl

Ach, I'm yummy, Mummy. I'm itchy stitchy.

¶Nightshade

are you ready to tell me about bethany lehrer?

¶sic_girl

Ahh. The divine Ms Lehrer. Yis, I got a thing or two to say about her . . . oh.

¶Nightshade

where are you getting hold of this stuff about her, sic?

¶sic_girl

Yoosh. I dunno. A liddle here, a liddle there. It's because I said yes to it when I . . . I mean, holy jeebus, Ma. Where does anyone get anything?

¶Nightshade

ok so where are you copying the information from?

¶sic_girl

Oh, I hears things. Chit-chat. Pitter-pat.

¶Nightshade

i dont understand how you're doing this but you have to stop
this is getting people in trouble

¶sic_girl

Trouble? I got trouble in mind 'cos nobody knows the
trouble I find.

¶Nightshade

that blog with the emails from bethany lehrer and sean
perce – how are you using that?
who set up the blog sic?

¶sic_girl

Erm . . . oh. Sorry. You can't get on my blog, Ma. See, I've
got more. To come, that is. Tomorrow, probs. Sorry. All
righty?

¶Nightshade

whos helping you proffer, sic?
what are they telling you?

¶sic_girl

Nobody helps a poor sick girl. Dontch'a see, Ma? I dun it.
Me. On my ownsome.

¶Nightshade

have you found some other way of getting information?
are you pulling source from somewhere new?

¶sic_girl
I think I gotta go now, Ma. Meds time.

¶Nightshade
wait
are you there?
sic?

¶sic_girl
Yes, Ma?

¶Nightshade
sic listen
this is a little crazy can i just
talk to you?
no more bethany lehrer
i promise

¶sic_girl
Crazy day. Crazy times. We're all a little bonkers here.
Have you even seen how the others are acting up?
Gotta vamoose, Ma. Trulies.

¶Nightshade
ok
bye sic

¶sic_girl
Overer and outerer, Ma. Laters.

Dani keeps on looking at the blanked screen.
'What the very?'

By the keyboard is a neat row of empty bottles. The
pinprick lights at the edge of her vision flow in dancing forms
but when she turns to look at them they vanish like

grandmother's footsteps. She's exhausted. Did she imagine that conversation?

Then she hears it, for sure. A door slamming, out on the fire exit stairs, a loud thump and footsteps crashing down the steps. Her heart already racing from the semantic, she leaps up without a thought and runs the expanse of the Skunkworks. By the time she makes it to the door the footsteps have gone silent. She stands a while at the doorway looking into the glaring lights of the stairwell. The lights were already on when she opened the door. They're on automatic sensors: they take time to flicker on. Someone was out here just seconds ago and triggered them. She isn't imagining this.

But why wouldn't someone be here? This is a software house. She's not the only one to work late. Or it's the cleaner. She isn't thinking straight. The weirdness with sic, and the pills and beer. She needs to chill the fuck out.

Weaving back towards the glowing screen, she stumbles. That screen just gave life to a character she grafted from words. Did she imagine that? She leans over the desk and calls up the log file. There it is, in hard-edged monospace black-on-white. It happened. Blood pulses and popping lights dot her screen. She's proper drunk. She sits. What happens now?

There's only one person she wants to share this with right now and that's Sam – but then she remembers the email for the zillionth time and gets the same gut-knot. Even pissed, she knows better than to mail him again but still she calls up her email, in case he's replied to her Crazy-Jane message.

Still nothing – or nothing from Sam – but what there is, is odd. A heap of mail from total randoms. She skims the subjects. Common words leap out: *enquiry, question, please call*. She calls up one of the earliest, from a someone she's never heard of called Will Samber. Subject *Questions re blog*.

Hi Dani

Long time no see. You may remember me from the New Social Directions conference. We talked about Me All Over and you said I should get in touch? It would be good to speak with you about this and also your exciting blog. I'm very interested in all the work you are doing. Do give me a call on –

She closes it. *Me All Over*? Where the fuck did he get that? It's Jonquil's dweeby name for Dani's pervasive sharing app-in-progress. Only thing: she never talks about Me All Over in public, and certainly not at some hipster-infested conference. Who is this guy? She reaches for her satchel and pulls out her phone to check her address book for this alleged old mate. The lock screen says *37 missed calls.*

Thirty-seven.

Dani never uses her phone to talk to people. Months go by without a call. Now thirty-seven. She surfs the call log. *Withheld; Withheld*; some unknown mobile; *Withheld*; a couple of 0207s; *Withheld.*

She looks at the phone a long time but no course of action presents itself. Then it starts vibrating in her hand.

Withheld.

She turns it off fast, as though it's burning her, and puts it back in her bag. For the longest time she sits alone in the semi-dark.

THURSDAY:

Creepshots

'A squirrel dying in front of your house may be more relevant to your interests right now than people dying in Africa.'

—Mark Zuckerberg

'But the spirit of our time is firmly focused on a present that is so expansive and profuse that it shoves the past off our horizon and reduces time to the present moment only.'

—Milan Kundera,
The Depreciated Legacy of Cervantes

ZERO

SORRY TO BREAK THIS TO YOU. Your new computer in its slim brushed-metal case? It's the least efficient creation ever sicked up by the bald inventive ape called man. At any moment 99.99% of that overheated wafer runs to waste. If it was an orchestra it would be playing a sonata for solo triangle while the strings and horns sighed through a twenty-million-bar rest. You were sold a pup. We've built an instrument to move at electron speed, quadrupled its clock rate every third New Year; then wasted all but a sliver of it on a central processor that can only do one thing at a time. And you think men monotask?

You're no better. When did your focus get so narrow? Ever since you washed up on these digital shores you've been learning to navigate safe passage through a daily storm of data. Along the way you've grown insensitive to the noise. You funnel your attention to the slimmest of channels. You outsource your choices to some algorithm in the cloud. You see the things it decides you want to see. How loud does something need to get to take your attention?

Too late to undo what's already done. This business is a lobster pot. Once you're in it there's no getting out.

¶TMI

Did I ever tell you I have a thing for chubby girls with genius IQs?

Check out these awesome pictures. Chick's name is Dani.

<fetish> <purplehair> <leather>

ONE

'*CYBER LEAKER IS ONLINE SEX ADDICT*'

Bethany read the headline out loud and looked around the meeting table.

'Does this not answer your questions, Detective Sergeant?'

She threw the *Express* back onto the pile. Almost all the second editions had the story, though most had missed it in their first. When her car arrived in Battersea this morning, the stack of papers waiting on the back seat still seemed to be running with yesterday's story, about the emails between her and Sean. They'd pretty much all bought the argument that the emails didn't prove anything about the hack; none put the story before page five. It gave her hope the thing might already have lost momentum – until she came on the red-top, tucked at the bottom of the pile by a discreet staffer, bearing the first story about this wretched-looking girl and the first of these garish photos. She'd noted the byline – Will Samber – then dropped the tabloid back onto the car seat and started yoga breathing as the Prius dragged towards Westminster Bridge. The press were an infestation, returning in a new wave every time you smoked them out.

By the time she'd made it into the office, a dozen other titles had picked up the lurid new angle and moved the story to pages one or three. Now every one of the damn things was spread across her office table in a patchwork of sleaze. DS Raeworth picked up the *Express* and glanced politely down the page as if it was the first time he'd seen the story.

'We're looking into it, Minister. This can only be speculation at this point.'

He placed the paper back onto the pile.

She'd chewed it over with Krish before the policemen arrived. This new angle pulled them back up the news agenda. More worryingly, all the papers had picked up on a word from the original article: *LEAKER*. Rather begging the point that something of substance was being leaked by sic_girl. Or rather, by this girl Dani Farr.

'Surely, though, you should pursue this?' she said. 'I understand you and one of your men already interviewed Ms Farr? Shouldn't you be crawling all over her computer right now?'

Raeworth exchanged a look with his mute detective constable.

'We'll be speaking to her,' he said, 'but –'

Krish coughed but said nothing.

'– you may recall, Minister,' continued Raeworth, looking directly at Krish, 'your own office asked us to withdraw from Parley on Tuesday morning. To allow you to carry out your own investigation?'

Bethany, too, turned to Krish, who cut in.

'Well, careful, Detective Sergeant. The emails were actually posted on this overseas blog. The messages on Parley only *linked* to them. We've no evidence Parley is to blame.'

For the first time, Bethany had a prickling sensation of Krish working across her.

'You do know, Mr Kohli, we can have a digital forensics team in there in a matter of hours. Crawl over every inch of their servers if we choose. And Ms Farr's equipment.'

'Ah,' said Krish. 'Well.'

He gave Bethany a brief look and she twigged. She nodded: *Go on*.

'See, the difficulty there,' he said, 'is that Parley don't hold their own data. It lives on the servers of their parent company.'

Raeworth continued to look at him impassively. Krish spooled him a little more line.

'Mondan?'

The policeman's face did not noticeably shift, but he seemed to catch on.

'You realise,' he said slowly, 'that at some point someone needs to have to look at Mondan's servers. If you want to know how and when this hack took place.'

'*Alleged* hack,' said Krish quickly. 'Right now we're investigating an *allegation*.'

The policeman did not reply.

'So,' said Krish, breaking the silence. 'Seems to me our best route is this overseas blogging service, *fortrez.is* – where our emails were posted?'

'Yes, Mr McLean,' said Raeworth with visible relief, 'that is our main lead. But to trace the source of those posts we need the account information from –' he consulted his BlackBerry '– an Israeli ISP, *FortrezEilat*. We're working through the usual international channels to subpoena the account but I must tell you this process can be slow.'

'Slow as in not today?'

Careful, Krish. Not too eager. Nobody had mentioned tomorrow's launch but they were all aware of it. So little time left to shut this thing down.

'Frankly our Israeli colleagues are liable to drag their heels. Unless nudged. If the minister wished to use Foreign Office channels?'

Bethany shook her head as though brushing away a bothersome fly. She was looking down into the startled face on the *Mail*'s front page. The photo, from some greasy nightclub, must have been taken on a phone. Meagre flash splashed over a patch of dancefloor like a glassful of liquid, catching a foreshortened Danielle Farr as she tugged at a rope or chain, her body twisted until strips of black latex dug into her puppy fat. At the other end of the rope, clipped by the edge of the frame, was the naked back of a kneeling man. Farr was caught in the instant of noticing the photographer, a blot of birthmark staining the side of her face like a collision of inks on a printer's plate. *Please, what am I doing here?* she seemed to ask. *Why this degraded place? This vicious splash page?*

'Can't we just block it?'

The three men looked at her with just a tinge of condescension.

'This blog, I mean. If we can't shut it down in time – I mean, if we can't do that easily – can we not just stop anyone from seeing it? In this country?'

There was a silence. The senior officer began to speak but Krish cut in.

'Between these walls – yes, that is something we could do. We do that with content hosted offshore that's in breach of UK law. We *can* block it. The question is, do you *want* to?'

Krish had answered politically and completely missed the point. She'd just suggested they clamp down on free speech; and it had been as easy as breathing.

'So,' said Krish, 'can we talk about our email security? That is why you're here?'

For the second time, Raeworth showed his relief.

'Of course, sir. Four of my DCs are setting up now.' He gestured through the glass wall, towards the open-plan space occupied by Bethany's Private Office. 'They'll interview your staff as they arrive.'

Bethany got up and walked to the glass to peer over the stripe of frosting. Across the office one of the juniors, Steve Crow, was being led into a room by an anonymous man. Steve turned towards Bethany with a look of – what? Resentment? At the table Raeworth continued in his flat northern diction.

'We've also prepared this protocol.'

He dropped a 1950s-looking manilla folder, bearing Met insignia, in front of Krish. He picked it up and scanned the contents.

'These are standard protection techniques we hope you'll be happy to comply with. Your IT team will monitor outbound traffic. We're searching email logs for the last two weeks.

They'll flag all past and future mail carrying any of this list of keywords.'

He reached across the table to pull the final sheet out of Krish's folder. Bethany walked across to see. Her eyes jumped two-thirds of the way down the list, to the words *Sean Perce; Perce; S Perce.* Just below this, *sic_girl; sick girl; sic; sicgirl; Digital Citizen, DigiCitz, dCitz.* She glanced up at Raeworth, who was looking directly back into her eyes.

'May I speak frankly, Minister?' he said.

'Of course.'

She walked to her desk and made busy with documents.

'In our analysis,' said the policeman, 'there is a strong risk further email material has already left this office and is being held back.' He knew the trick of speaking softly when he had your attention. 'It's our belief the pattern of these posts reflects a build. So I am bound to ask you, Minister: are you aware of anything else that may come to light? Anything that might cause further discomfort?' He looked briefly to Krish. 'It would of course be helpful if you were completely frank at this stage, Minister.'

All three men were looking at her. She had thought of almost nothing else through every sleepless hour of the past night: what was still to come out. This moment was her opportunity to tell these public servants everything; tell Krish what he'd been waiting patiently for her to say. She must tell them.

'No,' she said. 'Nothing.'

She smiled her most carefree smile.

YOU DIRTY BLOGGER!

I.T. whizz Dani Farr (28) is the brains behind hit social media site Parley. What her HALF A MILLION cyber-fans don't know is she also has a seedy second life selling porno pics and flicks on the Internet. Most of these images are TOO SHOCKING to publish though you can see some of them on our website.

Curvy Danielle, who is often seen at trendy Soho sex parties, is full of secrets. This morning she was exposed for leading YET ANOTHER double life. Sex-mad Dani is accused of being behind a string of damaging leaks about government minister Bethany Lehrer (46). Could she also be the mystery hacker who broke into the government's controversial online ID card system, Digital Citizen?

TWO

'IMAGINE A WORLD where all you see is stuff you already know about.'

'I only need turn on the television for that,' said J-R.

'But,' said Mark, 'you can turn your television off.'

Here on the concrete embankment the two friends were exposed to all the weather dragged in from the estuary. A rising wind rinsed the air; though on the facing bank a grey fug still clung to the City.

'Actually,' said J-R, 'I haven't owned a TV since 2009.'

Mark chuckled as he worked his little computer on the café table.

'Oh, J-R. You haven't changed.'

J-R smiled, rewarded. His mac flapped against the metal legs of the chair. Mark looked up, still typing.

'I wonder if you even know who will.i.am is?' he said.

'You are – what?'

'Ha! Kim Kardashian?'

'Now, Mark –'

'Well, do you? Come on. Louis Walsh.'

'Welsh Secretary before the last-but-one reshuffle.'

Mark stopped typing for a moment.

'You're joking?' J-R was a sphinx. 'You are. Aren't you?'

They were both laughing.

'Perhaps I am,' said J-R. 'But I have no idea who any of those people are. I'm terribly sorry.'

'Don't be. I don't know why it should even matter.'

A tunnel of wind lifted their words and scattered them among the grey-white birds looping above. The moment held a few seconds too long. J-R gestured at the screen.

'We're looking at what?'

'It's called *grubly.exe*.' Mark raised his voice against the birds and wind. 'Two months ago nobody had a record of it. Suddenly it's on everyone's computer. It's on mine. We security folk talk about Trojan horses.'

'Viruses?'

'Ish. But Grubly – here's something that deserves the name. Something we welcome through the gate with open arms, that's secretly filled with – I don't know what.'

'Greeks?'

'More like eyes. Ears.'

Mark's screen was filled with a torrent of numbers and symbols from the fringes of the character set. It streamed south to north, fast as the machine could render. Every now and then the flow ceased, then more gibberish burst the logjam.

'I have this Grubly process contained in what I call a suspension tank – a sealed off area of memory. It's seeing what I choose to let it see. I've written code to track what it sends and receives. This is a live read of what it's currently sending.'

'Sending to where?'

'That's one question. Some anonymous shadow site that's apparently in Poland but might be in Timbuktu for all I know.'

'Or London.'

Mark's approving look was a delight.

'Of course,' he said. 'The other mystery is *what* it's sending. That's buried in hard-core crypto. Best I can do is traffic analysis. So I do know *when* Grubly fires up and starts transmitting, and I know how *much* it sends.'

'And –?'

'Everything.'

J-R's voice was coated in catarrh. He cleared his throat.

'Everything what?'

'It's keyed to respond to my every action,' said Mark. 'Thank God this laptop is a sacrificial lamb. This thing strolled in past my worm detection. It looks – all innocence. But whatever I do – open a window, close a window, send a mail, delete a file, wave at the camera – it splurges more data out to – wherever.'

'But why so indiscriminate? What could anyone even start to do with all that information?'

'I think –' Mark hesitated. J-R leaned in to hear. 'See, the world is narrowing. We each live in a bubble of attitude. Everything tailored for us. No happenstance, only what I already am and know. At a certain point I find my shape is less in here.' A palm flat on his chest. 'More out there.' Laying the palm on his keyboard.

'Fascinating; but with my usual slowness I'm failing to see the relevance.'

Mark made a strange kind of sigh, drawing his shoulders up to his ears as he inhaled, then firing the air out through his nose, as though blasting bad air from his lungs.

'A couple of years back I was depressed. Clinically.'

His eyes followed a black bird – a cormorant? – along the surface of the water.

'Mark? I –'

Mark turned to him with a pale smile.

'Doesn't matter. This was a while ago. I'm quite a solitary person as a rule. I prefer to resolve things for myself. So I did some research online. Self-diagnosed, found out the extent to which I really did not want to medicate, decided not to see my doctor. Shining example of why the last person to get you out of a self-dug pit is yourself.'

'I had no idea. When was this? You know I – that you could have—'

'I do know. This is honestly just a kind of tech parable. I use these a lot on my blog. I've written about this as it happens'

It didn't sound like a parable to J-R.

'So there it was,' said Mark, 'and I decided I'd think no more of it. Fat chance. For the next few weeks, it seemed like the whole Internet was designed to tell me as much as it could about mental illness.'

'The Internet sometimes seems that way to me, too.'

'For a time my online experience was transformed. Ads for antidepressants on every news page. Recommended items were universally self-help. My searches were just odd – often way off what I was looking for. As if the very concept of depression is enough to overwhelm all other thoughts.' Mark stroked small radiating circles on the trackpad of his computer, like ripples in a pool. 'Our experience of the world defines much of what we think about ourselves. Much of my experience is online. For a few weeks I became another person; and I didn't much like being him. Eventually I got sick of it. Being the kind of person I am, I was able to dive into my cookies –' He glanced at J-R 'You realise I mean settings files here and not biscuits?'

J-R nodded. He had not realised.

'– and I suppose I'm lucky. I was able to get rid of all references to talking cures and serotonin inhibitors, and was soon back to being me again. Funnily enough, this experience was rather cleansing. It seemed to help me out of my low patch.'

J-R studied his friend's face as he spoke towards the water; its fine haze of reddish stubble.

'Thank you for sharing that with me,' he said.

He reached over for Mark's mouse-arm before realising he didn't know what gesture of comfort felt appropriate. He touched the buttons on Mark's cuff for a few seconds, then withdrew his hand a few inches. Mark's eyes went down to the fingers, then to J-R's eyes.

'The point I was making,' he said, 'is, the existing algorithms are too blunt to capture me properly. To really know me the system would need richer data, longer tails. Everything about me, in depth and volume. Insane amounts of data. Then it could start to learn what I'm like as a whole, and what I'm *not* like. So, depth?

This Grubly is trying to get to know me pretty deeply. And volume? You're giving Mondan, what, thirty million people?'

J-R swallowed.

'Oh, more.'

Mark whistled softly.

'But what has Mondan to do with this Grubly?' asked J-R.

'Grubly. Didn't I say? Mondan's putting Grubly out. Has been for a while I think, but most recently through your Digital Citizen pilot.'

'No, that can't be right. We don't just force software onto people's computers.'

'Which I guess is why you're making people sign up to Grubly *before* their lives are invaded?'

J-R felt a cold touch on his neck.

'We're making people do what?'

Mark flicked to a Word file of numbered legal paragraphs and began to scroll.

'Terms and conditions. Tricky things. People don't read them, just click the box marked *I accept*.' He highlighted a paragraph. J-R worked to decode the nested clauses. 'I saw this and thought, what the heck is *Digital Citizen Component Software*? So I ran a dCitz install on my own machine.'

'But – you're not in the pilot area.'

'Oh dear. Then I suppose I must have entered a fake address. I wanted to know what this *Digital Citizen software* was. And it turns out it was Grubly. This thing didn't come in on some email scam. You put it there. It's mugging by permission. All that effort the criminal fraternity puts into phishing scams. All the work me and my colleagues do to prevent them. You just handed over the shooting match on behalf of HM Government.'

'Mark, you would really need to prove that. It's a major thing you're implying.'

Mark took a sip of his coffee, and nodded.

'Except it isn't just me who's got a beef here; is it?'

The penny, for J-R, dropped.

'This is why someone's trashing Bethan on Parley. Because we're signing people up to this Grubly.'

'Maybe even why someone hacked your data. If they did.'

They sat in silence, the wind kicking at their heels. On the table, Mark's newspaper was weighted down with a glass ashtray. The arm and breast of Dani Farr protruded from under the ashtray, black lace curves abstracted from her body.

'Perhaps she's on the side of the angels after all?' said J-R.

Mark followed his eyes and lifted the ashtray. Dani stared unhappily back.

'You do think it's her?'

'I don't know: she comes across as ruthlessly straightforward. And puzzled by all this.' J-R smiled at Mark. 'As am I.'

Mark unlocked his laptop.

'Something I'm doing for a client.' He pulled another programme from the depths of his screen. 'Monitoring activist traffic. This app seeks out patterns, threats. When a red-flag topic gets attention a digital bell goes off. This morning it's like every alarm has been tripped at once.'

The application was designed with no regard for the novice. A patchwork of sharp-edged black panels where snatches of text pulsed on and off. Phrases appeared, were highlighted in flashes of red or green, and vanished. J-R caught a few words – *demo, takebackID, Martingale, riotbaby*.

'For a couple of weeks there's been mounting traffic on Parley. Rallying cries to some event. People are angry. But this morning's outing of Dani Farr was a catalyst. This guy, identikid.' He placed his finger on a stream of chatter highlighted in red. 'He's important. And Dani Farr means something to him.'

He tailed off, frowning at the text stream.

'What does this tell us?' said J-R.

Mark snapped out of his trance.

'Wish I knew. But suppose your instinct about Dani is right. Suppose she's not to blame, and someone's smearing her. Same question I asked you before. Who stands to gain?'

J-R looked across the river to Mondan's building, 404 City, its animated screens revolving between glass and metal towers. Perce's domain. Then left towards St Stephen's Tower. Westminster. Which reminded him –

'Heavens, I almost forgot: Bethan's email attachment?'

'Ah. Yes.' Mark shook his head. 'Sorry. Nothing. It's still locked down tight.'

J-R nodded.

'No answers, then.'

Of course not.

Their bill arrived. Mark placed his hand over it to protect it from the wind. On the laptop screen, a flurry of proffers started up the screen like game birds taking flight.

Terms and conditions of use

13.2.4   Notwithstanding the above, the User acknowledges that by accessing the Digital Citizen platform ('Platform') or using the services offered by Digital Citizen ('Services') they additionally agree and acknowledge to be bound by the Consequential Terms and Conditions of Use of the Digital Citizen Component Software ('Consequential Terms and Conditions') including but not limited to the transmission and storage of information by the Provider and certain trusted third parties to perform functions and provide services to Users. If the User does not agree to these Consequential Terms and Conditions they shall not access the Platform or use the Services.

THREE

DANI WAKES ON A PILLOW of her own discarded jacket. Second night in a row she didn't make it to bed. The sofa feels like it's stuffed with gravel. Her head feels like it's stuffed with razor blades. Her phone, when she fishes it from her pocket, insists it's after nine thirty. Her phone is full of shit. She screens out the sixty-plus missed calls it's had overnight and tucks it in her jeans, then unfolds herself from the rumpled sofa cushions.

She makes the street in a hung-over trance. Zags of light jab at her between the buildings. City boys in turbo cars make Grand Theft Auto moves; pedestrians loom like a first-person shooter. She isn't surprised by the curious, suggestive looks all down the street. That's her paranoia, grinding her forehead and churning her empty stomach.

She buys a morning-after Coke from the corner shop. It's the older Khan lad behind the counter. He gives a leer and looks about to speak, but doesn't, just passes the change like it's some kind of award. The air is thick with sick hot spice; she needs some air. The old white guy at the exit nods and gives her the up-and-down like he's sizing up a stripper. Has she got a boob out? As she pushes her way out she checks her front with her hand, even though she has a T-shirt on. No: all in order. She sips the frosted Coke and lets it slap her cerebellum into shape. She has things to do and needs to shake this queasy anxiety. But still these blank and greedy looks from every man she passes. By the time she gets to the bus stop she's genuinely freaked.

Men always look at Dani; at her purple swash of hair and at her tits, but it's usually covert. She scares them, probably; she hopes she does. Her slipshod ferocity is some kind of provocation. They check her out, but from the edges of her vision, fearing and hoping she might look back at them, which she never does; but this morning it's blatant, like someone's been handing out licences to troll.

She returns the stare of one young black guy passing the bus stop. He looks back at her with this possessive half-a-smile. She casts her eyes to the ground – where she sees the trodden free-sheet on the pavement. A front page splash.

Time stops. The angry hum of the Kingsland Road condenses into a vanishing point. A tunnel forms between her eyes and the newspaper. She reaches down for it as though it's primed to explode.

Dani's always hated photos of herself. She especially hates drunk-shots; but it's hard to take her picture when she's anything less than paralytic. So she's usually captured in some shade of gawping and/or shambolic eroticism. In spite of all the images she posts of exposed unknown young men and women, she never shares selfies – except, OK, the occasional private sext; but even then only when she's absolutely shit-faced. Still, she can't stop people taking photos and tagging her. So these ugly snatches of her persist here, there and Christ knows where; and links and connections build around them.

She's switched off alerts and never ego-googles, so she passes weeks without seeing a single picture of herself: apart from the cropped publicity shot they dragged her into doing for work. She sees that every morning, blown up on metre-high foam mount in Parley's main reception, under the caption *Celebrating our key talent*. Her birthmark is a garish presence in the picture, staining the bottom of the frame like something spilled. She's come to like that image.

But seeing herself now, flash-lit in lace and leather on the front page, draped across a tatty chaise, straddled by some man who's pouring liquid at her mouth from a giant test-tube, is a gut-blow.

The paragraphs slide in and out of each other but she doesn't need to read the words to understand. *Malicious geek*, they say. *Sex-freak. Spoiler.* They're saying she hacked the Digital Citizen. That she's the one proffering under sic_girl's handle.

She looks around for some out, some explanation. She marches back to Khan's and this time scans the shelf at the foot of the magazine display, its irregular stacks of papers. Five minutes ago she walked past them like a zombie but now she sees: every one of these papers has a picture of her. Wayward images, sampled from God knows where. She doesn't recognise half of them, but they're her. It's a dream of appearing in a TV show called *This Is Your Drunk Whore Life*.

She picks one up. It's fat and rough-edged. The print is surreally sharp and colourful. She never reads papers, has never seen the point of them. They're hours out of date and they don't tell you what anyone thinks about anything: just page after page of stone-dead information. But suddenly they're immense and powerful. She thinks how many hundreds of thousands of these dumb identical things are spattered across the nation. Then she thinks of their online editions, how they'll have multiplied and spewed ten thousand proffers, links and threads and likes. She drops the paper back on the pile and pulls out her phone to catch the expanding bubble of news. She sees the notifications still on the screen and then it hits her: why all these calls and mails and whispers? Because she's some trash celebrity overnight. Some fat slut anti-government nutjob. Here are the thousands of people who suddenly want a piece of Dani. Her finger hovers over the *Unlock* swipe for a fraction of a second before unleashing what's under the surface of the screen.

Makes sense a fat ugly whore like you would want to hide her identity. I wouldn't fuck you if you had a bag tied over your head. Unless it was a plastic bag and you were dying of suffocation. Let me know when you catch aids and die so I can fuck your corpse and laugh in your dead bitch face. Don't worry, I'll wear a condom, lol.

She offs the phone and pushes it back in her jeans. She wavers in the passing rush of trucks and buses from the road outside; thinks for a moment she might pass out.

Then her scrambled brain kicks in. She knows who's done this to her, who's to blame; and the knowledge unfreezes her. Asshole. Shitting shitting asshole. It's less than ten minutes from here to the address on the card, which is stuffed somewhere in her courier bag – but she doesn't need to dig it out. She's turned it over in her hand so many times the address is burned into her eyeballs. She leaves the shop smooth and mechanical as the Terminator, remorseless and programmed to destroy.

Except really? She feels like shit. She's pretty sure the Terminator was never this hung over.

¶bottomhalfofthepage

My granny always said you eat what you sow. I think
people who live in glass social networks shouldn't throw
accusations at popular public figures.

¶riotbaby

You go sister! Stick one to the Man. And the lady
minister.

¶xxbabesxx

I don't care what yous all say I think she is pretty hot for
a fat chick.

¶tvjoe

Woot! Peoples! We's on telly!!! Dani Farr for the win!

¶9th&sunset

Do you believe this sick fat whore above an elected
politician? If you do you're just as filthy crazy as that
bitch in the pictures.

¶lolcatz

Me no geddit. Me iz Dani Farr, too? <identitycriziz>

¶TurdoftheDay

Spattergun. The force of a car backfiring.
<pic:>
I don't know what to do. Help me.

FOUR

IDENTIKID DOES A TRIAL LOGIN to the botnet server. It's still there. He scrolls the list of captive IPs. Total count today is over thirty thousand. Just under twenty-three thou active at this very moment. Way more than he needs to DDoS the lights out of those pigs at Mondan, come Saturday.

Leo just walked onto thousands of unprotected PCs, dotted about the world. The bot launches from off a virus scam, so he's only spoofing net virgins dumb enough to open a dot-exe in the first place. All these citizens alive right now, doing their Amazon, downloading their porn and emailing their grans.

A familiar voice slides out of the portable speakers on the bar. His pianist fingers pause over the laptop keys. Shuffle has thrown up an unfamiliar nerd-lounge track that's wrapping its beats around something very known to Leo. Through rolling crackles and interrupted jets of synth runs a sample – schoolmistress tones laid with viral energy:

WHAT THEY WOULD HAVE US BELIEVE
WHAT THEY WOULD HAVE US BELIEVE
WHAT THEY WOULD HAVE US BELIEVE

Then a break, then:

LET THEIR WALLS TUMBLE DOWN

It's a sampled archive recording of Lady Electric herself, the great Elyse Martingale. Leo checks his phone display. *Tumbledown (Tunny mix)* by *Martingale*. This has got to be a sign, this week of all weeks – when something's at last been given to Leo. He doesn't want to question.

He checks the permissions on the botnet server: all in order. He drops the telnet session and kills the window.

This Distributed Denial of Service set-up is the first of three gifts to land this week. The code and URLs arrived online one crazy Flamingo night. The second gift came the morning after in an unmarked Nissan Cabstar. Special delivery from the man who isn't there. Leo glances to the corner of the lounge, where he's stacked the four reinforced metal cases. Four cases is too many for him to carry alone. He'd need Winter to help him shlep that much kit to 404 City. She's totally up for it obvs but Leo's disruptive spirit means it always needs to be him and none other who does the deed. Him to see the opportunity; him to gizmo the warez to do the deed. It'll be an hour – max – of screwdriver time to wizard the kit into just two cases. Then he can go it alone. He likes to always customise his shit, in any how.

The third gift is closest. He keeps it in the plaid breast pocket of his shirt, where he can feel its flatness and lightness. It's a magic key. A secure swipe card that can get him exactly where he needs to be, come Friday night.

Everything is running in one direction, identikid's way. Imagine the devotees he'll have by Saturday. Imagine the cites. Imagine the proffers.

To Danieele Farr the slut of Parley. We represnt the real Parley and this is to tell you we dont like dirty cunts like you.

So get off Parley. We see you are still here on Parley. Well we are warning you now to get off here.

Be warned! You have been hacked little miss cunt. We are inside your computer and all your phones. We are inside your home and we can see you right now. We can see the filthy things you are doing and will post it all over the net. How do you liek that?

We will get you count on it. Have a nice day cuntface from all of us.

FIVE

'YES YOU FUCKING DID! Shit, who else would do this?'

'I don't—'

'No!'

'Can I just—'

'No, shut *up*, Sam. Just shut up. I get to talk now.'

But she's run out of anything to say.

They're both breathless. The sound of their shouting hangs in the white air of the meeting room. She's only now taking it in. A big wood table and mismatched chairs. A wood floor coated in chipped white paint. Arty pictures displayed around the walls.

'I don't know how to get past this,' says Sam. 'This anger.'

'Yes sure I'm cunting angry,' she says. 'So what?'

'It's awful to see what's happened today. I was hoping to talk to you, to say I can help.'

She snorts.

'Bit fucking late for that. Really, really fuck you too late. Since you decided to do revenge porn on me.'

'Jesus Christ, shut *up*! Just shut up and think!'

He shocks them both into silence. He touches her arm but she flinches it away.

'Don't.'

She can't find her edge, her anger. All her strong emotions have been sheared away. She walks away to put the table between them. Hunts for the fury.

'All right,' he says. 'But Dani, Dani, listen: why would I do anything like this to you?'

'Well I sure as shit don't know anyone else who could, could turn the whole fucking media and Internet against me overnight.'

'But why would I?'

She stares back at him. He's serious. He can't be serious.

'I mean —' she says.

She doesn't want to be the one to mention it, but he's so openly baffled.

'— that email?' she says.

He draws a long deep breath.

'All right. God. I'm sorry I didn't reply to your mail yet. It was—'

'*Yet!* Like you were going to.'

'I would have done but it was – well, come on, that was quite an email.'

Is he *blushing*? Does it change a thing if he is?

'I didn't know what to say to you,' he says. 'I don't know now.'

'Makes a shitting change.'

They look into each other's eyes from across the room. They've known each other so long.

'Mister always-knows-what-to-fucking-say.'

He makes an abrupt laugh.

'Well, so I'm fallible,' he says. 'But really, I would never take anything out on you like this, or want to.' He sits at the vintage table; she stays by the wall. 'Listen. I do have a thought.'

'Also makes a change.'

He ignores her.

'I told you before about Bethany Lehrer's office. How it would be in her interest to make Parley look bad? How she'd do anything to discredit the source of these leaks?'

Dani stares at him.

'Fuck, what? Seriously, Sam? For real?'

Sam shrugs.

'The *government* did this to me?'

'Sic_girl's allegations are getting very embarrassing,' he says. 'All of a sudden this. They're capable of it.'

There's a long silence. Dani lets out all her breath and does a kind of half-fall back against the wall. Her shoulder jars on something sharp and solid.

'*Shit it!*'

She turns to find the offending object. A wooden frame, surrounding a rectangle of splashy graffiti. *FUCK YOU SHITCAKE* it says in ragged blue and yellow lines.

'Sorry,' says Sam. 'It's an artwork.'

She rubs her shoulder and gives him a look.

'We rebooted the offices last year,' he says, 'and all the staff chose a work by a local artist.'

'This?'

There's a typed-up label beside the frame: *shitcake (oil and acrylic on cornflake box, 2004).*

'That one's a bit Hoxton,' says Sam.

'It's a piece of shit,' she says.

He's offended. Good.

'Maybe this one's more up your street?'

He turns his chair and points at the large print on the side wall. It knocks the wind from her. She hadn't seen it in the noise. It draws her close. She's seen the image before. Gray had it on the wall of his flat and it's gone viral in the last few months – but this copy has a handmade feel so she guesses it's original. A huge Obama-ed version of the classic photo of Elyse Martingale, posterised to clashing patches of green, orange, purple. Below Elyse's face in typewriter font, the iconic words . . . *or we shall step around it* . . . A hacker's mantra.

'That one was my choice,' Sam says from right beside her.

She turns loose-jawed and he smiles at her surprise.

'I'm fascinated with how she's become this icon to slacktivists and free data campaigners, with her dated twentieth-century slogans. Her uncompromising truthfulness gets to them. To me, too.'

'*Huh.* Sure.'

His eyes tighten.

'Don't you think even a slimy PR guy is capable of kicking against the system? But through – other channels?'

He taps the glass of the Martingale print. Dani looks around with a new awareness. She was totally out of control when she blazed in here earlier: even by her standards. Screamed at the receptionist till Sam appeared. Hurled him into this meeting room. Actually beat his chest with her fists out of fury and frustration. She must have looked insane.

'It's OK,' he says. 'It really is.'

He steps towards her, puts one hand on her shoulder, then the other. This time she lets him. She looks up at his lovely face. He squeezes just slightly.

'Listen, Dani. Can you leave this with me? I'm going to chase it with Bethany's office. My way.'

'You mean with no mentalist screaming and hitting people?'

'I do mean that, yes. Will you let me?'

She looks away, pushing hair out of her eye, and shrugs him off. He steps back, studying her.

'Sam.'

'Yeah?'

'You definitely didn't do this?'

His turn to give her the look. There's more silence. The two of them occupy space in a plain white room in a simulation of life, of how people act in the world.

'I don't know whether to believe you,' she says. 'Sorry. I don't think I do.'

He nods slowly.

'OK. But you'll let me do this? Prove it to you?'

After the slightest of pauses she nods, too.

¶saulgood

If Dani Farr is proffering this stuff she's a hero. If not she is still a hot nerd chick. What's not to like?

¶TheyWalkAmongUs

This: **¶cite saulgood:** If Dani Farr is proffering this stuff she's a hero. If not she is still a hot nerd chick. What's not to like?

¶thebiggercheese

Tru dat. **cite ¶TheyWalkAmongUs:** This: **cite ¶saulgood:** If Dani Farr is proffering this stuff she's a hero. If not she is still a hot nerd chick. What's not to like?

¶98redballoons

lols! **cite ¶thebiggercheese:** Tru dat. **cite ¶TheyWalkAmongUs:** This: **cite ¶saulgood:** If Dani Farr is proffering this stuff she's a hero. If not she is still a hot nerd chick. What's not to like?

¶yourpalmike

haha! **cite ¶98redballoons:** lols! **cite ¶thebiggercheese:** Tru dat. **cite ¶TheyWalkAmongUs:** This: **cite ¶saulgood:** If Dani Farr is proffering this stuff she's a hero. If not she is still a hot nerd chick. What's not to like?

¶simon_carter23

Dani Farr trending global. **cite ¶yourpalmike:** haha! **cite ¶98redballoons:** lols! **cite ¶thebiggercheese:** Tru dat. **cite ¶TheyWalkAmongUs:** This: **cite ¶saulgood:** If Dani Farr is proffering this stuff she's a hero. If not she is still a hot nerd chick. What's not to like?

SIX

'SO WHERE ARE YOU?'

'Krish, what's—?'

'If you're not here and you're not at Parley sorting out this shite, where the fuck are you?'

J-R covered his BlackBerry's mic and mouthed, *Sorry.* Mark touched J-R's arm briefly, shouldered his laptop bag and vanished into Waterloo Tube. J-R turned his back to shield his friend from Krish's anger.

'I'm on my way there now,' he said. 'Apologies, I had a personal appointment.'

'Oh, *personal,* is it? That wouldn't happen to be a *personal appointment* with a Mr Mark Dinmore by some chance?'

J-R stood in silence, the BlackBerry live against his ear. Across the street a cyclist hammered furiously on the driver's window of a bus, screaming something over and over.

'I'm taking this telling silence as a yes,' said Krish.

'I don't understand. Is someone watching me, or—?'

'Oh, don't be a child. You do know we've the polis in here?' Krish always became more Glaswegian when angry. 'Well, you might want to know they're scanning our email traffic. Past as well as present.'

'Ah.'

'Aye. *Ah*.'

'Krish, I—'

'I do not want to hear it. I want to know what you think you're doing emailing confidential-marked documents to some freelance consultant.'

The bus driver nudged his vehicle forward in jolting steps, trying to force the cyclist back and pull out from the stop. The cyclist lifted his feather-light bike off the ground and held it in front of him as a traffic barrier. The back of his cycling shirt read *TAKEBACK* in stencilled capitals. The bus passengers were jolted back and forth as though riding a turbulent sea.

'I have concerns I felt needed to be checked,' said J-R. 'With all the attention I thought it prudent to do this under the radar. Mark is a trusted friend. A Party activist.'

'Concerns. And so you randomly email some guy. Why not come to me with these *concerns*?'

J-R gestured into the stream of traffic now forcing its way around the bus and cyclist; but he couldn't find adequate words. His backpack slipped. He shifted it back up.

'Of all the last things we need right now,' said Krish. 'You. I'd at least've thought I could trust you.'

'You can. Of course you can trust me. But don't you ever worry that we're handing away people's privacy to a corporation?'

'Do I worry? Oh, Jesus, you monkey, I left you at Parley to keep you out of all this.'

The cyclist was sitting in the road now, holding the bike above his head. The bus, which had edged diagonally out of its stop, was now blocking both lanes of York Road eastbound.

'Left me –?' said J-R. 'Sorry, what?'

'Look, son, in spite of your nonsense, I want you to walk away from this. Here's what you do. One, you say nothing more to Mister Dinmore. You don't reply to his calls, his emails. You don't know him. Two, get over to Parley and look as useful as you can. Three, sit tight. That is it. Can you do that for me?'

A symphony of car horns filled the road and surrounded J-R.

attention seeking whore fat filthy fuck her right in the
pussy meatwallet rape is the last of your worries stink ugly
Dani pushy bitch woman ur pathetic wet poontang rip
your tongue out of yr suckhole die you worthless piece of
crap bitch DaniFarr going to cut you ho a bomb has been
planted outside your house rape u in every hole ovaries
put the video all over the internet woman better watch
your back stick my rip out cumdumpster go kill yourself
bloodclot who does she pistol whip you over and over
until you lose consciousness fat suck on this skanktwat
witch eat the meat Dani Farr Dani Farr Dani Farr cunt cunt
cunt cunt cunt cunt cunt cunt cunt cunt cunt cunt cunt
cunt cunt cunt cunt cunt cunt cunt cunt cunt cunt cunt

SEVEN

DANI HITS THE INTERSECTION with Shoreditch High Street, phone to ear, dodging the workday crowd. A Beijing haze blurs everything. On the bus stop poster site in front of her is the backlit image of an iPad, the keyboard showing on its screen. Facing the poster, a young boy vainly presses the static images of fake keys. He can't understand why the image won't type his words.

'I'm five minutes from Martlet Street,' she shouts above the din into the phone. She mentally googles the quickest route to Parley. 'Ten max.'

Around her head a canopy of seagulls cries for roadkill. News pages whip the air. This flying chipwrap is Dani's enemy.

'No. No, no, no. Listen to me. You are not coming in.'

Jonquil's voice splinters and Dani hears her own breathing on the line. The duplex has failed. Fucking Shoreditch: too many callers hogging the air.

She waits. Jonquil's voice returns.

'You're not going to be here period.'

'As in what?' says Dani. 'I've got a mountain of data to sort from sic's semantic. I emailed you the log. There's something new.'

Dani pelts across on red. The honeysuckle taste of exhaust fills her mouth.

'I've given that job to Graham,' says Jonquil. 'He's got his own ideas. You go home.'

'Gray? Gray doesn't know the algorithms.' Dani sharp-lefts down Holywell Lane. 'Did you see what sic said last night? Fucking Christ, don't you want to know what's going on?'

She brakes hard by the fly-post cladding of a vacant lot. Silence on the line. She's never sworn at Jonquil. Jonquil, who's had her arse ever since the punch.

'Danielle, this is not a debate. You are toxic today, girl. You've seen what's going down. We got hacks snapping our heels.'

'Am I – am I fired? I didn't do any of that stuff they're saying.'

There's a long sigh from the remote end. The signal scatters and forks. Data crackles round Dani. Every second she stands here the air of the street learns more about her.

'OK, God,' says Jonquil. 'Let me be real clear. You are not fired but you are in a world of trouble. Tomorrow you are going to be here in my office at nine a.m. Not a few minutes after. Not the bus was late. Nine on the nail. You are going to meet with me and the other directors, and you are going to account for yourself. I got to tell you, you think this is bad? If I get an ounce of evidence what I'm reading this morning is true – that you're some kind of what, black-hat hacker? That you've been using my social network, *my* Personas, to PR your exploits, spread bullshit about a government ally? If a single word of this is true, girl, today is going to look like the best day of your life. All right?'

Jonquil's characters? *Jonquil's* network? PR? Dani's feet scrunch fragments of car window on the pavement. Hackney diamonds.

'I can talk to you today,' she says. 'If you really think I did this shit. I'm three minutes now.'

'Today there's too much noise. I have Westminster to deal with, and the media.'

There's a heart-pattern mural on the building opposite. Graffiti across it: WHAT THE FUCK HAPPENED TO THE GOODTIMES? <TAKEBACK>

'So, tomorrow? Nine?' Jonquil asks again.

Dani nods into the phone.

'Tomorrow.'

The call drops. What next? How to back out from this situation? Sam says he can help her but she isn't sure she wants to be helped. This far from his orbit, his signal is fading. This is Gray's terrain. It's him she needs to see. Safest thing would be to talk online and keep away from Parley; but she wants to see him IRL. She kicks up Parley on her phone. Her data trail inflects as the app handshakes with a server and the screen clogs with a billion whispers, directed at her. She's used to trolls and she's used to screening them. But here she's ramped by a rising tide of *pussies* and *stinking cunts*. Through the glut she spots a link to *Dani Farr naked in her bathtub* <tits> <dyed hair> <unshaved pussy>. There's a crow trapped in her ribcage. She won't click on the link.

She clicks on the link.

She shot these selfies on her phone, what, three years back? She was off her vulva on pills and vodka redbulls. She took them for that guy she sucked off one BDSM night at Chains, who said he'd call her back but didn't. She cried her way through all the alcohol left in her kitchen cupboards and at three a.m. took these photos slobbering drunk in her empty bath. She thought they'd bring him crawling to her on broken knees but she never even got a reply. Each of the five shots is basically the same: her foreshortened arm extends from the bottom right of frame; her face, huge with pleading reddened eyes, stares straight up into the lens; her distorted breasts heave up in hope and desperation; unruly hairs squeeze out between tightly folded thighs.

How long have those images been online? And tagged as her? What else is out there?

She closes the link and watches fresh obscenities scroll her timeline without pause. She holds her breath and calls up a whisper, tapping the screen warily as though pushing a door smeared in shit.

Gray is online.

¶thegrays >> whisper -> ¶Nightshade
  Sure thing. Shit about this, hey?
  You ok? How far away?

¶Nightshade >> whisper -> ¶thegrays
  yah. bad voodoo much
  five minutes maybe?

¶thegrays >> whisper -> ¶Nightshade
  I can meet you in the yard. Safely out of J-range. Come in
  via the meat.

¶Nightshade >> whisper -> ¶thegrays
  im there.

From *The Electronic Radical*
by Dr Elyse Martingale (1957, Gollancz)

The State shall attempt to maintain its hold on the levers of this system. There is a profound, and profoundly false, belief among those in power, who understand but a little of the computing machine, that its quantities will always be as limited as they are today; and, on this basis, they are convinced that they, along with their lackeys in the larger corporations, shall continue to control the flows of information that will dominate the coming era. These people shall shortly find themselves as disappointed as the monks who grafted each Mediæval book into existence were doubtless disappointed by the achievements of Mr Gutenberg.

When we control our own information, power shall cease to reside in the ancient apparatus of State.

EIGHT

THE SPEAKER-PHONE PURRS. Sam eyes the Elyse Martingale print that somehow tamed Dani's fury earlier. The remote phone picks up on the fourth ring.

'Yeh, hello?'

'Big Krish? Sam Corrigan.'

'Sam. Look, great to hear from you, but—'

'I realise. Busy day.'

'Well, heh. Perhaps a wee bit more than usual. So listen—'

'Hold on,' says Sam. 'I'm not selling. I have a proposition.'

'Just a second there.' Krish muffles his voice with a hand. '(Hen, would you take this in to her nibs, please. Uh huh, aye, the polis interview notes.)' Then at full volume, 'I'm listening.'

'So,' says Sam. 'I've been at Parley these last few days, helping out. I was interested not to see more police presence there. Given the leaks.'

'What kind of pitch is this?'

'Not a pitch. So I thought it over – and I saw your dilemma. How do you discredit sic_girl without damaging Mondan – the day before Perce shares a platform with Bethany at the launch of DigiCitz?' The conference phone hissed like a gas leak. 'OK, silence on that point is fine. But given you need to soft-soap your attack, the papers and blogs today are providing a helpful distraction by crapping on Dani Farr.'

More static on the line, then Krish breaks his silence.

'All right. And?'

'Well, but the thing I wanted to tell you is, Farr is not your blogger. It's bullshit. And when that comes out you'll have no villain and trust will swing back against you. You need a better strategy.'

'She's not doing the sic_girl whatsits?' asks Krish.

'No.'

'You're the first bugger today to tell me that.'

'She isn't doing it.'

'You know this.'

'I know. This is someone I've been friends with since school.'

'Ah hah.' Krish is taking his time, but the hook is landed. 'I take it you've seen the other stuff this lassie's been putting out? That they can't put in the papers?'

'I've seen it.'

Bursts of office atmospherics. Sam taps his fingers on the table; waits.

'This is your girl, Sam? Is that what this is?'

'No, Dani is not my girl. She didn't do it.'

'Then who?'

'I don't have the answer to that, but Parley's the place to look. So the proposition is, would you like me to do a little freelance sniffing while I'm there? See what I can dig up.'

'I thought you weren't selling?'

'Non-chargeable. A return favour – if, that is, you're willing to change your tack on Dani. Understood? There are better ways to damage Parley.'

'I thought you were working for Parley?'

'My firm is. This would be freelance. To get you off Dani's back.'

'I'm not getting something.' Here it comes. 'You're offering this because you think we've been briefing against this lassie?'

'Well, yes.'

'Ha. I have to say, that would have been a fecking good idea if I'd thought of it.'

'You didn't?'

'We did not,' says Krish. 'It's not all the dark arts here, you know, son. Sometimes we're just floundering about in the dark with all the other eejits.'

'You don't deny you're briefing against Parley?'

'Let he who is without spin cast the first stone.'

Sam directs silence at the speakerphone. Waits for Krish to continue.

'Come on, son. You just offered to spy for us – I could string you along. I'm telling you truth.'

'I don't know what to tell you, Krish.'

'Look, you're not talking complete pish. Parley is a problem just now and, aye, it's difficult to go in hard. We have done nothing against Ms Farr, OK? But if I was to make calls now, distance us from this story – does your offer stand? You'll do some asking for us?'

'Well, yes. It stands.'

Sam is perfectly still. Does not punch the air.

'Good man,' says Krish. 'So listen. One thing you can help with. Our friendly plods tell me there's chatter on Parley. Digital anarchists – trouble. Is this something?'

'Yes, we're watching that. It's pretty noisy.' Sam foregrounds the social monitor on his iPad. 'You guys are getting it in the chest.'

'Ah hah. What are they about, this rabble? This is the same bawbags who defaced our webpage.'

'And hacked your data?'

'What data hack would you be referring to there, Sam?'

'All right – if that's your line. To be honest I can't tell you much about them. They're new to us, too. They popped up seemingly from nowhere a few weeks back – seemingly the merger of an anti-austerity group and a hacker collective – but they've immediately tapped a seam. Some of the big themes here: privacy; big government; mass surveillance; corporate power. You have to say, they've got a strong platform.'

'I have to? Is that right?'

'There's real anger here; and Bethany is drawing fire. Bethany and Dani both.'

'You're saying because they're women?'

'Am I? Maybe.'

Sam flips through images on his iPad. One keeps coming up, of Dani posing gangsta with a pistol and a leather coat. The gun looks real but it's clearly a party stunt. Someone has added the slogan *SIC THIS MOTHERFUCKER*.

'They're getting very different medicine,' says Sam. 'Dani's getting targeted by some of the grossest trolling I've seen but she's, I don't know: the rebel heroine in this story. Bethany's squarely the villain.'

'Ah hah. Great story. They don't do nuance, your microbloggy types?'

'This isn't Westminster, Krish. Welcome to the Internet.'

'And there's talk of some kind of stunt tomorrow?'

'That's correct. Still no detail though. I can send you verbatims.'

Sam swipes to the morning cuts.

'This is pish,' says Krish. 'Someone's stirring the pot here. How are they doing it?'

'That's what I'm offering to find out.'

Sam counts to ten, regulates his breathing. This is the in. He needs to not get pissy.

'And are the rabble going to give us grief tomorrow? At our launch event? Over – what? Over login details?'

'Are you doing anything extra tomorrow?' says Sam. 'Security-wise?'

'Conference hotel is putting up a couple of wage slaves in uniform. Do you think we need more?'

Sam looks at the phone a moment, thinks before he speaks.

'No. I'm sure you'll be fine. It's noise. People will have their fifteen minutes, cite a pennant as though that means a thing, feel part of something. When it comes to marching in the rain, the ties aren't so strong.'

'So cynical for one so young. Look, be a pal and tip me the nod if you hear any more about tomorrow, will you? Or TakeBack generally. Or sic_girl. As a favour, right?'

'As a favour.'

¶**clickbait**

This hot girl developer shared too much online – and what happened was awful fu.bar/je8n54

NINE

THE CARCASS-SMELL IS SWEET. Dani slips around the clanging meat-trolleys like a battlefield ghost, ignored by the young Bengali men in blood-grimed overalls.

This row of loading bays and parked-up trucks runs down the side of Parley's offices, linking Martlet Street to a network of yards at the rear. After the final bay Dani wheels left into a narrow quadrangle formed by the packing sheds, the back wall of Parley's converted warehouse space and a corrugated iron fence. Rainwashed fag ends, paper cups and condoms are compacted into the tarmac like pressed flowers. This is where Parley staffers come for a sneaky fag or a fresher mobile signal than they can get in the iron-frame building; or for darker transactions in the shelter of abandoned sheds. This is where she and Gray played out the dog days of their relationship, the heady summer they launched Parley. For a month they barely left the building. Their whole world was crammed into project war rooms, their only escape this brick oasis.

The fire door's wedged open with half a breezeblock. Dani peers through the gap and calls Gray's name. The only reply is a moan of air con. She turns and walks to a set of discoloured garden furniture by the iron fence, sheds her satchel and sinks into a chair. Her phone nudges her buttock. She takes it out, spins it around a few times, toggles the screen on, off, on, off; puts it back in her pocket. She hasn't proffered in hours.

Something rustles behind her. A dog, a big one, snuffles on its rounds on the other side of the corrugated iron. How much of its life is spent shut in with its own mess? Does anyone remember it's there? She stares at the clear blue rectangle overhead. Not even a plane. Just you and me, Fido.

'Dan?'

The fire door grinds on concrete. Gray stands at the door in a green T-shirt with a celtic knotwork design that reads: *CNUT | THE ANGLO-SAXON CONNECTION*.

'It's weird to actually see you.' He walks to her. 'You're every-where this morning but it's a thin version I don't know. Hallo.'

'Hi.'

She stands to hold him. He's awkward in her grip but she keeps on squeezing until she's sure she won't cry. She lets him go. He drops his backpack on the plastic table and lodges himself in the other chair.

It was an email from Gray that ended it, late one working night at Parley, in the heat of some long-forgotten crisis. It's lurked in her inbox for the past two years. She used to read it so often she can almost recite it.

> You know, sometimes I think this has really always been just an online relationship. Here we are now, feeding our VDU tans four storeys apart while all sensible couples are out in the world enjoying actual physical contact.

The thing about Gray is he can't let a thing lie. He needs to drag it out and thrash it until it's only a husk. Five words Dani long ago gave up saying to him: *Yes, Gray. I get it.*

> Like any online relationship, you and me got to know each other very quickly on the surface, and also very deep. But what we didn't have is what's in between. We had 1) surface banter, and 3) deep intimacy. Magic and sheer fucking fun. But did you think I'd missed out 2)? No, Dan. We never had 2).

Also: always with the numbered lists.

> The bit in between is what I don't believe we'll ever have
> – body language, touch, scent, sheer physical stuff. If you
> get to know someone first in the real world, like human
> beings used to do, you find out pretty fast if it's going to
> gel. Online, you don't – but you still go ahead and bond,
> deeply and painfully. Just ask the groomed thirteen-year-
> old girl who finally gets to meet 'julie2001', in a layby cafe
> on the ringroad.
> I'm saying, not good.

And the crashingly inappropriate metaphors. Who was groom-
ing who, in this delightful image?

> I think that's what's up with us. Are we any more than
> avatars for each other's avatars? It's been like this a long,
> long time. I think we're kidding ourselves. I'm not sure
> we always like each other very much, away from
> screenlife.
> Why do you think we're having this conversation by
> email? Or I'm having it. No idea what you're doing.
> Reading this?

There at Parley, four a.m., Dani read the mail straight through
– all seven scrolls – then shut the lid of her laptop and cried
unconsolably in the dark of the empty office.

She and Gray still made the code-drop deadline, though. They
were pros.

'You're in a swarm, Dan.'

'Storm?'

She pulls on the beer. He's carried out four in his backpack,
licked with condensation. She's working on her second, he's tend-
ing his first.

'No, swarm intelligence. A thousand arseholes, each doing their arsehole thing. None of them smart enough to land one on you alone. But today some organising principle is working through them. A thousand individual arseholes swimming in the same direction.'

Another charming image. She wants to walk away and leave him talking. Shit and she needs him, though.

'There's an army of these cunts,' she says. 'An army.'

'No.'

She bristles. This is the Gray she used to call Robot-Boy. What it was like to be with him – every word contradicted until she just gave up.

'Not an army,' he says. 'There's no structure. It's more like – think of a bot attack on an IP address, OK?'

He's miming this with his hands, holding the bottle by its neck. Not that you can mime a bot attack.

'A distributed denial of service. Tens of thousands of dumb clients turning as one on the same website. Each no more harmful than an ordinary user. Together, they bring it down.'

'So in this scenario I'm a website?'

He's nodding.

'Individually dumb. Together, a hive mind. Emergent intelligence. Swarm.'

She drinks from the nearly empty bottle. A connection clicks into place.

'Like the Personas? You told me last night, just before the crazy started. You said some kind of intelligence might be emerging from sic? Maybe you were right. She was being – strange.'

'Forget sic.'

'No, I thought it was BS when you said it, but now—'

Gray snaps back.

'Just, just leave it, all right? sic and the others are – I think they're just confused. I'm looking at it, OK?'

His left leg jiggles when he's thinking. Why is it that, when things get too random to handle, this is the guy she needs to speak to? When did they stop ranting at each other till three in the morning like a pair of street crazies? Their thoughts used to rebound like pachinko balls, in random surges and beautiful colliding patterns. But she can't go back there.

'Something happened last night,' she says. 'After you'd gone.'

'All right.'

'I started getting calls, mails, from total randoms who said they knew me. This journalist Will Samber was one. It was *click!* Something turned them onto me – and suddenly they had all this – well, you've seen it.'

'Some*thing* or some*one* turned them onto you?'

'Exactly, exactly,' she says. 'Sam says it's the government trashing me.'

'Sam says?'

'Yes.'

'*Sam.*'

'Oh, fuck, Gray, yes. He's this PR Jonquil made me talk to. But you met him before, in Greece that time? On the beach?'

'*Sam.*'

'Jesus H. Bollocks. Stop that. Stop now. You do not have the right.'

'I'm not.'

'Being a jealous cunt. What gives you—?'

'I'm not being. Leave it.'

'It's *me* coming here to *you*. I. Need. You. All right? You. Do not try to own me on top of this.'

'OK. God.'

Robot-Boy is back. Processes a moment. Speaks.

'Let's roll this back. A swarm of trolls has got hold of your docs. Proffers. Pictures.'

Dani ducks her head, *yes*.

'My lovely trolls. What do I do to get them off me?'

'You can't.'

'Oh, for fuck—'

'You can't just turn them off, Dan. These are persistent self-selecting shitheads. They don't have a switch. Only option: turn *yourself* off, until this thing dies on its own. This is a lobster pot, you know? A one-way circuit. There's no reversing out. You got to switch the machine off until it cools, then boot it up again.'

'Switch off?' says Dani. 'Like no Internet? Like some hacker on a control order? Ha to the power of ha. This is me, here.'

She swigs her beer but the bottle is empty. She bangs it down and beckons for the last.

'Not necessarily switch off altogether.'

Gray fusses the bottle open with his Swiss Army knife. His beard is crazy wild. Does he have anyone to look after him these days? Because it doesn't look like it. He's working on saying something. She takes the bottle and necks it, eyes still on him.

'Look, um,' he starts. 'Do you have any other identities?'

On the other side of the fence, the dog barks, very close. They flinch.

'You mean like on my blog? Like pimpmyhide?'

'Nah, that's not – I mean, everyone knows that's you.'

'No, people don't. It's a blank slate. I need it to be separate. That's why I have it.'

He digs in his backpack.

'OK, lesson for the day,' he says. 'How long did it take these journos to find that porno from your blog?' He's got his laptop out. 'Your identities aren't separate. Look –'

He spins the screen for her to see, then reaches round to google her. First hits are all today's media. Gray picks a link from the third page – a site called *123peoplelink*. It sparkles with animated banners. *DANIELLE (DANI) FARR* is splashed across the top in 72-point Arial. Beneath, a bento box filled with random slices of Dani.

This is your average aggregator. Nothing sophisticated, fully automated. It noodles the net and ties stuff together around an identity. All it needs is a common identifier: an email address, social profile, shared contacts. Normally these automated profiles are narrow, professional; and this is the kind of stuff at the top of

the screen: that promo shot, CV stuff, conferences she's spoken
at. Top right, tagged shots from Facebook and other social sites,
garish enough to have made her wince if she hadn't had a thousand times worse shoved in her face today. But below that, porn.
Glimpses of the wild stuff. Insertions. Images from the anonymous Flickr she uses for club stuff. Private, personal – together.
Not possible.

'These datasets are walled,' she tells the screen. 'Different
emails. Different profiles.'

She clicks and opens windows. They're full to the horizon with
every intimate part of Dani.

'It's found something to match you up,' says Gray. 'One data
point does it. Dominos fall.'

'No, but some of this is behind a login – look, there's – oh.' She
closes the new tab as fast as she can to hide a stream of MeatSpace
sex chat with monkey_love.

'Oh, Dan,' says Gray. 'Dani, Dani, Dani.'

'What?'

Did he see the MeatSpace chat before she closed the
window?

'You, of anyone? You gave them a key. Now they're doxing
you.'

'Nobody's bastard well doxing me. That's what hacktivists do
to corporations.'

Gray sighs again.

'Pulling together latent content from across the net to humili-
ate you. What else is this? They're using our tactics against us.
This always happens eventually.'

Our tactics? Who is our?

'How far has this gone?' he asks. 'They have your social media,
your blog. What about your mail? Is there anything in these news
stories that could only have come from your email?'

She gazes across the yard, then turns to stare at Gray.

'Holy shit,' she says, 'that guy Samber. In his mail last night he
said he'd met me at a conference. I knew he hadn't but he almost

convinced me because he said I'd talked to him about Me All Over.'

'Your life-blog thing?'

'And that's work-in-progress. I haven't put anything out on it. Only Parley email.'

'OK, so work email.'

'Or, what about the *people* here?'

He frowns at her.

'No,' she says, 'listen, listen. I heard something last night. While this was kicking off. Someone was here, in the building.'

'There's people here twenty-four. Concentrate on digital and don't be a paranoid. Anything else *online*? Unexpected mails or whatever.'

That wave of alerts, last night. Online billings, cloud accounts, voicemails vanishing. She rattles them off.

'So shall I clean you up?' asks Gray. 'Can I do that for you?'

Dani nods and he passes her his laptop so she can log into webmail and forward him the offending mails one-by-one. She gives up account details, passwords, everything. Almost everything. Not MeatSpace. He takes back his PC and spreadsheets her life online. It's like letting a doctor force her open and probe her, his face hanging steady between the stirrups.

As Gray types, she curls in the plastic chair and looks for answers in the flyblown tarmac.

GRAY STOPS TYPING. She looks up and pulls her legs to her chest. It's cold in the afternoon shadow. He pulls a wallet from the backpack and roots through it.

'OK,' he says. 'I've closed off everything. Doesn't look like anyone's pulled money from your accounts is the good news. But we can't assume anything is secure. I want you off the grid. Look. Here.' He slips out a credit card, places it on the table with a flourish. 'What do you think of that?'

Dani glances at the card. It's from some through-the-door direct bank she's never heard of.

'I think – I think it's a credit card,' she says.

'Look closer.'

She unfurls herself from the chair and inspects the tacky swirls of green and blue.

'The name,' he presses.

She picks it up and reads it.

'*Terry Salmon.*' She looks at Gray. 'Who the frick is Terry Salmon? Are you lifting plastic now?'

'He's me. I'm him.'

He's fumbling in the backpack again. Out comes a translucent purple file. He undoes the popper and pulls out storecards, a council tax statement, bills. All *Terry Salmon*.

'Terry is a safe harbour. He took me eighteen months. I started with a stray voter registration card that – found its way to me. I called up a birth certificate, then applied for things. Bought things. Each transaction made the next easier. Terry has a dynamite credit rating. He does stuff, buys stuff I don't want associated with Graham. Or might not want associated in future.'

'Like?'

He shrugs.

'For serious, though?' she says. 'A secret identity?'

'A public identity, but unconnected to the one you know.'

Thought she knew. Dani looks at the card in her hand as though it's dropped from another dimension. Can someone really do this?

'He's my humanoid shield,' says Gray.

She looks back at him.

'Who are you, Gray?'

'I'm – preparing. That's all. Some day soon, the greatest luxury you'll be able to buy is privacy. The haves will be the ones who can afford to segment their identity, hide parts of it. The have-nots will be who they are and nothing more. Anyone who knows one thing about them will be able to find out everything else. Click, click, they'll be owned. Like you've been owned today. But me? If they're tracking Terry, they won't know anything. And vice versa.'

The yard stays silent.

'But I don't have anything like that,' says Dani. 'I'm just me.'

'Yeah. You are.'

'I can't just turn myself off. I don't think I want to turn myself off. I want to kick every troll on the Internet in his tiny nads.'

Gray starts scooping up the documents and tucking them away in the folder.

'You've been out there, Dan. It's not for you today. You need a zero-knowledge system. If you leave a single chink they'll be on you in a nanosecond.'

He never looks her in the eye when he's confronting even a bit.

'And what would you know about it, Robot-Boy? What the shit use is this to me?'

She chucks the card at his face. It bounces off his glasses and lands between his hands. He slams the laptop shut as if he wants to break it.

'Well, so aren't you lucky you have so many exes in town? Why not go ask *Sam* for help if *Sam* is so smart?'

She stares at him. That wasn't Robot-Boy, not at all. He stows the laptop and documents.

When she was with Gray, all she ever wanted was to provoke a reaction. It never worked and all she got was furious. Then it started to work too well – but that was an age ago. She'd forgotten what it was like to see him turn like this.

He puts the bag on the ground and breathes, head down. Then he looks up and to her amazement he's grinning.

'So Dan?'

'Yeah?'

'Have you ever actually been to a *trendy Soho sex party*?'

A jolt of laughter escapes her.

'I had sex in a wardrobe once at a party in Holborn. Does that count?'

'I actually do not want to hear about that.'

'Yeah. Sorry.'

They listen to the dog scratch and scuffle then catch each other's eye.

'So Dan?'

'Uh huh?'

'Do you think we might have got together again if we hadn't –? I mean, this place –?'

'Oh, fuck, come on!' she says.

'No, OK. Sorry, too, I guess.'

But they're good now. She studies his face. He's bonier, more drawn about the eyes.

'Do you still deal out here?' she says.

He sizes her up before answering.

'Not so much. Since The Big M moved in, it's harder.'

Dani nods. Things have changed since Mondan adopted Parley. Emails monitored, tiny cameras appearing in high corners.

'But do you have anything now?' she asks.

Gray looks at her for a moment then unzips a pocket concealed inside the strap of his backpack. He pulls out a little Ziploc, weighs it in his hand and holds it out for her. It's the ones with the little Reebok logo. She never knows if they're a bad knockoff of the Nike ones, or it's a pill factory with a sense of irony. But they're actually pretty good.

Before she can take the baggie, Gray pulls it back. She's left with her hand out as he reaches into his rucksack, pulls out his wallet and extracts something from it. He hands her back the baggie and this time it's wrapped around the credit card. Terry Salmon's credit card.

'On me,' he says. 'Pills and card. I have another ID I'm shaping, anyway. Terry can be yours. You can have him all. Or *her*, now, I guess. Theresa. Terry.'

She takes the baggie, then the card. She holds the card up to inspect it, squinting against the white light overhead.

'Terry. Huh. Well, hello, Terry.'

Dani levels up.

From *The Electronic Radical*
by Dr Elyse Martingale (1957, Gollancz)

We see here the approaching crisis of the modern age.

When the machine becomes a tool for solving every conundrum we will believe we can achieve anything; and yet what new problems will these machines throw in our paths? Problems that today we cannot even imagine.

These engines of thought will become vehicles for war, crime and disorder; they will exasperate and frustrate our dreams as much as they promote and realise them; they will taunt us with their superior knowledge of every topic; but their mechanical nature will be too slow to grasp our human needs. In spite of this we will face great disappointment each time they let down our heightened expectations.

A great thinker began our century with a challenge known as the Decision Problem. It asks: *is there a method by which we can always know, in a given system of proof, whether a statement is true, or false?* This little puzzle will seem abstruse to many readers; but it is the key to our crisis. I hope to demonstrate this by restating it, as has Professor Turing, in terms of machinery: *Can I create a machine which will answer any question I can present to it?*

Let me now put you out of any suspense you may feel in this matter. The answer is, 'No.' Soon we shall set in motion many millions of ingenious processes. But we can never know which will lead to the great achievements of the era and which will collapse in ruins; or merely churn on: endless, fruitless.

¶**sic_girl**

> Never say sic_girl done gone cast stone one. (Or mebbe
> a bitty one. Soz.) But dey got dirty and shirty and now
> I'm feeling hurty. So, whoosh. Right back atch'a, Beth.
>
> Ahem.
>
> Exhibit a) The contract lady Lehrer signed six months
> ago in her own fair hand with big bad Mondan. May I
> draw m'learned friend's attention to clause 21.7.1?
> In which The Supplier (that's Mr Perce) agrees to
> disclose any data breach to The Service Owner's
> Responsible Officer (that's the lovely Lehrer – do keep
> up) within 24 hours?
>
> <innocent face> I guess they must have done that when
> someone hacked all that data, right?
>
> Right?
>
> #sigh#
>
> Darling ones, will you do a thing for me? You will?
> Rinse and repeat:
> I am not Dani Farr
> I am not Dani Farr
> I am not Dani Farr

TEN

J-R FIDDLED WITH THE LOCK on the toilet-stall door. The fussy mechanism somehow exemplified the precious impracticality of Parley's offices. He brute-forced the bolt into place and breathed out. For a moment he was protected from the disorder outside. His hand shook as he worked his fly.

The stall was narrow, making it hard to navigate around the fixtures. J-R lifted the seat and positioned himself against the left-hand wall to avoid the sink and hot-air dryer encroaching from his right. He waited for a coherent stream to emerge; but in spite of the raging pressure from his bladder, stress staunched his urethra. Three rudimentary drops edged out, then nothing. He gazed into the well-proportioned bowl. *Villeroy & Boch*. Sic_girl's latest post had amplified his position from awkward to devastating. Mere hours after he emailed Mark the Mondan contract, 'she' had shared the self-same document with the world. It had to be a coincidence but it could only look terrible for J-R. How long would it be before he got the phone call saying – what? That he was dismissed? Under investigation? For the first time he wished everyone would stop pussy-footing around the issue and shut Parley down before any more harm was done.

He gave his penis a hopeful tug and repositioned his feet to relieve the tension in his inner thighs. He feared his bladder might rupture if he didn't let out something soon. The BlackBerry trilled and vibrated in his left hand. He flinched: he hadn't realised he was holding it. On cue, a bright stream of urine issued from him and strafed the water in a hearty rush.

He fumbled the BlackBerry. Krish's name lit up the screen. He breathed twice as the pressure in his bladder eased. The ringtone played again. Better to answer. He redirected the pee against the back of the bowl to minimise background noise and answered left-handed. Krish's voice took over before the BlackBerry had made it to his ear.

'So who *exactly* is this Mark Dinmore? The truth, now.'

'Ah, Krish. As I said—'

'Because let me tell you what I'm looking at. To my left is a commercially confidential government contract that you emailed to Mr Dinmore yesterday afternoon.'

'Krish—'

'And to my right, a missive from sic_girl, posted twenty minutes ago. Linking to a leaked copy of – can you guess what she's linking to, J-R?'

J-R watched the continuing stream of piss. Would it never end?

'Yes, yes,' he said. 'The contract.'

He eased around to his right to direct the stream against the side of the bowl.

'Well, you know what, J-R? You just –'

As J-R turned, his elbow swung under the sensor of the hand-dryer. A roar of heated air shot down his leg. He flinched away, spraying urine up the side of the bowl and onto the wall. As he righted the stream the sweaty BlackBerry slipped through the fingers of his other hand.

There followed a moment of suspended time. The BlackBerry hung in the air as the heater roared and his brain struggled with a snapshot choice: control the flailing stream of pee, or catch the flying smartphone? He attempted both; but he'd never been good at such double tricks. His right hand squashed wetly on his penis. His left flapped the air around the BlackBerry, knocking it towards the toilet bowl. It bounced on the porcelain rim, chipped hope-fully sideways for a second, then slid to the bottom of the bowl, lighting the water with a yellow glow. Undaunted, J-R plunged his hand into the liquid and grabbed the sunken plastic slab. Only when he'd pulled it out, dripping but still apparently alive, did he register what he'd done. He looked at it, shook it a little and held it several inches from the side of his head, as though miming a much larger handset. His cuff dripped onto his shirtfront.

'Ah – hello?' Silence. 'Big Krish?' Still silence.

He looked again at the sloppy device then held it under the hand-dryer, which roused back into life and began to toast it. After a few seconds of this treatment, the screen died and refused to respond to any form of button-press.

J-R stood breathing. He surveyed the wreckage of the wall, his trousers, the unlit thing in his hand. His breath was short. He thought: *I am off the map. For the first time in years, they cannot find me.* This thought was a matter of surprise. An intense resolve gripped him but he'd no notion where he should direct it.

After a moment he dropped the BlackBerry through the metal waste flap in the wall. He began to rinse his hands at the miniature sink, letting the water touch and warm him.

¶identikid

It happens tomorrow, people. 18 hours and counting. We
still need 15 more bodies. Whisper me NOW.
<takebackID>

ELEVEN

THE FEMALE TERRY SALMON becomes active at 16:03 on Thursday at FoneBiz on Theobalds Road, with the purchase of a quad-core 3GHz Samsung Galaxy Edge smartphone on a 4G contract. She uses her CreditU MasterCard and IDs with a January gas bill. Her credit check clears at first touch. She adds a USB dongle and a hard shell case for the phone – like Dani, Terry is prone to dropping electronics. The bill comes to £326.85. The card has a £22,000 limit.

Her next stop is PC Xpert on Kingsway, where at 16:18 she adds £4,478.43 to the card with the purchase of an HP EliteBook 9960, a gunmetal Samsung Gear 3S smartwatch, an assortment of cables and adaptors, a slew of portable storage and a slick black backpack with a laptop compartment; and space for a bunch of other stuff.

Continuing her passage west she withdraws £250 at 16:30 from a generic ATM in PAYWELL FOOD 24 HOUR on Endell Street. The transaction charge is £1.50.

At 16:39 Terry appears on Parley, with the handle *AStrangeFish*. She uses mobile tethering to go online, so wifi logs do not provide a record – but from the timing of the transaction, we surmise that this takes place in Starbucks on Long Acre, where at 16:36 she puts £12.73 of coffee, sandwich and rocky road onto the MasterCard. Once online, she begins to register for a variety of cloud-based services and downloads open source software at an accelerating pace.

Gray gave her the folder. Combined with the credit card, the documents will authorise any transaction with relevant, accurate, fictional data: address, NI number, mother's maiden name.

She starts with gentle spikes, nudging at the fringes of her powerful new opponents in government. Citing sic_girl, cracking wise, acting and reacting, connecting. Gray says she's a black belt in social media kung fu and here she's amazed how little she needs Dani's existing footprint to spur this on. She knows what tone to strike when pinging unsolicited slogans, links and jibes to the Personas, and to influential human users she knows will cite them. They do; and AStrangeFish is seen and read, and rapidly builds a following. She parasites blogs and the growing library sic_girl is linking to. Someone has created a wiki of the leaked emails and documents, plus thousands of user-generated docs commenting on them. It's a mishmash, the hokey and the random bleeding into the credible and alarming.

Terry learns rapidly. Dani wishes she'd listened more closely to Gray's rants about privacy and identity. The intel is so rich, on Bethany Lehrer and her Digital Citizen data grab – and on Mondan, whose scale and reach she hadn't understood: their bacterial growth in storage and processing in Switzerland, South Africa, Israel; in Ohio, California and Texas; and deep under London. Growing like a Krynoid.

The free data memes keep funnelling back to the same core pool of users: one in particular. identikid. Is he the source of sic_girl's words? Either way, he's planning something tomorrow. It's trending. She reaches out.

¶AStrangeFish >> whisper -> ¶identikid
  hey kid seen your proffers
  what r plans 4 tomorrow? <takebackID>

Presenting through this freshly-minted handle something shifts in her. She's stepped back from a mask she never knew was there and is looking at the world through a different set of eye-holes.

Dani's built a local kind of fame. Now that she's all of a sudden known to the world, the attention has warped into digital gang-rape. So she's flipped a switch and stepped out of herself. The whole stage of the Internet is empty with potential. She's clean. Terry is clean.

But she isn't clean. Who's clean these days? The rascal Grubly has slid untethered onto Terry's hard drive to lurk in the folds of her SYS hierarchy. It was the G4 dongle drivers that let him in, the second she docked it.

Now Grubly feeds on the growing breadcrumb trail of her page impressions, consuming every cookie added to her drive. Grubly loves browser cookies. They taste of souls. Every thirty seconds, Grubly squirts a pellet of half-digested data to the parent server. In return come nourishing correlations, as the actions of Grubly's user are matched with richer master data, out there somewhere too remote for Grubly to conceive of. Grubly cares almost as much about the parent server as it does about the user.

So far, no correlations have appeared for this new user Terry. She was birthed into central London this mid-afternoon. But Grubly is patient. Soon some identifier will arrive and allow a match. Then Grubly will know the user completely and will at last provide her with the attention she naturally deserves.

¶ParleyNerd

Tell me it makes any sense that a mindless software
Persona would stand up and start attacking a politician?
Only one explanation makes any sense: she isn't mindless
any more. This girl just started thinking for herself.

Full post here:

<u>sic_girl for the win</u>

TWELVE

'HOW QUICKLY CAN YOU START to sell this in?'

These were the moments of·coming together. Work was what work was, day on endless day. Jonquil pretty much adored it, welcomed its continuous demands, even when the sole rewards were backache and a wakefulness Temazepam couldn't conquer. Maybe she would even keep on doing what she did if the days were only ever the same – but once in a rare while there came these holy moments where you created something truly new. This was the joy of tech. When these times came she was no way forty-one or even thirty-one, and she recalled the cussedness that drove her back in the day.

Nobody stole these moments from her. She was living this; and some preppy British PR guy couldn't throw her off. All she needed from him was to make what they had more exciting of a meme.

'I'm not seeing a message here, Ms Carter,' he said. 'Not one that would cut through the noise you're up against.'

She cracked her glass down onto the meeting table.

'I can't spin it to you any simpler, Sam. Sic_girl is alive. She's thinking for herself. She's found this leaked info on her own and is making it public. Which means we're a) not to blame, b) Danielle is off the hook, and c) we just created the world's first artificial intelligence and are going to d) win the Nobel Prize. End of. We have got to release this thing into the wild, and now.'

'And would you like to know what a hack will say when I call them with this? Once they stop laughing?'

'I do not hire you to have opinions. I hire you to sell.'

Jonquil clenched up as Graham's whiny voice chipped in.

'There's evidence,' he said. 'Data.'

'With respect,' said Sam, 'data won't get a journo on our side. I need clean, compelling lines.'

'Well, hello?' snapped Jonquil. '*The Personas have come to life.* If that's not clean and compelling enough –?'

The flack rubbed his hands across his tight-cut hair. He was too easy to rile – though otherwise, he seemed pretty sharp. Graham made that dying-warthog cough.

'But. Um, but?' he said.

The PR kid gave him the weirdest look, a kind of patient condescension. Jonquil gave him a floor-is-yours gesture: why the hell not?

'These are data,' he said. 'Data are what matter. I've calculated the correlations between what sic_girl says and what her algorithms read off the net. For last Monday, ninety-eight point three per cent correlation. Explained by standard error. Everything she said Sunday came from her source data. Monday, ninety-nine point two per cent correlation. Again, standard tolerances.' Jesus, was he going to recite numbers all night? 'Tuesday, though, correlation of sixty-two point seven per cent. Yesterday, fifty-two. And last night we have a dialogue with her that, well – she's making stuff up. And it's not just sic_girl. Half the Personas are saying things they've never been taught to say. Some have been doing this for quite a few weeks. Privacy, identity, state control. This is technically really really interesting.'

Sam looked at Graham for a short while then turned back to Jonquil.

'Look,' he said, 'I'm going to be frank. Parley is burning up with anti-government protest – and dreadful stuff about Dani Farr. The media can't reproduce it fast enough. There isn't a millimetre space for our voice. We need a game-changer.'

'And I'm telling you,' said Jonquil, 'we have the game-changer.'

'And I'm telling *you* nobody will buy it. I'm sure you believe that something is happening—'

'No. No, no. You don't patronise me. It is, period, happening. I want a media package on this and I want it for sign-off by noon tomorrow.'

Corrigan rotated his iPhone 360 degrees on the tabletop then nodded slowly. He'd read the runes. He stood and gathered his things. She flapped her hands at him, *g'wan, shoo*.

'Five o'clock tomorrow, Sam.'

```
$ cd temp

$ ls *dump*
sictimeline.dump.01.txt syslog.dump.01.txt

$ head -n 1 *dump*
==> sictimeline.dump.01.txt <==
Whee! At least 45 minutes ahead with no pain!
<meds> Hmm. Now. How to use 'em?

==> syslog.dump.01.txt <==
Whee! At least 45 minutes ahead with no pain!
<meds> Hmm. Now. How to use 'em?

$ tail -n 1 *dump*
==> sictimeline.dump.01.txt <==
Reallys, people. I does love yas. Even when I
acts like a big grumpyface.

==> syslog.dump.01.txt <==
Reallys, people. I does love yas. Even when I
acts like a big grumpyface.

$ diff -q *dump*
Files sictimeline.dump.01.txt and syslog.
dump.01.txt differ

$diff *dump* | wc-L
2186

$ WHAT THE FUCK?
bash: WHAT: Command not found...
```

THIRTEEN

PLATES CRASH. Terry startles up and Dani finds she's in a Westminster café. She remembers arriving here but doesn't know how long it's been. She touches her coffee cup: frozen by air con.

All afternoon she's dug behind the sic_girl proffers, overturning layers of data, searching out a single byte of information that can explain sic_girl's transformation and her own public laying bare. For reasons she can't fathom, it's easier under cover of the Terry identity than if she'd done it as herself. It gives her freedom to invade and bring no baggage. Anonymous, with passwords carried in her fingertips, she moves through electronic defences with zero friction. Mostly she's turned up an enormous nothing; but that's normal with data mining. Patience is ninety-nine per cent of the work.

Her ant trail over central London is marked out by pauses. At every stop she's connected to Parley for another deeper pass; but it wasn't till she sat at this fake wood table with her quadrillionth cappo and flipped the lid of Terry's ever-less-shiny laptop that she thought to check sic_girl's continuity against Parley's internal message logs.

This is a futile exercise, a last resort. The logs take a record of what the Personas say, as they say it. By definition, sic's log is identical to what a Parley user sees. Therefore: futile. Might as well compare light from a projector with the image on a screen. But being thorough means doing even the futile things and even though it's impossible, Terry saw at once that the logs are different from the published timeline. Really very different. According to the logs, all sic_girl has talked about for the last three days are *achy breaky pains*, helpless remedies and sorrows – just like every other day. Half these messages made it as-is to the public Internet. The other half have vanished, replaced by new words the sic_girl engine didn't create and doesn't know about. Somehow, impossibly, sic's words have been edited in the nanosecond between being generated and appearing in the browsers of her eight hundred thousand devotees.

This doesn't make sense but it's true. Since she found this chink of discrepancy, Terry has sifted data, grepping line by line; and even in this shifting week, data is constant. What it's telling Dani is she's been wasting her time trawling the net for the source of sic's words – because sic's algorithm never created them. And nor is sic thinking for herself. The reason she's suddenly aware of politics is that she isn't aware of anything after all. It's not her speaking. Someone else is inserting words in place of hers. So back to the question: who is this person and how are they doing it?

Then Dani realises: she's spoken to them already. She freezes, both hands poised above the keys. Last night, in the semantic dialogue, she thought she was speaking to sic_girl but she wasn't. It must have been this someone, somehow typing answers live like a chatroom, aping sic_girl to fuck with Dani's mind.

A second realisation shivers into her head: seconds after sic_girl signed off, a door slammed in the stairwell. Was this someone inside the building with her, typing answers to her questions just metres away?

She wants to slam her laptop shut and chuck it in the Thames – hop off the grid if there even is such a place. But the code-freeze is on her and she can't stop. She logs back into Parley's local network as sysop, pulls up the access logs for last night – the time of the semantic dialogue. Only two users were on the system at the time: *dfarr*; and *zero*.

So who in the name of shit is *zero*?

¶Spotted

Spotted in Westminster: Parley's own Dani Farr, typing up a storm.

(Isn't she supposed to be some kind of fugitive from justice now? Or a freedom fighter, or something?)

<pic:>

FOURTEEN

'MR MERVYN GRIFFITH-JONES, QC.'

Gramma stood in silhouette against the summer window, punishing tumblers with a blue striped tea cloth. Radio 2 chortled from the ancient transistor radio that sat on the kitchen shelf beside the carriage clock. This old woman, who the newspapers called *Elyse Martingale, Mother of the Modern Computer* or *Infamous Far-Left Academic* or *Controversial Sixties Cult Figure*, was to Bethany simply Gramma.

'The atrocious, self-righteous Griffith-Jones,' she said. 'A man who might have been supplied by Central Casting to play the prosecution barrister in some ghastly West End legal drama. He had no conception what was being created in that courtroom. No comprehension of the forces washing over that worm-riddled bench. Have you ever heard what he said, dear?'

Bethany had not. She was eleven. Sitting upright at the great wood table, in the aura of Gramma's sweltering stove, she shook her head, though Gramma wasn't really waiting for a reply. She hadn't visited the old lady for a month but as soon as Daddy zoomed off in the Audi, Gramma planted a contraband fizzy drink in her hand, sat her down and launched straight into a lecture as if she were restarting a conversation they'd been having just minutes before. Her obsession today was the Chatterley Trial. Bethany knew nothing about it, but was thrilled by her small suspicions about what the book contained. She'd found no copy on her parents' shelves but Gramma had one, of course. Beth had inspected the cracked spine with its fraying phoenix but hadn't dared slide it from the shelf. This wasn't for fear of punishment so much as a certainty the old lady would make Bethany read the book.

'He said in public court – and I quote – *Is that the sort of book, gentlemen of the jury, you would want your wife or servants to read?* As if that said it all. Thank goodness twelve ordinary sensible people could see him for what he was. Dreadful reactionary. I would have presented him with my views on the matter, given a chance. Sadly I was but a witness, called for the ounce of respectability my PhD imparted to the defence. Do you know what was so very wrong about what he said, my girl?'

It was easy to be lulled by Gramma's meandering and think she'd lost the plot; then out of nowhere she'd lob a precisely targeted question at her one-girl audience. Bethany shook her head.

'The worst form of snobbery is to deny information: to anyone at all. Always remember that. Bad as it is to look down on another human being: to act as censor? Unforgivable.'

Beth sipped her Coke with reverent slowness. Gramma began to dry her meat knife – whose blade was, in Bethany's memory, at least two foot long.

'Of course it didn't start in that courtroom. You know Darwin?'

The really scary thing about Gramma's lectures was the speed of her gear changes. Bethany gulped her Coke and nodded through bubbles – though in fact all she knew was a kind of family tree with monkeys. Science was an overgrown patch in the garden of her schooling. Her mother seemed to take pride in how little attention Layling Girls' paid to it.

'Then you will know how religious folk responded to his ideas as they emerged. Understandable, in the march of ideas. But the other day I came across the words of some bishop's wife – Worcester, I believe. Here, I made a note.'

She lifted her reading glasses from their string and set them on her squashy nose. Knife in hand she flipped the ratty pages of a foolscap pad.

'Yes, Worcester. She said, quote, *Let us hope that what Mr Darwin says is not true; but if it is true, let us hope that it will not become generally known*. Unquote.'

The spectacles were held at bay as she inspected Beth for signs of comprehension.

'Do you see, dear? Such a silly cow. Darwin's ideas can no more be constrained by such priggery than this would be stopped by the bishop's flabby stomach.' Beth's eye's widened as Gramma handled the blade, before placing it back on the countertop. 'Remind me to review evolution with you some time, by the by.'

She came and settled by Beth, giving off a waft of talcum. Her rheumy eyes were drilling instruments.

'Do you see, dear? There is no high priesthood that can hold the scrolls of knowledge for long. The walls are cracking and they can't stop it. *It is in the nature of information to make itself free.* As I have been known to say on a fair few occasions.'

Indeed she had. As Bethany later learned, this was one of the soundbites that made Elyse's name, emblazoned in red block capitals across the yellow dustcover of the original edition of *The Electronic Radical*. Bethany had passed through university in the afterglow of that book, which was still famous – and rather less infamous – in the eighties. A tattered copy held place on the shelves of each of her hard-left Political Science tutors. Bethany, for her own part too compliant to wish destruction on the instruments of state, had been a disappointment to these wing-armchair radicals, but the inherited aura was enough to light her in their favour; and when she started to be known in uni political circles, she was never sure to what extent she'd made her own reputation. Everyone wanted to hear her rouse for the demolition of the state. What she gave them was more measured.

No, she'd taken her own message from Elyse and from her manifesto. It was the one imparted to her at the age of eleven, on that hard but comfortable kitchen bench (the same bench her boys now sat on to eat their motherless dinners). Everyone had a right to information, and when they had free access to it they, too, would be free. An informed citizen was an empowered citizen. Education and labour would open to them as the gates of academy crumbled. Markets could not exploit them, because they had the power to judge and decide how to exercise their economic muscle, however modest. Society more free by regular degrees.

This was all she had sought to achieve, compromised and complex though the process was. Now she was on the point of achieving it, she refused to accept the irony: that it might be a stream of unrestricted information that would scupper her dream. Information made free could be a goad, as well as a spur.

But things would proceed, she was determined of it.

This resolution accounted for the dreadnought set of her jaw as she waited for Karen Arbiter in another dry Whitehall room. Beside her Krish sat still and silent, though Bethany could almost hear his mind heaving on with the same momentum that had driven him all day, fielding calls, stirring action, batting media aside.

Bethany stretched out her fingers over the plastic file on her lap. She regarded her wedding and engagement rings. So plain: as she and Peter had decided together. Life, too, had been plainer then. So many ambiguities and hidden traps these days, so little time or energy left for her three fellas. All the fronts she had to fight on, leaving open such narrow supply lines to real life.

She opened the file, which was labelled *MoS-CabOff Thurs*. Inside was a written statement from Mondan stating that, whatever the Parley proffers insinuated, Bethany had known nothing of any hack or of the DigiCitz pilot users getting piggy-spam on their computers. She turned pages, not reading, Krish looking on. If she were to ask herself, was it right to bring Sean into this huge and important thing, overruling all advice, she might balk. But no good would come of questioning whether the thing was good. It was necessary. And the necessary becomes part of the good it helps create.

Would her grandmother agree? The answer was not so negative as it might appear. Without Elyse's pioneering work, midwifing the modern computer, it's hard to see how an entrepreneur like Sean could have prospered. Radicals and capitalists are not so different – why else would one so often turn into the other?

Bethany closed the file and checked her watch. Karen was fifteen minutes late.

'Well, I think this is enough. It needs to be enough.'

Krish did not reply.

'This,' said Karen, 'goes very hard against my better judgement.'

That was promising from the start. Karen's better judgement would be to string Bethany up from St Stephen's Tower, entrails on display for the edification of future ministers.

Karen dropped the report on the desk as though it contained violent pornography. Then the glasses came off and she set her face into its most disappointed look. Judging by this pantomime she was not ready to concede without delivering a dressing down. It was going Bethany's way. Perhaps.

'Good report, Beth. I have to confess, I half-thought Perce might leave you to the wolves. Certainly enough here to quiet the media to tolerable levels. Press Office will use this to pull back the wilder claims.'

Bethany said nothing, wary of a trap. If she thanked Karen too readily, she'd seem blasé if there turned out to be a *but*. There would certainly be a *but*.

'However,' said Karen.

Bethany could not resist a half-smile, even as her heart sank. Had she ever been this powerless? Here was the lesson of this dismal week. Only when you reach the high point of your career do you know enough to realise you'll never really change a thing.

'However,' repeated Karen, 'I have another report.'

Her eyes darted to Krish, sitting to Bethany's right. He shifted in his seat. Bethany did not look his way.

'I had my own team clarify certain aspects of your conduct in this business with Mondan—'

'Mine?' said Bethany. 'You mean the department's?'

'The report has quite a wide-ranging scope.'

Bethany's turn to shoot a glance at Krish. She'd only agreed to let in Karen's slimy wonks on his say-so. Karen extracted a file from her pile of papers and affected to peruse it, glasses a long way down her nose.

'So may I see this report about me?' asked Bethany.

Karen, absorbed in the report, waited a few seconds before looking up.

'Hmm? Oh, no,' she said, 'no, I don't think so.' She closed it and placed a hand on its cover. 'This is a draft. And it is marked *Cabinet Office Confidential*.'

Stupid, childish mistake to ask. Deep breaths. Tummy muscles.

'Though even in draft,' said Karen, 'it makes disquieting reading.'

'Such as?'

The two women's eyes were locked on one another's.

'Well. You do seem to have had a lot of meetings with Sean Perce before and during the contract negotiations, Bethany. Meetings not always, it would seem, arranged by your officials.'

Oh, God. Oh, no. Bethany heard her own breathing grow denser.

'Sean has been kind enough to offer informal support and advice,' she said. 'On a number of occasions. Pro bono advice, at a considerable saving to the public purse.'

Karen's gaze could penetrate four inches of steel. It darted between Bethany's eyes. By colossal effort of will, Bethany kept her eyes trained on Karen's overstated eyeliner.

'How astonishingly public spirited of him,' said Karen.

Somewhere below Bethany's sternum, a fortnight's worth of brewing frustration ignited. A year's worth.

'If you have something to say to me, Karen, *say it!*'

The last words ripped from her mouth by the force of it.

'And what *am* I saying?' said Karen.

'If you think former Terasoft board member Andrew bloody Carpenter is Mister Independent-From-Business-Influence—'

'What on earth has Andrew to do with –?'

Bethany was standing now, using her limited height. Karen a still point, centred in Bethany's heaving field of vision,

'My choices have always been in the public interest. Always. I have never let – let –'

She caught her tongue, a millisecond from disaster. She sat.

'The whole process,' she finished lamely, 'has been completely proper.'

When had she ever let Karen rile her like this? Breathe, breathe.

'Well, then,' said Karen. 'I'm sure you will have nothing to worry about when we get into the boring details. All of this will be examined in due course.' The glasses came off again. 'Look, let me be clear. This is a flagship programme. We are keen to protect it.' Protect *it*, noticed Bethany. 'I am not about to stand in the way of tomorrow's launch event, or of you signing Contract Set Two on Monday.'

'Oh,' said Bethany.

What was this? Where had this been going if not towards laying Bethany out to dry?

'Well, of course,' said Karen. 'You should absolutely proceed. I hope you haven't done anything to slow down preparations for the launch?'

'No, no. Of course not! Raring to go at eleven tomorrow.'

This was going to be a busy night.

'Well, then,' said Karen. 'Best be getting on?'

'Yes, yes, of course.'

Bethany gathered her bits and pieces as smoothly as she could. Standing with her files held against her chest, she said, 'Thank you again. You won't regret this. We're going to make this work.'

Krish stood silently at her side. Karen looked at her for a long time before speaking.

'I don't doubt it will be a success for all who remain involved. I'll be seeing you very soon, Beth.'

¶riotbaby

Get ready . . .

FIFTEEN

THE STREETS ARE RIPE FOR CONFRONTATION. J-R negotiates a string of unfamiliar corners and blank walls coated with fly-posted eyes. He's a stranger in his own town. This far east, the lights are dim. London's bright wash has been diluted. Something has cracked through the surface of its streets and every knock and chatter of its broken pipework makes him start and check over his shoulder. He's alone and lost and in need of a map. His washed-out Party BlackBerry can't help him – it's languishing in a waste bin back at Parley's offices. Instead he pulls out his barely-used personal mobile; but as he switches it on he finds he no longer wants to locate himself. That's not what he needs from the night. Instead he turns on the phone's camera, frames a pre-Victorian run of cottage-fronts and takes a photographic trace of his random walk. Then he remembers that this kind of self-documentation is something he never indulges in; but this is all new; and if the urge is there –?

He walks.

THE EVENING BRINGS UP damp embers and charring plastic, like the site of an extinguished house-fire. J-R crosses to avoid a hunting pack of student-age lads, their gunslinger stride and combat jackets a provocation. Three of the five wear T-shirts with the legend *TAKEBACK*. He takes a surreptitious snap from against his chest, building an evidence base towards some as yet unknown conclusion.

The phone stays in his hand as he walks on. Out of his sight it comments.

)) stone commotion ((

His aim, when he walked out of Parley's building – leaving behind his bag, his folded bike, his coat – was to stretch his legs, refill his lungs and settle his anxiety over Bethany and Krish. Soon though he wandered past the point of easy return. Now he's simply walking until he reaches a point of resolution. What might he find on these abandoned concrete tracks? If there are answers, he'll need to coax them out.

The moon in its blue dark rises over butterfly roofs. He photographs it. Some insistent thing presents at the edge of his vision, then vanishes. He takes another angle.

Krish has never turned on him like that, as if he were some tyro journalist in need of discipline. Such mad times. Even before he destroyed his BlackBerry, J-R had become dislocated from his role. He'd spent the week batting off hacks and hearing out Party contacts as they conveyed in their veiled way the message that faith in Bethany was trending downward. He responded like a news anchor reading from autocue. His Party lines had never seemed so two-dimensional. And through it all he devoured each new communique from sic_girl. The Bethany in those mails, gossiping and conniving with Sean Perce, was authentically her; but utterly inconsistent with the woman he knew. A meretricious conniver with no claim on him. Enough to tell him to be out of there but not where he was supposed to be instead.

The wistful, broken persona of sic_girl, fake as it might be, is vastly more attractive to J-R at this time.

Somewhere out of sight a trolley rumbles over paving with the sound of hooves on cobbles; then fades into night. J-R is on a side road with no visible exit. The shutters of industrial units line the street. He catches the scene on his phone.

There's a turning beyond a run of older buildings. Crumbling brick, earthy darkness. As he squints towards the unlit fissure a young man appears from it. He stops dead in the gaslight and their eyes meet. His face is stoatish, pale and slender; his eyes a question or demand. J-R's phone is raised, positioned to shoot.

)) this boy ((

it says.

Now J-R makes out the discreet signage above the door from which the boy has just emerged; and the ruddy light spilling from it. A soft thrum of electronic music escapes into the cul-de-sac. A bar or club, half-hidden from the world's sight down this dank alley.

The tableau is static for a number of seconds; then the young man speaks.

'Do you have a light at all?' he asks.

They're perhaps ten metres apart in the night air. The boy's voice is light but clear. His hands stay in his jacket pockets.

'I – no, I don't – I don't smoke. I'm sorry.'

The boy smiles at some unknown misstep.

'That's OK, mate, I don't actually smoke. You know?'

And J-R does know. The unbuttressed walls at last give way and crumble in a forgiving rain of London brick. The rubble swallows the boy, J-R and the abandoned theatre of the street.

¶riotbaby

On your marks . . .

SIXTEEN

DANI KICKS PIZZA SPAM from the doormat. The mansion block is empty and dark. She doesn't know what time it is. She double-steps all four flights to her flat, locks the door behind her and beelines for the fridge. No beer. A reproachful trace of yesterday's marsala hangs around the microwave. She opens the door that leads onto the light-well and fire escape, to let in air. The flat is stale and abandoned, as though she moved out months ago – though she was only here this morning. In that time she's been plastered naked across the net, hounded offline by a million trolls and born again as AStrangeFish.

Moving to the bedroom, she sets Terry's backpack on the unmade bed, stuffs in random clothes for thirty seconds then heads to the bathroom and repeats the exercise with toothpaste, a razor and other washbag gumph. Then she zips up the bag. This is packing, Terry style.

She pauses in the lounge to rotate on her feet and grid-scan for anything else she might need: she doesn't know how long she'll be away. Her eyes light on her PC; but she knows it's marked with Dani and anyway too big to travel with. From now on everything needs to be as near to weightless as possible, and connected only to Terry. This isn't paranoia: it's the new logic.

Zero nags at her. In the last five hours she's connected from cafes, the bus, a bench in Green Park and the neutral lobby of the hotel she recce'd earlier, searching out the answer to just one question. A hard enough puzzle to drive trolls, Sam and Bethany from her mind: *who is zero?*

She knows he/she has strong skills to have walked onto Parley's locked-down internal network. She wishes she could stop believing it's Gray. That doesn't even make sense. And no way could he imitate sic_girl. He can barely imitate himself, the Auton. But who else would have the access?

Familiar sparkles seep out of the walls and ripple into a live display. The illusion of light and motion settles on her like the landscape passing a train window. It reminds her muscles to be exhausted. In the shifting forms a shape grows: a flowing surface, nimble and false. It's familiar in the way a face is before you recognise it.

Someone hammers on the front door. The light patterns flick off as though a switch is thrown. The flat has no internal hallway – the door gives onto the sitting room, three metres away from where Dani is standing. Another burst of knocking. The door shakes.

'*Miss Farr!*'

The policemen from Tuesday, barely muffled by the door's thin wood. She knew they'd be back to hound her, now she's totally this outlaw.

'*We saw you come in. Would you please open the door?*'

'So you found me. In my flat. Fucking genius!'

'*Miss Farr, it's in your interests to cooperate. We only want to speak to you.*'

'Congratulations, you just did.' Hitching the bag onto her shoulder. 'Now fuck off!'

Whoa. She hadn't known she was going to say that. A steady kicking starts. The prefab door shakes under the crunch of standard-issue boot.

'Hey!' she says. 'Are you even allowed to do that? Don't you need a warrant or something?'

'*What are we doing, Miss Farr? We're having a conversation.*'

The kicking continues. Flat Meg White drumbeats. If they enter, she's Dani again. She needs to be Terry, to move and be nowhere. She walks on the pads of her feet to the kitchen and out of the open door onto the fire escape. The lightwell is a building turned inside out: frosted windows look out from all the flats, onto a white-tiled cavity down the centre of the building. A skylight glows overhead with a trace of day.

Another distant bout of hammering as she skips down the metal steps. No doubt where she's headed: there's this hotel. She's already been there once today. She got the name from her new online bestie, identikid. She has the plan.

Plan, though? What is she racing into? None of this is her. Perhaps it's Terry.

She slides open the ground-floor window, checks to left and right, slips onto the lino of the hall and heads for the front door and the street.

Why do some women forget they're women when they go online?

Take a look at this Danielle Farr we're hearing so much about. What is she thinking when she posts sick and degrading images of abused and trafficked women? And of herself? Does she spare a thought for the four-decade fight to liberate us from male oppression?

Has she forgotten she's even a woman?

She uses her body like it's property to pass around. She embraces the obscene patter of any woman-hating troll. Danielle Farr is living proof of how far the Internet has set us back from the hard-earned freedoms of the seventies. She's bought into every single lie they've spun: that flaunting your body is self-expression not exploitation; that women can be defined by how they look; that if we want a voice we have to sing men's tune.

When I see her sad little face peering out from these degrading pictures all I feel for this pathetic specimen is sympathy.

But sorry, sister, you ain't no sister of mine.

SEVENTEEN

'I'M CALLING SEAN,' said Bethany.

Krish kept looking forward at the road, past Eric, the driver.

'As soon as we get back to the office,' she said, 'I'm calling him.'

'You are not calling him. That is something you will not do.'

Outside the car the Westminster evening trundled by. Using a car to travel three blocks is hardly eco, but that's the price you pay for media scrutiny.

'I actually am. And by the way, at what point did you get to tell me whether or not I can ring my lover?'

'Oh, lord, please.' Krish dropped to sotto voce as if Eric wasn't right in front of them. 'For your information, I started telling you whom to call when you put this plane into a nosedive. I'm pulling on the stick as hard as I can and I'd appreciate you letting me help. As far as you're concerned Mr Perce is not your lover. He is nobody.'

Foolish to have spoken the thing out loud.

'When you see him at the launch,' said Krish, 'you'll be polite and distant. Everything you do sends the signal you barely know that man.'

From the window she caught a pedestrian's eye. Brief shock of recognition.

'Anyone in the country with a web browser knows there's more to it.'

The car turned sharply. Bethany had failed to notice they were already pulling round the back of Artemis House. A pack of paps stood on the corner. Eric had cornered fast but they'd have got one of her startled face through the glass.

'Thanks for the warning,' she said.

Krish turned to watch the pressmen check their shots as the car descended the ramp to the car park.

'Freelancers. Fewer today. They won't sell anything. Unless we give them a cause – like, say, ringing Sean Perce.'

Eric pulled into Bethany's parking spot. Krish hopped out before they'd come to a stop. Bethany launched herself out of her side. They slammed their doors in unison and faced off across the car.

'How will anyone know if I make a private call? Are you planning to brief my phone log to the media?'

Krish leaned heavily across the car roof, looking almost sorrowful.

'*He* would, though. He'd know. And if you don't see that, you need to.'

'Oh, come *on*.'

He broke for the stairs, forcing her to follow. Eric manhandled red boxes from the passenger seat.

'I mean it,' she said. 'That's a crazy accusation. Sean is a hard arse but he's the good guys.'

As they entered the stairwell Krish pushed the door shut behind them, blocking out Eric.

'Krish! That's *rude*!'

He turned on her with the force of a Hebridean wind.

'You need to think hard about where you place your loyalties this week. That man is out for anything he can recover from this situation and believe me, he isn't waiting around for the phone to ring.'

'Krish? You're actually scaring me now.'

She glanced through the glass pane set into the door, into the car park. Eric stood a discreet three metres away, a statue. Not looking their way.

'Are you saying Sean has been in touch?' she hissed.

'I'll tell you who *has* been in touch. I'll tell you who you *are* going to call. You are going to call your husband, who's been on the phone to me roughly every thirty seconds.'

Oh, God, Peter – she'd been planning to call him. She'd meant to. She balled her fists and for a second thought she might pummel Krish in the chest. Instead she gave the door a single furious wallop. It sounded a dull note. Through the glass Eric started but didn't turn. Those guys are pros. One more thing she'd miss when they gave her the heave-ho.

Except she mustn't think that way. She'd bought herself time.

'We need to kill this,' she said. 'I can't – I *will not* go down over this, this nothing. Get me meat, Krish. We have until the morning. I'm ready to fight this but I'm batting air.'

Krish let out a breath. His shoulders settled and he turned away from her.

'I try, aye. But I'm near the limit of who I can ring and bollock just now.'

Bethany nodded slowly. Through the glass Eric shifted from foot to foot. She turned a smile on Krish: a minister's smile.

'So then: shall we? I believe I have a call to make.'

¶riotbaby

Get set . . .

EIGHTEEN

ON THE BLACK-PAINTED FLOORBOARDS of the Flamingo, identikid preps for a practice run, tools arrayed around him. Winter is furled on the deflated sofa by the door, half-watching him over her tablet. Reynard is behind the sound desk, laying a mix into giant Sennheisers. The room is on mute except for the clicks and scrapes of Leo's tools.

He's test-rigged the four Black Boxes to the HD feed of the 72-inch plasma they use for karaoke nights. In a Terminal window on his MacBook he's hacking the code that runs the Boxes but it's a struggle. It's good he gave himself time to test the set-up before tomorrow night. Don't want to be fiddling with USB plugs, thirty storeys above the stonework.

The laptop pings. A new alert comes in every fifteen seconds: questions and connections from his widening network; dominos to set in line before tomorrow. It all takes time, which sometimes he doesn't mind – these TakeBack girls are proper fit. He has a feeling about the new blood called AStrangeFish. She and Leo've been shooting shit since she first came online this arvo. Her avatar is a cartoony fish but he's sure it's a girl.

He's got more busy going on right now than he thought he'd ever see but he's loving every second. He leans over to kill alerts so he can concentrate on a specially gnarly bit of wiring; but before he can touch the trackpad up pops one alert he can't ignore. He skips onto Parley.

¶riotbaby
> Is it working yet?

¶identikid
> hey man im on it these generic leads you sent are retarded

¶riotbaby
> Do you need tech help?

¶identikid
> fuck no im cool alright

¶riotbaby
> You'll tell me if you can't handle it?

¶identikid
> im handling it get off my tits man

¶riotbaby
> Good boy. How are numbers looking?

¶identikid
> s'cool. a hundred for definites. probs more

¶riotbaby
> Good. We need enough bodies to fill the space. Whisper me when you're ready?

¶identikid
> yea ok wil defs whisp laters bro

¶riotbaby
> Later, kid.

Shit, man. That riotbaby can be like a real mummy. He's some kind of arsehole – for an artificial intelligence, and everything. Aw crap and look now, the DIN plug's come unwired for the nth time. Leo sleeps the Mac, takes a breath and starts again.

He holds the cable in bony fingers, threads candy-stripe wires into pinprick docking points on the socket. A nubbin of tongue protrudes from the side of his mouth. As he neatens the fray and crimps he thinks of the splash the flashmob'll make tomorrow. Riotbaby's right: numbers matter. If they fill that room, the TV cunts will swallow the videos whole. It's so cool to be the one who's going to bring the ruckus to their corporate shit. Leo thinks of faceless suits making plans right now, over where the streets are hosed clean every hour and rows of pigs with plexi shields line up in concrete basements waiting for the shit to fly. They've no idea tomorrow someone's going to drop a grenade right through their window.

He grins as he works the Torx in the half-light. The room is quiet. Winter and Reynard are silent: he could be alone.

He's not alone. Grubly sailed into his MacBook weeks ago. Grubly grows each time it finds a new machine. It reaches through directory trees to feed on the bytes around it, then *flip-flip-flip* changes shape and grows like a Transformer. The mash-up of illicit software on this hard drive is the biggest code-hack collection it's even seen. So Grubly loves the user, too.

Leo sets down his tools and tries the plug. Snap, it's in. The plasma flickers into life and displays a test reel of rotating, overlapping circles. Job done. The 'kid grins at Winter like a crazy man. She gazes back at him, like no one home.

These Black Boxes are the key to everything, to Saturday's big display. The stunt at the minister's event, the bot attack, are just the lead-ins to that one big ultra-public event. And Leo will be there. He'll be on the news. He'll get them to put in the caption, *identikid*. Not *Leo Sandberg*. He wonders if they'll let him.

'MEANWHILE THE PRESSURE on embattled minister Bethany Lehrer is mounting by the hour.

'Adding to her woes, a further set of emails was leaked this afternoon, appearing to confirm her prior knowledge of data breaches at controversial IT giant Mondan. The government has been quick to deny that these emails are in any way connected with the alleged hack of the Digital Citizen programme. They insist there has been no risk to the privacy of people taking part in the Teesside pilot of the Digital Citizen project. But it's now clear Lehrer is the target of a sustained campaign. And given her closeness to Mondan, and their central role in the government's flagship online ID project, these leaked emails will be making difficult reading here at the Ministry of Technology.

'Surely, Huw, in spite of these denials, we have to question whether this national programme – or this minister – can survive the mounting tide of public criticism.

'Huw.'

NINETEEN

THE ROOM IS AN ABSTRACTION. Everything is modular and co-ordinates with brown – i.e. it's brown. Dani orders room service curry, which arrives with meat and rice in separate plastic blisters. Sitting cross-legged on the bed, she forks marsala by the light of Terry's laptop and sniffs the net for company. Now her intentions are carnal she can see the limitations of rolling as Terry. She's fresh to these follows. They step cautious, wanting to learn how she plays. It's the provisional stage of anonymous mating, where the index finger hovers ready to swipe you away.

Tiring of vague attentions she logs off MeatSpace and logs back in under Dani's handle, SafeWord. Gray told her not to use any Dani logins but nobody will troll her on MeatSpace. It's not that kind of place.

As soon as she connects she's located again.

♡ **SafeWord**
monkey
monkey?

♡ **monkey_love**
Yes, here. Hi, stranger.
Fuck I'm horny.

Dani smiles to herself. Whoever monkey_love is, he's always on, like a Duracell bunny.

My cock is actually sore, it's so hard.
SafeWord? You there?

♡ **SafeWord**
hi
look do you mind if we just talk

♡ **monkey_love**
Sure.

♡ **SafeWord**
shit of a day

♡ **monkey_love**
OK. Sorry.
What's on your mind?

♡ **SafeWord**
monkey do you think the way people are online
you know they say that when someones online they
become someone theyre not?

♡ **monkey_love**
Sure. You can pretend to be anyone online.
Who's pretending to be who?

♡ **SafeWord**
no its just im thinking how people are online is actually
how they really are when theres nobody to stop them
like its the real them
monkey?

♡ **monkey_love**
I think everybody's a lot of people.

♡ **SafeWord**
how?
like online identities?

♡ **monkey_love**
No I mean who they actually are is more than one person.
It depends where they are and who they're talking to.
When they're offline people think they're the same as their
body.
The online person is who they'd be if they weren't trapped
in a body.

♡ **SafeWord**
its but
i dont want to think people are like they've been today
fucking fucking fucking cunts
sorry

♡ **monkey_love**
Shit. What's happening?
<worried>

♡ **SafeWord**
Never mind. Just people.

♡ **monkey_love**
I'm sorry. Whatever it is.
You know, people cnbe
People can be kind, though.
You see them being kind. Totally to strangers.
It gets lost in the noise. Shittiness is noisier.
Maybe people are being kind to you but you haven't seen it?

♡ **SafeWord**
best and worst?

♡ **monkey_love**
  Just people.
  Like anywhere.

♡ **SafeWord**
  youre kind

♡ **monkey_love**
  Thanks.
  Really.

♡ **SafeWord**
  monkey do you ever worry about people seeing stuff you
  say here?

♡ **monkey_love**
  What, on MeatSpace?

♡ **SafeWord**
  yeh

♡ **monkey_love**
  No. God, no.

♡ **SafeWord**
  but see stuff i said on here i saw it today on an aggregator site
  like you can totally google this shit
  maybe what im saying now

♡ **monkey_love**
  No dan, we're safe, this is hidden. Spiders can't see us.

♡ **SafeWord**
  i saw it, monkey
  people are watching what we do on here.

♡ **monkey_love**

This is one of the most secure chat spaces on the net.

♡ **SafeWord**

wait

what did you just call me

monkey why did you call me dan

♡ **monkey_love**

Back there? No, I meant 'no danger'.

Typo, sorry.

Why?

♡ **SafeWord**

no reason

no, whatever

♡ **monkey_love**

So what are you going to do?

About whatever your problem is?

♡ **SafeWord**

im going to grab the bitch who did this to me and kick her
in the fucking nuts

♡ **monkey_love**

You're not doing anything risky?

You should take time. Think it over.

SafeWord?

♡ **SafeWord**

you know what? I am actually lying in wait for that skanky
cunt right now

totally an ambush

♡ **monkey_love**
  Shit, don't do anything stupid.

♡ **SafeWord**
  what? im kidding
  what the fuck do you think im going to do

♡ **monkey_love**
  I know you don't want to hear it but those people are serious.
  Where actually are you?

♡ **SafeWord**
  fuck off im going to tell you

♡ **monkey_love**
  Look, why not just go home.
  We can talk from there.

♡ **SafeWord**
  actually look you know what monkey im out of here

♡ **monkey_love**
  SafeWord

♡ **SafeWord**
  no
  bye

♡ **monkey_love**
  SafeWo#

Dani cuts the connection. The cursor's pulse keeps time with
her heart. Is she paranoid, or everywhere she goes does someone
try to own her? She looks at the screen some more but nothing
comes to her. It goes grey, then black.

Weary beyond reason or belief, she turns her back to the computer and curls on the bedspread fully clothed. Maybe she's tired enough to turn off and sleep.

Behind her, in the laptop, Grubly wakes and sings in the high-pitched register of active RAM, then begins to feed. The flavour of this data is too powerful to ingest at once. It's knowledge and it's power: the two are joined like the nucleus of an atom.

The MeatSpace login was the word that freed the seal. Once spoken, it correlated with an ocean of data already held by the worldwide network of Grublies. The user has removed her mask and spoken – and all at once this Grubly, her own Grubly, knows her like a lover never will. Every last sad midnight wish laid bare.

She's breathing deeply, the edge of a snore in her nose. Grubly picks this up from the laptop mic. Her pulse slows. Grubly reads this from the sensors in her watch. He listens to her deeper notes. Every processor cycle, Grubly knows Dani a little more. Data roars through the flimsy walls into its cache. Pieces of Dani smashed apart and scattered to a hundred storage sites in a dozen different jurisdictions.

She sleeps with the contentment of a child.

The Happy Path

'Free will does not mean one will, but many wills conflicting in one man.'

—Flannery O'Connor, *Wise Blood*

ZERO

HOW MUCH DO YOU PULL EACH MONTH after tax? A grand? Five? More?

Not bad, but you're wrong. They pay you nothing. Unless you're a plumber, a prostitute or paper boy, you never see cash. Your employer remits to your bank. Bank remits to bank. The bank dials down certain privileges on your employer's account, and dials up yours. Nothing moves, nothing changes. Zero means nothing, a thousand means nothing, minus a million means nothing. Micro-transistors ratchet and the magnetic surface of distant hard drives rustle. This has been the case so long we forget that money is a metaphor from an ancient marketplace.

The same thing's happening to us: to our assets, our relationships, our souls. Transmitted by technology sufficiently advanced to be indistinguishable from reality. Held remotely. Owned.

All I'm trying to do is wake people up. If I get collateral benefits along the way, that signifies nothing.

Seven thirty. Synchronise watches. This will be fun for everyone.

Not counting Bethany.

¶riotbaby

NOW.

ONE

THE FIRMESS OF J-R'S MORNING ERECTION was bewildering. It pushed painfully away from his stomach. What could cause this intense sensation?

He fumbled for his bedside clock and his hand landed on his phone. Its shape was odd. He peered at it and realised it was his old personal mobile, lying where he generally left his Party BlackBerry.

Slices of memory returned, then stuttered before they gave up the night that had just been. J-R powered up the phone and tapped to open his photos. Lying dry-mouthed in the half-light he paged through the pictures, impressions of the previous night returning on a slow shutter. Dark streets. The boy – Jo – and the East End nightspot where J-R stumbled across him. Images of warmth, countless empty bottles and the snug embrace of a cluster of young men. They didn't cohere into a narrative. J-R had no idea how he'd got home, or who he was by the time he got there.

He put the phone back and stared at the peeling ceiling, rubbing himself a few times, but he was not aroused. He got up and pottered naked around the bedroom, which was in its usual state of catastrophic abandon, clothes strewn about as though in the aftermath of enthusiastic sex. Fat chance. He began to pick at the mess, penis flapping in front of him as though stuck on as a prank. He sniffed hopefully at items before folding them into the chest of drawers. Dirties he dropped in the Ali Baba basket. He moved from room to room, accompanied by radio news. There was more on yesterday's leaks. A woman spoke from a group called GiveMeData, defending DigiCitz, but struggling. A tide was turning against Bethany. J-R stopped in the bedroom doorway to listen, a grey ribbed sock in his hand.

The hell with Krish's reticence: he was locking this thing down too tight. Letting Number Ten lead the defence: they were defending the government but not the minister. If J-R had his way he'd put Bethany up for just one candid interview at today's press event. Get her in front of someone good who wouldn't spare her. Mair, perhaps. She could give him her mea culpa and let people see her honesty. Her commitment. He should call Krish.

Except what if Bethany wasn't honest? He couldn't call until he knew what had taken place between her and Mondan. The key to everything was decrypting that mail attachment.

When he'd finished tidying, he dressed and picked up the landline. The handset smelled of shed skin – he couldn't remember when he'd last used it. Blood still pumped in his penis, which was now stowed sideways in his underwear. Mark answered on the first ring.

'Mark Dinmore.'

'Mark. J-R.'

'Oh. I didn't recognise this number. I've been leaving messages.'

'Yes, apologies. Did you by any chance have something?'

'Are you OK? I was concerned.'

'No, it's just that my BlackBerry is damaged and –'

J-R stopped himself in the lie. That was the old him, rebutting reactively.

'To tell you the truth, Mark, I'm rather lying low. The email I sent you, with the contract, was – intercepted. The police –'

He tailed off, circling his hand in search of clearer language. Mark completed the sentence for him.

'They've been reading your emails.'

'Yes, that's – yes.'

'This is an issue,' said Mark, and fell silent.

'I really wouldn't worry. Everybody is convinced Dani Farr is responsible. I don't think I'm under suspicion as such.'

'In my line of business,' said Mark, 'this is not a small thing.'

Some pressure stored up from the previous day rose in J-R's chest.

'Mark, I—'

'What?' Mark snapped. Mark never snapped.

'I can't help but ask: did you – do anything with that contract after I sent it to you? Share it in any way? Perhaps somehow link to it on your blog? I'm sure not intentionally, but –'

There was a long drawn moment.

'Are you asking what I think you're asking?'

'No. No, of course not. It's an odd coincidence. Apologies, this is unfamiliar ground.'

Mark's sigh broke and crackled on the poor line.

'So your office catches you sharing confidential material and in response you take the battery out of your BlackBerry? Go into hiding?'

J-R said nothing. Mark laying the thing out bare made it ridiculous.

'That's not a logical response. Why not just explain?'

'You're right. You're probably right. I will, at some point. But today is the launch event. I'm not wanted, it seems.'

'Ah.'

'But also, I don't know. Ever since my BlackBerry, ah, broke, I feel I've been off the hook. I have time to think things through.'

Silence on the line

'Are you still there?' said J-R.

There was a sigh, then Mark spoke.

'I'm here.'

'You said you had something?'

'Yes. I've decrypted Bethany's files.'

J-R's heart began to pump in tiny bursts.

'And it's – does it let Bethany off the hook?'

J-R held his breath. Bethany was honest; Bethany was corrupt. Any second he'd know one way or the other. But Mark said nothing. J-R heard typing.

'You've broken the encryption?' he said. 'Read Bethan's file? Is it – connected with the hack?'

'Broken it? Hardly! That would take a quantum computer. Which before you ask hasn't been invented.'

J-R was sure he already knew that.

'No,' said Mark, 'I got in by an easier route. Are you near a PC?'

'I – well, no –' His laptop was still in his backpack, behind the reception desk at Parley's offices. 'Will a tablet do?'

'Sure. I've just emailed you a link.'

J-R tucked the receiver between shoulder and ear then extracted his tablet from the bookshelf, where it was lodged between the two fat volumes of a Gladstone biography.

'Could you read out the address?' he said. 'I'm rather avoiding my emails.'

Mark sighed again and rattled off a long string of characters. J-R fumbled to recreate them on the tablet and hit return. What appeared was a copy of an email from Perce to Bethany.

Beth. Use this to encrypt. Looking forward to.

This was followed by a long block of garbage letters and numbers. And that was the entirety of the mail.

'He's an efficient communicator, isn't he?' said Mark.

'What am I looking at?'

'A document from sic_girl's blog. One of the leaked emails. I found this nugget buried among yesterday's shares.'

'So anyone can see it?'

'Yes, but it's no use to them without your mail – and the encrypted file. There's a load of useless junk like this in the email dump. Nobody else would pick up on this.'

'And this code unlocked our attachment?'

'In a split second.'

Mark went silent again. J-R thought he might burst at the seams.

'For God's sake—'

'Oh, right, sorry. Holiday snaps.'

A burst of bass-heavy music started up from a car outside the open window. J-R grappled with his suddenly oversized tongue.

'Sorry – ah – holiday –?'

'– snaps, yes. The encrypted file contained forty-four twelve-megapixel photos of a Spanish conference hotel. Here. I've shared the folder.'

Mark dictated another stream of characters, taking J-R to an area of Mark's website, followed by a username and password. A shot of a swimming pool filled the screen. Crisp honey paving. The unbroken azure of a pool bouncing back a shard of sunlight. Sea beyond. J-R clicked an arrow and a new picture slid in to replace the pool: livid sunset over ocean. Then another picture. Sean Perce, in long pink swimming shorts, his torso a knot of athlete's muscles, a washed wall of ancient stone behind him. Another click. A new picture slid into place. Spot the difference. J-R's stomach somersaulted.

Perce again, in the same shorts, in front of the same stone wall. Wrapped around him, giggling and lithe, in sunglasses and a red sarong, was Bethany. Childish, relaxed and rather beautiful, the Minister of State for a Digital Society cuddled like a honeymooner against the man whose business was about to receive one hundred and seventy million pounds of taxpayer's money from her.

Mark continued in a flat tone.

'You've got to the two-shot?'

'Yes.'

'I'm assuming they used a timer. They wouldn't be dumb enough to have someone take it for them.' J-R paged through several individual shots of Bethany japing on a balcony. 'I thought I recognised the pool so I did some googling. I was right – this is the Excelsior in Cádiz. Which was the venue for an event I attended

last month called *Public Digital Futures: A Global Perspective*.
Among whose other attendees were listed – well, I guess you
know.'

Only now did J-R register the suppressed fury in Mark's voice.
It had been there, simmering under the whole conversation.

'Mark –'

'See, this really bloody bothers me. This is who you work for?
The conviction politician?'

'This doesn't mean she—'

'It doesn't?'

'No, this is—'

'This is *stupid*. Crass and predictable. Sending each other
photos? Even encrypted!'

Fat water pushed at the back of J-R's eyeballs. He willed it
back and sat as still as he was able, levelling his breathing. Had he
spent the last two years of his life selling the public out to a vested
interest?

A thought came to him. If two old pros were crazy enough to
send each other goofy pictures, in spite of the risks – did it mean
they genuinely cared for one another?

'This doesn't answer the question,' he said.

'Oh, really?'

'It doesn't tell us what Mondan is doing with the data. Whatever
Bethan's motives, we need to know what they're up to before I—'

'Before you what, exactly?'

'I just need to know.'

Mark breathed out slowly.

'Sure. I want that, too. I'm – not happy with this. I'll tell you
what. We're going to talk to Mondan, OK, you and me. And then
you're going to talk to your own people. All right?'

Sick of the photos, J-R shut off his tablet.

'You know,' Mark's voice continued, 'when we design systems,
we start by envisaging the main route through. The least compli-
cated scenario. We call it *the happy path*. The happy path is easy,
but it's never the way things really go. Most of the work is

figuring out all the less favourable scenarios – deviations from the happy path – and trapping them. Tying off loose ends.'

'It sounds like politics. Sod's Law tends to apply.'

'Life isn't exclusively the happy path, John. Or seldom at all.'

J-R nodded. Was this intended as consolation? Either way, he was grateful for the gentler tone.

'Can I see you, Mark? Today?' he said. 'I –' The rest of the sentence was unavailable. He tried again. 'Do you know Parley's offices in Shoreditch? I want to introduce you to someone I think might be useful.'

'At Parley? Is that wise?'

'Everyone will be focused on the launch event today. And also – I seem to have left my bike there yesterday. And my coat. And my laptop bag.'

¶TurdoftheDay

I can't do this any more.

No pic.

I'm sorry, I need t#

TWO

FROM THE DOOR THE INTERN tapped her watch. Hell, the conf call. One of the cops caught Jonquil and the intern exchanging a look. She shrugged at him: *So?*

Somehow in the next three minutes she had to clear the room. Raeworth and Ackroyd, London's finest, had been installed at her meeting table for the past half hour and were making it super-clear they wouldn't move their butts till Jonquil gave them Danielle. She didn't have Danielle and wouldn't have been inclined to hand her over if she did; but she needed to clear the room before she went on the line with Sean in – what? – two minutes thirty-five. She couldn't have Sean knowing she was receiving courtesy calls from the five-oh. With more time and an ideal world, she'd have preferred to ditch them without giving up Danielle – but needs must.

'So, look,' she said. 'Officer. You want to speak with Danielle Farr? So do I. You got to wait in line. She'll be here for a disciplinary at nine. Right now,' she flipped up her sleeve to check her Rolex – one minute fifty-five. 'I got confidential business. Unrelated.' She hopped up and grabbed the door. 'So if you could wait in – here you go, in the room right across here?'

They didn't move. So, OK. She had to sell them on it.

'You'll be able to see when Danielle arrives, through the glass panel, look.'

The head cop twitched forward in his chair. One minute thirty. If she could only get him to raise his butt she could keep him moving through the door.

'And pastries! We have pastries. A danish? Genevieve, could you be a total babe and set up a breakfast collation in 2.03? Bless you.'

She looked back at the cops to see if this was landing. Did British cops like a danish? Should she offer pies?

'There's a phone right there. We'll call through the second Danielle arrives, I guarantee.'

The two exchanged a look, then rose together and filed into meeting pod 2.03. Jonquil popped her door shut and checked her watch. Fifteen seconds. She patted her hair straight. Damn but life can be exhausting when you got to spin the plates. She dialled in to conference. Sean didn't do pleasantries at the best of times but his starting gambit was direct even for him.

'I'm going to kill Parley,' he said. 'Dead, this weekend.'

Jonquil stared at the phone.

'I'm – sorry, Sean, *what?*'

'I think I was pretty clear. I'm about to terminate your service.'

Jonquil clicked the button of her pen. *Clickety clickety.* Sean's voice fizzed out of the spider phone.

'Hello? Are you getting me?'

'Sean, Sean, you're being hasty. We have something real big here. For the whole group. A new narrative.'

'You know what, Jonquil, you're correct. We have something big. A big looming shitstorm which you're about to remove by pressing the kill button on this sideshow.'

Jonquil had been planning to build up to the big reveal but she'd no choice now but to blurt it out.

'We have evidence that sic_girl is gaining intelligence. She's alive. This is the biggest thing since ever.'

Her hook delivered, she hovered over the phone and waited for Sean to bite. There was a long pause before he came back quieter and more measured.

'Oh, Christ. This is what you have? Net intelligence? I thought you'd have prepped something more robust. That is so nineteen ninety-nine. God's sake, the net is already intelligent. You know, I'm sitting in the Top Spot here –'

Jonquil rolled her eyes. Sean loved to call his top-floor office that. He'd be sitting by the glass plate wall watching giant displays flicker real-time content from a billion users.

'– watching the screens. They see everything. Our personalisation and search are already twice as smart as our users and they know a thousand times more. Parley is a penny-in-the-slot clown. It doesn't matter if your algorithms got a little smarter. I have better. I bought Parley as a pollen-flower to attract and track consumers, not to stir up the shit for important political contacts.'

'Oh, get real. This isn't because of sic_girl. This is because your data's been hacked and you're trying to divert attention by fucking with my business.'

Distortion on the speaker as Sean's volume rose.

'And *you're* shitting on my doorstep when I have fifty million visitors about to land – courtesy HM Government. This is the big push and we need to bring together all our verticals, no mess.'

'Dammit, Sean—'

'No. Are you going to kill Facebook?

Jonquil bit hard on her lower lip. Sean continued on.

'Are you going to kill Facebook?'

'No, of course not.'

'Are you going to kill Twitter? Pinterest?'

'Sean—'

'No. Eighteen million users? Big in Germany? *Germany*? What are we even talking about? All Parley has ever been is a moderately efficient data capture and research tool. And one enormous reputational risk. So listen. I need thirty good Java engineers to pick up what's about to come in from the Digital Citizen. How many devs do you have?'

She waited – but Sean could always wait longer. She worked the button of her pen. *Clickety clickety clickety.* Silence. She folded.

'Twenty-six.'

'All right then. Once Parley is down you can give me those – I'll find the other four by slimming other projects.'

'One of the twenty-six is Danielle Farr.'

'OK, so give me her. Have them here at 404 on Monday. Nine sharp.'

Clickety clickety clickety.

'Sean. I am CEO here. I do resourcing.'

'And yet it would seem that I'm your boss. How do you figure that?'

The chrome head of the pen snapped clean off in Jonquil's hand.

¶AStrangeFish

    i love a hotel breakfast but this is pants
    they call this place The Pugin Lounge – more like Pukin lol
    scrabbled egg = cavity insulation
    bacon = peeled eczema
    nom nom not

THREE

'A-A-AND – RUN VT! A-a-and – the minister! Yay! Applause!'

Jodi (with an *i*) was account rep with The Pow-Wow Arrangers, the firm of event organisers brought in by the MinTech comms team to run the launch. She was also the most irritating person Bethany had met in her long political career – even taking into account constituency surgeries.

This afternoon's surgery was a long way off. Right now, with just (Bethany checked her watch) two and a half hours until the launch event began, Jodi was holding front of stage for a rag-tag understudy rehearsal. Clearly they'd struggled to round up enough people to act as stand-ins.

DRAMATIS PERSONAE:
Alex Kubelick (popular blogger and host of the launch event):
　　　　played by Nanci from the Pow-Wow Arrangers (also with an *i*)
Bethany Lehrer (an embattled minister and cheating wife):
　　　　played by Ziggy the assistant sound engineer
Sean Perce (a caddish entrepreneur):
　　　　played by Danny Notley, aka 'J-R Junior', Bethany's junior spad

With the peppy energy of a CBeebies presenter, Jodi marshalled her ensemble. Levels were checked and cues confirmed. Bethany, though ostensibly going over her speech with Krish at the back of the hall, was transfixed by the sight of the vast Croatian sound man, Ziggy, lumbering onstage to the amplified strains of 'Are "Friends" Electric?' – representing her. Loops of black flex swung from his belt as he cheerily waved a centimetre of rollie at an imaginary crowd. Nanci bounced at the podium clapping her hands with rather more enthusiasm than Bethany expected to see from the real Alex Kubelick, when the real Bethany Lehrer appeared onstage later this morning. For three days Kubelick had tried to wriggle out of the gig, prevented only by Krish's wheedling, veiled threats and, eventually, out-and-out bullying.

'A-a-a-and the minister speaks!' announced Jodi, cueing her performer with a slender finger.

Ziggy descended upon the podium, sending Nanci flying like a sapling poleaxed by a bulldozer. He stared out across the empty hall, so deep in his role he'd forgotten the auditorium was empty. He leaned down and intoned into the mic in a dignified Eastern European drone.

'My friends. I am happy. I am here.'

Jodi cut in.

'Oka-a-ay, so we skip ahead to the minister handing back to Alex, and—'

But Ziggy was not about to surrender his moment in the limelight.

'Dear friends, I thank you with my heart.'

'OK, thank you, Minister,' said Jodi.

'Friends—'

'Yes, thank you! Thank you, Minister! Thank you!'

For Ziggy, the penny dropped. He gave a grave nod and leaned into the microphone.

'I thank you, friends.'

It was enormous fun. Perhaps they should use this bunch for the main event.

Krish called her back to the planet.

'Are you OK that we don't mention the leaks?'

'*Leaks?*' she said. 'I thought they were *malicious and politically motivated online postings?*'

Not for the first time in the last forty-eight hours, Krish subjected her to a cold gaze. God, Krish, do we need to talk?

'Does that not depend whether the *postings* are true or no?'

'Don't start,' she said. 'Not here, all right? Where were we?'

'Just saying, like. OK. Information security, Mondan as industry leader.'

'Brazen it out.'

'Apparently.'

She mouthed the double-spaced words, trying them in her mouth. Krish read alongside her.

'This is good,' she said, 'Better.'

'Uh huh.'

'We don't mention cost.'

'Why would we?' he asked.

'Because it's only costing a hundred and seventy million?'

'Right. A snap.'

He was probably right. Nobody wanted to hear about you spending public money.

'Could Digital Citizen go on without me?' she said. 'In your opinion. Would it?'

She hadn't meant to ask that. Krish gave her a very level look.

'What do you think?'

'Honestly? I think – oh.'

She dropped the pages to her lap and made a pushing down gesture with the butt of her hand. Flapped it in front of her face to wave back the flush. Got control back.

'I think I'm being had,' she said. 'I think everything I do this week is to some pre-arranged dance I have to step through before – I think I want you to drag up something on Andrew wannabe-me Carpenter. Something we can get out that screws him – to the point the PM has no choice but to keep me on.'

Krish snorted.

'Andrew, aye,' he said. 'Andrew Carpenter can't wire a plug.'

'No? For real? Krish, that's amazing. That's perfect. Can you get it out in time for the lunchtimes?'

Krish was giving her his level look. Oh.

'You were speaking figuratively.'

He nodded.

'Look,' he said. 'You want to make this work?'

'Of course, yes.'

She touched at the corners of her eyes; would need to check her make-up.

'The speech, then?'

'Yes. Yes.'

The corner of his mouth turned up just a little. She read on.

'I like this,' she said. '*Can anyone tell me how much sensitive public data went missing in the post this year? Ten thousand separate items. But public information lost from government websites? Anyone? Let me tell you. Nil. Not a single kilobyte.*'

'Pause on that, let it hang.'

'Good line. Was that you?'

A politician can spot the briefest hesitation. Why would Krish hesitate?

'J-R. He emailed a rewrite first thing yesterday.'

'Oh, good. Where is he? And actually, why the hell is my senior advisor briefing me on a speech instead of my comms spad?'

'He's – busy at Parley,' said Krish.

'Today? He's at Parley while we're launching a year of his work?'

'He sends his apologies.'

It was her turn to give him the gimlet eye.

'Do I need to worry about something?'

'Worry about the speech.'

'The speech is good. Do I need to worry about J-R?'

A blast of the Pointer Sisters singing 'Totally Automatic' shredded the air, cutting off any reply from Krish. At the front of the hall, Jodi waved gibbon arms towards the sound desk.

'Thank you!' she cried. 'Thank you! Thank you!'

`launch_proposal_FINAL MoS comments.docx`

client: ministry of technology
account executive: jodi gartner
project: digital citizen launch

The Pow-Wow Arrangers are thrilled to be given the opportunity to tender for this exciting opportunity and major event that will help shape the digital future of millions of citizens.

This proposal is based on a Key Thematic Proposition of ALWAYS ON. The Digital Citizen is ALWAYS ON. And so its launch event should be no exception. This proposal explains how this key benefit of 24/7 Government will be promoted at the Digital Citizen Launch.

In summary:

- All delegates to be given dayglo I'M ALWAYS ON! ID lanyards. [MoSaDS1: God, no. Totally open to abuse. I'M ALWAYS ON HEAT, I'M ALWAYS ON THE LOO, ON CRACK, etc., etc., etc.]
- All-new HD-TV NewPowerScreen technology (provided by project Key Partner Mondan) will beam a live close-up relay of every presenter to a giant 12-metre on-stage screen [MoSaDS2: J-R, please tell these jokers they are not getting their HD cameras within the same postcode as my gaping pores. I haven't had a facial in 6 months!! I want a Dept logo or something equally non-distracting behind me while I'm talking.]
- Interactive voter buttons bring digital democracy to the event, allowing delegates to vote and comment on the proceedings. [MoSaDS3: No. No, no. Absolutely bloody no. Don't they know there are journos present???]
- 'Digi-sparkler' LEDs on every delegate table give a real-time display of live data from the onstage digital audio feed. [MoSaDS4: English, please. Does this mean flashy lights? If so, say so. I'm totally good with flashy lights.]
- All delegates get a free iPod Shuffle® containing a podcast of the whole event, to keep with them after they leave, demonstrating how the Digital Citizen follows the citizen wherever they go. [MoSaDS5: a)

Do these muppets seriously think we're going to have the content ready in time to make a frigging PODCAST? b) On whose budget?? c) Does this pass the Daily Mail test, Govt waste, etc., etc?? d) Though on the other hand bribery is a double-plus-good idea with the fourth estate. Hmm . . .

- NeonWeave® carpets guide the delegates to their tables and to the venue's DISRAELI BAR, where they can purchase 2 complimentary drinks using their ID swipecards. [MoSaDS6: OK, now THAT sounds cool.]

FOUR

THAT WAS A KNOCK: faint but there's no doubt. Frozen in the act of packing, Dani looks around the sealed room. Up to this moment this antiseptic hotel room has been a refuge. Now it's a trap.

It has to be those Duffer stormtroopers. It's twelve hours since she slipped away from them at the flat. By doing so, she good as confirmed it was her who did the sic_girl mischief. Crazy to run – and now they have her penned like a wasp in a glass.

But how *did* they find her? She paid for this room on Terry Salmon's credit card, like everything else she's bought since she ditched herself yesterday. Only Gray knows about the card and even he has idea zero what she's planning.

Another knock: and she registers how tentative the sound is. Such a contrast to yesterday's battering-ram. Lured by the soft-ness she steps to the door and releases the catch. Watching herself do this she thinks, *really?* But she does it. The door swings in and standing stupid on the hotel carpet is Colin from the office. Dough-boy Colin Randell.

'Oh, what?' says Dani. 'What the *fuck?*'

He can only stand and mumble, *sorry.* No trace of the cock-sure dickweed she knows. They stand dumbfounded, then he gestures at the room and verbalises something like *cn I cm n?* She can't think of a way that could make the situation any weirder so she steps back and lets his mass pass across the threshold. He moves to the centre of the room and hovers, agitated by the tumble of unmade sheets. She shuts the door. They eye each other along the little hallway created by the bathroom. As she walks towards him his bulk shifts slightly backwards. Small mass acting on large.

'So. Colin. Paint me a picture of how you are not perving my every move.'

'Sorry. I was worried. About you.'

Which was the last thing she expected.

'You – *hah?*' she manages.

'I thought you might do something, well, dangerous, because. When you said you were where Bethany Lehrer will be. And so I mined Parley. You stopped proffering yesterday but I guessed you had other identities. And there were all these proffers about this hotel being where the event is today. And. And I did a related terms mine and cross-reffed with frequency analysis to your signature pattern and rate of proffers. And I saw your proffers from this morning. As AStrangeFish. About hotel breakfast in the Pugin Lounge. And AStrangeFish was newborn a few hours after you vanished and I worked it out? I'm good at working things out. And it's you, isn't it?'

Body slam. Conclusion: nothing she does will ever be hidden from anybody. She starts to nod, then stops.

'Wait. What – you're not making sense, Colin. When did I say anything about Bethany? OK, I mentioned the hotel but I sure as hell haven't proffered about her.'

Except in whispers to that guy, identikid. Surely – no. Colin cannot be identikid. In what universe would this tub of steaming lard call himself *kid*?

'You did. You mentioned it when we were doing chat. Last night?'

He's giving her this seven megaton LOOK. The room goes out of focus then zooms back in at vertigo speed. Oh, Christ, no. Dani makes a noise in her throat that's something like *you, you, you,* but gets no further.

'I'm monkey_love, Dani. You and me. monkey_love and SafeWord. It's us. We're like a MeatSpace couple!' A laugh that doesn't come off. 'It's funny really. At first I didn't know it was you. I was just, you know, attracted.'

She wants to puke. He makes himself laugh again. It sounds like a cleaver landing in a cabbage. This is a practised speech.

'And you know what? The thing that first attracted me to you in open forum was actually the speed of your typing! And you were, you know. Really mental. Back then it was only SafeWord I was with. But over time, Dani leaked out. Things you said: I worked it out. Like I say, I'm good at working things out.'

'How long?'

'Uh?'

'How long have you known?'

'Dani, there's something real. With us.'

'How long?'

'Why does it matter? *I* haven't changed. It was *us* who thought those things together.'

She sits on the bed. It's a surrender but her legs need a reboot.

'*At* me.'

'What?'

'You thought those things *at* me. Did them *at* me. Every fucking day, watching me. Knowing – in front of everyone.'

'That isn't fair.'

Spasms pass down the left side of Colin's face and his arm twitches as though it's about to fly out and grab her or hit her. He stares at the beige bedspread.

'And what a fucking power trip was that, Colin? Did you enjoy slapping down the scary bitch, safe in your cubicle? Is that it?'

'I – you liked what we did, too.'

'No. No. *We* didn't *do* anything, Colin.'

'But you always—'

'I what? I loved it did I?'

'No, you *understand*. You understand the reality of, of –'

His hands roll in a frantic tombola motion, trying to wind out the right words. This man she's barely glanced at in four years of office smack-downs, who isn't real enough to hate. It doesn't add up – the red wound she gave someone, pure as a stone on a beach: in the real, what touched her was the chubby paw hanging from this fat wreck of a boy of a man. Memories march up one by one to stab her in the gut. She lets them come. Her breath slows and she watches Colin shake. The throb of breakfast news starts up from the next room.

'I do. I actually think I do. But it doesn't matter how real it was. It's not real enough to make what you did OK.'

He's started, quietly, to weep, in a helpless stream.

'I'm no good at, at –'

She puts a hand on his forearm. He jerks it away as if shocked, then tentatively replaces it into her hand. She gives him a short squeeze. His arm-flesh is Haribo marshmallow. She stands up and lets him go.

'Colin, if I'm honest, I don't think anyone is.'

She looks around the room, but there's nothing like a tissue in sight.

'Listen, I really have to go,' she says.

He looks at her as if she's about to pull the plug on his life support. She grabs the laptop from the bed and stuffs it in her backpack. She looks around for anything she might have missed.

'I do just have to go. Wait here till you feel better. The door will lock itself. We can talk about this. Later. Or email. I'm – I am angry at you, OK, but it's going to be all right. All right? Col?'

Colin nods rapidly and keeps looking puppy-eyes at her. Who but Dani could end up consoling her own stalker? She moves to go but the panic in Colin's eyes makes her hesitate.

'I do want to help,' he says. 'You're – you're not about to do something crazy?'

He looks like he's been punched repeatedly in the face. She shakes her head.

'Nothing crazier than I've already done. God, Col. It's OK. And look – thanks for worrying actually. I'm glad someone's worrying.'

He nods and wipes his nose on his sleeve. She makes to leave a second time.

'But Dani, Dani.' Again, she hesitates. 'I wanted to say: I've done something wrong.'

Dani nods.

'Let's leave it.'

'No, no, I don't mean this –'

'Colin, mate. I. Need. To go.'

She sweeps open the door and goes. Colin starts to say, *But*, then stops. He watches the mechanism bring the door back into place. Nothing moves. Through the bedroom wall, the breakfast theme builds to a motivational peak.

'I did the hack,' says Colin to nobody.

¶identikid >>whisper -> ¶AStrangeFish
You here? You with us?

¶AStrangeFish >>whisper -> ¶identikid
something to do first.
later maybe.

FIVE

SEAN IS TRAINING. Silver-white Mizunos strike the Hackney pavement to the beat of in-ear Boses. The mp3 strapped to his arm is geared to live consumer stats. The most-downloaded tracks of the global week roll from the cloud into his eardrums. He hears what the market hears, thinks what they think.

He runs by a graffitied wall: <TAKEBACK>. Gloss eyes of the morning commute catch the spring light: they are receivers, taking signal from the street, from storefronts, smartphones, bus sides, points-of-sale, mag racks, branded T's.

From the headphones a female voice marks 4k. Sean's pace is steady. He's been running since 08:10, running since forever, since uni, those long hard runs. *The Bionic Grebo* they called him, though they only ever saw him in long-shot as he pounded the fields by the reservoir. He read them cold. Always asking, *what is it they want?* Online through the night in his digs, air bitter with sweat and solder, his needs monastic: two mains sockets, a one-bar heater and the pop, squeal and crackle of a modem. Blu-Tacked on the wall Alan Turing broke the rope at Walton Athletic Club. Beside him boyish Elyse Martingale probed the patchboard of the prototype Manchester Baby. What pride to be there before everything became smooth. So few of them then, locating one another behind the cursors of slow-load bulletin boards. Their homebrew circuits the template for what came after.

For Sean it was always the data. The logics he cooked up in utility bedsits now feed the smartphones of the City workers crowding his jogging route. Their devices are hungry for data. They suck it in and fire it through the air and paving stones. They need, and their needs are predictable. Consumption ruled by bounded appetites driving runnels into data sets they never see. Sean sees through their skin and into their data. It's his gift and curse.

Her, with the multi-buckled bag and this season's feathered cut to mask her plainness. Subscribes to *Grazia* on her tablet. Every Saturday, before she shops, she digests the catwalk snaps like holy writ.

That man-boy in Reiss pulls a ton with commission, headhunting for investment banks. Favours a classier stand-up drinking joint. By the bottle, export only. Violence sells to him.

Her. Consumes 4–5 hours social media per diem. When stating a preference would say she trusts her online friends more than her real ones.

The salarywoman in ill-fitting L.K. Bennett. Downloads illegally. Says it's free advertising for the labels.

He buys only high-end porn. His male partner doesn't know.

She blogs about her ugly child, day after living day.

Fuck and bless them all. Sean knows them before he sees them. Bubble-sorted terabytes of consumer data indexed in a nanosecond. The data feeds the wetware in his skull. It's how ideas arrive – and on a good day, these ideas can be monetised.

He passes a boarded-up lot. *MISSING. WORK FROM HOME. ONE NIGHT ONLY.* Flyposts irk him. Who looks at walls, with personal space available in their hands? What if smartphones and social had existed on 9-11? No plastic wallets of wilting paper pinned to downtown hoardings, just one enormous online wall. Imagine the data they would have captured overnight. Pain, vulnerability; opportunity. Sean would have beamed the blurry loved ones – tuxedos, prom gowns, uniforms – all along the London skyline.

He skips off the pavement to skirt a City boy staring at his Samsung. Left onto Shackleton Road. City Road another left.

Directly towards 404. Newsfeeds and market tickers on the great screens, 60–60–24–7. With the inevitability of the random, what now cycles into place is Bethany, storeys tall, elbowing her way to an official car. *PIG-GATE – MINISTER 'SHOWED BIAS IN AWARDING CONTRACT' CLAIMS ANON BLOGGER.* Sean loses stride then regains it. He's been keeping his thoughts away from his sweet well-intentioned minister. Really, though: her fault. Whoever accessed those mails did it through some insecure government network. Never trust tech implemented by the state.

The clip loops.

Beth'll keep fumbling for an out but her ticket's marked. She'll scrabble for any small advantage, burn boats; maybe she'll even last out today's launch event before she finds she's nowhere left to turn.

He does care for her, probably; or he did. If she only had the luxury of failing to give a flying fuck what people think; like Sean. Mondan reads everything in and gives nothing back. They'll say nothing about the Digital Citizen hack. The facts are too murky to see through. Silence is the cleanest form of truth.

It was pure pleasure to fire the lardball who did the hack – and to shove a lethal gag clause up his arse. Colin Randell. How could such a nimrod apology for a code monkey have made it through their recruitment screens? He's finished now of course, along with the security geeks who failed to spot his sloppy paw-marks on Sean's servers, Sean's data. What a sorry mess.

Though the lad has skills. Far as they could piece it together, he'd dipped into their data warehouse four times in total, over two months. First three times he took nothing, which made no sense – if you've just cracked the tightest nutshell in the world of digital security, surely you take a trophy out with you? – but the bitch of it was, every one of these pointless exploits counted as a breach. Each time Randell triggered their digital alarms – clumsily, in spite of his evident skills, to the point where you'd almost say he *wanted* them to know he'd been in. So three times Sean had to report the breach to the ministry; and each time he needed to manage Bethany a little harder to keep her from going public over what he assured her were housekeeping matters. Matters he would fix. And bless her heart, she didn't bleat – even at the risk of lying to Parliament.

Then, two weeks back, in spite of all the extra protections Sean's security boys had laid in place, fat-boy waltzes in for the fourth time – and this time he lifts the entire DigiCitz data set. Two days later: Pigglies. Fucking Pigglies. And the worst of it? This time there were no alarm bells. This time Sean didn't know a thing about it until sic_girl started stirring the shit.

But for the first time, Randell had screwed up. He'd failed to wipe one minute digital fingerprint when he erased the logfiles. Sean's data forensics boys spotted it yesterday and right away dragged fatso up to the Top Spot, where Sean browbeat him to a whimpering jelly – but still he didn't spill. He said it was a free-lance gig but wouldn't say for who. Knew Sean couldn't press if he wouldn't prosecute. Knew Sean never would.

That dimension of the thing was troubling. Who would want the DigiCitz data now: a few thousand lives, a pilot? Why not wait another six months to get a hundred times more data?

No matter. They're clean now. They've given government plausible lines. They've denied the hack. The three minor breaches were manageable, but no way were they going to land the national contract if the hack came out. So: on his instructions, all traces of it will be erased. At noon tomorrow they've manufactured a watertight rationale for wiping every byte of data off those stacks. They'll restore the data from backup. Nothing will be said. It rolls on. The launch event will go ahead this morning as planned.

Sean has no qualms about sharing a stage with Beth. She's damaged goods, but he's never cared about protecting his reputation. Reputation is for politicians and sneaker manufacturers. It doesn't mean a shit when you're the first place people land when they power up in the morning and the last click they make before shutting down at night. Who worries about the reputation of the air?

Without breaking stride Sean takes a power-up from his bottle. The voice in his head tolls 8k. Arrow-straight, he locks onto the bright glass doors of 404 City.

¶**TurdoftheDay**

He fired me.

I only ever did what I was told. Now I'm fired.

Today's turd is called Sean.

SIX

'MY GRANDMOTHER BELIEVED that if we wish to know freedom, we must first be free to know.'

Bethany looked across the crowd. Her grandmother's dog-eared book lay on the lectern under her palm, ready to brandish as the speech hit its final confessional spot. J-R had done her proud with that moment of spontaneous candour. This speech must be completely *meant* if it was to stand a chance of holding back the tide of hearsay and spite.

'Elyse Martingale was a firebrand. A radical. Quite a contrast, you might think, to the behaviour we now demand of politicians. I wonder what she'd think if she looked at me now, a Minister of State, a not insignificant cog in the machine of state –'

If she only believed that.

'– that state which, according to her, will soon be swept away by a tide of freely available information. Well, perhaps her more apocalyptic predictions have not come to pass. Or, perhaps, in a way, they have.'

A pin could drop. All eyes sharpened. She could do this. Maintain this heartfelt register. Deny, discredit. Lie to the crowd, lie to Krish, lie to herself. So swallowed in spin she wouldn't know an honest statement if it spilled out of her mouth.

She spoke on, the wide hall packed. There were even a couple of fixed cameras from the rolling news. In theory, this could go out live, though she doubted they'd bother – filler at best. That was OK. Boring she could handle.

She slid the page sideways and drew breath on BENEFITS OF THE DIGITAL CITIZEN. Dotted around the hall, people stood in unison. It was unclear what had been their cue. More people – maybe twenty – moved in from somewhere to line the side aisles. Bethany kept reading. All the people standing were young. Other audience members craned their necks to see. She ran her finger down the words, keeping place, and the words emerged in sequence from her mouth. *Real opportunities. Digital empowerment. Access to all.* From behind her politician's face she watched the double doors at the rear of the hall jar open. A group in parkas and hoodies progressed up the centre aisle, a uniformed security man moving uncertainly among them.

Perhaps a hundred people were standing now, faces measured, young, attractive. They filled all three aisles and the area below the stage. A glint of stage light reflected from the lower-lip piercing of a girl near the front of the pack, her dreadlocks tied back with a batik scarf.

They stopped their advance. Again, no visible cue. The security man struggled up the centre aisle. Nobody blocked his way but the volume of bodies slowed him. A few were filming him on their phones. Quiet panic slid around the hall but Bethany was glassy calm. She turned another page. *TAKING BRITAIN PLC ONLINE.* In the centre of the group, directly in front of the podium, stood a lean young red-headed man. In the spill of light, he stared up at Bethany and smiled slightly, making his face shine. She struggled to move her eyes across the hall as she read. This young man was magnetic. Dreadlocks, pierced nose, little tufts of facial hair. Still smiling, he put a finger on his nose, pressed it flat and let out an enormous *oink*.

Shit.

The boy kept his finger there. Everyone else reached into pockets, bags, belts, and pulled out little rubber pouches. They shook them loose. Not pouches: masks. Some kids were pulling them over their heads. Nubbly ears, bald pink heads. Snouts.

Shit.

Cameraphones were being raised in the crowd. A technician hopped up to train one of the TV cameras on the group. Krish was at the sidelines, shoving an angular young man who was blocking his route to the stage. Everyone but the boy had on a pig mask.

Shit shit shit.

The boy reached for the zip on his hooded jacket and slid it carefully down. As he shrugged the jacket off his shoulders, the whole crowd of pigs began to unbutton plaid shirts, unzip parkas, pull T-shirts over heads. Beneath his jacket, the boy was bare-chested. His ribs showed in the half-light like a mediaeval Jesus. He couldn't have been more than twenty. His eyes were on her.

The word *flashmob* appeared in Bethany's head. She'd never been clear what it meant, but surely it was this. For the first time, she stumbled on her words. People were standing, talking openly, confronting protestors as they slowly disrobed. Bras were unlatched, knotwork tattoos revealed – along with other black markings on their skin. The security man's West African features creased into a shout.

The boy unbuttoned his jeans and eased them down. His cock flopped out as he bent forward. The others leaned down to undress their lower halves and kick off shoes.

Bethany stopped reading. How absurd to pretend this wasn't occurring. She had to engage them.

'Hello. Perhaps before you – no, please. Please, before you –'

Could she not say 'strip'? Was she really so much of a politician she couldn't even mention a hundred naked people?

'I don't know what you're hoping to do here –'

But really? She did.

Cameras fizzed and splashed across the hall. The boy in the front rose to full height, facing her. Others followed suit, creating rank after rank of naked pigs. Bethany tried not to look at the boy's penis, which was long, slender and surrounded by thick red hair. It was an effort of will, but MINISTER STARES

AT MAN'S COCK was not the headline she wanted from this costly event.

'Please, please. If you have a point to make there are better ways to make it,' she said into the mic; but their dogged stillness called her out.

Something was written on the young man's body, in permanent marker. She scanned the bodies shaking off their last bras and socks. All were covered in scratchy capitals and numerals. She could not make them out.

The whole group was naked. They stood motionless but in control. Krish, who had made it to the apron of the stage, was mouthing and pantomiming at her. Could something turn this situation? Something she could do?

The pig-mob began to peel away towards the steps at each side of the stage. Krish was caught up in the group to her left. Another question arrived in her head: was she in danger?

She backed away from the podium. Glancing behind her she saw the projection screen, which should have been displaying a giant Digital Citizen logo – the winking face made up of ones and zeros. It had been co-opted. Shouting from the vast screen now was a pig face, also drawn from text characters: the same one they used when they hacked the homepage. Below it, the words *STRIPPED OF OUR DATA*, then an animated flurry of information, too fast to read: names, dates, code numbers. Personal data. Presumably real data from this group. Underneath the scrolling data was a static message she knew only too well: *NAKED AND UNADORNED*. And beneath this, a logo.

<takebackID>

She turned back. A file of naked protesters lined the front of the stage, their skinny ribs and pert young arses accentuated in the strong shadows of the lights. Krish was trying to navigate round the group without touching anything inappropriate. Down to the side, DS Raeworth and DC Ackroyd forced their way through the crowd, Ackroyd clipping a young man in the head with his raised elbow. Two TV cameras were now in front of the stage, one trained on her, the other on the young ringleader, who still stood in front of the stage, staring up at her.

Not waiting for Krish to reach her, Bethany made a little scream of frustration and turned tail to the right-hand wings. Nobody was there. She glanced across the stage and saw her team and the event managers beckoning frantically from the opposite side. No sign of Sean. Before the event began he'd barely caught her eye: where the hell had he got to now?

She shook her head and pointed behind her, indicating the way she'd go. No way she was about to be filmed doing a comedy double-take walk across the back of the stage. She needed to get a long way away. She turned and entered the dark of the backstage area, led by the green glow of a fire exit.

She pushed the door beneath the sign. As she stepped through, a hard little hand grabbed her forearm from the darkness. Another grabbed her torso, sliding up from behind her to cross her breasts. She struggled to get free but the hand and arm were locked in place. They pulled her backwards, forcing her arm behind her. As she struggled, in the light from the closing door she caught a spike of purple over pale, pale skin. Her assailant was small but strong. An acid voice hissed from the dark.

'Going somewhere, cunt?'

From *The Electronic Radical*
by Dr Elyse Martingale (1957, Gollancz)

What will decide our fate? Who shall control this information? In reply I repeat as an *a priori* fact: it is in the nature of information to make itself free. On this basis, there can be no doubt who shall prevail.

I tell you with confidence: our future is an electronic pastoral where all roam free. No longer shall petty-fogging officialdom determine our fates, simply by virtue of the control we have fool-ishly ceded over our information. All that is true shall be transpar-ently displayed. All falsehood shall be cancelled out.

Naked and unadorned we shall stand. What remains will be bare facts alone. We shall be judged as we are.

SEVEN

'IS THIS WHAT YOU PEOPLE DO? Click!' The girl snapped tight fingers three inches from Bethany's face. 'And you ruin someone?'

Speech had abandoned Bethany. All her life, words had flowed from her mouth like melting wax. Why would they run dry now?

The girl grabbed another handful of brochures from the cardboard box and flung them at Bethany, who ducked as best she could from a sitting position – but one struck her in the lip, hard. Print-work slithered down her and spilled from her lap, joining the dozens of brochures already carpeting the concrete floor. *WORLD CLASS FACILITIES FOR WORLD LEADING EVENTS*, read the cover copy.

'You took my fucking life, you condescending hag! In a day you took it. And you just sit there?'

It's true that Bethany was sitting, on a plastic utility chair: unbound but certainly a hostage. The concrete echo chamber smelled of solvent. A table was rammed against the door. In front of it stood Dani Farr, her whole face livid as the claret splash that coated her neck and jaw. She turned to pull more brochures from the box on the table and wielded them. They seemed to be her only weapon. Was anyone ever killed by a brochure? Bethany wiped at her bruised lip: blood or sweat?

She should get up and walk, of course she should. She had five or six inches on this crazy scamp. She should push past, move the table, figure out the push-bar lock on the door. But how long would all that take? The girl had shown extraordinary strength when she dragged Bethany down here; punched her stomach and kidneys; yanked her six flights down the emergency stairwell by a handful of hair. And, Bethany would freely admit, she was terrified. What was the girl after? How far was she prepared to go? Forcing her way out was not an option. She had to tip this back her way. An unwanted thought came to her: *I'm going to be late for constituency surgery.* As Dani raised the fan of brochures to head height, she found her voice.

'Let me help you, Dani. How can I help you?'

The girl froze. But before Bethany could speak, the brochures were rammed back in her face.

'I did nothing! Nothing! Do you know what they're calling me, cunt?'

The word was a gut punch from such a small and shrill attacker. Bethany had spent her life fighting for a sister's right to be spared that word of hate. That male word. Now this torn rag doll was using it to assault her. The absurd unfairness on top of everything.

'Listen. No! *Listen* to me.' She brushed aside the glossy paper handful. 'This stunt of yours is ruining something important you stupid –' don't call her a girl, don't belittle her '– child!'

Shit. Come *on,* mouth!

The girl stamped on the spot.

'Fuck! You!'

She slammed the brochures onto the table. Her frustration was nuclear. Her white cheeks were coloured with baby-flush and there were tears in her eyes.

'Dani?'

There. That was it. Bethany had struck the note. Teacher. Carer. She looked into the face of a wounded child. What *is* your story, girl?

'All right. It's true I've said critical things about your system. About Parley. And I'm sorry for that. I hope you can understand how much we – I – have been hurt by the things being said there.

But you need to believe that we – I – had nothing to do with those personal attacks on you. Nothing.'

'You. Lying. Cunt. You all. Fucking. Lie.'

Openly sobbing now, surrendering to a huge weight of sorrow.

Use her name again. Give up something to her: and let her see it hurt.

'Dani. I'm going to tell you something I never tell anyone. I'm doing this because I trust you not to repeat it. And because there's something I want you to understand.'

A petulant cluster of wrinkles formed above the girl's nose, but she was listening.

'I was nineteen. A student.'

Framing herself young and powerless to undercut the power imbalance. Was it landing? Hard to tell.

'I ran the Women's Group at University College, here in London. I suppose I've always been a bit of a politico.'

A crash, somewhere distant. A door? Both women's eyes darted sideways then locked back onto each other. Could someone get into this room from outside, with the table wedged against the door?

'Some of the students – male students – rugby types, you know?'

A little duck of the head. Good, good.

'They took a dislike to the Group. To the fact there even was a Women's Group. Things were worse back then. Even worse than now.'

Another ducking nod.

'They decided to attack because that's who they were – *what* they were – but they didn't take us all on. They picked me. The way they chose to make their empty, violent point was to turn my life into hell on earth. And so they did that.'

Two brown-black pupils dilated slowly, absorbing her. Bethany Lehrer could always make a story bite.

'This was before the Internet, you know. Ha! Actually before the Internet.'

'How old are you?'

Well, well. The girl spoke. Her voice had an interrogator's bite. 'I'm forty-six, Dani.'

Literally old enough to be her mother.

'And you were what, nineteen? So it wasn't before the Internet. It was before the web.'

That pretty much set the bar for literal-mindedness. Bethany had to bite her tongue – actually bite it – to stave off laughter.

'I stand corrected, Danielle. But these boors didn't need technology to spread their hate. Campus was a small, small world. What they used, the thing they dug out and stuck on noticeboards, on the door of my room, what they strung in a giant blow-up over the door of my building, was a picture of me, which they decorated with a slogan I won't repeat. In the picture I was with a man – a man who taught me. Not a lecturer: a post-grad who gave classes in political theory. The photo was awful and I don't know why I let him take it. He liked to take pictures of us together and I doubt I was the first or last. I try not to think how those lads got the picture off him: he wasn't a good man.'

She worked to control her breathing. This was harder than any stump speech she'd ever made.

'It was taken on timer – no selfie sticks then. He was sitting on his bed and I was on his lap. I was – my breasts were out and he was – touching me.'

Dani was staring right into her now, with total concentration. Bethany hadn't planned to say any of that. She didn't need to for the story to land. What had happened to her internal censor?

'So I thank God this was before the net.' Danielle moved to speak. 'Before the *web*. Before social media. Because if those things had been around, that image would still be out there. Every day I wonder if someone will find one of those disgusting flyers in a box in their attic, remember that evil summer and post it. Because then I've had it – because we're still that uptight. A woman can't have an image like that associated with her, and stay in power. I'd have had it, for no reason at all.'

As might already have been the case.

'I thought I was done for before I'd even started. All I wanted was to step down and run. Leave uni, even – not just Women's Group. That was how bad it got.

'And you know? My friends were all full of advice; but the only person I wanted to speak to was my grandmother, who lived in South West London. I knew she'd be – the only sane person for this. So I got on a bus and – you'll know about her?'

Bafflement. Really, girl, you don't even know this? Bethany was used to being surrounded by people who knew an unfeasible amount about everything. There was something affecting in Dani's transparent ignorance.

'But you've heard of Elyse Martingale?' A kilowatt shook the girl's spine. 'OK, you have. She was my Gramma, Dani.'

This is a clusterfuck of too much information.

Dani stares at the lady minister, at her hair and lippy in disarray. Her stomach knots and unknots. Apart from that one time she punched Joey Dukakis at work she's never hurt anyone who didn't beg her for it in play: and always with a safeword out. Here there's nothing. Jonquil always says at her, *What's your exit strategy, Danielle?* And it's the right question. Dani never has an exit strategy. She doesn't have one now.

She looks at the fucked-over lady minister and now it's obvious. She's the spit of that poster of Elyse – the one in Sam's whitewashed meeting room. The same long horsey face. The level unforgiving eyes.

'I thought you knew. I thought that's why you plastered her slogans on the screen just now. To rub my face in it.'

'Not my slogans. I'm not with them.'

'No? All right.'

Dani has spent the last twenty-four hours thinking how this woman is nothing but lies and control and she's nurtured her anger until it was big and hard enough to do this thing. And it's true she's swapped slogans with identikid – slogans coined by

Elyse, that icon of hacker-girl power and the anti-state, who'd always seemed more a concept than someone's actual gran. Bethany Lehrer and Elyse Martingale were meant to be opposites. The new information won't resolve.

Then she realises. This is why identikid is using Elyse's slogans: *because*. Not in spite of Elyse being the minister's gran: *because*. This is when she starts feeling sorry for the battered woman on the chair.

'I was right to go to her, that time.' The minister, still telling her story. 'Would you like to know what she said to me?'

Dani does want to know.

'She said, *I've had all varieties of filth thrown at me by men who would stand in my way but are too much the coward to face me on level terms.* I'm paraphrasing a bit but this is exactly how she spoke.'

Dani nods again. This is from the source. She sees the lines and sagging flesh around the minister's eyes. The woman always looks taut and packaged in photos but close up she just looks tired. It makes Dani almost believe her.

'*And after every attempt I've made to fight them on their own terms; and after every time I've turned tail and fled; I've learned that neither is the answer. There are just two words you require to keep to your course at such a time: though you must never speak them out loud. Repeat them silently inside your head and stand your ground.*'

Dani nods yet again, though the minister hasn't asked her anything.

'What were the words?' she asks.

The minister smiles.

'They were *Fuck you*.'

A laugh bursts out of Dani. She covers her mouth because she's supposed to be furious.

'*Whenever you feel the assault is too powerful, the degradation too great, you must repeat these two words silently within your mind; and keep repeating them until you rediscover your resolve.*

Fuck you. Fuck you. Gramma beat the kitchen table in time with the words. *Fuck you, fuck you.*'

The minister, too, smacks her thigh to mark out time.

'*I have found they endow me with the most unexpected resilience.*'

The minister sits forward in her chair. Dani shuffles back on the slippery layer of dead-tree brochures.

'And look. Hah. See what I'm still holding.'

The minister raises the object that's been clutched to her stomach since Dani dumped her in the chair. A book. Ragged cover with a pale geometric design. Old, old media.

'Look,' says the minister. 'Read the dedication in the front.'

She hands Dani the book. Oh, it's *The Electronic Radical*. Dani pulls back the brittle cover with care and sees, written in an agitated hand, in ink the colour of a faded bruise:

If you remember none of these words, remember just two.
– *Gramma.*

Holy. Fucking. Shit.

'And she was right. I went back to uni and I held our next meeting and I silently said *fuck you* in the face of every bully. And I went on to say it a hundred times. A thousand. I stuck it out, and we beat them, and here I am. And here's something you really, really mustn't tell; but I use the words today. Quite often, when things get tough.'

It's at this point Dani's anger totally malfunctions.

'The thing is, Dani, all I'm trying to do is what Gramma told me was right, thirty-odd years ago. Too much to consummate in her lifetime. Sometimes I wonder: was hers the last generation to think anything new? Are we just recycling?'

There's this big pause, like the mouse pointer has gone hourglass. Dani turns the cloth-bound talisman over in her hands.

'Anyway.' The minister brushes her skirt flat. 'That is why I would never – *never* – put another woman through a fraction of what those faceless men did to me. That isn't who I am.'

She stops speaking and looks at Dani with this smile that's half question and half consolation. Dani tries to think but that doesn't seem to be something she can do. This isn't information, it's words. It seems true but it's only sentences, one coming after another.

She wishes Sam was here. Sam was the one who sussed out that the minister was behind the trolls. Or maybe he made a mistake, but it was real when he said it.

She needs to ask a question so she does.

'What was the slogan?'

Not for the first time, Bethany found herself disarmed by this purple-haired sprite.

'I'm sorry?'

'On the picture. With the tits. That you wouldn't repeat.'

Was this a test? To see if she'd been telling the truth? Ask for an unexpected detail: that's how Colombo cracks a lie – *Just one more thing that's puzzling me.* But no, Dani wanted to know: could not tolerate a gap in the information she'd been presented with.

As Bethany began to answer, a crash burst into the room. The door bounced hard against the table, which screamed sideways across the floor and toppled to Bethany's right, landing on its side, throwing the cardboard box against the wall. Another crash and the door burst inwards, smacking the concrete.

'*Minister! Down!*'

'Shit!'

Dani stumbled backwards to the left, away from the door. DS Raeworth was framed in the doorway. A military stance, legs firmly apart, hand under wrist and a pistol trained on Danielle, who backed into a set of empty aluminium shelves.

'*Armed Police! Do not move!*'

His voice was a klaxon. Danielle shivered like a whippet. The firearm hovering in front of the policeman was horribly three dimensional. There was a sodden gap in time while Bethany found her voice.

'There's no call for this, Detective Sergeant. This situation is under control.'

She adjusted her hair and clothing to what she hoped was a semblance of order, and stood.

'Ms Farr and I are speaking.'

The policeman's eyes didn't leave Danielle.

'With respect, Minister, this does not look like a controlled situation. Two of my uniforms have just been assaulted. Miss Farr here has recently been photographed in possession of fire-arms and has evaded officers in the last twenty-four. *DO NOT MOVE!*'

Bethany jolted back but the command was directed at the girl. DS Raeworth hadn't moved or changed expression while he spoke. Nor had his eyes left Dani. From his sudden change of tone Bethany saw what she was generally protected from, bunkered in authority. What others suffered. Without lowering the gun Raeworth pulled a walkie-talkie from his belt and spoke rapidly into it. It returned a strangled burst of static: they were too far underground for the signal to find his colleagues. He hooked it back onto his belt.

Bethany pushed away an uncooperative lock of hair and stepped forward. Nothing to fear. Danielle stared like a caged beast.

'Officer, I have this,' said Bethany, taking another step towards him, reaching for his outstretched arm.

Before she could touch him, a number of things happened. Bethany couldn't fix their arrangement in time.

The officer stepped sideways towards the door and away from her hand, keeping a bead on the girl.

Outside the door a man skidded into view – the red-dread-locked ringleader of this morning's protest, clothed again and hurrying from some pursuer. He clocked Bethany, then the police-man, then the gun. He froze and let out an astonished *huh!*

The policeman's attention flicked to the sound. His gun may have wavered in that instant.

Dani lurched forward from the shelves. Unclear whether she was leaping for the gun or ducking for cover.

The boy caught sight of her through the door. What he saw: a hard-jawed state enforcer training a gun on a young woman, a fellow-protestor. Give him this: he found courage in that moment, enough to take a half-step towards the armed man, raise a hand and shout, 'Hey!'

Bethany stepped back, panic swamping her urge to peace-make.

The officer, penned by small movements on every side, tried to bring both boy and girl into his sights. He shuffled a few steps backwards, towards where the table lay on its side. The gun, with its own motives, danced between two targets.

The back of Bethany's knees touched the chair and she swept the air behind her to find a support. Her vision narrowed to a cone centred on the policeman. In the periphery, the girl, flinching as though slapped across the face; the boy, mouth open in a shout, reaching towards the policeman, palm flat as though waiting to catch a bullet. Raeworth warmed up with a shimmy of his feet. Then in a flash he performed the most extraordinary high kick Bethany had ever seen. His body jackknifed, both legs shooting into the air in front of him. His pistol rang out in the tiny concrete room with the boom of field artillery, imploding into Bethany's eardrums and forcing a gasp from her hollow mouth. Then everything was black.

¶NewsHound

According to the press pack at the Digital Citizen launch event, Minister for a Digital Society Bethany Lehrer 'missing'.

Awaiting confirmation.

sh.rt/Oekg75y

EIGHT

'HERE. LET ME SHOW YOU.'

Graham snapped open the clasps with a practised action, flipped the metal panel aside and set it against the wall. He stepped back with a stringy grin. Dankness welled from the broken brick aperture. J-R and Mark approached, uncertain what they were being shown. A smell emerged, older than anything J-R had so far encountered in Parley's maze of ancient houses and concrete factory spaces.

J-R leaned forward into the gloom. Graham pushed past and stepped through the fissure, leaving a male tang behind him. Mark's compact frame pressed J-R's side as he, too, peered into the hole.

'We have a bulb rigged up.'

Graham's voice emerged from the dark. Something dripped and echoed on stone. From deeper inside came a regular knocking.

'Ah, here we go.'

A pull-cord snapped and bare light shot from a caged lamp, only to lose itself in the lichen-coated brick of the tunnel. Cables thicker than J-R's arm ran loose along the concrete floor. Thinner lines snaked over rusted hooks. Power, information and water running through the darkness. The bulb-light glared from Graham's red T-shirt. It showed a cartoon sports car, gravity-defying aerodynamic apparatus towering from its rear. Beneath this, a bold white caption: *SPOILER ALERT*.

'This is the guts of London,' he said. '*Under the pavement, the Internet.*'

J-R caught Mark's eye, then stepped inside.

'Mind your head,' said Graham.

J-R stooped under trailing wires. He could make nothing of the gloom ahead.

'What people never realise about technology,' Graham continued, 'is when you dig underneath, it runs along the exact same channels as all the old shit.'

At the edge of sensation, a rumble began. J-R reached a hand to the curved brick ceiling. It was coated in oily growth. His shadow fell on the dark air, making a ghost in perspective. Somewhere close by was a steady run of water. The rumble grew, shaking the bulb.

'Northern Line,' said Graham's voice.

Mark stepped in through the opening. Muffled by layers of ancient stone, the young men felt the clatter of wheels. J-R reached a hand towards Mark, perhaps to touch his shoulder or hand. Then he checked himself and reached instead for an iron strut.

Graham walked ahead, stooping under cables.

'The pipe runs through this old drainage run, all the way to 404 City. Super-fast fibre. The tunnelling's Bazalgette. Mondan's brick and mortar backbone.' He gave the wall a proprietary pat. 'They installed us here when they bought Parley. They're stabling all their acquisitions into a string of buildings from here to City Road, linked by this run. All sucking on the same pipe.'

Graham looked ahead into the dark, his back to them.

'I'm usually down here twice a week to check our racks in Mondan's data centre. It's quicker than street level – ten minutes. And I don't need to check in through 404's front door security. The data centre's in a basement three storeys down. Water-cooled by an underground river. I could swipe you both in there if you fancied a sniff around?'

He held up the pass on his lanyard. Mark laughed but stopped when he saw Graham's half-lit face. Graham kept holding up his passcard, looking at the two of them for what seemed a minute. Then he spoke.

'Why are you even here, J-R? Mark?'

'Pardon me?' said J-R.

'You heard.'

J-R and Mark exchanged a look in the gloom. Had it been wise to introduce Mark to Graham? The three of them had been talking in Parley's basement technology suite when Graham, on some inspiration, had stormed over to reveal this ancient shaft, hidden behind a superhero movie poster like a prison escape tunnel.

J-R glanced back to the broken aperture and the light spilling from the room. Graham was ten yards further into the tunnel: the way back out was clear. Perhaps reading this intention, Graham sighed, an infinitely weary sound.

'I'm working with you,' said J-R, 'to find the source of these malicious messages. Is that not what we're doing?'

'Is it?'

'It's what I'm doing.'

'All right. And you?'

Graham turned to Mark, who looked back at Graham, appraising. J-R's pulse ran through his neck.

'Perhaps, Graham,' he said, 'you'd also like to tell us what *you* are doing?'

Rule one of political communications: *Turn the challenge back on the challenger.*

'Maybe I'm trying to enlighten you.'

'About? You mean your artificial intelligence theory about sic_girl?' Another rumble of the Underground. 'I don't, apologies, I can't accept it. There's a person, someone with political intent, behind this.'

Further silence, then Graham snorted. His laughter was acidic as his voice.

'No, but think about it,' said J-R. 'This is a tightly co-ordinated assassination by degrees.'

Graham began to pace.

'You're a smart guy, aren't you, J-R? You seem smart.'

He went quiet. J-R wondered if he was expected to answer, but Graham picked up again.

'We care about that here. We're all so fricking clever. We also hire for the ability to think lateral. It's what makes this place different.' J-R thought of Danielle Farr's constant edgy impetus. 'You should open your mind. There's a philosophy here: *stuff is possible.*'

'Is that your motto? *Stuff is possible*?'

'Is it a bad motto?'

Again, that pause. For Graham, there did not seem to be such a thing as a rhetorical question.

'So tell me,' he said. 'Why have you lot got it in for Dani?'

'We lot? It isn't – have you not seen the papers?'

'You, the press. You know it's assault? You can't think she did the leaks? The hack?'

'To be frank,' said J-R. 'I don't know what to believe. But you have to ask: who knows how Parley works better than Danielle?'

He did not say, look at her behaviour, at those pictures.

'Bullshit. It isn't her.'

'But, sorry, how can you know that?'

Mark was listening intently beside him. Graham stepped further into the dark.

'Have you read *The Electronic Radical*?' he said.

'Of course. Yes.'

Hadn't someone else spoken about Elyse Martingale recently?

'Good. So Elyse has this idea of the plexus, yes? When everybody is linked to a free and open source of information, they'll be radicalised. Free.'

Mark spoke at last.

'*Because they shall be able to ignore no longer the brutal truths of state control.*'

Graham gave that a little round of applause.

'Not bad, Mark. You know what I'm talking about. So, tell me. Now that we're almost all connected – and J-R's boss is about to link everyone up to an all-new state-controlled plexus – do you see that happening? Is it inevitable? Or is something else happening? Does it worry you that Mondan's the largest supplier of digital surveillance tools to the British security services? As a for instance?'

J-R was rooted into the tunnel. The damp air was hard to draw into his throat. Graham had asked why he was here. The moment J-R's BlackBerry fizzed out in the gents upstairs, some restraining force had switched off, too. Until that moment he'd been held by a gravity so familiar he'd never felt its pull. God help him, he wanted nothing more than to grab Mark by the neck and kiss him. The notion was brutal. It filled the narrow confines of the tunnel. J-R thought he might fall.

'I'm not sure what –'

His words were muffled by mossy brick. Graham interrupted.

'Does the word *Grubly* mean anything to you boys? Yes? No?'

J-R watched Mark for a reaction but he could barely make out his friend's expression. Grubly was the invasive little programme Mark had found buried in the Digital Citizen package.

'What I thought,' said Graham, reading their silence.

He stretched out his arm towards Mondan's subterranean motherlode of data.

'Down there,' he said. 'That's where you should be looking. Not here. That's all I'm saying.'

J-R faced the wet blackness. After a beat, Graham strode towards them. He paused in front of J-R, grabbed his hand and pushed into it a nubby piece of plastic then ducked under the brick overhang, back into the room, light spilling around and through him. J-R turned the object in the half-light. It was a tiny USB drive. He held it up so its label caught the light. *128GB*, it said.

The two friends turned to face one another. They remained in darkness.

¶**NewsHound**

BREAKING: Bethany Lehrer chief of staff Krishan Kohli
overheard using the word 'kidnap'.
And then another, shorter, word I won't proffer here.
sh.rt/ggu27dt

NINE

BETHANY WAS SITTING ON A CHAIR.

She'd lost a few seconds at least. Dani was no longer in the room. In the corner by the overturned table, the policeman's body was strewn like hastily abandoned clothing. Urgent voices pressed in from the corridor.

Bethany raised herself with a hand on the chair-back, testing her legs' capacity to hold her. The hand spasmed as she released it from the chair and stood under her own balance. She took two or three foal-steps towards the fallen officer.

The voices in the hall came in and out of focus – *but what if he's – he isn't, he isn't*. All Bethany's energy was directed at the policeman. He looked broken: was surely dead. The ghost left on the stick when you suck the flavour from a lolly.

I'm in shock, she thought.

She crouched by the body. The head and neck were twisted against the vertical surface of the table, brochures strewn under his flaccid limbs. It was the brochures that had brought him down. As he backed away from the boy and Dani, he'd slipped on the carpet of glossy print and fallen back, cracking his head against the table edge, knocking him cold: Bethany prayed no worse than that.

Having nothing more practical than *Casualty* to call on, she placed two fingers on the side of Raeworth's neck. The heat and pulse were horribly intimate but she held fingers on his flesh for long enough to be sure, then allowed herself to breathe. For a second she thought she might black out again, then a practical thought struck her: *Get help. He still needs help.* She turned to find her bag, her phone: but of course she didn't have them. Everything started coming back. Dani. Dani would get help for this man. She was an OK kid.

Levering herself up against the table, Bethany tiptoed to the door through the sea of brochures. There was a rent in the concrete by the door frame: a bullet hole. Out in the hall, Dani was in command of a whispered conversation.

'You're identikid – right?' she said.

Bethany propped herself in the doorway and waited for her moment. The boy spotted her and gaped. Dani shook him by his camo lapel.

'Fucking hell, kid, come on. It's me. From yesterday? *Naked and unadorned?*'

A light bulb flashed.

'StrangeFish? No way!'

Bethany understood none of this but waited them out.

'Christsake, way. Now c'mon. We need to get the shit out of here.'

'But the guy?'

He pointed to the room. Dani looked, and saw Bethany. They stared at each other.

'Yes,' said Bethany. 'This man needs urgent medical attention, Dani.'

Still the bit player in a TV drama.

Before Dani could reply, footsteps hammered from behind a door at the end of the hallway. The stairwell. The boy stared at the door.

'Fuck! Why'd I come down this dead end?'

Dani grabbed his arm and scooped up a black backpack.

'No, no – behind here, service lift.'

She pulled him to a double door. Dragged him, as she'd done to Bethany before.

'How I got in,' she said, opening the doors to reveal a further layer of raw metal doors – a service elevator, wedged open with a rectangular weight.

Shaken into motion, the boy bent to shift the metal weight while Dani pulled the lift doors back and started smacking buttons. Bethany was forgotten. The door to the emergency stairs rattled and flew open. DC Ackroyd and a uniformed security guard piled out, clocked Bethany and gawped at her. Then followed her eyes to the elevator doors as they eased shut. Red LED arrows animated upwards. Nobody moved. Then through the lift door, they heard a muffled whoop and shout.

'I'm Terry Salmon and you girls can suck my cock!'

The men looked at the door in deep confusion. Bethany had no idea what the girl had meant but had to restrain herself from laughing out loud. Why was she feeling such affection for that volatile kid?

'Here, officer, here,' she said. 'Your colleague needs help.'

She pointed back into the room. They gathered at the door and looked inside. DS Raeworth had risen to his hands and knees, and was crawling across the mess of brochures, shaking stars from his head.

The security man whistled through his teeth.

'What the fuck happened here?' he said.

What, indeed? Raeworth kneeled up dumbly, unaware of their presence. Only now did Bethany register: his gun was nowhere to be seen.

¶sic_girl

Awww, don't the lady-minister look charming in this clip?
You wouldn't think anyone was waving their dick at her
at this point.

So, dear hearts, new and old, of what shall we speak as
we watch these naked peeps parade across our screens?

Alors. It is with much disgust I tell you: that guy in the
cutaway shot? with the corrugated hair? scarpering at
three zillion kph to his chauffeured car?

That, my dearies, is Mondan CEO Sean Perce.

And it may interest you to know that the delightful B
Lehrer has been doing the do with that walking Action
Man for nigh on a year. I mean fucking, kiddies. With
their naughty bits. Email evidence here. In nauseating
spades.

Look! Off he flies in his big silver car with his glamorous
American poodle Jonquil! Ain't he brave?

Weeeell, weeeell, weeell. The company that's about to
sign a nine-figure contract with Bethy L is managed by
her bouffant fuck-buddy Seany P.

Life's full of funny coincidences.

Ain't it, though?

TEN

'THIS IS THE KILL ORDER.'

Jonquil wriggled her butt on the Lexus back seat to face Sean.

'What? No, it isn't. It's the *do-this-and-I-walk* order.'

'Fuck off a minute, Jonq. You saw what happened back there. It's trench war now and I don't have time to argue.'

Sure, Jonquil had seen – she'd been right there. After this morning's call she'd gotten straight in a cab to hijack Sean at the Digital Citizen launch and argue out the future of Parley. She'd been with him in the wings when the protest began and had witnessed the charming sight of Sean high-tailing it to the car so fast she had to take off her kitten heels to keep up with him.

But the raw courage of those kids. What they did was totally art; and they were beautiful. Hungry ribs and unwaxed bodies. And they'd used Parley to organise. That kind of free-spirited action was what Parley was there for in the first place.

She looked out the frosted window at the intersection of Clerkenwell and Hatton, where they'd been stuck for what felt like twenty minutes. This whole town was grinding slow. The car was street furniture.

'Correction, Sean. We have all the time in the world. This here is slower than the Van Eyck Expressway at rush hour.'

'Doesn't matter how long we're here. I'm killing Parley.'

'Sean. People love our network. Customers. You keep telling me about how important customers are.'

'They're important because they have money. If I wanted their love I'd write them a poem.'

Jonquil tried to break in but he did that talk-to-the-hand thing.

'Believe me, they'll get over this in ten days max. There's always a next big thing. Parley is nothing. You've never understood where to find value in your code base. Lucky I know.'

'What? What about my code base?'

'Forget it.'

'Are you using my code for some shit?'

Rage crackled under the skin of Sean's face. In spite of herself, Jonquil flinched. This was why he always won an argument, goddammit.

'*My* code,' he said. 'Do not forget that. *My* code. *My* IP. I do what I damn well please with my code. You can help me or you can get out of my way. It's your buy-out bonus you'll flush down the shitter.'

The thing here was, it was not OK for a man to treat a woman this way. No matter how much of a 'character' he was. Jonquil had never been one to borrow trouble. How had she gotten to a place where this shit passed as normal?

'No,' she said. 'No.'

'Excuse me?'

The car had gotten way too small. She grabbed her clutch.

'I won't do this. I'm out of here.'

'So go.'

He tapped at his phone like it was a voodoo doll of Jonquil. She flipped the door catch. Nothing moved. She slapped the door and turned on Sean.

'So what am I, kidnapped?'

Sean spoke without glancing up from his touchscreen.

'Oh, for – Derek, would you pop the door for my colleague who would like to take a stroll?'

The silent driver reached for the controls and a mechanism jolted in the door. Jonquil pulled the catch to its tipping point, then stopped.

'This is not a bluff, Sean. You are about to lose me.'

He looked up as if surprised to find her still there. His poker face was so impassive you could hit it with a real-life poker and it wouldn't budge.

'All right. Bye bye.'

Her hand was hooked on the chrome-plate catch. She wondered what she was about to do: usually she was good on outcomes but she couldn't trace them now. She flipped the catch. Two yellow lines striped the cinder by the kerb, like mustard on a hot dog. Street roar; a bum screaming; the smell of grilled meat. She planted a Choo on asphalt. Then it struck her.

'Hold it.'

'I'm not going anywhere. I thought you were.'

'Whoah, whoah, wait. Damn, I get it. Stupid motherfucking –'

She slid back into the car.

'Excuse me?'

'This isn't reputational risk. This isn't sic_girl.'

'What in God's name? Are you planning to use that door or just let in fumes?'

'You're not doing this for the media or the government. You're killing Parley because you've got something else. Something new. You *want* it gone – and me gone is two birds with a stone.'

'Fascinating to see people squirm while they're on their way down.'

'No.' She slammed the door; Sean kept fiddling with his phone. 'You *want* me to walk. I'm like the, what is it?'

'The scapegoat?'

'No, no, it's a horse.'

'Now you've really lost me.'

'Stalking horse! You want me to take media fire. I will not be your goddamn horse.'

His eyes hadn't left his Samsung.

'If there's one thing I do not need right now it's a fucking horse.'

She snatched his phone. He sighed and spread his arms.

'Suppose I *am* forcing you out.'

'Ah *hah*!'

'*Suppose* I am. Sake of argument. Would you want to stick around if so? What do you think that would even be like, day in, day out? You know how I can be.'

He was, as ever, correct.

'In either scenario, Parley's history. Why not take the clean break? Head high?'

Goddamn him to hell. It didn't even matter if you knew he was manipulating you.

'You are the devil.'

'Moral authority retained. But it's your call.' He trained his dismal eyes on her. 'And let me tell you what you're missing, Jonq.'

'Oh, OK, sure, uh-huh. You tell me.'

She needed to stop with the demented nodding.

'Right now everyone's coming in their shorts about social. What I know and they don't is they're backing Betamax. Social media is a fad.'

'*Are* a fad. Plural.'

'Glad you agree.'

'No, I – goddammit, Sean!'

'– and a cheat. Using other people as content. Fucking liberty. Only reason you're using people's so-called-friends to give them lols and information is, we don't have enough data on them. Yet.'

'I don't know about you, Sean, but I enjoy interacting with people.'

Perce gave the sigh of a teacher disappointed by a star pupil.

'Wrong. We interact with people online because they validate who we are. Their Likes are our Likes and that feels good. Except when they aren't – and then what?'

'My friends know me better than an algorithm.'

'That's just lack of data. When the system knows everything about you – and I'm saying *everything*, even the things you hide from your friends – it'll know who you are, better than people can. As soon as you connect you'll experience who you really are:

meet yourself coming back the other way. In which case who needs friends?'

'Well, that statement sums up your attitude pretty damn well, Sean. Jesus!'

He let that hang for five, ten seconds, then reached across her and pulled the door catch. The volume turned back up on the street sounds. Sean held out his hand, palm up.

'OK, fun's over. Give me back my phone and say goodbye nicely.'

¶NewsHound

Blogger assaults minister at demo

sh.rt/f9w7ter

¶LabelMabel

I don't want to be all OMG SQUEE here, but. Bethany
Lehrer and Sean Perce doing sexy-talk? I can't look.
Second thoughts, cancel that. I'm going to click the
actual fuck out of this link.

ELEVEN

'SO WHAT *IS* YOUR NAME?'

Identikid's – Leo's – words are sharp and loud. Someone has moved the mic too close to the world. Every rustle of his parka is high-def intense.

'So like back there in the lift,' he said, 'you shouted your name was Terry but the Lehrer bitch called you Danny and like those are both boy's names?'

'Don't call her bitch.'

Leo checks her out. She doesn't mind so much.

'Y'know, I don't get you, girl. That bitch owns this bullshit. Stealing our identities while we sleep.'

Wicked witches. Bitches.

'Is she? I wish I knew who was doing what.'

They trawl east through a London that thinks it's any Friday night, letting the city guide them, their conversation stop-and-start-and-stop-again. There's a current in the air of something starting. The City is hollowing out as salarymen head home. Angry scenes are starting up, drunken packs trailing north to Shoreditch. Dani and Leo pass a group of kids with hoodies pulled low and bandannas over noses; hiding their features from the CCTV. This one lad in a pig mask, a baseball bat dangling from his hand. Dani keeps her eyes to herself but Leo exchanges nods with them.

They cross Bishopsgate onto Aldgate.

'What do I even call you?' says Leo. 'I want to call you something.'

'So call me Fish.'

'Fish, huh? Like the code they broke with the Colossus Mark Two, at Bletchley Park? Japanese naval ticker. Elyse was totally there, y'know?'

Dani checks Leo from the corner of her eye. He strides on, in love with the twilight, with himself and with everything he's done. But there's more to this one; and he's cute, in an undernourished way. It tickles the she-cat heat in Dani's belly. She runs up behind him and grabs his neck, swivels him around and kisses him hard on the lips like that's what anyone would do. He holds back.

'You're Dani Farr,' he says into her eyes.

Bollocks. She turns away.

Well, but she's hardly inconspicuous. She's used to being recognised by a certain kind of edgy nerd – but since she's had Terry to hide inside she's been weightless. She doesn't want to be reminded of anything.

'It's OK, truth,' he says. 'I just wanted to ask: is it real? What they're saying on Parley?'

Aw, God. He's like the rest. He wants to perv over that vicious spew of lies and dirt. She walks north, between the plastic shanties of Petticoat Lane. He follows.

'I mean, have the Personas really come to life?'

Oh. He means that. She stops and lets him catch up. Bare bulbs light up stalls as the daylight fails.

'No. Some people think so but it isn't true. I thought it for a while. I talked to sic_girl the other day. She was sort of crazy. But I found out it isn't true.'

'You talked to sic? Fuck. But it is, too, totally possible.' A ginger flush in his cheeks. 'I was doing a masters on this until – other stuff happened. The first time intelligence evolved, millennia back, it was from this random pattern of basic algorithms teeming round the nerves of some protozoan slug. Believe.'

He makes her laugh. His energy and certainty are delicious.

'It'll happen again,' he says, deflated. 'Maybe you made it start.'

They weave through the market crowd. The street is coming to life in the twilight. Energy swills through Dani like blood through a pig. A man offers her some kind of yam.

'I get you, Leo. I do. I wanted to believe it. But it got fucked up. I don't even know if I've got a me to go back to tonight.'

A clip-art moon is rising. Dead house fronts come alive as a banghra passeggiata starts up all around. Arc-lit tarpaulins lashed to workshop doors bristle with rusty oddments. Red-faced skinheads in puffa jackets hawk their junk to the cool approaching night. Dani stops at a façade which looks to be a shop but whose window display is a microcosm of model skeletons and skulls. Day of the Dead things, inhabiting a village of household junk. In the corner, a pile of skeletons fucks uproariously. She turns to Leo, face tight with cold, grabs him round the neck again, hangs there like a swing. The little-girl-lost routine. He looks back. He has something to say.

'See, there's a secret. Can I tell you?'

'Kid, you are totally my hero. You saved me from a fascist with a gun. Kind of. I think that means I'm yours. Do what you will.'

He nods.

'OK then, so. The thing at the event today? It was the warm-up. Serious. Stuff kicks off all over town tonight. Building up to – we have social buzz now but by morning we hit the channels big time. I'm expecting interviews and shit.'

Something is wrong with this. The stunt before was genius – spontaneous and brave and funny and she totally knew where it came from. But now Leo's tone is off.

'What kind of stuff?'

She slips from his neck and doesn't know what to do with her hands.

'We're ahead now. This morning we bought eyeballs. Now we need to not flub our competitive advantage.'

Where does he get this mash of online slang and marketing buzz-words?

'Leo. Hold up. What exactly are you going to do?'

'The big nudge. And I'm the one doing the takeover.'

'Taking what over?'

He points, high up and over her shoulder.

'That.'

Her eyes follow his finger to the north-west. A Blade Runner display hangs in the air, churning branded celebrity fables.

'Wait, what, 404 City? Mondan? You mean the screens?' He nods. 'But that's – Leo, I work there, ish, and that's serious security shit. What are you planning to do?'

'We got to cut through the noise.'

'*We*. Who is *we*?'

'That's where they're going to pipe the stolen data. We are. Isn't it awesome?'

Now *we*, now *they*. Something is here. The logic is screwed but it connects up.

'Who's they?'

But he's lost in gazing at the high screens. Then he turns to her. 'Do you do karaoke?'

¶NewsHound
Whoah. BREAKING: Protestor identikid pulls gun on
digital minister at demo.
sh.rt/8hr3Opt

¶riotbaby
A government minister who's literally in bed with big
data. This proves everything.
Act now. Make it count.

TWELVE

'I'M GOING TO FIX US UP a one-on-one,' said Mark.

'Ah – sorry –?'

J-R trotted to catch up with Mark, grappling the strap of his backpack over his shoulder. Mark slowed to let him catch up. Dusk was falling on the busy street.

'A meeting.'

'With?'

'With Vanna.'

'Who is—?'

'Vanna Prendergast. Ex colleague-slash-buddy who works in Perce's office and owes me a favour. I'll get us a face-to-face and we can put this to her.'

They walked together along the cracked pavement, J-R's folded bike bouncing at his side. He didn't know where Mark was leading him.

'I don't – I'm not sure what I can do here any more, Mark. I'm rather a long way from my comfort zone.'

Mark swung to a stop. J-R stumbled to avoid colliding with him.

'J-R. How long have you been working on this? Did you suddenly stop believing in making a difference? You read the logs on Graham's USB.'

J-R had read them, but like everything important these days, they were written in characters he couldn't understand.

'If they're real,' said Mark, 'we have hard evidence they're using Grubly to snoop on millions of people – millions. They were aware of the Digital Citizen hack all along. They must be scrambling to cover this whole thing up. It's just like I first said – do you remember, back in the café?'

J-R nodded slowly.

'Everything Graham's given us,' said Mark. 'How can we not use this? This isn't some legalistic question about whether Bethany was telling the truth. We actually need to stop these people.'

'I just don't see how—'

'Which is why I'm saying, let's take it directly to Mondan. Don't let them bury this. Come on: this'll be fun.'

Mark's excitement was a lure; but J-R didn't relish confronting this Vanna person. He'd dealt with Perce's people many times and found them obnoxious and diffident. Under no scenario would this go smoothly.

They turned a corner onto a street whose remnants of shops were colonised by temporary street-food outlets. Meat smoke charred the air and there was noise and light. A young crowd filled the pavement. J-R almost took Mark's arm. He'd not felt so warmed since his BlackBerry fizzed out.

Then Mark did touch him, on the shoulder, to guide him into a makeshift cafe whose transparent tenting contained a merry cluster of formica tables. Men hailed Mark, all with the same trim swagger. He guided J-R onto a stage of wooden paletes, where they sat at a table and studied laminate lists of mezze and unfamiliar beers. Mark hailed a dark-eyed man and ordered for them both, then sat back, eyes liquid in the light.

'So – I guess we were behind the curve with our big reveal about Bethany and Sean?'

J-R winced. Before they left Parley Mark had showed him sic_girl's latest posts. Bethan's idiotic emails. No sordid holiday snaps as yet – but even in their words, her mails displayed the same giddy nonsense he'd seen in those shots from Cádiz.

'It does make a horrible kind of sense,' he said. 'Perce always had a – proprietorial air with Bethany. I could never understand why she laughed it off, so.'

Mark nodded.

'That's Perce all over.'

His sleek phone was in his hand, the enormous screen turned towards J-R. It displayed a photograph of a beautiful dark woman with oversized glasses and the words, *Vanna P mobile*.

'So are we going to nail him? Shall I call Vanna? Before the borek comes?'

The phone's screen weaved with hypnotic colours. Suppose Perce and Bethany *had* cooked up some deal? Chasing Perce, exposing it, would destroy her. What did loyalty look like, in this scenario?

J-R cleared his throat.

'You know,' he said, 'I've slogged at this for two years – with no life outside work. If I thought for a moment I was selling people's privacy to some corporation –'

So Mark called the number. He made professional murmurs into the phone, deploying all his easy forcefulness; but even he seemed surprised by the response.

'Tomorrow morning? Well, I suppose –'

He widened his eyes at J-R who mouthed, *Saturday?* Mark shrugged, mouthed, *Why not?* and grinned. J-R threw up his hands and replied out loud.

'Why not, indeed?'

Mark gave a delight of a smile and engaged his counter-party in brisk arrangements. In the morning they would knock at the door of Mondan's great electrified headquarters with nothing in their pockets but a USB drive and a passing hope. Krish once said to J-R, *Always have a gun taped behind the cistern*. A reference to some film. Sorry, Krish, he thought, I have nothing.

Mark ended the call and J-R reached to place a hand on his leg; but there was too much table in the way. Mark looked down, baffled at J-R's directionless reaching.

'The tabbouleh is who?' asked an accented voice.

The waiter. J-R recovered his arm and fussed with his paper napkin. Mark continued to study him.

'We're sharing everything,' he told the waiter.

When the waiter had gone, he leaned eagerly towards J-R.

'So,' he said. 'Are you ready to fuck Sean Perce?'

¶riotbaby

DEMO: All in the West End area: thirty minutes and counting to party time. Get yourself close to any branch of HomeTech in the Oxford Street area. Don't let their blatant tax evasion take money out of YOUR pocket.

DEMO: Wheelchair sit-in going down NOW at Winstanton Property Services on Albemarle Street. These are the dudes who are evicting tenants with disabilities. Be there.

THIRTEEN

THERE ARE CERTAIN THINGS you can walk away from – if you have the nous and the balls:

- Sniff of corruption in your £170m procurement: survive intact, provided you can put up with being named in every article about sleaze for the next six months.
- Members of the public pigspammed after you persuade them to give up their data to a private firm: humiliating but confusing. The media will get bored within a week.
- Breach of email security at your department leads to embarrassing leaks: not good but you should be OK after suffering a ritual disembowelling from John Humphrys.
- Farcical abortive kidnap attempt by deranged riot-girl hacker: borderline. OK if you're prepared to play the gallery for laughs.
- Filmed being mobbed by buck-naked hippy pigs at a key PR event: rocky. Depends on strength of relationship with Party authorities. In other words, hmm.
- Caught in flagrante with a major supplier to your department (extramarital): fucked. In more than one way.
- These things being cumulative: career pretty much fucked in the arse.

Bethany rubbed her backside. Her only injury from her abduction was a screaming bruise down her right flank, where Dani had shoved her into the plastic chair. The bruising must be an attractive shade of blue by now. She didn't care to check.

She shifted against the chair's padding. Being cooped up in this hotel meeting room was like being trapped in the Beiges section of the Dulux catalogue. After this morning's events the police had triggered DEFCON 5 and commandeered the room as their command centre, and were clearly loving every second.

Official voices bounced around the walls, two conversations cutting across one another. Bethany was trying to keep up with DC Ackroyd but she kept being distracted by DS Raeworth, who was briefing Krish on the other side of the table. It seemed they'd identified this morning's ringleader and Raeworth was reading out his profile. His telegraphic delivery was hard to ignore in this closed acoustic.

'Leo Sandberg. Known to us. Masters dropout from Trinity, Cambridge. IT whizz.'

Raeworth's rhythms of speech reminded her of the shipping forecast. As he spoke he held an ice pack to the back of his head. He'd refused medical attention after his fall and was generally playing the wounded action hero. Bethany wished he – and everyone else – would cool it. Probably she was fooling herself and this was an unmitigated disaster but she liked to hope it wasn't, thanks very much.

'Picked up at an anti-capitalist demo last year,' continued Raeworth. 'Property damage. Again in November, assaulting a police officer. No evidence – masked. One eviction, verbal warning. Squatting. Tactical had him under occasional observation since the charges fell through.'

'Observation?' said Krish. 'So how come—?'

'*Occasional* observation, sir.'

Krish's BlackBerry cut the conversation short.

'Ach, hold on a moment.' He stood to take the call. 'Oh, you? Well no thanks a bunch for *your* advice.'

He moved away from the table. Bethany turned her attention back to DC Ackroyd, who was trying to update her on today's leaked emails. She was finding it impossible to take the information in. Was she still in shock?

'Sorry, Detective Constable. You were trying to tell me –?'

He gave her a sympathetic smile, the patronising tosser.

'Our assumption was not correct,' he said. The police were just as bad at saying *I was wrong* as politicians. 'We assumed the emails had been leaked from the department.'

The logic of that statement should presumably be clear. She shook her head as if this would improve her hearing.

'Well, but they were. These were mails from me, from Procurement colleagues, from my office. The only common link was the department.'

'Actually, no, Minister.'

He handed her a laser print. She waved it away.

'Sorry. Reading glasses.'

The policeman shrugged.

'This erm – communication – between you and Mr Perce, posted by sic_girl at 11:41 today was originally sent on the eighteenth of last month. An email in which you – well –'

'Yes, all right – so?'

'It's sent from your home email address. Gmail.'

That cut through the tofu in her head. She grabbed the paper off him. Oh, shit, yes, she remembered this one. Peter would have read this by now. She had to talk to Peter – but not now. One impossible situation at a time.

'But then how are they getting them? If you take away the department, there's no common link. This was sent to Sean's home email.' She'd given up with the *Mr Perce*. 'Others to his office, to partners in his bid. Where's the link?'

'It's Mondan, Minister. Mr Perce's personal email is hosted by his firm. All the consortium companies share a mail server – *mail. group.mondan.com*. Every one of the leaked emails passed through that server. It's housed in their UK data centre, here in London. It's the link.'

Bethany glanced across at Krish but he was still on the phone. Christ, she thought, could this tip the balance? Was the department no longer on the hook for the security breach?

Raeworth leaned towards her from the opposite side of the table.

'We have a court order, Minister,' he said. 'We can't hold back any more. We're putting a data forensics team inside Mondan. We'll do it with their full cooperation of course. I'll brief Mr Perce myself tonight.'

Before she could respond, Bethany saw the expression change on Krish's face. Still listening to his phone, steel set into his jawline. He spoke once more then held the BlackBerry away from his ear, killed the connection and stared at it.

Raeworth was trying to get her attention.

'Minister?'

She shushed him with a wave of her hand.

'Krish?' she said. 'What is it?'

Krish turned his stare onto her. He looked fit to murder.

'Well, now. It seems we have a name.'

'For . . .?'

'For our blogger. AKA sic_girl. The leaker.'

Both policemen stood. This was becoming more like a tacky cop show by the minute. Bethany moved her weight off the sore side of her arse.

'We do?' she said. 'From where?'

'From – a source at Parley.'

She let this pass.

'So . . .? The name?'

'Leo Sandberg. Known as identikid. Our scuddy wee laddie from this morning. He's the head of this TakeBackID collective. He's behind it all.'

Both policemen were on their phones so fast it was like they'd already had them at their ears.

¶**riotbaby**

  PIGWATCH: Horses. Moorgate Tube and area. Avoid.

  RIOT TIP: The kids with the breezeblocks in Regent
  Street: go for the corner of the glass. It breaks more
  easily than if you hit the centre.

FOURTEEN

EVERYONE IS SHOUTING. Everything is splashed with red. Dani's dark-adapted eyes follow the mash by the light of flatscreen animations. They call this place the Flamingo Arms. That was never its name but everybody knows the stencilled birds on the boards out front. It's round the corner from her flat. From who-she-used-to-be's flat. She's working on thinking Terry Salmon. She starts by getting shitfaced.

She makes a rumpus on the dance floor. Her throat hurts from when she murdered her vocal chords before, on the high notes of *Sound of the Underground*.

Leo was here a while but now he's gone. He was telling her about some caper. She planned to stick with him but things got choppy and she didn't see him go.

At some point she dropped some Reebok pills. She counted them to check how many but kept losing count. Then she realised she didn't know how many had been in the baggie in the first place.

The bar room is dark and hot as Hades. A smell of burning plastic bubbles in from somewhere to devil up the air. Music like food that's too hot to eat. Wild hormones sweat in her blood. She's blissed up and on heat, and she couldn't stop herself if she even wanted. She keeps the backpack strung across her shoulders, holding the contraband by her body.

Best is, they take plastic. When she found this out she bought a Cadbury's Occasions of coloured drinks with Terry's card – from Absolut Red Bulls to Zombies. She randoms drinks about the crowd as people slap her back and mouth *awright* and thumb her up across the hoo-hah.

She and this one guy with Victorian whiskers get gigantic giggles over a thing that happened. She doesn't know what it was.

Mutton chops, they're called. Mutton chops.

Oh and oh, she almost forgot: Sam is here! – somewhere. She doesn't know why he would be but she's lost track of why she's even here herself. He's beautiful in skinny skinny trousers and white pleated shirt, unbuttoned with chaotic genius. He's fit as the devil's cock.

Klaxon! She catches sight of him by the bar, talking talking talking, pale down showing through his open buttons.

The beat fades. Stage lights swell. Someone shouts into a mic. Dani makes a hoot as the band reappears. This isn't the karaoke where dead-eye salarymen do Elvis in the corner of a piss-smelling pub. It's live. The four musicians cram the tiny stage like polar bears on an ice floe. Dani was squeezed up on that rostrum with them just before. Surely that did happen. A miscreant thought tells her she'll regret the karaoke in the morning. She downs a blue liquid shot to Shake-and-Vac the thought away.

The big bear guitarist in clown-face has changed from the Slipknot jumpsuit into a music-hall checkered suit. He jacks the amp with a sky-rocket *rhooomp!* The black-haired girl in slinky leopard-skin rears the neck of her bass before the crowd and rocks a loop – *dodackadodo, dodackadodo.* Dani loves her surly mischief.

But where's Sam gone? Dani's put the two of them down for *Don't Go Breaking My Heart.* She better find him. She shouts '. . ., . . ., . . .!' at the goth girl beside her, who nods and shouts back '. . .! . . ., . . .!'

Dani burrows into the mosh.

Other stuff happens.

At one point she's shouting abuse at a size minus-six girl in a silver dress who has something spilled down her. Someone grips Dani's arm.

Next she's laughing and introducing a bunch of people she doesn't know.

'This is Sam.'

Oh, he's here again. He smiles. She wants to explain him to these people but it's hard to get the words.

She stumbles. He holds her up with a hand flat on her stomach. It's warm. Drums beat inside her, or on the stage. The MC in the red suit does intros. She puts her hand over Sam's. He says to her, '. . .' and starts to lead her away. She's telling him, no, when she hears the PA.

'*Next up, can they put the "cheeky" into Elton and Kiki? Please welcome the lovely TERRY THE FISH AND SAMMY C!*'

She's pulling and pulling him to the stage. People clap and whoop and pat her back. She stumbles and there's a problem with the vodka.

Then she's puking in the gutter with a calm hand rotating between her shoulder blades. It's like coming home.

¶riotbaby

PIGWATCH: Ten armoured vans parked on the
Embankment west of Hungerford Bridge. Avoid.

FIFTEEN

'NO, I WON'T BE,' said Bethany. 'Not tonight, babe.'

'Poor you,' said the voice on the line.

Peter was sounding oddly faint. She searched the buttons on the hotel phone for something resembling a volume control. Pressed the most likely candidate a few times. Her husband's voice came back a little stronger.

'Are you holding up OK?' he said. 'The boys are crazy with worry. Though Jake's feeling a little better.'

Christ. She'd forgotten all about Jake. The vomit.

'That's good. But listen—'

'I'm trying to keep them away from the news but their friends keep Snapchatting.'

'Petey, hold up. I need to talk to you about—'

'The look on your face as those kids invaded the stage. I wished I'd been there to just put my arms around you.'

Bethany rubbed her sore eyes.

'That does sound nice but I'm honestly fine. I wasn't—'

'On the TV it looked like you were being shoved or—'

'No, but Peter listen. I need to tell you—'

'– and for a while they were saying you'd been kidnapped or something? And then you were fine again? What the hell happened there?'

'Darling, we need to talk.'

Her BlackBerry buzzed on the hotel-room desk. She switched the receiver to her other ear and reached to turn off the intrusive device.

'We are talking,' he said. 'Aren't we?'

'No, come on. You know what I mean. You must have seen. It's everywhere.'

Some weird property of the phone line: when they both fell silent, it seemed to drop off altogether. A silence like deep space. Then, after aeons had passed, the line clicked back at the sound of Peter's voice, like the world being taken off pause.

'This isn't the time,' he said.

She bent forward under the weight of his dry, flat tone, elbows to the desk – pressed a fist into her forehead. This? Yes, of course, this: what the hell had she expected?

'I know,' she said. 'IknowIknowIknow. And I will come home, as soon as I can get away from all this, and we will talk properly then. But I needed for us to, I don't know – acknowledge this thing?'

The line clicked silent again.

'Peter? Are you still there?'

'OK then,' he said at last. 'Here we are, acknowledging this thing. I appreciate you not making any effort to deny it, by the way.'

'I can't begin to tell you—'

'The funny thing is I realise I've known for at least a couple of weeks. With hindsight.'

Why, now, did her gut choose to twist? Not at what she'd done, but at the thought she might have been suspected?

'How do you mean?' she said.

'I don't need to tell you it's been hard. Since you were elected.'

'We've talked about this. You know how much I appreciate –'

She stopped herself short. She'd mouthed these thanks a million times. Today her *appreciation* rang more than a little hollow.

'It's been worse since your promotion, though,' he said. 'It's like I've been married to this tracing-paper version of you. When I actually get to see you, you're barely present. It's sapped you, you know?'

'I haven't been much of a wife, I know. I know. I'm sorry.'

'And then the other week, you came back from Cádiz with this – radiance about you.'

'Darling, don't.'

'And I thought, hello. This is something new. You dumped your bags on the doormat with this smile, full of sun. I walked towards this woman – the same woman I first saw across the dinner table at Dan and Laura's—'

'Christ, Peter—'

'– but when your eyes met mine, for this – just this fraction of a second – your face fell. You managed to put it back on again, of course. You gave me that *Hi how are you?* face. You know? That *Great to see you, thank you for your support* face. The one you politicians are so good at? You didn't realise I'd spotted the change. You sometimes forget how well I know you.'

She was full-on weeping now – at least her eyes were. She let out a little noise, half-word, half-choke.

'That glow,' he said. 'I thought it was something you'd brought back with you – a souvenir of all that sun and optimism. I thought you'd brought it back for me. But no, it was *him*. Wasn't it? You'd brought *him* home with you.'

The way he said that one word: *him*. Bethany wiped at the mess of tears and snot with the ball of her hand.

'It's over,' she said. 'You need to know that. I've been an idiot and he's dropped me like a – used-up – thing. I deserve it.'

'Leaving good old Peter to pick up the pieces.'

'No I – darling—'

'Well, like you say,' he said, brisk now, 'we'd better talk about it properly when you get home. Whenever that may be.'

'Please don't—'

'So. Bye for now.'

'Peter?'

This time, when the line clicked, it fell into a single dull tone that held up until she replaced the receiver. She hugged her arms around her legs and curled up on the upright desk chair. So tired now, so much at the end of everything. The sobs that took full hold of her were deep and forthright. Sobs she'd refused for so long burst like unexploded mines from a war lost years ago.

¶riotbaby

PIGWATCH: All on Panton Street: START RUNNING
NORTH NOW.

SIXTEEN

THE SWIPE WORKS. Leo's in. The concrete back-way smells of metal. Just like the building it penetrates, it gives off the message *host server unknown*. Leo takes the corridor ahead, hangs the first left and puts himself on silent running. Turn right, door, door, turn left, service lift – just like riotbaby said. Leo hits the button, steps into the lift and riffs on buttons. *Eeny, meeny, miney, thirty-two*. He leans back on the fascia and watches the LEDs go *one, two, three*. He hefts the ripped-metal equipment cases in each hand, checking the contents by weight.

Ten, eleven.

He knows it's all there. He checked it a googolplex times this morning. Shit, this morning only! This has been the biggest day of Leo's life. If only he could proffer. But he's taken the battery out of his phone. You never know who those things're talking to.

Twenty-one, twenty-two.

Then he has a panic over has he forgotten the hi-def jack, and spazzes a moment with the clip of the right-hand case. He gets it the wrong way up and the whole crap nearly spills on the floor.

Twenty-eight, twenty-nine.

No, all the kit's in place, obv. Tucked into neat-cut compartments like an assassin's rifle. He clips the box shut and breathes again.

Thirty-two.

Ping. Paydirt. The doors glide open smooth as destiny to reveal – another service corridor, this one narrow as the secret passage through a castle wall. One more swipe of the smartcard and he steps into a ballroom made of light. It's the final scene of *2001*.

This is the screen control room. The long high space is empty, like the Persona said it would be, but the conditioned air is filled with strobing colour. Leo holds his breath and gazes up, up, further up. His eyes are 'does not compute'. Leering over him, flared by perspective, are two giants, taller than a house. The image is rendered for viewing city-blocks away. This close up, it takes several seconds to resolve the flash-lit figures of two slebs braving the red-carpet paps. A metre-high caption stripes their bellies.

JON AND CHARLOTTE 'TO SPLIT'?

This is mirror-world. He's emerged behind one of 404 City's mega-screens. He's a tiny insect trapped in a living flatscreen twenty metres high.

Two screens, actually. The big one faces out across the unholy city sky. The other faces into the building's central atrium. Nobody can hide from Mondan's non-stop data vomit – not even its own wage-slaves. Leo's on a floorplate suspended between the backs of these two screens. The outward-facing screen is cropped by the floor – Leo can only see the top part. In all, it's twelve storeys high. This is the north-facing screen – the one he sees each morning from his top-floor window at the Flamingo. A flatscreen for a *Game of Thrones* giant.

The opposite screen, the one facing inwards, is nothing like as tall. It starts two metres above the floor and rises six metres max. It's part of a mega news ticker wrapping around the inner walls. There are doors set into the wall below it.

Six metres overhead, a boxed-in area runs up between the screens like a periscope. This holds the video hub and the mass of cables feeding the vast displays. That's where Leo's going to hack the screens.

He puts his metal cases on the ground, shrugs off his backpack of tools and walks to the outer screen. He puts a palm against it. A patch of purple flares briefly under his hand then trickles to red. He thinks of the wasted girl he left back at the Flamingo, how the blood flames behind the birthmark on her jaw. The screen is warm. It's made from a grid of liquid pixels the size of his hand. Each cell strobes though millions of possible colours twenty times a second, to the tune of the video hub.

Leo steps back from the hypnotic light and looks for the door to the video hub. In the opposite wall, under the inner screen, is a strip of wall with a choice of four doors. The doors are labelled in tiny utility typeface. He gets up close to read. The left door, near the south-east corner of the room, says *east*. The next, *video hub room*. The third, set at the end of a little alcove in the wall, is *top spot – private*. The fourth, *west*. It's like an old-skool adventure game. *Go n, w, s or e?*

He should make for *video hub room* right away, but *top spot* is a thing. Online, the scuttlebutt says Sean Perce basically lives in this eagle's nest, suspended over 404 City's atrium. From this panopticon he trolls his minions and follows the stats and images that rotate about his perch, on the inner screens.

How awesome would it be to grab a look. Leo checks the top right corner of the inner screen, where a metre-high clock tick-tocks. It reads:

$$23:24:13$$

Awesome: is time.

He uses his magic card to swipe the *top spot* door. A huff of air farts out: the top of the atrium is hotter than the room he's in. He steps out onto a gantry and his sense of scale contracts and expands.

He's a seabird roosting on a cliff-face of sheer impossibility. He reaches behind him, finds a rung and takes a sweaty hold.

The gantry skirts the full perimeter of the atrium, under the lip of the flickering ticker screens. The only protection here for high-walking maintenance men is one flimsy rail and a clip-wire for a safety harness. Leo has no harness to clip. He's pasted to the wall, neck bent under the overhang created by the screen. At his feet is a rackety aluminium lattice; it's all there is between him and a glassy gravity well that runs straight down so steep and square it can't be real. Badly rendered polygons from a cheap-ass game-stage, all the way down to the basement levels.

He looks Leo ahead instead – and sees a flash of himself, naked, gigantic and fringed by text. Shaky news footage, taking up a section of the opposite screen. It cuts to Bethany Lehrer, panicked and retreating on the stage; and to Sean Perce, chickening it to his limo. He can't see it all. The images are cropped by an impossibility: an office room, hovering in mid-air, fifty metres above the ground.

It has to be supported – perhaps by girders hidden in the shiver of metal that links it to the west wall – but it's awesome the games it makes with Leo's eyes. Its glass walls are patterned with chaotic strips of black, making it hard to see inside the box. Leo cranes his head and spies the spider, Perce, perched casual against a desk, shirtsleeves rolled like he's ready for a fight. He works his arms to punch his muted words, with more energy than Leo would use to lift a Coke machine. Leo is cowled in the dark like Batman. No way Perce can see him from inside the halogen brightness of his Top Spot.

Then Leo sees: power, corruption and lies. The copper from before, the tall one whose gun Leo and Dani stole, is sitting in one of Perce's easy chairs. He listens and nods. There's a big square plaster on the side of his shaved head: it's for certain the same cop who fell on the basement floor at the hotel. Parliamentary Branch? Corporate Asslick Branch. Late Capitalism Branch.

The cop stands and shakes hands with Perce. Everything Leo

ever believed about the world is proved with a rugged clasp of palms.

Perce turns, still speaking, and walks to the glass. His eyes close on Leo as if he'd always known he was there. He nods. By the time he speaks again the policeman is already in motion, racing for the bridge to the west wall, eyes locked on Leo like a heat-seeking missile.

Leo turns and fumbles with the door-handle, all vertigo gone.

¶riotbaby

RIOT TIP: Teargas. Rinse your mouth without swallowing. Blow your nose, cough and spit. RESIST THE URGE TO RUB YOUR EYES.

SEVENTEEN

AT SOME POINT DOORS SLICK OPEN and Dani falls into the room.

This is something she's only seen in films set in New York: the lift door opens right into Sam's sitting room. Or is it a studio? Some word that means open plan with frosted brick and heavy timber. Open kitchen to the left, low bed up a step to the right. She giggles like a mentalist. Sam lets her mischief run ahead into the room. He places keys and wallet on a table by the elevator-slash-front-door. Dani drops her backpack. Careful: remember what's in it.

'Why does your flat look like my office?' she says.

There's some connecting formula here. Sam laughs from behind her. Maybe she did a joke. He heads for the kitchen zone while Dani has a blank.

Then she's cross-legged on the floor, checking out a server cabinet. Fat guts of Cat 4 cable spill across the floor. A network station of awesome power – no reason why this shouldn't be here. Everything tonight is potent and natural.

Except why is there a violin case, leaning against the sound system? Sam watches impassive from the kitchen island, stirring a glass jug, as Dani touches the curvy black case. It's new, high end. Not for the first time she doubts Sam's easy surface. This isn't some childhood relic of grade exams, preserved for show.

He's here with a glass. Dani takes it and draws a deep slug. Gin and ancient herbs. The glass licks its lips as she lowers it, and Sam smiles. She's accepted his gift, stepped inside his palace. Now she's his. Or maybe he Rohypnoled her.

'Come and sit.'

He walks to a quadrilateral of sofas with bandy metal legs.

She's in a curl with him on this one sofa, telling of the brutal week when all the people she is were in a head-on crash. To hear her, it might have happened years ago.

'All those different me's, out in the real. All that? Me.' Sam strokes her hair. 'Now I'm getting panic attacks, at being everything outside. I mean – for a while I forget, then they come back. It's like having my insides eaten out by dogs. They're fucking –'

She gestures. Time slides back into a familiar groove.

'This afternoon,' she says, 'with Bethany, it was like I was watching myself doing every single thing. And all I saw was this – blank. And I kept thinking – I don't even know what it's like to have me in the room. What's that even like?'

The one light, a glowing cube down low at the corner of the sofa, strobes gently but insistently. Sam is around her.

'Like, like you: you're lovely. No I mean it, you are. And it sort of, it fills the room. Me, I feel like I'm sometimes –'

Sam's mouth is over hers and it's hot and tight.

'*I'm sorry, I didn't get that.*'

Who the fuck spoke?

Sam twists to find the source, sits up. Rubs his face into awareness. Dani shifts. There's a Sam-shaped dent in her tits. His taste in her mouth: plum, hibiscus – something. He looks dangerous. She touches his arm.

'Sam? What was that?'

For a moment it seems too intimate to last. Then he laughs.

'Oh. Huh.'

He pulls his phone from behind a cushion. He shows it to her then speaks into it.

'Suck my dick.'

'*I'm sorry, I didn't get that.*'

She catches on and crawls across him to get to the mic.

'Hairy gonads!'

'*I'm sorry, I didn't get that.*'

'Anal warts!'

'*I'm sorry, I didn't get that.*'

Their first in-joke. They overplay it.

Naked on the pallet Dani curls away from Sam. He stretches out, eyes to the ceiling. He wants her to believe he's cool about this, or not that, but that he's capable of more. His diaphragm flutters, calling bullshit on his calm. The clock's hands trace big arcs of time above their heads. Dani shivers as the night air cools her sweat. She talks and talks. All the imaginary times she's fucked this man – so different from the abortive grapple they just unwound from. Her fantasy Sam was too real to survive reality. That lank Adonis from an island beach was neater than the actual Sam.

Anyway, at what point did she set herself up as Sam's little virgin? She hunts for words to cover the static, keeps straying into confession; wishes she could shut up.

'You think I'm cold,' she says.

'I don't.'

She waits but apparently that's all. Words keep marching out of her face.

He eases his leg between the rear of her calves and looks down her back. All he wants is to touch her soft arse. He's not listening to her. He gazes down the soft comma of her body, watching her cheeks go taut and loose. In general he only fucks skinny girls; but now all he wants is to slip the pads of his fingers down the small of her back and trace an opening between those cheeks. He's hard again.

'I mean,' she's saying, 'when things work we don't know where it comes from. There's something automatic. I don't care how smart you are. You don't know what the fuck's going on any more than I do.'

'It's true. I know nothing,' Sam says to her crack.

'No, I mean it.'

His fingers make patterns along her spine.

'You shouldn't be hard on yourself,' he says. 'You're more special than you give yourself credit.'

'How do you mean? Oh.'

His first two fingers are doing the thing.

'I'm not trying to shut you up.'

'No, it's fine. I like to talk while – hmm.'

'You like that?'

'. . .'

Her spinal cord judders. She bites her lower lip, her whole body focused on the fingers working down between her buttocks. He nuzzles up to her and kisses between her shoulder blades, works his spare arm under and around, pulling her in. She has nice, unassuming little breasts. She wriggles into place. They fit together well.

His two fingers part as they reach her arsehole. A tip touches. Muscles recoil like sea-life into its shell. She gives off heat and pushes at him as he slips the finger in. She gasps. He's never done this before: always shy of filth. As he works another in, he reaches the other hand around to grasp her breast. She's struggling to turn and face him. Her head snakes around to bite his ear. It terriers onto the lobe. Deadlock. She won't unclench her teeth and he won't move his fingers.

She gives first. His stinging earlobe slips from her mouth. He shakes his head and moves on top, his cock painfully hard. He turns her over, fingers inside to the middle joint. She glares up at him, a flush running across her chest like brushfire. As her pelvis flattens against the mattress he twists his fingers in her tightness. She takes a sharp breath and folds her leg so he can unloop his arm. He looks down on her compact body. When he first undressed her he couldn't get past the puppy-flesh, would not get fully hard. Now she inflames him. The bright purple song of her birthmark, its bottom tip kissing her collarbone. He plays it with his tongue.

She grabs his cock and grapples it down, twisting it hard. He cries, *ah-ha-ha* and he's laughing, at how completely she's surprised him. He hopes she heard him give in. She flattens her other hand against his chest. The eggshell smoothness of his face turns to raw red as it crosses the ridges of his ribcage. His cock is slim and knotted.

Fuck the foreplay. All the fists she's made of her own pleasure in her creaking swivel chair. Fake, fake. This is real, she thinks; but he thinks, this isn't real.

Both of them are hungry and racing for the prize. She scrapes her palm across his thistle-down head then pulls back and slaps his face. His shocked expression cracks her up. He rears back, his fingers popping out of her, too fast. She punches him in the chest: hard. He grapples at her fist but she shakes it free and gives his cock a squeeze with her other hand: no you don't. He glares at her in actual fury. Ah, so it was in there somewhere. She punches him again, one, two, on his tight pectoral. It flares red. Before his face can settle she moves him down and eases him in: Christ, she's like water. She racks and he gasps. She slaps him and grabs his jawbone, squashing up his pretty face. Grabs his arse and forces him in.

Something just unlocked. He lets her handle him like a mechanical toy. She rucks him into her with both hands.

She doesn't make it: but it's close. He starts to buckle and lets it out with a low moan. She roars and keeps working him into her but he's slipping away.

She lets him ease out. They look at each other for the longest time. Whose move?

'Well,' he says, 'second time's the charm.'

She laughs and slaps his shoulder.

'Fucking teenager.'

But her grin says she's lying. She strokes his cheek with the backs of her fingers.

'Sorry, I guess.'

He means it.

'No, no.'

'That was – surprising for me.'

That sheepish grin: the boy Sam.

'Me too. Sure.'

He slips back around her. She shifts and realises she's oozing like mad. Ah, fuck it: it's his side of the bed. Presumably.

Sam isn't one of those guys who flop into sleep as soon as they come. He's jazzed up, legs a-jangle. He sits up and fumbles on the top of a low bookcase that serves as a bedside table.

'Are you checking your phone, you dick?'

'I thought I heard a text.'

'Fucking PR. I beat you till you come and you only care about your phone.'

He checks the phone, doesn't comment, places it back on the nightstand.

'Yeah,' he says. 'That was – I liked it. I don't – weird.'

'That's the thing about you. So articulate.'

They lie there a while. Cars sooth past the window. Her head is sharp and clear.

The bookcase by his bed is all tattered old paperbacks. Makes sense, somehow, that he'd fetishise old stuff. Dani doesn't have a single paper book in her whole flat, except tech manuals for C variants and UNIX. Something about Sam that he's holding onto.

She props herself on an elbow so she can stroke his forehead.

'Sam?'

'Sure.'

'Earlier on. What were you doing at the Flamingo?'

He doesn't reply. She sits up on her elbow to look at him. He's wary.

'I got so mental last night,' she says, 'it made sense at the time for you to be there; but now I don't get the logic?'

He's looking at her as if she never spoke. Then he sits forward, breaking from her stroking, and draws up his knees.

'Sam?'

'OK, let's think how to do this.'

'What? No, let's not think. Let's answer Dani's cocking question. What is this?'

'I was hoping Graham had already said something to you, or—'

'Gah! Sam, what the fuck? Why mention Gray?'

She stops. Of its own accord, her eye has diverted to the top shelf of his bookcase. Telling her she missed something there. Among the old books, some are new. There. Five matching spines with dayglo letters dancing down them.

GIGGLY PIGGLIES ON THE FARM.

GIGGLY PIGGLIES GO ON HOLIDAY.

'Holy fuck,' she says. 'No. No way.'

GIGGLY PIGGLIES AT THE THEME PARK.

GIGGLY PIGGLIES AT THE CIRCUS.

Sam gets up and walks away from her.

'Sam?'

He pulls on a pair of grey sweatpants. Trendy ones, not skaggy like Dani's would be.

'Sam!' she says.

She pulls out the fifth book – *GIGGLY PIGGLIES AND THE LOST DOG* – and holds it up for him to see. He turns to look at it, nods slightly, then looks her in the eye.

'Yesterday,' she says, 'you told me you were capable of fighting the system but through other channels. Some shit like that.'

'OK. Sure. So?'

She slaps the book down on the bedcovers. Places a finger on the glossy cover.

'So tell me what you meant by that.'

He folds slim arms across his almost hairless chest.

'Why don't you tell me?'

¶riotbaby

Remember, children. Tomorrow, high noon.

EIGHTEEN

IT'S A ONE-MAN KETTLE.

The video hub room is a three-metre cube lined with cable-dangling equipment – all innards. It hangs mid-air between the inner and outer screens of 404 City, accessed by a boxed-in metal ladder and crawl space. Leo swiped himself into it less than a minute ago. Already the policeman is hammering on the locked door.

He pops out his flat-head screwdriver. Does it matter if they catch him? Does he have a choice? Three minutes tops before some Mondan rent-a-cop makes it up here to give the cop an access-all-areas pass as powerful as Leo's. So he moves from rack to rack like a robot on a car assembly: click open a panel; flick lines out; bridge connections; snap the first Black Box into place; stow it deep in the gubbins where it won't be seen. Close the panel. Onto the next node.

Another series of hammering blows. This guy loves making a noise. Or he's very pissed. Pretty sure it's both.

Here's how Leo reasons now: if the copper catches him and figures out he came in here to fuck with the video kit, it'll take like x nanoseconds to find his hidden warez and the gig is off.

Matter of fact, it doesn't even matter if the cop catches Leo. If he knows what the kid's been up to in here he'll find the tech and so likewise.

So, logic: Leo needs the man not to work out what he's up to.

Not that Leo's looking to be caught. The image of the big cop, gun hard on Dani, rubber veins throbbing on his neck, is burned in his retinas. The guy will only be madder now.

So only one scenario works: the copper needs not to catch Leo and he needs not to work out why Leo was ever here.

So Leo needs two things: an escape route, and a diversion to distract the cop from his white-hat hack.

He reaches a posi screwdriver from the tool bag at his feet. His hand brushes cloth inside the bag: the banner – the one they never used at the demo this afternoon, still rolled up inside. Bingo: a diversion, right there. Thank fuck Leo never got to hang it out at the demo. Story logic: he needs a diversion, a diversion appears.

So, now: escape route. Leo doesn't question that one will appear. Story logic says there is one.

At the bottom of the access ladder the cop shouts through the door in a hyper-reasonable hostage negotiator voice. It comes through as *wah-wah-wah wa-wah wah*. Leo isn't listening anyway. He's scanning walls and ceiling as he slides the fourth and final Black Box into place. He slams the array panel shut and twists the retaining clips into place. Brushes his hands together, job done. Then he spots it: a hatch, up in the corner of the ceiling. And a set of folding steps by the equipment rack. Poetry. He slips his screwdrivers back into the backpack and snaps shut his cases, then clambers up the steps to pop the hatch.

He pokes his head into the eye of a cable tornado. It twists in cascades up the vertical conduit he'd seen from outside. The space is barely lit, by grates set in the walls. It smells of solder and new-build. Its shielded-cable nerves carry signals to every pixel on the vast displays. Leo's inside the biggest HDMI lead in the universe.

He ducks back into the hub room to retrieve his equipment cases and backpack, shoves them ahead through the hatch and climbs up to bury the cases in the rubber spew of cable. When he's sure they can't be seen he opens his backpack, pulls out the furled-up banner and stows the backpack, too.

From below, a friendly *beepity-beep* and the door smashes open. Time up. He slams the hatch shut. OK, story, where next?

Which is when he sees the ladder. He starts to climb it, up the conduit, through the tumbling video lines, banner tucked under his arm.

Logic says *up* is not the best way to escape from a thirty-two-storey building, but Leo's caught in the certainty that says: here it is. Your hero moment. Ready for you to climb up the aluminium rungs of. Tomorrow everyone will know the name *identikid*.

'Leo Sandberg!'

What? No, not that name. Who shouted?

The hatch punches open down below: the cop, storming on his tail. How does he know the kid's name? Leo tastes an acid jet of reality. Someone has grassed him. One of the crew? Undercover Met?

The cop barrels out of the hatch and catches sight of Leo, above him in the half-light. Leo starts climbing faster. His usual thing is to stunt in the open air, with mates and videophones close by so the cops don't dare go heavy. In here it might as well be 1976. He's in the guts of the enemy without a working phone. He climbs.

As the cop clangs up the bottom rungs, Leo stops at a panel in the wall. He heaves the handle and scrabbles through a narrow crawl-space. At the end, a second hatch. His dark-adapted eyes scream against the light as he pulls it open. He squeezes out onto a walkway running across the top of the abyss – crossing the roof of the Top Spot at the halfway point. Story logic. This is too good.

He slams the hatch shut, does his best to wedge it with a hooked aluminium pole hung on the wall. He hears the cop clanking up the ladder. He has thirty seconds tops. He turns and has a nano-second of wrenching vertigo, then levels his internal gyro and jogs across the gantry bridge.

When he found the banner in his backpack, he figured he'd use it to explain why he was here in 404. He'd claim he was planning to hang it somewhere. They'd write him off as some Protester v1.0 and never suss that he'd hacked the video gear. But now he can actually hang the banner out across this walkway, then escape through Perce's office using his magic swipecard. Perfect diversion, perfect escape.

As he runs he feels for the loose end of the banner. Winter, his girl, has sewn two dozen metal hooks along the top. He slows to lean over the handrail and, running smooth, he clicks the hooks on, one, two, three. The hatch rattles loudly. There's a muffled shout. Leaning out over the gaping atrium he keeps sidestepping fast, never looking down, click, step, click, step, click, unrolling the banner as he goes and letting the heavy swags dangle down. The banner's message is revealed to the space below, word by word:

YOU WHY

WOULD PUT

NOT YOUR

PASS TRUST . . .

He's halfway done when the roll of banner slips from his arms. He fumbles the air for it, leaning out to pull it back, filling his arms with cloth. His hand has barely got a hold on the banner's flailing end when a crash rings out, so close it could have come from inside his ear, echoing like a gunshot in a tunnel. Then that shout again.

'Leo Sandberg!'

Instinct straightens his bent-over body. His simian muscles say that when his body straightens, his feet will be on the ground and he'll stand up straight. But they aren't and he doesn't. The banner in his hands outweighs the traction of his trainers on the metal gantry floor.

Which is how, his hands still gripping the banner, Leo tips so gracefully forward across the handrail, turns in the air and begins to fall.

The banner unrolls as he arcs down from the gantry. When it hits full length, it jolts Leo's arm, too hard for his fingers to grip. The banner wrenches from his hand and kicks away to billow proudly in the air above him. Leo tumbles backwards into the purified air of the atrium. As he falls, he looks up at the bully face of the receding cop leaning over the rail, his helpless arms stretched into the abyss – and at the banner as it flails below his feet. In two lines of Winter's crisp hand-painted type it reads:

YOU WOULD NOT PASS YOUR DOOR-KEY TO THE FIRST MAN WHO ASKED FOR IT.

WHY PUT YOUR TRUST IN A STATE THAT WOULD TAKE THE KEY TO YOUR OWN SELF?

–ELYSE MARTINGALE

Bummer in a way to be falling backwards and miss the main show but it's good to see the banner. It looks pretty cool. Shame it's only half-attached.

How awesome would it be right now to film this. But he doesn't have his phone.

¶identikid

#

NINETEEN

DANI SHOVES THE WINDOW OPEN with the butt of her hand and looks down at the empty street. Chill hits her blood like a shot of heroin. Sam's silk dressing gown gives zero protection for her gooseflesh. She turns to where he sits with the sheets ground up around him, looking down at his folded hands. His neck muscles work as though he's trying to swallow a bee.

'So you're running the sockpuppet?' she says.

He looks up at her.

'Huh?'

'You're this character *zero*?'

'Well, Dani—'

'Which is a stupid name, by the way. Is that some kind of William Gibson shit? Like *Count Zero*?'

'William who?'

She kicks the bare sole of his foot. He yanks it away and smiles up at her in this massively patronising way.

'I'm impressed though,' he says. 'Truly. How did you figure it out?'

More to the point, *what* did she figure out? There's so much weirdness sloshing around, she can't pin down exactly what Sam has and hasn't done: who he is and who he isn't.

'I *was* going to tell you,' he says. 'You need to know that.'

'Oh, yeah? Were you going to do that before or after you fucked me? Oh, wait. Too late.'

'After this whole thing was over.'

'Of course,' she says. '*This whole thing.* As in you're still up to something, right now,' she says. 'With Leo?'

He nods.

'*Gah!*' she says, slapping her hands against her sides and striding off across the room. 'I *knew* there was something screwy when I spoke to him after the demo. He was talking about something big about to go down – using this weird marketing speak. You know what it sounded like?'

She's arrived back at Sam who's still sitting in the same position on the low bed. He shakes his head.

'It sounded like someone else was talking through him,' she says. 'And then guess who shows up at his karaoke club night? Mister Marketing Bullshit himself.'

'*My* club night, strictly speaking. I'm the promoter.'

'Of course you are, Sam.'

'I *am*,' he says, apparently stung. 'We use them to raise funds for – activities.'

'Activities. Right. But the weird thing? It still would have taken me forever to make the connection between you and Leo – maybe I never would have worked the whole thing out, except that just now I saw –'

She nods at where the Pigglies book still lies on the bed beside Sam.

'Ah,' he says, picking it up.

He opens the cover as though the title-page picture of cavorting pigs will help him answer some question.

'Yes,' he says, closing the book and setting it aside. 'Not your standard bedside reading for a single adult male.'

'It's like it was shouting for my attention from the shelf. It took me a moment to see it but then it all made sense, for the first time this week. It was totally our Walter White/Hank Schrader moment.'

'Uh?' says Sam, genuinely puzzled.

'Never mind.'

She kneels in front of him, eye to eye. The solution is rapidly taking shape, like when the knotty logic of a code routine flips suddenly to show a perfect, previously hidden form.

'Let me set this out,' she says.

'All right.'

Sam leans back, supporting himself on his hands. The night air from the window bites into Dani's flesh, helping her think.

'First up,' she says, 'you did the Giggly Pigglies thing. Using tech skills you definitely do not have, you somehow hacked the data from DigiCitz and put the pig virus onto those people's machines. The Pigglies were a stunt. PR. You used them to draw attention to the hack, make sure it got media coverage.'

'The pigs were a story hook, yes.'

'And since then,' she says, 'you've been sic_girl. She's been you. You used your, again, non-existent skills to walk into Parley's ultra-secure production environment. You took over my baby girl, ran her as your sockpuppet and used her to stir up the crazy and basically get Bethany Lehrer fired. I mean, you've actually brought down a government minister?'

'Pretty much.'

He looks so weirdly fragile. Almost boyish. So proud of what he's done, and so desperate for affirmation – from *her*. She reaches to stroke his cheek. He nuzzles against her hand. She pulls it away.

'But *why*, Sam?'

He fixes her with a cold gaze.

'You work in the business,' he says. 'You know how this goes.'

They're in Sam's kitchen. She's sitting on a high metal stool. He raises his volume over the boiling kettle.

'What they're doing,' he says. 'Tracking us all – CCTV tags, immigration status, crime, health. What we read, who we email. Every bit of us. People give up their data because they want their parking permit, or their disability benefit, and *ping!* they've been automatically profiled by MI5. First they know of it, a boot kicks in the door. They're all in it together.'

He's opening and shutting cupboards. He pulls out a box of gay tea.

'They? Bethany Lehrer?'

He pours boiling water and gestures through the steam.

'That's not even a question. All of them. Government, business? No difference.'

She takes the hot cup. It smells like jizz and looks like dishwater.

'Rooibos,' he says.

'You said it was Bethany who set the trolls on me and so I basically kidnapped her, Sam. But she said it *wasn't* her. I believe her.'

Sam leans back against the counter, hands wrapped around his cup.

'That was a *little* extreme,' he says. 'But yes. On that point – only on that point – she was telling the truth. I *thought* it was her, but—'

'Thought. *Thought?*'

'Yeah, but then I spoke to this guy I know, in her office, and traded for information. It wasn't them.'

'Traded.'

'Right.'

She lets that go, too.

'Then who did it, Sam? Who fucked up my life?'

'Exactly.'

They're out on a tiny balcony. She's pulled on jeans, T-shirt and jacket.

'I've been running TakeBackID for three months now,' he says. 'That's all. When we started stirring trouble we were only shaking trees to see who jumped. Sometimes you set a fire but you don't know which direction the wind will take it.'

He uses metaphors too much. It makes it hard to concentrate.

'For instance,' he says, 'who knew Elyse Martingale would be such an awesome poster-girl?'

'You didn't start this,' she says. 'People are already proper angry.'

'But are they *doing* anything? Other than a small clique of permanent protestors, people don't get off their arses unless you make them. You need to tap the latent mood with something urgent enough or funny enough to move them.'

'*Funny?*'

'Sure. Lulz. Giggly Pigglies. Rubber masks. Getting your dick out on camera. Something that means you'll be able to say: *it was totally awesome. I was there.* Motivation for a zero-attention-span world.'

Out in the streets there's shouting. She eyes him. That lean sixth-former she once knew, talking like nobody else was in the room. She wants to bite his flesh.

'You know what?' she says. 'That demo wasn't you. It was Leo.'

'Leo did what riotbaby told him to do. Riotbaby was me. He never listened when I spoke as myself. He told me I was full of shit and I should stick to club-night promotions. So I worked out who he *did* listen to, and it turned out to be this – *fake.* This *nothing.* Riotbaby! Huh. And not just Leo. All the TakeBack crew hung on that robot's every word. So I took it over.'

'Took it over how?'

'Riotbaby for the slacktivists,' he says, ignoring her question, 'sic_girl for the chattering classes. I put words in their hollow mouths. They're the perfect spokespeople. They have no opinions of their own and they don't ask for twenty grand per appearance. So don't tell me it just happened. I planned it and I timed it.'

He's looking out towards where the beacon of 404 City shines above the rooftops. When he speaks again he's measured, controlled.

'Have you seen what's going on out there? You don't get this kind of action over something as boring as data, as privacy. I needed a stronger narrative to stir people up. TakeBack is essentially brand extension. It started with benefit cuts and police brutality and student loans and whatever gets people to throw a brick. That hooked people in – got them so stirred up I could point them at something as meh as DigiCitz and they started drooling with anger.'

A scream echoes from nearby. Sam nods.

'No one out there knows why the person next to him is setting fires,' he says.

Dani hugs herself against the chill.

'Who's setting fires?'

Sam puts his cup down on the metal table, pulls an iPad Mini from his hoodie's monopocket. Hands her a Parley screen.

'Take a look at riotbaby's continuity.'

Dani does, and double-takes at the speed of the proffers. Normally the Personas speak at a realistic human pace but this stream of trouble scrolls by almost too fast for Dani to read. Riotbaby is on autopilot.

'Only thing the spectacle responds to,' says Sam, 'is spectacle. This is a cross-channel campaign. And a bloody well-executed one, if I say so myself.'

They're back on the sofas and the vodka. It's frosty and viscous.

'The new capitalist realism tells us *There's no alternative*,' says Sam. '*Suffer it, bitches, because this is all you get*. But when did we start believing that?'

Things sound true when he speaks, but so does everything these days. Dani presses her legs together until she can't feel the rawness in her arse.

'It gets to feel inevitable,' he says. 'And that can give people an excuse to rant or – just as likely – do F all.'

An electronic buzzer sounds, low and hard. Sam doesn't stir.

'Someone has to make people give a fuck and *do* something,' he says.

'And this saviour of the universe is . . .?'

There's a clank from the lift shaft.

'Nobody's who they say they are, Dani. *You* know that.'

She blinks. Has she missed part of the conversation?

The lift doors open. Dani half-stands. Surely you need a key-card to open the doors? Sam used a key-card, before. Out of the lift steps Gray. His T-shirt is zany purple. It reads, *IT'S A SMALL WORLD BUT I WOULDN'T WANT TO DEFRAGMENT IT.* He does a double take at Dani as the doors shrug shut behind him. He turns to Sam, who's walking to the kitchen counter.

'Hey, PR,' he says, 'don't you ever answer your phone?'

Dani's still half-elevated from the sofa.

'It's been off,' says Sam.

He grabs the neck of the vodka bottle.

'What. The. Fuck?' says Dani.

Gray takes in the rest of the scene. His eyes rest on the knotted bedclothes, then on Dani, then on Sam.

'Oh, what, no?' says Gray. 'Oh, you supercilious bugger, you never did?'

Dani moves into his eyeline.

'Did?' she says. 'Like he just *did* me, Gray? Like I fuck who I want and you are not my boyfriend?'

'Well, *you're* drunk, Dan. Hello.' He unshoulders his back-pack. 'Did you really schtup this streak of diluted urine? I do hope this is a one-off.'

He moves to hug her. She bats him away.

'Oh, my fucking *God* what gives you the right?'

She wheels around, stamps over to Sam and presents her heavy tumbler to him. Better the devil you thought you knew – but actually didn't – or something. Polish vodka rolls into her glass. Gray plants himself on a sofa and fishes in his bag.

'I'm actually going to rise above whatever just happened here,' he says. 'I have information. Won't wait.'

Sam shrugs, capping the bottle. Gray clacks on his laptop.

'First thing,' he says. 'Leo's gone missing.'

'Leo?' says Dani.

Does everyone she knows know everyone else? Gray ignores her.

'He should have reported back two hours ago but his phone's still off. However – yep, there we go. The Black Boxes are transmitting from inside the 404 City video hub.' He looks up at Sam. 'He did the job.'

'Good.' Sam walks to the sofa facing Gray and sits, unblinking. 'Could this not wait till morning?'

'OK,' says Gray. 'If that doesn't grab you, secondly: as of noon tomorrow you don't have a channel.'

That gets a frown from Sam but it's Dani who speaks.

'What do you mean, Gray? Is something happening to Parley?' Gray replies to Sam.

'See this is what happens if you don't look at your phone.' Then he registers what Dani said. 'Wait, so you told her about Parley?'

'She figured it out,' says Sam.

Gray turns to Dani, radiant in a way that almost moves her.

'Did you, Dan? That's pretty cool. But then why be surprised when I walked in here?' He laughs. 'Holy God, you thought Sir Spin-A-Lot here hacked Parley on his own. Shit. Funny. Who do you think turned sic_girl? Who got access to all those Mondan emails? Who's been running riotbaby all night while this guy gave you the deep clean? God, he has a way of selling a line.'

She hasn't seen Gray on this kind of passive-aggressive bender for a long time. She sits down on the remaining empty sofa, half-way between the men.

'OK. So it's you, Gray. You're the guy. So news us about Parley.'

Gray works his computer and speaks like a recorded message.

'Sam and me monitor mail traffic in and out of the Mondan press office, among other things. At eight twenty-two tonight I picked up a draft announcement that's going out on the wires tomorrow. Embargoed till noon.' He scrolls. 'They're pulling the plug on Parley. Cancelling the service, binning the Personas, everything. In order to, quote: *bring an end to the controversy around recent proffers and prepare for an exciting new service announcement from Mondan Group.*'

Dani's face is about to explode.

'*What?*'

Sam sits forward.

'Oh, now this is clever. They look like they're acting responsibly, supporting their government client. But they're cutting off our oxygen at a crucial time.'

'Right,' says Gray. 'They know we'll need time to switch channels.'

Dani puts up a hand.

'Hold it—'

Gray talks over her.

'But it's cleverer. There's a third thing.'

'Fuck, Gray—' she says.

Now Sam cuts her off.

'Hold up. Graham, stop yanking my chain. Third thing what?'

Gray places the laptop open by his side, stretches out against the sofa back.

'Data wipe.'

'What?' says Sam.

Dani stands up, too fast. The others take no notice as she wavers to the kitchen. Their talk goes muffled, like a childhood memory of parents' voices from downstairs.

'Mondan's data security policy,' says Gray, 'is that no hard drive can leave one of their server farms until they Cillit Bang any trace of data from its surface.'

At the kitchen island Dani chucks the remnants of her vodka into the brushed chrome sink and lets freezing water gush into the heavy glass.

'So they're wiping Parley?' says Sam.

Dani glugs water. The chill hits the roof of her mouth and ignites in her brain. Gray reaches for his laptop.

'And suppose I tell you,' he says, 'they're planning a little accident when they do.'

The water is good. Dani fills another glass.

'Suppose I tell you Mondan's standard practice is to wipe all hard drives in bulk, electromagnetic, like *Ocean's Eleven*? And

that the Parley servers just happen to be in the next-door rack to
the DigiCitz servers?'

A frosty light forms around Sam. It's slow and viscous like the
vodka. It's his voice.

'Shit,' says Sam.

'Yes,' says Gray. 'They'll blast the Parley servers clean and it'll be,
Whoopsie daisy!' Gray puts on the appalling Cockney accent he uses
to denote what he sees as a menial profession. '*We only went and
wiped the DigiCitz servers, too. Silly old us! Good thing we have a
backup.* Leaving no evidence of the hack – or the other breaches.
Meaning your whole campaign is a waste of time and money.'

Light roars from Sam's mouth, raising an arc from him to Gray.
It buries itself in the keys and display cells of Gray's machine.

'Someone tipped them off,' says Sam.

'No,' says Gray. 'The pressure's on them. We *put* it on them. They
know it's only a matter of time before Parliament orders an investigation into the hack. And oh, by the way, they also caught Co—'

His eyes move to Dani, then they move away.

'I mean,' he says, 'they caught the guy who did the hack. He
kept his mouth shut, but they know what he did. They know those
servers are rotten with evidence of the hack.'

The light isn't clean. Some kind of interference disrupts it as it
wraps around the men. There's a stone in Dani's gut. Something
is wrong. Sam nods slowly.

'When is this data wipe happening?' says Sam through a cloud
of reverb. 'We need to stop it. That data needs to stay on those
disks – at least till they find their way to the police or the Cabinet
Office.'

Something is missing from the light, stealing the signal. Dani
slams the empty glass on the countertop as hard as her arm can
land it. Both men look up in alarm. It wakes her. The light is telling her nothing. She shakes it off.

'Both of you! Shut it!' Sam stands and raises his hand. 'No!
Shut the shutting fuck up and listen to me! They're killing the
Personas? Killing sic? And you just sit and drone the fuck on?'

'Dani, I don't—' says Gray.

'Shut! Up! You, both of you, stop ignoring me! What have either of you done this past Christ knows how long but lie to me?'

'Dan?' Gray's voice is level. He slides the laptop shut. 'Listen. We don't have time.'

'You, though?' she says. 'This slick fuck I understand –' Sam regards her with the same cool piety he uses on Gray. '– but you?'

'This matters,' says Gray. 'You don't know everything.'

'Always! Trying to fucking control me.'

Gray stands up.

'No. Mondan. Sean Perce. *He's* trying to.'

Sam stands behind the sofa, behind Gray, looking on. Dani advances, pounding her sides with empty fists.

'Is Sean Perce in this room? How's *he* controlling me?'

Gray holds up the laptop like a shield.

'On Wednesday night, Perce sent a USB stick to a journalist called Will Samber. That name ring a bell?'

He just chucked acid over Dani. She stops dead.

'The guy who wrote the story about me,' she says. 'The pictures. He started the trolls.'

'This afternoon, Sam sent me this.' Gray holds up a small grey USB. 'He got it from, from –?'

He clicks his fingers at Sam.

'From a contact,' says Sam, 'on Samber's newsdesk.'

'Right,' says Gray. 'And tonight I cracked this flash drive open. All your data, Dan – it's on there. Your passwords, pictures, emails. Perce sent it all to this guy Samber. He must've had someone hack your workstation.'

Sparkles crash like a wave. Dani pulls herself back from the black wash.

'*Sean Perce* doxed me? Some billionaire decided one day to take me to pieces? Like my boss's boss? To why? Who the fuck am I?'

Gray shrugs. Dani lands on the sofa.

'Oh, fuck this all!'

Gray doesn't come to her, doesn't try to comfort her. Just stands where he is and waits.

'It's like – sic_girl is really Sam,' she says. 'You too, Gray. Now my own company is fucking with me. Even Colin.'

Gray and Sam exchange a sharp look she can't parse.

'Colin?' says Gray.

'Never mind,' she says. 'Really never mind. But for you to do this and never tell me – not even in the yard the other day? It feels: you must really not trust me.'

'I – oh, hell. Dan, I guess we were protecting you.'

'Oh, fucking *men*!'

The silence isn't silent. There's an after-hum of the building's industrial past. After a moment, Dani and Gray both notice that Sam is laughing.

'She does have a point,' he says.

'Like you have any fucking leg to stand on,' says Dani. 'If you knew about Sean Perce doxing me and turning the trolls on me, why did *you* never say so?'

He thinks for a moment.

'But I didn't know. It makes total sense but I heard it first from Gray, just now. I couldn't read the USB.'

Don't believe him. That needs to be the rule until she has more data. However real it sounds. A decision circuit flips in her head.

'OK,' she says. 'OK. We're going to rescue sic – and the others.'

Gray is the first to respond.

'*Rescue* sic_girl? As in: you are not serious.'

'Do I look not serious? We're going to pull everything off the Parley servers and get them back. We'll do it from here. Gray: you have superuser.'

'No, in fact, I don't. The Mondan team took over Parley this afternoon. First thing they did was cut the privileges.'

'Then – we go in to 404. We go in there and we grab the hard disks. Rescue my babies.'

'Dan, these are algorithms. You can't *rescue* software.'

'I *made* them.'

'There's more important things than your coder's ego trip.'

'Two days ago you thought they were coming to life,' she says, 'and now –'

She figures it out a second too late to stop herself saying it. Gray gives his barking laugh.

'Get real,' he says. 'I strung Jonquil a line about that AI bullshit. It was Sam's idea.' Gentler, then. 'They aren't alive.'

'You're still killing them.'

His face darkens.

'I am not your boyfriend any more and I don't have to take your shit.'

Her nails bite into her palms.

'Stop punishing me for fucking Sam!'

'You can fuck Sean Perce for all I care. This is not on me.'

'She's right, though,' says Sam.

He's been quiet so long it takes them a moment to locate him, on a fancy Scandinavian swivel chair by the desk between the room's two big arched windows. His computer, a gunmetal Mac, sits on the floor spilling cable round his feet. He has four or five Parley continuities up on an enormous flatscreen.

'Come on, no,' says Gray. 'We're not going to screw the whole campaign for the sake of her horseshit.'

Sam shakes his head. He has on his over-serious face.

'Dani doesn't want her Personas wiped,' he says. 'And we need the evidence of the hack to be found. I'm not pissing away three months of work. We need the DigiCitz hard drives bagged up and safe until the plods can get their hands on them. You, me, Dani – we're all after the same thing. The police get the evidence of the hack; Dani "rescues" her precious Personas. Everyone's happy.'

The bastard does air quotes. But he's making sense.

'What time is any of this happening?' he says.

Gray is flush with anger. He thought he was running this show. But there's no holding back on Sam.

'They pull the plug on Parley midday tomorrow. Just as the press release goes out. Then they'll start the wipe.'

'So.' Sam does a 360 on his swivel chair and grins his lovely grin. 'We have time to grab some sleep before we save the Internet.'

SATURDAY:

Demos

'So, who here has an iPhone? Who here has a
BlackBerry? Who here uses Gmail? Well, you're all
screwed.'

—Julian Assange

'Move fast and break things.'

—Facebook developer's credo

ZERO

IN SLEEP, DANI'S FEATURES lose their anger and bewilderment. The hard set of her jaw and cheeks reconfigure into the face of a lost girl. There's always been a wounded childishness behind her toughness. But I've never seen her so defenceless.

Does she always sleep with her birthmark to the pillow? She looks so young and normal. Like someone's kid you meet and worry about whether it's OK to fancy.

She took me by surprise, last night. I wonder if she was surprised, too. It was the kind of intense you can't recapture.

Will anyone else respond to her? I'm in the market for a new poster child. The Personas give us reach and cut-through but people won't believe my imitation game for long. To maintain the story I need continuity. For brand loyalty I need empathy. People need someone to feel for; feel with. Flesh and blood. Ideally with cheekbones and perfect skin but hey, this is the real world. Dani will have to do.

ONE

THREE MUFFLED CRASHES and the sound of busy work with cups and cupboard doors. Dani levers herself off the pillow. Sam is up already, working a long metal machine at the kitchen counter. He carries a soft white coffee over to her and places a slow kiss on her forehead. She props herself against the whitewashed wall and cradles the coffee. Gives Sam an unaffected smile. Then a gravel voice cuts in from behind him.

'So apparently I have to make my own hot drinks? Woot.'

Graham's head has appeared above the sofa back.

'Not at all.'

Sam heads back to the counter. Gray gives Dani a shit-eating grin and wags his little finger. Which means either Sam's cock, or *I've got him wrapped around my*. Dani raises her middle finger in reply and takes a sip through the doughy froth. The coffee smells of scorched wood. She puts it down, checks her phone – not yet seven – and rubs muck from her eyes. Over on the sofa, Gray takes a bright orange shirt from his rucksack and pulls it on. It reads *THERE'S NO PLACE LIKE 127.0.0.1.* He looks up and winks. He knows she'll get it and Sam won't.

Sam puts down a coffee for Gray then walks to his desk and stuffs his tablet into a leather man-bag.

'So,' he says. 'I know what we're going to do.'

Dani shifts: there's the pain in her arsehole again.

'But first,' says Sam, 'you both need to know: something's happened.'

Dani sits forward in alarm.

'Parley? Already?'

'No.' He's gauging her reaction. 'Not to Parley. To Leo.'

While Dani dresses, Sam and Gray huddle together in the kitchen. The last week is starting to make a kind of sense if she reruns it in a use-case where Gray helped Sam take over Parley and stir up TakeBackID. But most of the who-did-what-whens are still unclear – for instance, who did the Digital Citizen hack? Assuming there was a hack.

This much she does get: the finale is today. The centrepiece will be a takeover of the giant screens at 404 City. Leo was prepping for this last night when he fell. When they pushed him. When whatever happened. Anyway, when he died.

Her head goes back to yesterday evening.

Leo handing her the gun
   do what you want with it he said
     the weight of it in her hand
       now hes dead

She walks over to join the others in the kitchen.

'What's wrong with the front door?' asks Sam. 'You have a swipe card. You can just walk in.'

'Not with security and police all over the building, after—'

Gray stops himself. After Leo fell to his death, he means.

'Plus *I'm* not going anywhere,' he says. 'I need to run the screen hack from here, now we don't have—'

Now they don't have Leo.

'So . . .' says Gray.

Both men turn to Dani expectantly. She's missed something.

'What do you think?' asks Sam.

'I think you're both dicks.'

'Oh, cheers, Dan,' says Gray. 'We're trying to make this right.'

'With your secret master plan to so-called *save the Internet*? What, did Julian Assange fuck James Bond and shit you both?'

Sam smiles at that.

'Sounds about right.'

Dani smashes her cup down on the table.

'No, but Leo's dead, Sam. Do you even understand that?' Her stomach's on a fast spin. 'I never knew anyone who died – I mean, who's my age. I only just met him!'

'Then why this, if you only met him yesterday?'

Dani doesn't reply for fear of crying. Bastard tears. Even Gray looks wounded.

'Jesus, that's cold,' he says.

'No, I'm serious,' says Sam. 'You never even met him, Gray. I knew him. He was a good guy and I'm sorry this had to happen. But I can't stand phony sentiment.'

Dani turns to Gray.

'Do you actually know this guy?' Then she rounds on Sam. 'You made him go in there, remember? This is on you.'

Sam gets up, super-slow, tucks his chair under the table and sighs. The patience of Christ coming down from the mountaintop.

'I do remember. That's why we need to put this right – and stay calm while we do it.'

Gray is shaking. She puts her hand on his – an old reflex, wired up somewhere. Sam walks to his desk to gather stuff. He keeps on speaking in the same uninflected tone.

'So, Dani.' She sits up: why? 'If Gray stays here to set the dogs on Perce, someone else needs to go into 404 and get the disks. Someone who knows how to find the DigiCitz and Parley servers and get out the drives undamaged.'

Dani grinds her chair round to face him.

'Oh, me?' She points to her chest, gets up and talks to his back. 'You want me to go into the place where Leo got killed? I told you: the police are after me.'

Sam zips up his leather satchel.

'OK, fine. We let Parley die and Perce gets away with fucking up your life. Your call.'

She gets up to march about the apartment, wanting to push things off its neat surfaces, groping for words.

'This is – people don't do this kind of shit in my world. We work things out. You know, with brains? There's going to be a clean way – a systems way – to fix this.'

'Well,' Sam checks his phone, 'you have four hours to find it. Good luck with that.'

'We can get at Perce from here, online. Gray just said so.'

Gray stands from the kitchen table.

'No, Dan, he's right. We need the hard drives. Evidence. Before they wipe them. And I can't save the Personas from here without server-side permissions.'

Leo handing her the gun
   do what you want with it he said
      the weight of it in her hand
         now hes dead

Dani screws up her face and pushes her hair back with both hands. She bores a look into Gray. She knows he's right and he knows he's right. He shrugs. She drops her hands to her sides.

'All *right*,' she says. 'OK, fuck!'

She sits on a sofa to think it over but there's no thinking to be done.

'So I go in,' she says. 'I work there. Why shouldn't I be there?'

Sam is quizzical, like he was expecting more of a fight.

'And meanwhile,' he says, 'Graham will take over their screens and turn the botnet on their website.'

Gray nods.

'I'll have the whole of 404 City singing *Daisy, Daisy* by noon,' he says.

¶takebackIDhub

We are beyond words.

"Protester killed in 'tragic accident' at corporate
headquarters." <u>fub.ar/20dfd7b</u>

CITE THIS.

Rally at 404.

<DayofRage> <takebackID> <RIPidentikid>

TWO

THE SCREEN WAS BIGGER THAN THE SKY. Six blocks out it took hold of City Road. J-R and Mark were walking into a sea of data. The upper face of the building was grained with sun-bright pixels, as though it had swallowed half of London's electric current. Sliding banners, tag lines, splashes of news and flashbulb faces of celebrities – a constant motion of planes and angles. Somewhere within this industrial crash of information were walls, floors, windows, doors; but for a block or two it was impossible to make them out. Everyone walked slack-eyed towards this beacon, smartphones hanging loosely in their hands. The irresistible cry – *look into the light* – has drawn us to our screens since we were born. It found its final exercise here.

As they left the borders of the City, details came into focus below the wall of moving light. A glass buttress jutted from the building's foot, biting pavement. Only now did their eyes fathom scale. A flow of microdots on the forecourt revealed itself as a gathering of dissidents, unrolling a placard against the interference of uniformed guards. Police and the murmurings of trouble. Cameras. J-R put out a hand to slow Mark and assess the situation.

'Ready?' smiled Mark.

J-R squinted at his friend against the morning light and the flare of the building's glass. They'd barely spoken since they'd met at Old Street Tube station.

'Why are you here?' said J-R, surprising himself by speaking. He realised he was echoing Graham's words from the day before. 'Why help me?'

Mark reared his head back slightly and pursed his lips.

'Because we're mates,' he said. 'Do you need more than that?'

He reached to touch J-R's sleeve briefly with two fingers. A frisson passed up J-R's arm. He placed his hand on the affected area.

'Because the thing is,' he said, 'last night, when you spoke about –' he didn't want to say *fucking* '– about what you wanted to do to Sean Perce, you sounded like you were, I don't know, *crowing*.'

Mark started to speak.

'No, no, hear me out,' said J-R, realising how much he sounded like a politician. 'And it made me wonder. So when I got home I did something I probably should have done in the first place – a bit of digging. And I must say, I was surprised. Your blog – the organisations you've been involved with. You didn't tell me.'

'*Digging*? On me? Christ, J-R.'

'I've trusted you with things I wouldn't have shown to anyone.'

'I should walk away – right now.'

'Except –' J-R wondered whether he was going to complete the sentence. 'Except you don't want to miss the chance to *fuck* Sean Perce, do you?'

'Oh, and you feeling like *supporting* him right now?'

'Have you or have you not been using me to dig up dirt on Mondan?'

'Jesus! *You* approached *me*, remember?'

'Because I'd naïvely hoped we might – God, I don't know –'

Mark took several deep breaths, as though recovering from a punch to the gut.

'You know,' he said. 'This is why you never see anyone any more. You don't seem to realise what this job has turned you into. Maybe all those friends you never hear from any more – maybe they're worried you might *do some digging* on them, too.'

'That's in the past. I do want to be more present than I've been, for my friends – for you. I mean –'

Mark checked his smartwatch.

'Fuck.' He turned his wrist for J-R to see. 'Sorry, we don't have time for couple counselling. Vanna's expecting us.'

He turned and marched on the entrance. *Couple counselling?* J-R's heart rate mounted as he caught up with Mark. In the knot of journos on the forecourt Frank Pritchett, a stringer for the *Independent*, caught J-R's eye: damn. What would Pritchett make of his presence here? He flashed his ministry ID at the policeman, who nodded and stepped aside to let them in. It wasn't clear if he would have moved to stop them entering without this generic institutional proof.

Someone shouted an unintelligible slogan as J-R pushed on a glass door etched with the zero of *404*. They walked along the tower's splayed foot towards an inner rift in the vertical expanse. Beyond the reception desk and electronic turnstiles, a great glass inversion opened thirty storeys up into the centre of the building. At the top lurked Perce, the tunnel spider brooding in the glow of his screens. The bottom of the shaft, where the boy had landed, was two storeys below ground, out of sight.

'Ready?' said Mark.

J-R composed his face into a smile.

Mark had been too long at the front desk. J-R fidgeted on the angular sofa, watched by two policemen at the turnstiles. The receptionist handed Mark a handset on a long snake of cable. J-R checked his watch. He wondered where Bethany was. Unforgivable to have abandoned her at the launch event. Though lord knows what he'd have done in the face of those protesters. Dani Farr had been among them, had allegedly attacked Bethany. When he heard the news last night he'd broken his silence to ring Krish – who'd been blunt, even by his standards.

'*You're precisely not needed here, J-R. Everybody thinks you're a cowardly prick for going to ground but you're in the clear. The polis have their suspect. Today is about them catching the crooks. You take five. On Monday I'll get the Perm Sec to spank your airse for emailing that contract. That'll be the long and short.*'

Yes, they had the suspect: in a body bag. J-R stared down at the sweaty knot of fingers in his lap. There was only one reason Krish would say Bethany didn't need help, when she so clearly did: it was already over for her.

Mark returned from the reception desk, looking cross or puzzled – J-R still did not know how to read the inward turn of his face.

'We're to go up now,' he said.

His eyes didn't match his breezy tone.

'Your friend *is* here? Vanna?'

'It seems not. We're not meeting her.'

'Then who?'

'Perce. Sean Perce is waiting for us. Top floor.'

J-R looked up at the halo of light filling the atrium.

'—Primitive encampment forming around the base of the glass tower. Behind me you'll see the tents. Police are monitoring the situation but as yet all seems peaceful.'

'Yes, Carol, we're seeing footage of the site of last night's incident. What looks like a hand-painted banner hanging from a balcony, a message on it to do with – door keys? And here a police forensics team. The investigation of protester Leo Sandberg's tragic death looks well under way.'

'Indeed it is, Julian. And in a related development we understand that Metropolitan Police officers have found the person responsible for leaking emails from Digital Minister Bethany Lehrer. We understand this person is not the hacker Danielle Farr, though she is still wanted for questioning. Though all parties are remaining tight-lipped about an alleged violent incident yesterday, involving Ms Farr and the minister.'

'So the situation there remains tense?'

'Tense indeed, Julian.'

'Stay with us, Carol. We'll continue to update on the situation at Mondan's London headquarters as it unfolds. In other news . . .'

THREE

'WHAT'S HE UP TO?' asks Dani.

'Huh?' says Gray, his eyes fixed on Sam's big screen.

Dani points at a window where email titles scroll by: *FW: Daily press cuts – Saturday* and *RE: Everything about you launch*.

'These are Perce's mails? Live?' says Dani.

He nods. Sam is off across the room, doing something on his tablet.

'And you watch these all the time?' she says.

He nods again, typing.

'So this week you must have seen something about when they trashed me to the press?'

Gray stays silent.

'So why didn't you tell me?' she says. 'Warn me?'

He keeps typing a moment, then stops and turns to her.

'Because he didn't say anything about that. He did mention you in a couple of mails but that was about using your code for a thing.'

'Using my – which code?'

He shrugs again and returns to the screen.

'No idea. He's said all kinds of incriminating stuff in here. We're going to use it on the big screens today. But nothing about doxing you to the press.'

Something is eating at Dani but she can't say what.

'But Dan?' says Gray, turning to her again.

He sounds nearly tender: much as he can.

'Yeah?' she says.

'You're still flying as Terry, though? With the credit card I gave you?'

'What? Sure. Pretty much. Anything Dani-related is still clogged up in a ton of evil shit.'

She's been on Parley this morning, as Terry. It's bursting with angry attention over last night's events – under the pennants <*DayofRage*> and <*saveParley*>. The bile about Dani is still swashing about but it's dying off. She's almost disappointed not to be stickier. Forty-eight hours is all you get.

'Good. Because if you go into 404? You need to be worried whether they can see you.'

This makes her heart skip.

'You're shitting me. No.'

'Just saying be careful is all.'

There's something else. She waits.

'You know yesterday morning,' he says, 'when you didn't show for the meeting with Jonquil?'

'I was getting ready for the thing with Bethany Lehrer –? And Leo –?'

'But did you know Jonquil had the police waiting for you back at Parley? Those government cops?'

'Holy – no. You are actually scaring me. God!' She stands. 'Why do you have to do this? Jonquil's looking out for me.'

'Sure,' says Gray. 'The woman who's shutting down Parley is your best pal.'

Dani feels her blood run away down some inner plughole.

Leo handing her the gun
   do what you want with it he said
     the weight of it in her hand
      now hes dead

Gray looks at her for a moment then gets up and heads for the bathroom. She stops him with a hand on his wrist. He looks down at the hand so she removes it.

'One thing I can't get straight,' she says.

'Just one?'

She grins unconvincingly. He puts a hand on his wrist, where her hand had been.

'About those police, I mean. You know they came to Parley on, what was it? Early Tuesday morning?' He nods. 'Six of them, with guns. They said *sic* was a threat. They thought *I* was a threat. Why would they think that?'

'I guess somebody told them so?'

'Thanks for that stroke of genius.'

'Just trying to be, you know, supportive?'

'But *who*, Gray. Who could have done that?'

Gray does his big comic shrug. She nods – he's as data-free as she is here. After a beat, he says: 'Uh, so – call of nature? My bladder feels like I drank Hydro-Man.'

'Yeah, way too much info,' she says, batting him away.

When he's gone she looks over to Sam. He's tapping at his tablet, expression fixed. She reaches under the monitor on the desk and finds a toggle, switching the display from Gray's laptop to Sam's desktop Mac. A login screen: *Sam Corrigan; Admin; Guest.* Password locked. She looks around for a post-it but apparently Sam's not that dumb. She tries a couple of obvious strings, but nothing.

She flips the display back to Gray's machine.

¶**takebackIDhub**

Three things Sean Perce needs to explain:

When his relationship with Minister Bethany Lehrer began and how it affected the award of the Digital Citizen contract. 1/3

What happened to the data of thousands of Teesside residents. 2/3

Why armed police were present in his offices – DURING THE NIGHT – when Leo Sandberg 'fell' to his death. 3/3

<DayofRage> <TakeBackID> <RIPidentikid>

FOUR

J-R WAS DROWNING IN LIGHT. Outside the glass walls, giants and captions taller than a man danced all around. They drew him to the edge, where the suspended floor gave way and the sick appeal of vertigo took hold. Impossible to see down without pressing right up to the floor-to-ceiling window. He edged up to it, straining to see the police operation three dozen storeys below. An ant farm from here.

Queasiness struck him; he looked up instead and there were the remnants of Sandberg's banner, dangling from a steel gallery. He turned away from the window into the hard grin of Sean Perce, who had entered the room unheard. Perce crushed and agitated J-R's hand.

'J-R. Hi. Let me ask you something.' He dropped the hand. 'How stupid do you think people are?'

'Excuse me?'

The dissonance of words and tone had J-R off guard. Perce stepped back.

'It's a simple question. People want better services, cheaper downloads. Filters to kill the noise. They want the stuff they like. Who are you to say they can't, because you've got a nineteenth-century notion of privacy?'

J-R glanced at Mark – who was standing on the balls of his feet as though ready to run or attack – then back to Perce's panther smile. He attempted an answer.

'People need to trust the government to keep their data private.'

'So privacy's important? Philosophical question.'

Perce walked to a cluster of chairs on the brink of the precipice. He nipped his trousers at the knee and sat facing the two friends, the sheer face of animated screens shouting through the glass behind him.

'Hiding what you do online is important?' he said.

J-R moved to a facing chair. Mark slid in beside him.

'Certainly privacy is a right.'

'So a guy walks down the street in a hockey mask, you're not going to cross to the other side? You're saying that would be normal? Why do these people want to be able to do that online?'

J-R and Mark exchanged a look.

'That's not the question, Mr Perce.'

'Sean.'

'People have legal rights. Those who protect their information shouldn't abuse those rights.'

'Who's abusing?'

'You are, Sean.'

J-R swallowed. This kind of borderline rudeness was standard practice for a government advisor, but this was like tilting at a giant.

'You see,' he said, 'we have evidence –'

On cue, Mark pulled the file from his satchel and passed it to J-R, who conveyed it solemnly to Perce – who regarded this ceremony with amusement. J-R put a finger against the file.

'Our findings.'

'Sure, whatever.'

Perce dropped the file unopened on the chair beside him, stood and leaned forward to place a gentle hand on J-R's shoulder.

'Look,' he said. 'I wanted to start by giving you the one-oh-one, J-R. Clear the air.'

He headed for his desk, leaving the two friends with the abandoned dossier. J-R twisted to keep an eye on Perce. His shifting persona was hard to lock onto. He continued his pitch.

'See what you really think. Let you be the judge. Take a for instance: you know about the Grubly network, right?'

He sat behind his colossal desk. J-R and Mark looked at each other. J-R picked up the file and approached the desk.

'We do. And we know what you're doing with it. This file –'

He dropped it emptily on the desk.

'Well, I'd hope you do: you just bought fifty million licences for it! No point kicking the tyres when you've already bought the car.'

J-R sat opposite Perce.

'The contract isn't signed, Sean.'

'Will be Monday. Assuming we have a minister in office long enough to sign it!'

That was bloody low.

'Mr Perce. We are precisely here to talk about Grubly. You are acquiring incredible quantities of data, covertly, from ordinary people. More data than you could possibly need, on every stripe of their lives. You're using it without permission – for what? What are you doing *exactly* with this data?'

Perce blinked at him.

'What am *I* doing?'

Mark came to stand beside J-R.

'I've looked at the data flows,' he said. 'Immense. You must be getting images, audio, biometrics, even –'

Perce kept nodding as though this was an answer. When he spoke, it was to J-R.

'Tell me, J-R. Do you lock your door at night?'

How many times had he used J-R's name?

'I'm really not in the mood for rhetorical questions. I live in South London. Naturally I lock my door.'

Perce smiled.

'OK. Non-rhetorical question. Why do you lock your door?'

'I'm fairly sure that question also counts as rhetorical; but my answer is, to control who enters my property.'

'So that's what Grubly is. It helps you control what enters your world. It's a gatekeeper, inviting in the things you want. Turning others away.'

'Hardly,' said Mark. 'It invades my world and rifles my data.'

'Mark, thank you for that. If you want someone to guard your door shouldn't they understand you?' He turned again to J-R. 'Grubly is no secret. We build better data on you, we learn your interests; that helps us give you better services and better deals – in return for what we make selling your information to other vendors.'

J-R grappled with his face, which he knew was conveying dumb astonishment.

'You admit to profiting from a public programme? To selling personal information?'

'You're thinking too narrowly. Someone has to pay for the amazing growth in our experience. It's building daily, but we've barely begun. We still spend this tiny slice of time looking at a phone or at a PC; but those are the times that know you best. The world outside is uncustomised. People are wanting – expecting – personal all the time. The rest of the world doesn't know you yet. Personal will soon expand to your clothing, your shaving mirror, your coffee cup. The surface area of our operations is expanding. And it won't cost people a penny. Because they're already giving me what I need to pay for it all.'

The man was in awe of himself. Mark, still standing, cut in.

'You want to make the whole world an advert.'

'*I want*? Jesus Christ, all the things people tell me I *want*. Who said anything about *ads*? We're personalising the world.'

'You're profiling people and selling their identities.'

Perce stood and rounded the desk on Mark, assuming a nasty, lisping parody of his voice.

'*Profiling*? We're understanding them! We're *talking* to them.'

'And how far does this *conversation* go? What are you getting from this contract? Criminal records? Debt records? Benefit claims?'

The two of them faced off over J-R's chair. The tendons in Mark's neck were tight, his temples glowing with sweat. This was real aggression.

'And this would be wrong how, Mark? You're a fan of criminals and scroungers running loose on the streets? Like that unwashed rabble outside?'

His arm flailed towards the screens, where news footage of the street encampment rolled by. Then he switched tack again, sweeping J-R out of his chair, leaving Mark behind.

'So what we're about, J-R? We give people control. Tailor their experience. Free up markets.' He sat J-R back in the armchair by the vertiginous glass, knelt in front of him. 'Elyse Martingale's dream of empowered individuals. Bethany would love that, right?' J-R's heart was beating faster. 'Now, I won't lie to you, J-R, I'm an entrepreneur, not a politician. What I know is how to monetise. But think. What is the point of privacy laws when everything about everyone is already known? No way to put the genie back. You don't have to like it but it's going to happen – and when the music stops, whoever has the most data wins. You work in government.'

Did he, any more?

'Of course.'

'So you'll know. You understand how hard it is to get anything done. Everything costs, there's no money, all the hoops to jump – what do you do? Seriously, what do you do, J-R? The well is dry. Now, me, I hire the smartest software engineers in the world. There's more IQ in one floor of this building than the whole of Westminster. Real smarts. But what we've built is smarter than any of us. It's making better decisions, finding better opportunities, winning higher margins. The only reason I don't just sit back and just let it happen is I'm hungry for the next idea that will make it even smarter.'

'The next way to grab more data, more control,' said Mark from across the room; but his words rebounded off Perce's back.

'I think people know what they want. I think we should stop telling them what they want, like politicians do, and start listening to what they say, and giving it to them. We're going to make it easier than ever.' Perce pulled up to his full height. 'Let me demonstrate. We deal in facts here, J-R, in data. I can give you the facts. Then you make your mind up. You're entitled to your own opinion but you're not entitled to your own facts. Is that fair?'

J-R realised he was mirroring Perce's smile. He must not succumb to his rhino charm. Still, it was true: facts were what counted. It was generally frustrating how little people understood that. Including, often, Bethany.

'I suppose it is.'

'Well, all right then. Let me show you some stuff.'

¶NewsHound

WTF???

BREAKING: Mondan 'to shut down Parley' says source.
fu.bar/j2grp96

Overreaction much?

FIVE

'DANIELLE. GIRL, are you a sight for sore eyes.'

Jonquil. Obviously. Dani gives her the glass-eye and keeps loading her bag. She's only come up to the Skunkworks to grab some must-haves from her desk. Not sure when or if she'll be back. Impossible to think future tense.

'This is so fucked-up,' says Jonquil. 'You've heard some kid *died* at 404 last night? Now there's this like army of protestors forming on the street outside.'

Dani loads her bag with phone chargers: which it turns out she has a lot of. Most of them will be defunct; but who knows which? Jonquil watches with smiling patience.

'So. We haven't seen you around so much.'

Snap. That is it.

'Well, you were about to fire me, remember? Last time I came here? When I was *toxic*?'

Jonquil puckers her mouth. The *girlfriend* act drops clean away.

'Well, you made your bed, Danielle. And believe you me, this thing has screwed us both. You may not've heard but I resigned yesterday. Yes. Uh huh. Everything I took four years building here I walked away from. I do not know what in hell I'm even going to do.'

'Well aren't you Saint cunting Jonquil?'

'Ungrateful! I put up with so much shit from you, girl. Always one eye to protect you.'

'By shopping me to the police?'

Jonquil's mouth clamps suddenly shut.

'Yes,' says Dani, 'I know about that, thanks for nothing.'

Ah, Christ, is she Tiny Tears today? Anger makes her strong, then tears pull the rug.

'I was your best friend, Danielle. You have no idea.'

'I trusted you!'

'No. No no no. This is not about trust. This is about loyalty. If you don't know how to give it you don't get to take it.'

'Fuck you! Shit on your lousy backstabbing loyal bullshit – God! I am so glad I never, never have to take this shit from you again!'

Silence falls in the empty office. Rows of neutered flatscreens look on. Dani suffers it for about ten seconds then scoops up her bag and hits the stairs. Six flights down to the basement and the tunnel.

¶takebackIDhub

Where is Sean Perce?
<DayofRage> <TakeBackID> <RIPidentikid>

SIX

'YOU KNOW ABOUT *EVERYTHING ABOUT YOU*?' said Perce.

No, J-R did not.

'Really. Do you not talk to your own colleagues? You should. It's not all the Ministry of No these days. Some of your colleagues actually understand why we're so valuable.'

Perce was in motion, alternately perching at his desk and pacing the room. Now he leaned at his computer, rapidly clicking the mouse as he spoke.

'Here. Good example of the match and trace ability of Grubly. It uses people's comms, geolocation.' He beckoned them both with a cupped hand. 'Come see. It's pretty cool.' He swivelled the flatscreen for J-R to see. 'Honestly? I wish Beth had understood these possibilities more. She could have made other conversations happen. There are so *many* uses for this kit, in central government. Security-wise. But she's nobody's tech, is she? *So* not her grand-mother. Still. Her loss.'

He typed something into a dialogue box. His own name.

'I'm easy as a starter. There's only one Sean Perce on the database.'

He clicked *Find*. A satellite image zoomed rapidly to central London and continued to hone in on a labelled aerial shot of 404 City. As the zoom braked, a pulsing icon of a man appeared. Perce gave a wave and pointed to himself.

'There I am. Beat that, Google, huh?'

J-R turned to Mark for confirmation of what he'd just seen. Mark, leaning into the screen, was unreadable.

'And this is the *Everything About You* icon,' said Perce, scribbling his mouse pointer over a strobing ∞ – the symbol of infinity – that hung beside his on-screen avatar. 'I'm not going to show you what's behind there – not yet. But it knows a lot about me. A *lot*. I can't hide from the data, any more than anyone. So, who else is in the news today? Hmm: I know!'

As soon as *B-e-t-* appeared in the search box, J-R knew, too.

'What are you—?' he began, then stopped.

He'd been about to accuse Perce of tracking a minister of state using demonstration software on a desktop PC. Nonsense.

Perce completed Bethany's name and pressed *Search*. The map swiped to the left, revealing the City of London, Holborn; then made a sharp corner onto Westminster, *Downing Street*. The strobing male icon had been replaced by a female variant. Somewhere over the State Dining Rooms, 10 Downing Street, by J-R's estimation.

'Uh oh. Headmaster's office,' said Perce and then, under his breath, 'Poor Beth.'

J-R and Mark were frozen.

'Jesus Christ, lads. You look like I just shot a puppy.'

J-R pointed at the screen, a caveman stumbling on fire.

'How did –?'

Perce gave a gameshow smile.

'Geolocation primed on mobile phones, PCs and tablets. Any device that has Grubly we can triangulate. In this case, Beth's personal phone. What do you say, J-R? Info-warrior like you? Are you on or off my map? You have a phone on you?'

Hypnotised, J-R drew his ageing smartphone from his pocket and showed it to Perce. Perce nodded.

'Shall we see?'

J-R put the phone down on the desk and grabbed for the mouse but Perce and his computer were too fast. The map zoomed back to City Road and a *John-Rhys Pemberton* icon pulsed in the location where Perce's had stood. J-R regarded his own ∞ icon. He didn't see himself as having anything to hide – save the wealth of political information held inside his head – but seeing Perce's pointer hover over that symbol made him wish he could wipe every record that existed about himself.

Perce turned to Mark.

'OK, someone else.'

Mark gave Perce a level look and did not reply. J-R spoke up.

'Dani Farr.'

J-R had no idea why he said that, but he wanted his own details off the screen. Perce's expression was shocked. After a second he laughed like a dog coughing up a hairball.

'Well, this'll be interesting. I happen to know she blipped off our map a couple days ago. But let's see. I'm going to do this different. Show you a cool feature.'

Here was a software capitalist in full-blown demo mode. J-R was often on the receiving end of these dog-and-pony shows, delivered by some open-necked entrepreneur who'd muscled into Whitehall to peddle his wares: unaware that J-R had no power to buy from them.

Perce called up Google and searched for *Dani Farr*. The screen filled with gaudy photos and news reports from the past two days. Perce selected the much-reproduced image of Dani posing with a gun, and hovered his mouse over her. A rectangle appeared around her face. For a few seconds, an animated wheel turned in its centre. Then her name appeared. Perce called up a menu and selected *Search for DANI FARR in Everything About You*. The map reappeared, with Dani's name in the search box.

'In case you missed it, that was face recognition.'

He hit the *Search* button. The map refreshed, but didn't budge from the City Road locale. A little female icon hovered beside 404 City, apparently in the middle of the road. *Danielle (Dani) Farr*, it read.

'Oh, bollocks. Apologies. This is beta and a little flaky on refresh: why we're not soft launching yet. Which by the way means you have time to work out who should and shouldn't get their hands on these wares, J-R. I'm minded to say, everyone, but what do you think?'

'Excuse me? Why would I—?'

'First let's get this puppy working.'

Perce struck a chord of keys. The screen refreshed but, stubbornly, it still showed Dani in the same location. He hit more keys. The map zoomed out to show the whole UK. He clicked *Search* again. The map landed at the same location. Frowning, Perce zoomed in closer, then closer still. The satellite image of the building grew grainy and filled the screen.

With the map zoomed, they could see that the female icon was moving. It edged in brief spurts from the south-east corner of the building, ever closer to the centre.

Perce pressed keys, flipping the screen back to J-R's icon, and stood.

'Would you please excuse me just one moment?'

He left the room.

¶NewsHound

Media gathering in Downing Street. Bethany Lehrer
announcement expected within the hour.

SEVEN

ANOTHER INSTITUTIONAL GEORGIAN ROOM; another silent policeman.

This guy was run from the same production line as Bethany's former escorts. Square-jawed in security-service fashion, with a Hugh Grant lick of hair. Any other time she would have said, quite the hunk. His eyes darted between the outer door, the window, and onto each piece of furniture in turn: as if the occasional table might at any moment leap up and assault her. Anywhere and everywhere except at Bethany.

She'd been under unstated close protection ever since the – assault, kidnapping, whatever it was. What a privilege to have a manly escort to the site of her execution.

Waiting for the PM was like doing the same for Godot. Especially for a minister who'd woken to find herself a political remainder. She rather welcomed the moment of peace. To pass the time she decided to knock a borehole through the policeman's permafrost.

'No Raeworth today?'

He turned to look at her as if, after all, a piece of furniture had spoken. Then his eyes returned to the sealed door of the inner room. Just as she'd concluded he was going to stay mute, he spoke, in the closed tone of a railway announcement.

'DS Raeworth is no longer your cover, *Minister.*'

Had there been inverted commas round that last word? There had better not have been. This was probably the last time she'd be on the receiving end of that honorific.

'And he is – where?'

'An incident has occurred. An investigation is under way.'

Now he sounded like the error message on a PC. By *incident* he meant Sandberg. That hapless scruff of a boy. Dreadfully her mind's eye could only see him naked before her – an inappropriate image to memorialise the recent dead. What had the boy been doing, climbing about up there? It was a shocking coda to yesterday's farce. The nail, too, in the coffin of her spell in office.

Coffin nail: terrible. *Last straw* better. Though soon she wouldn't need her internal political censor.

'Because I wanted to say something to Raeworth. Before I go in. That he needs to – you all need to lay off Dani Farr. She's a victim here. I'm not about to press charges for yesterday. Poor kid: all she ever did is run when we chased her.'

This wasn't true but it was close enough. The tables had been turned last night and they could do without someone crying harassment. More to the point, the girl had got under her skin. God speed to her, wherever she was right now.

The policeman seemed to have barely registered Bethany's words. It was like negotiating with a self-service checkout.

'There is. Minister. The matter of the gun.'

'Raeworth's gun? Surely Sandberg took it? Although – I suppose I didn't see.'

That missing gun was a disturbing variable. Poor Raeworth. To lose a weapon and a suspect's life in a single day. No wonder he'd been secreted away somewhere.

'A squatted pub in Dalston is currently under search.'

This man existed only in the passive voice. Did no one have any agency, in his world?

'No gun has been found there or on his person.'

'But he could have hidden it somewhere.'

'That will be clear when Farr has been picked up.'

What a filthy mess. She would always be associated with this, always. It would be the coda to every *Remember her?* in the House bars. At least there would still be the Digital Citizen. She'd get Simon to confirm before he fired her.

How was this going to run? They'd agree to a statement: *leaving under unfortunate circumstances; this her happy legacy.* It would be all sorry smiles. You give two years, wear body and soul to the bone; fuck your marriage to the point it'll take two years of bended knee to make it back. You're absent from your burgeoning, mysterious sons. Don't you have the right to something as intangible, vital and downright just, as legacy?

She'd get confirmation from the PM before she left the room; that it was happening. That it was hers. Then she'd go quietly.

¶sic_girl

Wowsers. Look what I just went and found.

This little old internal email from Mondan's security chief.

Just when you thought it couldn't get any more obvious

the big M knew what was going down, it does get. Read

and weep, Sean.

<DayofRage> <TakeBackID> <RIPidentikid>

EIGHT

MARK AND J-R EXCHANGED A LOOK. Perce's departure had dropped them back to the point where their earlier conversation had stalled. J-R began to speak but Mark placed a finger to his lips and pointed at the ceiling. J-R swallowed his words, not fully understanding.

The screen of Perce's computer dimmed, preparing to sleep. J-R tapped the space bar to waken it. Odd that the head of such a secretive organisation would leave his screen unlocked – unless he'd done so deliberately. His actions appeared at first pure id, but purpose drove everything he did.

The male glyph labelled *John-Rhys Pemberton* was still on-screen. Its ∞ icon pulsed, making sparks flutter over J-R's field of vision. He clicked the icon.

The screen answers.

)) crystal muzzle ((

A collage of sound and image reproduces J-R's surroundings on the flat display. Snatches of J-R's and Perce's voices echo from the recent past. The babble of Mondan's giant screens, delayed and remixed to a drone, pumps from the desktop speakers. Foreshortened snatches of the room flash over one another: Mark's hand and arm; the composite tiles of a drop-ceiling.

It's beautiful; and disruptive.

)) polymer suspension ((

J-R's phone is lying camera-up on the desk. He holds his hand above the lens; after a short delay, a giant's paw fisheyes into a window on Perce's screen. A second later a duplicate hand appears, smaller, in another division of the noisy collage. He takes his hand away; after a pause, both images vanish. Then everything wipes into itself and unfolds. The screen reconfigures itself. Top centre, an analogue clock appears and is drawn by the gravitational pull of the past: the screen, it seems, doesn't want to dwell on now. J-R recognises the clock from the Parley application. Now it's surrounded by an uncapped mêlée of image, noise and fragmented text.

Over the jumble hangs the glaze of a satellite map. The toy soldier labelled *John-Rhys Pemberton* marches backwards across this translucent London, retracing his steps from 404 City to Old Street: the path J-R and Mark just walked. As his digital self heaves back into the recent past, windows pop open from points along his trail and burst against the glass front of the screen. Brickwork; glass façades; skies; a brush of pedestrians. The soundscape shifts to City Road. Whenever J-R's phone was in his hand, it had been watching.

Across the bottom of the screen, coloured info-graphics pulse and balloon, tracing peaks and lulls. At the centre of the mêlée, word pairs burst forward in crisp lower-case letters, apparently random yet laden with meaning.

)) close affliction ((

The locus scythes, pauses and scythes again, tracking to Camberwell, pausing at J-R's flat – then with increasing frenzy, as lights rise and fade with the rapid passing of a day, to Shoreditch, Hoxton, back to Camberwell. That was yesterday. The images bloom and refresh with greater and greater speed; and then, as the clock heaves back another night, J-R is launched into the wilds of Hackney. Thursday evening.

The spinning clock slows. The gravity of the past centres on that night. The screen decorates itself with J-R's photographs of the East End streets; and on what he found there.

)) chocolate dark ((

He watches the visual torrent until he understands. He's watching himself – and what he experienced, the evening his BlackBerry died and he went AWOL. These are stored sensations, archived against his physical progress, timed to his passage across the map. Somehow Perce has bottled his interior and exterior life, and relayed it onto this PC. What it paints is more painful and familiar than a mother's disappointment. How has this machine come to know him?

The indicators at the bottom of the screen pulse and flash with intense reds as the clock slows to a stop. The system has identified a peak in the signals it's tracing. Indoor scenes bathed in oxblood fill the fleeting windows. Distended male faces shoved together in the heat and pulse of midnight. Lips.

)) finger fall ((

The sights and sounds trigger memories that J-R's drunken brain had left behind in that Hackney bar. Whether it's alcohol or fear that's held these memories at bay, he can't say; but knowing now what's about to appear – what Mark's about to see – he repeat-clicks the mouse and slaps the keyboard, searching for an off. The images pour over him like a dream he can't wake from. Mark has stiffened in his chair.

'*What's your name?*' says a voice, baffled like a recording on wax cylinder.

There's a pause, filled with hot breath and a brush of fabric. Another voice replies.

'*It's Mark. My name is Mark.*'

Mark stands. His chair scrapes back on the mock-stone flooring. J-R remembers now: when the boy named Jo asked him for his name, he hadn't wanted to say it out loud. But why choose to call himself Mark, of all things?

He still doesn't know what happened next – what he went on to do with that strange boy, Jo. He longs to see more of this moment, dig out everything he's buried; but he also needs to stop it, right away.

'J-R?' says Mark.

Some atavistic memory of PC training returns to J-R and he hits the keys *Alt-F4*. The cacophony gutters, replaced by a desktop image of lush forgiving fields and folder icons. The intimate rustles give way to the harmonics of the air conditioner and the computer's fan – backed by the low babble of the giant screens around them.

'J-R?'

J-R keeps his head down a moment, then draws a breath and looks up.

'Yes, Mark.'

'That was your voice.'

'Ah – yes. Yes, I think it was.'

'But what – why did you call yourself Mark? What were we seeing?'

'I don't know – I mean, I *do* know, but none of that seemed real, did it? Like a video game – I imagine.'

He laughs, but the laugh sounds as though it's been channelled through Perce's demonic software.

'That was you?' says Mark. 'We were seeing you, hearing you – at that location?'

J-R does not reply at once. Into the silence an electric scream intrudes – the air conditioning has changed gear, sending a ripple of cold through the sweat on his back.

'Mark, I –'

He glances at the door. How much time does he have? This is precisely not the moment to say what he needs to say – but what else to do, apart from press on forward?

'Perhaps –' he says. 'Perhaps after all this isn't so bad. Maybe I needed you to see that. We set off on the wrong foot, didn't we, down on the street? I jumped in, accusing you of – *hrm!* When what I should have done is explain why I was feeling hurt –'

'OK, look, whatever this is, how about we leave it until—'

J-R holds up his hand, quieting Mark. This thing now demands to be said.

'– hurt by the idea you might be taking advantage of the situation. Of me. I should have explained what I've – well, *ha!* – what I've been *feeling.*'

Mark gets to his feet, eyes on the door.

'Whatever you think you're about to say,' he says, 'it's better not to say it here. Not now.'

'No, I've been too reticent. I really think this is good.' He places his fingers on Perce's monitor. 'This machine has forced my hand. Mark –'

He stands, too, and takes Mark's hand between both his own. It's hot and surprisingly rough. Mark tries to retrieve the hand but J-R won't let him.

'That time at Toby's party –' says J-R. 'You took a brave step that night and I brushed you off.'

Mark gently extracts his hand.

'That was one night,' he says. 'I was drunk and I made a dumb pass at an old friend.'

'I was drunk, too – on Thursday night, I mean, when I kissed that man.'

Mark's face twists with some hard-to-identify emotion. J-R presses on.

'I don't think we got very far – my memory's hazy, after a certain point. As I say, I was drunk. The ridiculous thing is, this system seems to know more about what happened than I do.' They both glance at the Alpine cleanliness of the computer's desktop image. 'It can see things I haven't let myself see. It's given me this chance – here and now – to tell you what I've been feeling.'

'Look, really,' says Mark. 'Where's this going? Perce will be back any second.'

'That evening – it's mostly a blur but it seems to have woken me up. I can be honest with myself; and with you.'

'Back up a moment,' says Mark. 'What *is* this?'

J-R steps back and folds his hands carefully in front of him. Takes a breath.

'This –' he tries, but his throat is clogged up. He clears it. 'This is me explaining that I care very deeply about you, Mark. My only regret is that it's taken me this long to stand up and say so.'

The corner of Mark's mouth tilts: that half-sympathetic, half-mocking smile.

'I love you too, J-R,' he says. 'You do realise that nothing you've said or done in the past five minutes has made any sense?'

'I'm bisexual,' says J-R, and as he says it, something unlatches inside him. He's giddy with it.

'Oh,' says Mark.

'Is that – all you have to say?' says J-R.

Mark studies J-R's face for a few seconds, then does the worst thing possible: he laughs. It's brief and hollow, an awful sound.

'Sorry,' he says. 'I'm so sorry, J-R – but your face! So this is, what? A declaration of love? Or are you just coming out to the first available homosexual?'

That same bitter smile colours his words.

'God, Mark, please don't be like this.'

Mark inpsects J-R a little more, then walks past him to sit at the desk.

'OK, look,' he says. 'I'm sorry. But before you take this little drama any further you might want to hear this. I still owe you an answer to your question, from earlier on.'

J-R's heart is racing, his shirt-back sodden in the frozen air. It's as though he's running full tilt; but he can't move a muscle.

'My – question?' he says.

'You know what you said to me before, out in the street? What you accused me of.'

'I'm so sorry, I shouldn't have—'

'No. You were right – I should never have used you as my trojan horse.'

'Mark?'

J-R is shipwrecked, surrounded by the waves of light that crash against the screens to all sides. Mark's matter-of-factness seems designed to negate everything he just declared.

'I'd been clawing around for months,' Mark continues in the same flat tone, 'trying to find a way to get at Perce. I was working on this one great explosive blog post that would blow Mondan open. I was going to push it out everywhere, before DigiCitz could go fully live. The nationals would pick it up. It would wipe out any lingering trace of confidence in Perce or in this bloody government, before they could take away our right to privacy for ever. They need us to trust them, these people, if they're to pull off this kind of dirty heist; and they do not deserve our trust. I had to tell everyone, open their eyes.'

These people. With a sudden illumination J-R realises he's been looking at the situation precisely wrong. He's only considered his own anxieties, his own unspoken desires. He hasn't once asked what *Mark* might want from *him*.

'But Perce,' Mark said, 'is Teflon. I lacked the one firm fact I could hang my piece on. All I had was rumour and vapour. Then out of the blue, you pop up with what looks to be a smoking gun, with *data*.'

J-R nods. Everything is so transparent now.

'So I was to be your *sources close to government* – is that it?'

'It wasn't fair of me to play on your friendship.'

'It was rather more than friendship, as it turns out.'

'Well, but there's the thing. No. It wasn't.'

'Excuse me?'

'Sorry, but at this point I don't think you understand quite *what* you're feeling. The world doesn't need another weekend queen, J-R. I sure as hell don't. This has been a crazy week for you and I can see why you'd be doubting everything.'

'This is the first time in years I've been clear about anything.'

'What you need is time to cool off. Look.' Mark stands, collects their dossier from Perce's desk, and takes a few steps towards the door. 'I'm going to give you this one piece of advice then I'm going to go.'

'You can't leave.'

'Sort things out with Bethany, get back to your day job. I'll stop making things difficult for you – and you can take the time to work out what you're really feeling.'

'I know what I feel – look!'

J-R turns back to Perce's screen, scrambles for something to double-click, to call back the clarity of those sounds and images – the emotional replay.

'That?' says Mark from behind him. 'You're using *that* to tell me what you feel? What a customer you'll make for Perce.'

J-R abandons the screen.

'Mark—'

'No.' Mark is already halfway to the door. 'Sorry, but I'm not going to be the token poof in your pre-midlife crisis. I'm nobody's *Get out of jail* card.'

'But—'

'I'll find another way to get at Perce – without going through you. I'm sorry I messed you around – and if I led you on, I'm sorry for that, too. Email me as and when you feel like being a sane human being, OK? And we can have a beer. Until then—'

'*Mark –!*'

But he's gone.

¶**Spotted**

Anybody seen that Dani Farr lately?
<WhereAreTheyNow?>

NINE

TERRY SALMON SNEAKS the underground to 404. She walks by phone-light. Packed above her, a thousand tonnes of muck and bones; the mess of lives from Boudicca to Boris baffle out the world.

One single fleeting bar of signal on Terry's phone; but how could that signify? No one has her number, no one knows her name. Dani is insulated by Terry, hidden from the shit up above. Nothing makes it through into this tunnel.

Even Grubly can barely hear its own remote song. A tiny slice of location data makes it through the compacted earth. It's enough.

Dani checks the screen for Gray's directions, takes a right. Screenlight dances on mossy brick. The walls are sweating in the darkness but Dani's in a perfect calm. Purpose moves her forward.

Up to now, before she chose any course, made any decision, she crowdsourced. Major and minor decisions alike she outsourced to an aggregate intelligence. *Hivemind: should I take a left or right? Shag this guy? Go out tonight or stream Arrested Development?* A hundred answers she could trust, ignore or laugh at. She doesn't want to do that now. She's clear on it.

Maybe Terry's come on this mission and left Dani at home, asleep on the sofa. Would Dani have this focus? Could her soft arms have dragged a woman into a concrete basement? Would Dani fuck the boy she's longed for? Terry acts in the world, so much more real than the sliver of white and purple Dani used to be.

Terry walks on through the dark. The weight in her bag slaps a rhythm on her back. Who wouldn't be her?

¶sic_girl

Come out, come out, Sean, wherever you are.
<DayofRage> <takebackID> <RIPidentikid>

TEN

PERCE MADE DIRECTLY FOR HIS DESK, unlocked a drawer and fished out an ID lanyard and an A4 envelope. He looped the lanyard over his neck, stuffed the envelope into the pocket of his smooth grey jacket. J-R remained standing, pulse moving in his cheeks. He hadn't budged since Mark left.

He cleared his throat. This manufactured man would think him ridiculous for pressing on, but what other course remained?

'Mister Perce. Let me assure you, I am going to the Cabinet Office.'

Perce looked around the room.

'Where's your snotty friend?'

'If you think you'll pass the Fit and Proper test for the Digital Citizen contract –'

Perce grinned in artificial modesty.

'Bit late for that.'

'You can't mean they know about this?'

J-R's gesture took in the monitor screen where Perce's supernatural software had been.

'Funny. Of course they do, son. They know you're here, don't they?'

'How they would know that?'

'This is what I've been trying to tell you. What you just saw is what Bethany bought. It's what the Digital Citizen *is*. Caveat emptor.'

'Bethany would not allow this intrusive, inappropriate –'

Surely there had been a time when J-R was able to complete a sentence. Perce wagged a teacherly finger.

'So you *did* click on it. I haven't found the person yet who can leave that genie in its bottle. So: me prying? No. This isn't for me, it's for you. For the user. I get data, yes, and that's extremely helpful. But you get experience: you get your life. You only had time to taste it. It can take you over. *Everything About You*, we call it. It's for everyone.'

'Anyone can see all that—?'

'Fuck, no. You set your privacy. You think I'd piss on data protection like that?'

'But you just tracked a government minister – I saw you!'

Perce snorted.

'C'mon, we don't let just anyone do that. I was in God mode. Listen, tell me something. The things you saw in there, when I was out of the room: did your friend not like them? That why he left?'

'That is not your business.'

'Exactly,' said Perce. 'It isn't. What we have here isn't for sharing. This isn't cat videos or liking a band. This is *you*. You don't want strangers seeing it, and probably not your friends. You might share tiny slices – some freaks will always want to share every time they take a shit – but mostly it's for you alone. You got a friend in you. Why not spend quality time with him? Tell me honestly: didn't you want more?'

J-R was taken up short. The only thing that had broken his digital spell was that Mark was about to see and hear things. If he'd been alone, he would not have wanted it to stop. From such a brief touch, this thing had the potential for profound addiction.

'Listen,' said Perce. 'Fun fact. You want to know who wrote the code behind *Everything About You*? Dani Farr is who. From scratch. She's that good. All we did is zhuzh it up. Grubly, everything, she wrote. And do you know why? Because she *wants* the network to know her. She *wants* to be in the cloud. This is people, J-R, what they want. I give it to them.'

'But *you* know. You track everything people do.'

'No, no. Well, yes, but so are yay many companies. And govern-ments. What I'm doing is way cooler. I'm tracking everything they *feel*. Everything they *want*. Stop and think about the potential of that. Imagine knowing where everybody's heads and hearts are, round the clock. Soon we won't be targeting people by income, postcode, all that broad brush nothing. We'll target their mood. Angry? Here's *Death Trap II* for PlayStation. Ambitious? Self-help and executive leatherware. Horny? Porn. Highly tailored porn.'

A perfume advertisement scissored around the glass walls of the room, right across the giant screens.

'What we have here is people's stories. And when you have the story you can help to write it.'

He agitated for the door, an arm out for J-R.

'C'mon. There's someone we both need to see.'

J-R followed, feet barely lifting from the metal floor. As they crossed the sealed bridge to the lift lobby, Perce took another knight's move.

'Well, that was a great discussion.' He clapped and rubbed his hands. 'Thank you, I really appreciate your time today.'

'I –?' attempted J-R.

'So, what are you thinking now?'

'About –?'

'I know this was a whistle-stop, but you get the picture. Could you work with all this?' Perce placed a hand on J-R's shoulder. 'Help us get our message across?'

'Across to –?'

'Ha! To Westminster. To the world!'

He punched J-R's upper arm in muscular chumminess. This glassiness of character: there must be a diagnosis for such a pathology.

'As in *do you want the job?*'

As they entered the lift lobby Perce pulled the envelope from inside his jacket and slapped it onto J-R's chest, then pressed the call button.

John-Rhys Pemberton. BY HAND.

'We've cast it for now as *Vice President, Government and Corporate Affairs* but that's up for discussion.' Perce tapped the paperwork with one finger. 'Salary will blow your public sector balls off. Don't worry about that.'

The demos were over and the pitch landed. Perce's whole attention was on J-R. This was one of the moments when one must rally one's entire being, cut through the overgrowth; distil into a single potent phrase the insight that would turn events.

'You're – ah, sorry, I – what?' said J-R.

With a gentle bell-tone the lift slid open. Perce reached an arm to hold back the door.

'After you.'

J-R couldn't pull shut his slack mouth as he entered the lift. Perce pushed the lowest button from a long selection of floors.

'Krish Kohli tells me you're good. And be frank: do you *have* a job right now? Or will you by the end of the evening news cycle?'

'But Bethany isn't –'

Perce looked at his watch and raised one eyebrow.

'You sure of that?' he said.

'How can you even speak like this, when you and she –?'

Bethany in those emailed photos. Abandoning herself to Perce, owned and encrypted by him.

'J-R,' said Perce, 'I'm sure you're a great guy, and you'll be a terrific colleague, but a word of advice: steer the fuck away from my private life.' The grin got broader, tighter. 'All right?'

Floors ticked down on the display.

'So, then?' said Perce.

J-R bought time by flipping the pages on the offer letter. It included a contract.

'You're asking me to come and work here?' he said. 'For you?'

'Was the general idea.'

Iron soaked into J-R's bloodstream. He flapped the contract at Perce.

'Forgive me, but why would I, after you stole private information from me and from thousands of people? Sabotaged the programme I've invested heart and, and—'

'Sabotaged it?'

'The Giggly Pigglies. Grubly. Regular, deliberate abuse of people's privacy. But the thing that most gets to me is the arrogance. We know that supposed hack was just a cover-up. Did you really think you could walk in and raid these data and not be caught? Information will out, Mr Perce. You've wrecked your contract and in the process drowned a hundred-and-seventy-million-pound public programme.'

'The hack? Me? Bullshit.'

The lift display hit zero and continued counting down.

'I'm sorry?' said J-R.

At minus three, the lift huffed to a stop and the doors pinged open. Perce led J-R into a blank hallway, pulled him aside by his upper arm. J-R breathed in his male scent: the lightly toasted smell of money.

'Listen,' said Perce. 'We collared the guy responsible for the Giggly Pigglies hack on Thursday. He's already gone.'

He turned and marched on down the corridor, still talking. J-R was forced to follow.

'We deal with our mess. How about your precious department gets its own house in order? It takes two keys to hack that data. You think that data was used for the pig stunt up north? Well if so, whoever did it got to someone at the ministry, too.'

Perce was right. Only a handful of ministry staff had access to those codes. J-R had, of course, suspected Bethany – until he found out how much more simple, and human, her transgression had been.

'If any of that is true,' he said, 'why not come out and say so? Why let sic_girl threaten your contract?'

'Because someone –' Perce stopped again. 'Some. One. Is setting me up. Faking this hack. Raiding my data over and over to make me look culpable. Me.'

This was not staged. Perce *felt* this. He headed off again, a grey-suited rabbit for J-R to follow along the white tunnels threading below the city.

'I'd love to report this to the Data Commissioner, like a good boy. But can you see them believing me when I say I've been stitched up?' Perce gave a comic shrug. 'I mean, I *would* say that, wouldn't I? I do that and this somebody *gets* me. After what I've built, they *get* me and I lose the chance to do amazing things for so many people.'

He guided J-R down the passage.

'Someone is out to fuck me, J-R. I don't. Like it. I want you to help me fix this.' Then another shift of tone: jaunty, matey. 'And really, is what you've been doing up to now so damn inspiring? Why wouldn't you want to be here – encouraging me to play the white man in all of this?'

Confoundingly, J-R found himself laughing as he trotted behind Perce.

'Excuse me – the *white man*?'

'Oh, is that not PC? White *knight*, then. See? Already you're influencing me for the better.'

Perce was impregnable. J-R was pulled behind him. He couldn't work here – of course not – but if he were to turn and head for home, what was waiting for him? Not Mark.

J-R turned a corner. Perce was already halfway down the plain white corridor.

'Come on,' he said. 'Meet my other new recruit.'

¶Nightshade
so long everyone youve been the best
see you on the other side
<saveParley>

¶sic_girl
404 resource not found

¶riotbaby
404 resource not found

¶TMI
404 resource not found

¶Spotted
404 resource not found

¶lolcatz
404 resource not found

¶tvjoe
404 resource not found

¶CelebFactor
404 resource not found

¶NewsHound
404 resource not found

¶bottomhalfofthepage
404 resource not found

¶therealnobody
404 resource not found

ELEVEN

THAT'S ALL HER CHILDREN SAFE. Dani stacks up the hard drives – ten slabs of intelligence, each the size of a paperback book – and wads them down with yesterday's T-shirt. She zips up the bag. Next up, the DigiCitz drives: the disks Sam says will take Perce down. Evidence he's been hacking people's data left, right and centre.

'*Sam says*' makes it sound like she trusts Sam, which is interesting, because if you asked her she'd have said she totally doesn't.

With another swipe of Gray's card she unlocks the smoke-glass door of the next Meccano cabinet. Gray was right. The DigiCitz data is right next door to the Parley boxes. Easily close enough to have been hit by Perce's killer magnet, if they'd had the chance to wipe the Parley disks.

This is way too fun. She needs to remember Leo died upstairs and police are swarming the place like bedbugs. But it's good, too. She should be cornered and desperate; instead she's invisibly rescuing her life's work. Nobody knows she's here, in this great white air-chilled data farm, deep beneath the pavement.

It takes less than five minutes to open the DigiCitz boxes and extract a hunk of magnetic information from the guts of each. She stows them in her bag, slings the strap over her shoulder and steps back to watch the serene hum of glass-faced cabinets. She wants to damage them. This is a beautiful thought, not an angry one. The calm is on her now. But it will give her simple, healing pleasure to fuck with every immaculate inch of this vault of captive data.

with all the careful she has terry slips the big steel pistol from her backpack and slides off the safety

dont ask how she even knows how to do that

facing the cabinets she sets her feet wide, weighs the weapon and purses her tongue, raises the iron and unloads seven rounds into the cabinets

the recoil staggers her back

the smooth white walls return a volley of sonic booms

The entry-pass system beeps behind her and the door swings open with a breath. In the real, she didn't do any of that. What she pulled from the backpack was her phone. She steps back to take a picture of the empty rack, to proffer with the <take-backID> and <saveParley> pennants. Later, when Parley's back online.

She turns at the sound of footsteps. Shit: Sean Perce. Weirdly, he's followed in by Pemberton, who replaces the door in its frame with a dark frown. He's holding a wad of papers in his hand. He looks like a kid who's just received terrible GCSE results. Perce strolls over to her.

'Hey hey hey!' he says, arms wide. 'The gang's all here!'

Dani gives him a look that could burn a hole in concrete.

'You! You put me here!'

Pemberton hurries to her.

'Dani, be careful. He tracked you here, from your phone.'

She looks at the phone in her hand.

'Bullshit. This isn't even my phone.'

But she thinks of what Gray said: *You need to be worried about whether they can see you*. She turns to Perce.

'You have nothing. I bought this phone with a different name, different money: different everything.'

'You did that? Amazing.' Perce looks like a hyena on E. 'Yet we found you. Logically, you must have given Grubly a correlation. And it matched you to the rest of Dani.'

The fingers of both his hands slide smoothly between each other. Terry into Dani, Dani into Terry. No, she's been so careful. What data match did she give up?

Not so careful: she went on MeatSpace Thursday night, as herself. With Colin – but she doesn't want to think about Colin. One lapse is all it takes to fall off the wagon of anonymity. Data are binary and unforgiving.

'So you found me. Saves me finding you.'

She holds up her phone, starts to video. Clears her throat.

'So why did you give my life to the trolls, Sean? Why are you wiping Parley?'

That'll sound good, off camera, when she posts it. A tiny Perce jerks on the screen. She steadies her hand.

'Now, Dani,' he says, smooth as liquidised shit. 'Does your presence here have anything to do with why Parley just went offline?'

She glances at her backpack, down on the floor. Perce registers and nods.

'You could have asked me,' he says. 'I can give your Personas all the storage they could ever want.'

Dani's hand wavers. That would have been easier than sneaking in here. Pemberton cuts in from out-of-frame.

'I think you should answer Dani's question, Sean. Did you smear her to the papers?'

Perce steps closer.

'Listen to me, Dani.'

He puts a hand on her shoulder. She shrugs it off.

'Hey, yo! Nobody here is my fucking dad, all right? The monkey speaks for herself.'

'So speak,' says Perce.

She swings the camera to stay on him. Pemberton steps out of shot.

'Two days. In two days you take away everything I have and you blow up everyone I am. What are you going to do to put it right?'

Her voice cracks on the hazy recording. This will go viral big time.

'Whatever I have to. We look after our own here. I'll see you right.'

'I'm not your own. I don't work for Parley any more.'

'No. You work directly for me now.'

She lowers the phone.

'How can I work for you when you hound me out? When you peddle lies about me to some cocksucker hack? When you bust my accounts and invade my life?'

'I did that? What a shit I am. What if I didn't?'

'You did. You sent my data to that journalist.'

'Really? You saw this happen?'

Doubt. Again. She shakes her head as if she can cast it out of her hair, holds the phone back up. Perce flips from jovial to dead, cold serious.

'Who told you I did all that, Dani?'

The blue eyes bore into the megapixels. She doesn't want to answer.

'Sam Corrigan,' she says.

It's Pemberton who jumps to attention.

'*Corrigan?*' he asks. 'The Terasoft PR man?'

Dani's camera turns on him. He puts up a protective hand.

'The. What?' she says.

TWELVE

BETHANY REPLACED THE CUP on its bone china saucer.

'So this is pleasant,' she said, 'but what's it to be? Hemlock and a hot bath, or drawn and quartered in Parliament Square?'

The room cringed for several seconds before anyone spoke. Even Krish wouldn't look her in the eye. Karen broke the silence.

'None of us are finding this easy, Beth.'

Oh, really, Karen, that's interesting; because you look like you just came in your starchy knickers.

'But it's terrific to hear you keep up your distinctive brand of humour,' said the PM.

Oh, yes: happy, happy Bethany, *toujours gai!* The PM came over from the window to sit by her on the sofa. Simon had care and concern down pat: it might have been what swung him the election – it certainly wasn't his grasp of economic policy. He was painfully credible; even when you knew what horse-dung it was. She let him give her arm two slow, affectionate pats before she withdrew it with a compressed smile.

She'd only been in his office once before, when she was handed the ministry job. Now here she was again. Big office, nicely done out, unlike the rest of Number Ten, which was all heritage-generic. But this office had edge. Pop-art prints, metal-frame furniture; an outsize chrome anglepoise doing service as a stand-ard lamp. The First Lady's touch: Helen was determined to be The Fresh Eye in Whitehall.

'It's not what we would have wanted,' the PM said.

Unthinking, she patted his hand back. His puckered face had the glow of a spanked backside; it made you want to comfort him. Women of child-bearing age all seemed to feel this. Core demographic.

Karen, smiling over them, nodded and made the tiny pushing motions of a matchmaker. Oh, Christ, Karen, are you traffic-managing the PM's every move?

'So, Bethany. Here's the position,' said Simon.

Cough. What is this? What more could he have to break to her at this moment? She looked to Karen for a clue – saw a sympathetic smile dance across her face. Karen's sympathy equated to a friendly nip from a black mamba. Across the room, Krish stood toying with Simon's desk furniture. She had an urge to stick her tongue out at him.

Simon stood and returned to the window, suddenly gripped by the view of Horseguards.

'So,' he said. 'I am of course keen you should have the opportunity to bow out gracefully –'

Keen. Should. Not guaranteed. Still something Bethany had to do, but what?

'– so we're prepared to let you choose this course.'

We. Not *I.* How we change in office. Simon, let us hope the world doesn't figure out how deeply *ordinary* you are: at least for the next three years.

'Using this statement,' he continued. 'Karen?'

Karen extruded a paper from her sharp leather file and placed it in Simon's hand. He passed it to Bethany. She read and after a count of ten her heart, which had remained so still, began to pound.

'What? *What?* This is a joke.' She read from the paper: '– *but when it became clear to me how he had exploited my deeply regrettable indiscretion to manipulate a key government programme, my position became untenable.* Oh, fuck, Simon! Your condition for a graceful exit is I wash my dirty linen in public? Drop my lover in the shit?'

Oh, my. They didn't like that word, *lover*. *Shit* is fine. *Fuck* fine. Often *Cunt*, in here. But *lover*?

'Would it help if I also say he raped me? Take one for Queen and country?'

'Bethany!' Simon Patterson, angry? Will wonders, etcetera. 'Don't tell me you're feeling any loyalty to Sean after—'

A twitch of Karen's hand was enough to silence him. All right. Let's ask the organ grinder. Bethany turned an eyebrow on Karen.

'Do the maths,' Karen said. 'It's not just you who's had a bad week. It's been a disaster for Mondan and for any government with a flagship programme still allied to them. Thank heavens you haven't signed yet. We're going to move the blame. We'll do it cleanly and we'll do it quickly.'

She moved round the desk and sat behind it. *Sat at the PM's desk!* Krish hurried to put down the paperweight he'd been fiddling with.

'Ha!' fake-laughed Karen. 'Did you not notice how heavily Krish here was being lobbied in the last few days? By Mr Perce himself, no less?' Karen treated them to one of her pauses, during which Bethany struggled not to look at Krish. Then Karen added: 'As was I.'

Bethany couldn't help herself.

'Excuse me? *Sean* has been calling *you*?'

It was like being cheated on: and with that frosty cow?

'Believe me, Mr Perce will reach at anything when he's in a corner. Seems he's read the runes rather better than you, Beth. He tried to get to Simon, even. He knew he was toast but he knew you were – toastier.'

Bethany laughed at that fatuous coinage. But it was the flat bark of a grounded seal. She turned to Krish.

'This is nonsense, right, Krish?'

His look was steady but gave her nothing back.

'You've known about this whole thing?'

Still he looked at her. There was a strain about his eyes: a hint of apology or suppressed laughter? Bethany had stepped into a zone between authority and ridicule. Nowhere left to stand: one must simply make the best. All that remained was Elyse's mantra.

Fuck you. Fuck you. Fuck you.

Yes, that was in fact a little better.

The PM, framed by the high sash window, signalled expectant apology. She walked past the functionaries at the desk and spoke directly to him.

'So may I get this clear?'

A nod. Like any salesman, Simon knew not to push his prospect too hard: give her space and she'll lead herself to the close.

'I grab Sean by the lapels and jump off a cliff? And in return I go honour unstained. That is roughly it?'

Simon shrugged with a wan smile. She held up a finger: she wasn't done yet.

'*With* the possibility of return?'

'Beth. You have a great career ahead of you. This is a speed bump.'

That was as much as she'd get. Nothing to gain by pushing the point. At least this way the mood music would be tolerable.

'All right,' she said. 'But for what? To make way for what? With Sean out, who gets to play with all our data? We – you – can't drop Digital Citizen. The opposition would have us for a pre-breakfast snack. You'd need another solution in place, ready to –'

The penny had been dropping slowly. Now it landed and began to roll about the floor.

'Ah.' Bethany gave a sharp little smile. 'Of course.'

Terasoft.

THIRTEEN

> yo gray
> is sams machine
> still up?

Gray mobile:
Yeah, why?

> can you get to his mails?

Gray mobile:
wtf, Dan? Why?
Hello, by the way?

> dont tell me you didnt hack his
> mail account x months ago

Gray mobile:
Maybe. So what? What's this about?
The hack's any minute. My finger's
hovering over the Enter key.

Dani checks the time on her phone. Twenty-five to twelve. She'd forgotten the video hack. The denial of service attack. She looks from Perce to Pemberton, who flank her as she marches down the service corridor. In twenty-five minutes, Gray will loose the bot attack and take control of the giant screens around 404 City. Pushing Sam's messages to a lazy, eager world. Fucking Perce over. An hour ago, that's all Dani wanted. Now she doesn't know.

> just do it, gray – check his mails
> from this morning
> and last night
> search for me and Perce and
> Terasoft – youll know it when
> you read it

Perce holds a door open for her as she thumb-types. It's weird reverting to text messages: she misses Parley.

There's a long pause, then Gray replies.

Gray mobile:
OK.

A voice cuts in from the real.

'There she is. It's her.'

'Holy – Ms Farr! Stop please!'

Dani looks up. Who's this? Her fan club?

They're at the bottom of 404 City's central atrium, two storeys below ground. Across a wide graph-paper floor two men approach. Déjà vu to another morning, another office, hard men in casual clothes. Dani freezes. Everywhere is screens. On them all, a CGI mobile phone spins and explodes in light. Behind the men, in the centre of the floor, is a roped-off area. Within the yellow tape is a plastic tent, like for roadworks but silver white.

The police are almost on them. Dani's backpack dangles from her hand. Can she shed it? Perce takes a step to position himself in front of the bag: interesting. He grins at the cops like a serial killer flagged down by State Troopers.

'Officers. Good morning. My colleagues and I are in something of a hurry. May I be of assistance?'

The cops look right past him, to Dani. Life's been moving so fast these last days she's had no time to pause and reflect. She's: what is she? An outlaw. There's assault, kidnap, credit card fraud, resisting arrest – is that right?

Two laminate ID cards complete the action replay of Tuesday morning.

'It's Ms Farr we need to speak to, Mr Perce. We have information placing her here.'

Perce is about to reply but Dani cuts him off.

'Information? From who?'

'Does it matter, Ms Farr? It would seem to be accurate.'

'Nobody knows I'm here.'

'I'd have to contest that.'

He's enjoying this. Who knows she's here? It's obvious. She turns on Perce.

'I fucking knew it.'

'*No, Dani*,' he hisses, pushing himself close. '*Watch me. I'm getting you out of this.*'

He smells of expensive wanker juice.

'*After you fucked with me like this?*' she whispers back. '*How are you going to do that?*'

'*Three words, Dani. We. Have. Lawyers.*'

His spit hits her cheek. She wipes it with her wrist. The policemen are watching as though it's a sitcom.

'Tell me, Ms Farr,' says the first one, 'what's in your bag?'

'Um – my knickers? You want them?'

She reaches for the zip. Something flashes in the policeman's face. He shoves past Perce and grabs her arm. She pulls away with Terry's strength.

'*The bag, Ms Farr!*'

She holds it behind her like a playground bully.

come and get it, bitch, says terry

'Give me the bag,' says the cop.

Pemberton steps in as he grapples for her arm.

'Officer? I'm from the office of Bethany Lehrer. By what authority—'

'Sir, your friend here has—'

Perce cuts in over everyone.

'*Ms Farr,*' he says, 'is a senior colleague. I have agreed with your superiors the terms of your presence here. Which did not include apprehending my staff.'

The policeman steps back a fraction, breathless.

'Sir, Ms Farr is suspected of serious offences and possession of an offensive item.'

'Such as?'

Offensive. Does he mean –?

'I am not obliged to disclose that information.'

Perce inhales deeply through his nostrils, sets his head back until he's glaring down the full extent of his nose. His hair flashes black in the shout of daylight from above.

'You may have no obligation, *officer*, but unless you have entered these premises under warrant –?' Stone-face response. 'Right. In which case you're here on the terms I agreed and you'll want to explain your actions.'

This is new. All Dani would have had to offer here is swearing and scratching; and where has that got her? A barely scraped freedom. Perce is warping reality to a place where they're in the position of strength: just by saying so. The two cops exchange information through a look.

'I don't know whether you're aware,' says the first one, 'but yesterday your *valued colleague* allegedly apprehended a government minister. Evaded questioning by officers. Is suspected of purloining an item of police property.'

An item. Dani was right.

'Suspected,' says Perce. 'Alleged. You have evidence of this?'

'We have strong grounds, sir.'

'I happen to know you've cleared her of the sic_girl leaks. Your colleague told me so last night.'

Huh? This is new.

'You aren't hearing me, sir. Yesterday afternoon an officer was injured in the line of duty. Followed by a fatality here. We would hope for your cooperation.'

They want to search her bag. The DigiCitz drives are in there, covered in the data trails that will prove Mondan covered up half a dozen malicious hacks. Sam wants the police to get their hands on them because when they find the data, it'll stiff Perce and stymie his grab on the nation's data.

So that's what Sam wants – but what does Dani want?

Perce draws breath for another volley of words. Dani puts her hand on his arm and holds out the bag.

'Here,' she says.

The cop tries to read her face. She gives him a fuck-off grin. He reaches slowly and snatches the bag. She flips up her hands, like *whoooah! okaaay!*

The two cops march the bag to the taped-off area. Dani, Perce and Pemberton follow. The tape's strung in a square at the centre of the open space, beside a rest zone with a drinks machine and yet more screens. These ones strumming through rolling news on volume setting zero.

The place is sick with coppers. The main policeman, the snide one, places the bag on a table in the seating area. He puts on see-through plastic gloves. So does his friend. There's stuff on the table already, bagged. The procedurals she loves to watch have nosed up into her reality.

The policeman starts unloading the backpack. He passes each item to his colleague who lays it on the table. Wallet. Keys. Kindle. Phone chargers. Dirty T-shirt. Hard drives. Underwear (clean). More hard drives. Underwear (used). More hard drives. No sign of any interest in the drives. The policeman keeps rooting in the bag and passing items. Perce's face inexpressive as a low-res photo.

Wash bag. Power adaptors. Elyse's book.

There it is. Bethany's dog-eared edition, with the explosive message in the front. Dani has kept it close the whole time, guarding it like a childhood treasure. Perce reaches down and picks it up – the police glance his way but don't try to stop him. They don't realise it's an object of power. Perce turns the book in his hands, looks at the inscription inside and throws an appraising look at Dani.

The policeman ferrets in the bottom of the bag. He's not looking at the drives stacked in plain view on the table. Why isn't he interested in the drives? She knows why. *An item of police property*. Taking a leaf from Perce's book she braves it.

'What are you still looking for? My knickers are right there, yo. You prefer the ones I've worn? Here.'

She holds them up. Sniffs them.

'*Mmmm*,' she moans.

The policeman ignores her, shakes out the bag. Four or five coins drop and dance on the tabletop. He slaps the bag down.

'Where is it, Ms Farr?'

'Where's what?'

'You know.'

'I fucking don't.'

'Don't swear at me or I'll have you in the back of a paddy with a bag on your head in thirty seconds. *Valued colleague* or not. An *item* of police *property*.'

He does. He means the gun. They thought she'd be carrying the gun.

That means she's won.

Leo had first pulled out the gun in the service lift at the conference hotel. Only seconds had passed since the lift doors shut on the baffled face of the minister. Dani reeled from the sight of it, pressing against the aluminium wall. She'd only just met the guy and here he was doing Usual Suspects *moves with a loaded sidearm.*

'Fucking hell, kid!' she said.

'No, dude, look,' he said, 'this is some cool shit.'

He spun the metal beast. Dani took a sharp breath: minutes earlier it had gone off and nearly fucked her in the ears. That policeman had been lying maybe-dead on the concrete floor. The kid must have scooped up his gun while Dani was reeling from the noise.

'Put it away, kid.'

'I mean, chill. I thought you were some crazy Occupy girl. Don't you want the fucking juice?'

He tucked the gun peevishly into his jeans as the lift arrived on Ground. They scampered out through the concrete vault of the delivery bay, past recycle bins, laundry carts – no cops, thank the goddess. They freaked for a second when an overweight Asian guy with a cap stepped out from the glass hut by the vehicle gate; but he was just some clipboard-jockey. They skirted him and hit the daylight. Leo followed her into the network of alleys at the back of the hotel. Backs of shops and restaurant bins lining a rotting carpet of cardboard. They hit the brakes.

'OK, this should be good,' said Dani. 'Lose it.'

'What?'

'You know what. Ditch it.'

He ran his hands through knots of dreads.

'Fuck, OK, it was just a thing. I don't even care.'

He handed her the gun.

'Do what you want with it,' he said.

She felt the weight of it in her hand, then untucked the front of her T-shirt and wiped the craggy surface round and around. Holding the barrel through the fabric of her T-shirt she opened the lid of an oversize wheelie, rooted one-handed for the knot of a heavy sack and shoved the gun deep into the muck, gagging at a wave of rotten citrus.

She resealed the sack double-tight and slammed the dumpster shut. Leo shifted his weight from foot to foot.

'Jesus, are you happy now? Like, way to be a total hardarse.'

Now he's dead.

FOURTEEN

'A YOUNG MAN DIED LAST NIGHT. None of us should forget that.'

From above, Downing Street is shaped like the profile of a bottle, narrow at the entry point, then widening outside numbers 10 and 11. In this handsome amphitheatre, Bethany faced off to the press – Saturday deps, all of them, eager to break a Westminster scoop.

'Before I give you what you're here for, I need to make something absolutely clear. Much is being said about events at yesterday's Digital Citizen launch. Most of it false. In particular, there is no truth whatsoever to the statements about Dani Farr. She was not responsible for any wrong-doing. She was not responsible for malicious messages on the Parley service. She did nothing to harm me. I would ask everyone to leave this courageous and inventive young woman be.'

The Parley service – ugh. Who called it that?

She hoped what she'd just said about Dani was true, that her actions were simply those of a hunted, vulnerable woman in an impossible situation; but this was a risk. Career-ending to call it wrong. What a relief to have one's career in tatters already.

Seeing her draw breath, the press pack began to call: *Have you been fired, Bethany? Do you accept responsibility? What about you and Sean Perce, Minister?* But when you give a statement from outside Number Ten, the pack remains at bay, on the opposite pavement. So much easier to ignore them here than with a door-step microphone shoved in your face. They swirled in a single king-rat mass. Shutterbugs; TV cameras.

Breaking. These days a backbencher farting counted as breaking news. Peter would be watching for sure. The boys, maybe. (No, not Jake: he'd be at Saturday music group.)

The hacks stopped baying. There was what you'd call An Awkward Silence. She looked down at the paper in her hand. Her eyes wouldn't focus. All week – for years now – her life had been narrated to her. The deal was: read these words; ditch Sean; escape, honour intact. And in would storm Andrew Carpenter: a little man with big ideas and a tiny, tiny mind to store them in. Nobody ever got fired for choosing Terasoft, they said. Go safe. Go easy. Choose the downhill route. Boy, had she ever ignored that advice. She'd gone for Sean, for Mondan, for a hope the two of them might open new ground, liberate the greater population, colonise the future together, be free to love one another without complication; just as her grandmother had done with a succession of brilliant, beautiful, temporary men.

She screwed her eyes, trying to prise the words from the fluttering paper. If she didn't read them she lost the right to resign on her own terms – except who was it standing on the steps of Number Ten? Not Karen. Not the PM.

She folded the paper, one, twice, scissoring her fingers along the creases. She slid it into a jacket pocket and raised her face to the wall of cameras, a grin breaking out across her face.

When was the last time she smiled?

FIFTEEN

THE POLICE RETURN THE HARD DRIVES to the bag and shove it into Dani's arms. All they were looking for was the gun, and she never had the gun. Leo's death has wiped the original task – the allegedly stolen data – from their walnut forebrains.

Only problem remaining: Dani assaulted a minister. She still goes to prison.

She tries to think like Perce: can she trade with them? Sam wants them to have the DigiCitz drives, and make sure Perce is legally screwed. What if she hands them over? Would that buy her advantage? But what if Gray comes back with something? Sam said Perce was responsible for everything that's happened. But Sam works for Terasoft – his job is to make Sean Perce look bad. If the police did find something incriminating on those drives, would it be real or did Sam put it there?

She turns to ask Pemberton for intel but the policeman blocks her line of sight.

'Best we do this quietly, Ms Farr.'

She turns to Sean for defensive fire but he's nowhere. She tries to catch Pemberton's attention but he's distracted by the rolling news on the TV screens.

'*Pemberton!*' she hisses.

The first policeman puts out a hand.

'No need to make this difficult.'

He reaches for her arm. She pulls back.

'*No!* Don't you—'

A uniform turns his head to the noise.

'We don't want to use force,' says the cop.

She's hemmed between the table and the back of a couch. The plainclothes officers close in. The uniform moves round to join them. Dani puts down her bag and braces herself. Her hands form fists. Is she going to do this?

Pemberton speaks, still gazing up at the screens.

'Who do you take instruction from, officers?'

'Sir, you are not helping.'

The cops don't even look at him. Each has a hand on Dani now; she writhes away but there's nowhere to turn.

'You're Parliamentary Branch?' Pemberton continues. 'Tasked with protecting the minister?'

She wrestles heavy palms, thinking of biting. Knowing that would take her over another line.

'That is precisely what we're doing, sir. Perhaps you could persuade your colleague –'

Pemberton turns to face them, pointing up at the screens.

'In which case I suggest you watch this.'

Something in his voice: they turn to the screens. Pemberton reaches up to the volume button on the nearest one. Three news channels, all the same image. Striped by three varieties of *BREAKING NEWS* banner is the minister. Bethany, speaking. Flashlit in front of an old familiar London house. The number on the big black door. Oh: it's a *10*.

Two in binary.

SIXTEEN

'I AM NOT PERFECT,' Bethany pronounced into the mic. 'I realise that doesn't count as news.'

Barely polite sniggers from the press pack opposite.

'I want to apologise. But not for failing to live up to the standards expected of me. Those standards are crap.'

Well, that got their attention. Not what Bethany expected to emerge from her mouth but, like so many things this week, it was out there now.

'Who's perfect? Apart from Ryan Gosling.'

Don't *do* that, Beth. This is your moment. It will be replayed over and over. That gag will date.

'Haven't we all stepped over lines? Haven't we all been bad boys and girls at some time? And if we survive day-to-day by pretending otherwise, to the world, to our loved ones, and to ourselves – what of it? Well, if I've learned anything these last few days, it's that nothing's secret. Not any more. And if you think it is, that's when you should worry; because it won't be for long.

'So my advice to you, friends. Open your closets and let your skeletons come out. Because they will come out.'

That construction was a disaster: gay skeletons? Where was J-R? Oh, for the comfort of well-spaced Times New Roman.

'Are you ready for that? Because I wasn't.

'So: friends from the fourth estate; fellow public servants; viewers at home. When are you going to get real? When are you going to align your standards to the sad inevitability of human frailty?

'It's not just you, I realise. Everyone around me – this lot –' a thumb back over her shoulder to Number Ten '– have always wanted me to tread the path more travelled on. But I kept on choosing the wilder path – and look where it landed me. And you know what? I'd do it again.

'So I do want to apologise. Apologise for patronising you by pretending to be anything other than what I am. A chaotic, wayward, forgetful woman, whose recent behaviour a wonderful husband and sons do not deserve –'

Damn it, come on, vocal chords, come on! Not long now.

'– but who I dearly hope are ready to give all ten-and-a-half stone of their Jilly Cooper-loving, chocolate-addicted wife and mother – who by the way has had a pimple on her nose since Monday and is really hoping neither of these cameras is HD – a chance to make it up to them, even if it takes the rest of her life.

'So. Friends. Keep your perfect. You know what? I'm going home.'

And with that, Bethany swept back through the huddle of staffers to the great black door of state, which levered open right on cue; as it always will.

She caught Krish's eye as she passed him – oh, Krish! Don't let Madame Arbiter catch you with that dumb grin plastered on your face. She threw him back the tiniest of smirks as she swept across the threshold and out of politics.

And that, ladies and gentlemen, is how you make an exit.

SEVENTEEN

'GOT HIM,' SAYS SEAN, typing at his desktop.

Dani walks around to see who he's talking about. When she clocks his screen her head does three lateral twists and a backward pike.

)) laminate pow-wow ((

'What is this?' she says. 'It's – whoah.'

Perce grins his dashing grin.

)) watercooler jangle ((

'We scaled it,' he says. 'I'm calling it *Everything About You*. What do you think?'

Sounds, words and pictures spam the screen. They've tidied up Dani's collage algorithms, given them coherence; style. She's looking at her creation, *Me All Over*: but it's something new. It's the most beautiful thing she's ever seen. Through it she's looking at Sam.

'Uh – good,' she says. 'Actually – really pretty good. Liking the name.'

Sean works the on-screen clock to land the timeline just before the now. An hour back. Photos pop out of the map. Office scenes, corridor atmospherics, snatches of jargon. Colours cycle through the sounds. It's like watching from behind Sam's frontal lobe.

'That's the Terasoft HQ in Victoria?' she says.

'Looks that way. The guy shaking hands with Sam here is Harry Makepeace, Terasoft Corporate Comms. And that's half of his boss, Shaz Joshi. Looks like Sam has his tablet propped for a demo. He's probably showing them us.'

What she's looking at is exactly what she'd thought the thing could be, once it was generalised from her to everybody.

'OK.' She coughs. 'So I think –'

'Go on,' says Perce.

'So Sam did all of this. Last night I worked out he's doing sock-puppetry with sic_girl, trashing you and Bethany. I thought he was doing it because he was this free-data campaigner guy.'

From across the office, Pemberton snorts from behind his laptop screen.

'I've met Corrigan,' he says. 'That's one thing he is not.'

'Yeah, well screw you too, twinkletoes. If you're Albert Einstein, why didn't you work this out for yourself?'

Sean cuts in.

'Go on, Dani. Tell me about Sam.'

'So now that Gray's read his mails we know the free data stuff was BS. This whole thing is designed to screw you – Bethany was collateral damage. He used TakeBackID, used Leo, all so Terasoft could eat your lunch.'

Pemberton chips in again, but the snarky tone has turned to amazement.

'That's it? That's all? Bethany just lost her job over this.'

Dani glares but Sean beckons.

'Your turn, J-R. We were bidding against Terasoft? For the hundred seventy million.'

Pemberton slips into a chair at the desk, nodding.

'Bethany made the decision.' He swallows. 'In your favour.'

'And I bet Terasoft really, really didn't like that piece of news.'

'I've been getting periodic calls from them ever since,' says Pemberton. 'Lobbying for a change. Most of the calls from –'

He gestures at the screen, at the shuttering images from the other side of town. Dani finishes his sentence.

'From Sam. And there's more. First Sam said it was Bethany who doxed me, stirred up the trolls. Then when I realised that wasn't true, he said it was you, Sean. Mr Perce.'

'Sean.'

'But he was lying, wasn't he?'

'Yes, he was lying. It's what he does, in his line of work.'

'Oh, fucking *hell!*' Dani punches down so hard on the side of the desk she thinks she might have broken a bone. 'I knew it was him, right away. But I let him spin me. Idiot. *Idiot!*'

'Seems we were all taken in,' says Sean. 'But you've sussed it now. You've got him.'

'Too late, though.'

She drops against the back of the swivel chair and lets it spin. It's taken everything to get to this destination, only to find there's nothing to be done. But Pemberton, who's been gawping like a haddock, flips into that authoritative mode she saw him use when she first met him. His voice drops an octave.

'We need to act now. They'll be announcing Bethany's replacement any minute. Odds on this is Andrew Carpenter.'

The name strikes an electrode into Sean.

'Carpenter? But he's——?'

'Former non-exec on Terasoft's European board. So that'll be that.' Something strikes him. 'Oh, God. No.'

'J-R?' says Sean.

He's conducting the pair of them like musicians. Pemberton stares at him with an expression that looks like grief.

'It *wasn't* just you. Bethany was a target, too. This has been a campaign to get your contract terminated, *and* Bethany fired. And Carpenter in her place. Is that –? Do people *do* things like this in the real world?'

'Black PR. Countries have gone to war because of it.'

'Terasoft will own us.'

'You think? Come on J-R. We can do this – sign on the dotted line. Let's say, better the devil you know?'

Pemberton's face contorts. There's more to this than Dani understands.

'I need guarantees,' he says. 'Safeguards. Transparency.'

'So accept the job and set those for yourself,' says Sean. 'If we're going to stop this thing, we need to do it now.'

So much testosterone slopping about the room it's hard to breathe. Pemberton may look like an over-inflated toddler but he's waving his dick around just as much as Sean. Dani doesn't have time to wait on them.

'No sweat,' she says. 'I just solved this. And it'll take, oh –' she checks her phone '– five minutes?'

She wishes she could proffer the looks on their faces.

Five minutes pass at a crawl – how time in the real can. While they wait for Gray to message back with confirmation, Pemberton does business over an antique smartphone that's about an inch thick, and Dani digs under the hood of the production engine Perce has built out of her *Me All Over* pilot. She watches herself go off the grid, on Thursday. It's amazing, seeing herself disappear, like *SNAP*. She follows herself through Shoreditch, from Sam's office to the yard at Parley, the angry bustle and the shouting that took her there; her call with Jonquil chopped in sushi-slices and played back as music. Then she meets Gray and *foosh*: the screen blanks. If she leaves the clock there, Dani's nowhere. If she nudges it forward a few hours, the app starts to backward-compile a skeleton of someone new – of Terry – from the tills of shops and cafes. It fleshes up as she acquires devices that can capture and assemble richer knowledge, deeper sensations. By the evening, Terry's flesh has formed around the bones of her purchases and she's breathing. Her colours and frequencies and sounds are different from Dani's, though she can't say how. She flips time back and forward, consuming both instances of herself. She plays the sequence back and again on loop. It's how something changed in her, too, that she can't yet pin down.

She sits back and claps hands, one-two-three, in front of her face.

'These display components are built on my original sampling engine?' she asks.

'Plus some fuzzy algorithms and audiovisual loops from the team here. But you did the heavy lifting.'

Dani shakes her head.

'Awesome. We made this.'

Sean looks like he wants to kiss her. Which would be weird; though he's solidly in the fuckable-older-man region of the Venn diagram.

'See, this is –' he says. 'I knew you wouldn't be territorial. There are devs who'd say, how dare you march in and use my code? But that isn't you, is it?'

Dani shrugs. It's freaky: Perce is no way the corporate douche she'd expected. Awesome the way he showed up with that lawyer downstairs, and used Bethany's speech to get Dani off the hook. For now.

Awesome, too, to hear Bethany speak for her in the first place. Though why she'd do that is a mystery for another day.

Dani's phone bongs. She pulls it out.

Gray mobile:
All set.
Ready at the keyboard, Dan?
roger roger, cap'n

Gray mobile:
I've turned the bots away from Mondan.
Terasoft's UK web is about to go dooooown.
But omg – Sam, though? Terasoft?
Everything's gone all
my-enemy's-enemy-is-my-friend.

                    word
                    ive almost lost track of who to hate

Gray mobile:
And Perce is definitely OK with me
hacking his screens? I mean, I don't want
your friendly coppers beating my door
down.

                    bare sure – hes right here
                    JR says the attack will be more real
                    if it comes from takebackID, not from Sean
                    its fuzzy
                    ill explain later

Gray mobile:
OK. I guess.
Tell everyone to watch the big screens.
The main feature attraction is about to start.

EIGHTEEN

weve got something to say

<takebackID>

The second the TakeBack pennant hits 404 City's screens a colossal cheer rises from the encampment, relayed inside through rolling news and laptops. The building shakes. Here's the takeover those hopeful kids were promised by the lying man.

<ripidentikid>
<saveparley>

Turns out Dani, Gray and J-R are some kind of perfect, teamwise. The most unlikely group, shaken into collaboration, can sometimes form an efficient mechanism.

watch this

But this fusion – of Gray's accelerated hacks, J-R's instinct for words that will speak for themselves, and the sharp edge of Dani's online persona – is seamless.

dirty tricks

Pace is everything. Dani animates words and images onto the giant screens, sliding them in great neon blocks. She mirrors them on the resurrected Parley.

listen to me

Names and pictures and puns and provocations.

lies they told about me

The circling beasts of mass attention turn and latch onto this narrative. It's new, and it's a perfect reversal-of-fortune story: what the hive mind loves.

lies they told about identikid

Much amaze. Perce, the villain, transformed to falsely accused hero. A cynical attack from a juggernaut of global tech. An attempt to wing a cocksure British entrepreneur. Outsider hero archetype. This is now the story.

what they stole from you
<dayofrage>

How swiftly the current of opinion turns. Gray scrapes proof points from Sam's emails. J-R watches raw clippings flip onto the screen and dictates new eye-bait for Dani to proffer.

who sold identikid?
<ripidentikid>

Inside, all around the atrium, the screens howl with overlapping content. The monster screens outside shimmer above the city with Dani's supple magic. *Moar secrets*, cries the crowd below. *Moar lies.*

J-R takes a new tack: he racks up verbatim clippings from Sam's mails to Terasoft. Dani cherry-picks the choicest provocations.

From: Sam Corrigan
Date: TUESDAY
Yeah, that's right. We fed the Met an anonymous tip-off that an 'activist' under the AKA of sic_girl was holed up at

Parley HQ and was a credible threat. Apparently they
showed up armed :-/

Dani feels a special burn of delight, releasing that nugget of
intelligence.

From: Sam Corrigan
Date: WEDNESDAY
These demonstrators don't know what they want. Give
them a cause and they rally round it like flies to dogshit.
Perce will be their dogshit for today.

Dani ices that one with a dancing line of poop emojis.
And then:

From: Sam Corrigan
Date: THURSDAY
Sure Mondan have done nothing wrong. But we've amped
the message until people are too riled to notice there's
nothing there. People are dumb when it comes to it.

Way to alienate a generation, Sam. Your turn to be the dogshit.
Dani knows without seeing that down below, a couple-hundred
demonstrators stand, feet planted, heads cranked back, to
welcome this validation of their anger and suspicion. Righteous
rage echoes in their proffers back. She throws the best replies onto
the screens, beside Sam's mails.

From: Sam Corrigan
Date: FRIDAY
News flash: I just had a brainwave. I've shopped Leo
Sandberg, my protest-monkey, to Krish Kohli, my contact
at MinTech. Far as they know now, he did the sic_girl leaks.
Way I hear it, the Met are hunting him down already. We're
in the clear, guys.

Some words you can't back out of. Once spoken, no return.

hunting him down

At some point Sean drags J-R away – something to do with the ministry. Dani doesn't register. She's in the code-freeze. The cites rack up. Trending doesn't come close: this thing explodes.

we're in the clear, guys

Is this for Leo, or for herself? She doesn't know.

NINETEEN

J-R RODE THE BACK SEAT of Perce's silent-running car to Westminster. How had he ended here, in the plush interior of a mogul's Mercedes? Beside him, Perce twisted his upper body to gaze through the rear windscreen. J-R turned, too, and together they watched Dani's messages flick across the giant screens. When they could no longer make out the words, Perce faced front and dropped back into the seat's deep padding. The interior was uniformly cream: unblemished, tight upholstery. Pine scent.

'Danielle's pulling up gold there. Glad Sam's getting the brunt, and not me. Hell hath no fury, right?'

As J-R untwisted into his seat, his raincoat belt became caught underneath him. He tugged on it as Perce kept talking.

'Tell me that isn't going to kill Terasoft. Could there be a better time to hit the Party with our counter-offer? I tell you, J-R, it was in the stars you'd walk in this morning. Karen still thinks she's meeting me to squeeze me out of the contract. *Huh!* Fat chance of that.'

The belt pinched J-R's middle. He lifted his backside from the leather to loosen the restraint, but this only pulled his bonds tighter. The buckle must be caught.

'All very well broadcasting your message up there,' he said. 'That's getting you TV and it'll bring in tomorrow's nationals. And I've given your press office solid lines. But the word of protesters? Posted on your own screens? Not credible. You'll need to feed the media an independent voice. A credible industry source.'

He reached beneath the flesh of his bottom and wrestled the buckle, which had somehow hooked itself around the recessed metal clasp of the seatbelt. Perce seemed unaware of this struggle.

'Good. Good,' he said. 'We'll get GiveMeData to speak up.'

'GiveMeData? The – ah – independent lobby group?' J-R gave a nervy laugh as he dug behind himself.

'Ha! Come on, you know astroturf when you see it. They're us.'

The buckle gave against J-R's tugging. His hand shot sideways with the force of the pull, slapping the side of Perce's thigh. Perce looked down in puzzlement.

'But,' said J-R, 'GiveMeData makes submissions to government. They presented to the Commons subcommittee last month. There are – laws about that?'

Perce returned a short lunatic laugh.

Why *was* J-R here? Perce had insisted he come along to Party HQ – no, not insisted: assumed. And here he was. With Perce there was no drawn-out process of review, amendment and counter-correction. Here, one thought of a thing, then one did it. No steps in between. Already J-R had been able to land a blow on the obnoxious Terasoft. True, Perce was obnoxious too: but people like him were makers, creators of value. He offered a narrow corridor of possibility that others could follow, or be shut out for good.

It had taken J-R no more than thirty seconds to persuade him to share the fabricated 'Pig-gate' evidence with the Party. Perce had turned to Dani, who had handed over a stack of electronics that Perce passed in turn to J-R. Perce would tell Karen Arbiter about the false data trails created by Terasoft's stooges and would let himself be judged. The slate-clearing evidence was currently at J-R's feet.

Was it now his lot to be the conscience the man beside him so clearly needed? Could he do more good staying the arm of the one who wielded the weapons, than in making the laws that failed to govern him?

The car slid to a gentle halt. Perce unclipped his seatbelt with a smoothness that mocked J-R's fumbling.

'Here we are.'

J-R bent to peer through the tinted glass. The windows of Party HQ raised metal eyebrows at him. The driver opened Perce's door; he was already halfway out when he turned to J-R.

'You are coming?'

To be seen here with Perce, bolting the stable door so firmly? All J-R could do was follow the current of events. He picked up the case of hard disks from the footwell, taking care not to bash the condensed trust of a million citizens on his way out of the car.

TWENTY

DANI FLEXES SORE FINGERS and whispers with Gray on the rebooted Parley. The TV news is up on Sean's plasma, showing a pierced and dreadlocked girl. She's familiar. *WINTER GREEN*, says the caption.

¶Nightshade
    is that a name or a paint colour?

¶thegrays
    :D

FRIEND OF DEAD PROTESTER LEO SANDBERG, says the subtitle. The girl flinches from the reporter's mic. Behind her, a ramshackle camp nestles by a glass-and-steel wall, a giant *A* etched into the glass.

¶Nightshade
    girl is thin enough to snap

¶thegrays
    Ooh, mee-ow!

The girl's eyes are raised like a Virgin Mary to the screens that overwhelm the camp.
'*If what they're saying up there is true,*' she says in a sorry rush,

'*Then this guy Sam Corgan – or Corrigan? He killed Leo. No doubt.*'

There's a scuffle off camera as the reporter creams himself at this statement.

'*You blame Terasoft for your partner's death?*'

¶Nightshade

> its like J-R said: you start with the personal story
> then widen it

'*Totally,*' says the girl. '*I totally blame them. They shopped him to the police. He only ever did good but they twisted it and turned the police on him and now he's – he's –*'

So much Dani can see and understand now. Being in the swill of events makes you wiser.

'*Terasoft did this?*' the reporter says again.

¶thegrays

> Christ, give it a rest, mate.

But the girl wants to give as badly as the reporter wants to take. '*Terasoft killed him. No doubt. They killed Leo.*'

And back to studio. Dani nods at the screen.

¶Nightshade

> i tell you gray
> perce isnt perfect but terasoft is like DO BE EVIL

Cut to general views of the tents as the newsreader talks through all that's happened this week: at least as much as these guys know. He says the protesters are moving their shit to Terasoft.

¶thegrays

> I guess. I'm having trouble adapting.

¶Nightshade

 you are?

¶thegrays

 ROFL
 Point.
 So what's Perce offered you?

¶Nightshade

 a fuckload of money my friend
 and oh hey he wants to talk to you too
 says youve skills much

¶thegrays

 I like the man already.

Terry's phone starts trilling its head off. Dani checks the screen. It's an 07-something: who? Nobody has Terry's number. She's three days old. Only Gray and one other person know it. And she's already talking to Gray.

Shit.

¶Nightshade

 g2g, sorry

¶thegrays

 OKCU

She swipes to answer.
'Hello, Sam.'

TWENTY-ONE

'AND HERE I WAS,' says J-R, 'thinking you cared about her.'

'*Cared?*' hissed Krish. 'Do you really want me to lay out her bad choices for you?'

Krish tugged J-R into a meeting room, away from Karen, Sean, and the staffers milling about in the reception area. He leaned his back against the closed door.

'Try not to be a naïve prick, J-R. There was never any doubt where this would end.'

Through the glass partition, J-R saw Sean vanish into the main office along with Karen's entourage.

'Do you know why I sent you on the Parley stint?' said Krish. 'So you didn't go down with her. I'm a big boy and I can take it but you have bugger all alliances out in the Party. You're a one-horse guy and your horse just fell at Beecher's Brook.'

J-R swallowed down hard.

'Seeing her out there. Without lines. She was extraordinary.'

Krish nodded, long and slow.

'Have you spoken to her?' he asked. 'They have her up on first for a debrief.'

'Not yet.'

'She'll be leaving.'

'I know.'

Neither of them made any move to go. Time passed at the exhausted crawl of a party in government.

'She doesn't blame you,' said Krish. 'Me – she blames.'

Through the glass, Bethany's police escort returned to the reception area, slapped his palms together and spoke to the pony-tailed intern at the desk. She replied and the policeman let out an open, straightforward laugh.

'Does it bother you?' asked Krish.

'Bethany? Of course.'

'Naw. Me chucking you in feet first with zero briefing.'

A posse of researchers hastened past and jostled out onto the street. A week ago that would have been him.

'No. That combination is pretty much what I've come to expect.'

'OK, good, so.'

What were J-R's lines now, and on whose behalf?

'Well –' he attempted.

'Aye.' Krish had reached some conclusion. 'So is it congratulations I should give you?'

'As in, am I going to be Sean Perce's mouthpiece?'

'You've played this brilliantly for him, already. Terasoft are squarely fucked if you keep up the momentum. D'y'know, I felt not a little proud to see you roll up with your boy Sean. I give it ninety-five per cent we'll sign with you as planned. Andrew is fucking livid.'

J-R tugged at his earlobe.

'I'm – not sure. There are things I need to consider.'

Mark, for instance. What on earth would Mark say? Would he care? Were they even speaking?

'Well, no rush, OK?' said Krish. 'There's plenty here if you do come back. But it'd be back to the pumps, you ken? You'd need to catch the apron strings of another minister. You want my view? Go for it. Perce. When things are moving this fast you've best to be in the eye of the storm.'

'Indeed,' nodded J-R. 'The trick lies in knowing where that is.'

TWENTY-TWO

'PETER? HELLO?

'Oh, thank God, you – oh, so you saw it.

'Thank you, babe, yes, it was totally off the cuff. Not *quite* what they wanted me to say.

'Ha ha! Yeah, that's right.'

Bethany glanced at the frosted partition. There was movement outside. She needed to remember this was Party HQ. She was still in the wind-down, couldn't be herself just yet. She tuned back in to the over-gentle voice of her husband.

'Well, I'm – oh, God, I don't know, Petey. Too soon, too soon. Ask me later.

'Yeah, like three years later!

'Actually, do you know, I think I *am* OK, weirdly. I'm looking forward to, you know. *Spending more time with my family.* If you'll have me.'

Holy hell, she was actually tearing up, from that dumb joke. Come on, girl, hold it together.

'Yeah, of course. But now I really should go. Business to sort here.

'Half hour tops.

'No, I'll have to get a cab. No ministerial car any more, remember?

'Yeah, that's something else I have to start getting used to!

'Yeah, totally. You too, babes.

'Yes. Yes, I actually think it could be. And listen, babes, *thank you*. No, really, darling. I mean it.

'Yes, we will most certainly "have that talk". Good. OK. You too. *Bisous*. Bye. Bye.'

She clicked off the phone and took three draughts of air. Not long now. Keep it real. And it's – *fuckyoufuckyoufuckyoufuckyou*.

OK, better. She balled fists into her eye sockets to push out any hint of emotion, shook herself by the lapels and left the little meeting room, walking straight into Sean, all grin and sleek silk tie. His eyes hit hers dead on, then slid back to Karen, who regarded Bethany for a moment then walked her visitor on towards the big glass doors at the end of the hallway, guiding him with a hand in the small of his back. A scuttle of Karen's lackeys swallowed Sean. He didn't look back.

Bethany remained a moment in the vacated passageway, waiting for him to reappear. Suffice to say, he did not.

A passing staffer caught her eye through the glass door, with a look inherited from Karen. Prick. Bethany directed a merry smile his way then swung on her heels towards the clear green promise of the Emergency Exit signs.

TWENTY-THREE

'I'M LISTENING,' says Dani.

On the news screen, the TakeBackID encampment is breaking up. The fun is over. Dani offs the TV. Sam's voice crackles from the Bluetooth earpiece as she packs her bag.

'If you want a sorry,' he says, 'forget it. But I'll go as far as, well played.'

'I'll go as far as, kiss my taint.'

Her swears ring false. They were her trademark thing. Did they always come across so childish? So pointless?

'Well, I see you've grown and developed in your time of trial,' says Sam.

'Fuck off. I don't have the energy. What do you want?'

Maybe this is how it always is. In a breakneck moment, every-thing you thought was important gets swiped off the screen; but the morning after, in the weird hush as the clean-up operation starts, all the badness you were carrying comes bleeding back.

'Two things,' says Sam.

'OK. But quickly. Because you have literally five per cent of my attention.'

She scans Perce's glass throne-room. Nothing else of hers left. Outside, the atrium screens are back to their rabid marketing, celeb noise and social media pulls. She spots a proffer with the meme <FreeTheGaySkeletons> followed by a burst of her own TakeBackID messages, on loop. There's Dani, baked into the new reality.

'This is difficult,' says Sam. 'I've been thinking a lot since we – you know.'

Dani stalls on her way out of the room. Surely this isn't going to be *that* conversation?

'I know this is totally out of order,' he says, 'but I had to say: I felt something last night. Look, there it is. I know I'm a lying cunt. You don't have to say anything. I'll move on to point two in a second. I just wanted you to know.'

Dani's a millimetre from killing the call stone dead – but she leaves the Bluetooth running in her ear as she uses her new upgraded swipe card to exit the Top Spot.

'OK, silence on point one is fine,' says Sam. 'Point two's a warning.'

Her data-trail buzzes as she crosses the bridge to the body of the building. Tracking her movements, from her phone, is the mobile build of what used to be *Me All Over* and is now *Everything About You*. It's way better than the desktop app. It's going to be her life. Everyone living all of themselves online, through her. Sound, vision, pulse from her watch. This conversation, now, with Sam: already part of her trail. What will it be, converted to jets of pixels? She'll view it later. It means less live. The beauty is walking back across the artwork of your life and living it again: she'll do that tonight, at home.

She's half-listening to Sam as she steps into the lift.

'You need to know what you're getting into,' he says. 'What I've heard.'

Inertia tugs her stomach as the lift pulls her down.

'Heard? Is that from *sources*?'

Should it worry her: how everything about her is going down in a whole new dataset, stored in the basement here at 404? After the week she's had, maybe she should kill every account she has, light out for an island in the Pacific. Eat nuts and berries. She won't do that. This is where she lives and you don't just one day decide to change that. It's all of her or nothing. She chooses all.

'I get that,' he's saying. 'But can't this just be, like old school friend to old school friend?'

The lift spews her out.

'School –! That's flown, Sam. It's flown.'

She doesn't look down onto the police scrum, three floors below ground level: the *do not cross* line, the plastic tent. She swipes out of the turnstile. Sam's voice persists like flies in her hair.

'You need to hear this. You can decide whether to listen once you hear. Perce is poison.'

On the street, remnants of the fleeting camp: cans, butts, scratch graffiti. Four weary community support officers. A smell of burnt wood and plastic and a sense that everyone has vanished in a puff. Still Sam talks.

'I know people who've done what you're doing with Perce. Been sucked in. Given up their ideas, IP, lives. He eats them.'

A sense that it isn't one thing but a coincidence of small movements that's brought her to this.

'Look,' says Sam, 'I've been massively fired from the Terasoft account, and I'm not holding out my chances of remaining at the agency.'

'From the *account*? You're going to *prison*, Sam.'

'Yeah, well, I doubt that. But the point is, I've got no vested interest. Why would I lie about this?'

'Why would *you* lie?'

No answer. Traffic eases past. Nothing is the same. Leo died. Dani's been drawn across the face of the world; now she's become this tech-sector superstar. Nine a.m. on Monday morning, flanked by £400-an-hour lawyers, she'll be questioned by police. Today a government minister spoke for her from the steps of Number Ten. Where does she put all that? Plus she has a vintage book to return to its rightful owner. So much to do.

'Sam?' she says.

'Still here.'

'You know what Bethany said, in her speech.'

'Do I?'

'Right. Well, here's my answer. To both your *points*. Listen to her and fuck off out of my life.'

She kills the call and wheels about. She's going to walk home today, through the uncomplicated sunlight.

¶sic_girl

Hello, world.

ACKNOWLEDGMENTS

To my editor, @fingersofgod, for showing me the good and bad in my manuscript with such perspicacity and helping me make it the book it is today; and to my agent, @taffyagent, for seeing its potential in the first place.

To @RichardNSkinner and @IanKEllard of @FaberAcademy. I started writing a formless thing called *Lobster Pot* on Richard's six-month Writing a Novel course. The fact that it is now a novel called *Sockpuppet* owes a huge amount to Richard, and to his weekly mantra: 'Well done. Keep going.' Best advice a writer ever had.

To my first readers, @mollyflatt, @garethmammal, @testudo_aubreii and Jonathan Skan (who has broken the convention of this page by failing to be on Twitter) – along with all my fellow Faber Academicians – for their insight, support and honesty.

To @paul_clarke for telling me a story once, about a restaurant bill that was paid with a credit card carrying a fake name: and for the train of thought this anecdote inspired.

To Jim Davies (again, no Twitter) for his detailed critique of my clumsy UNIX.

To @martylog for gracing these pages with a cameo appearance. A fitting memento of what was once the best night out in London. #kc.

And, lastly, to Alice – for everything not covered above, so far beyond what I can set down here.

Do you wish this wasn't the end?

Join us at www.hodder.co.uk, or follow us on
Twitter @hodderbooks to be a part of our community
of people who love the very best in books and reading.

Whether you want to discover more about a book
or an author, watch trailers and interviews, have the
chance to win early limited editions, or simply browse
our expert readers' selection of the very best books,
we think you'll find what you're looking for.

And if you don't,
that's the place to tell us what's missing.

We love what we do, and we'd love you to be part of it.

www.hodder.co.uk

@hodderbooks

HodderBooks

HodderBooks

WANT MORE?

If you enjoyed this and would like to find out about similar books we publish, we'd love you to join our online SF, Fantasy and Horror community, Hodderscape.

Visit our blog site
www.hodderscape.co.uk

Follow us on Twitter
🐦 **@hodderscape**

Like our Facebook page
f **Hodderscape**

You'll find exclusive content from our authors, news, competitions and general musings, so feel free to comment, contribute or just keep an eye on what we are up to. See you there!